Skyfall

Taken on the Wing, #2

Elizabeth Munro

Blue Swell Books
Nanaimo, B.C.
Canada

First Print Edition: June 2014
ISBN: 978-0-9879724-9-1

www.elizabethmunro.ca

Chapter One

Master Sky crouches in the center of her Memphis sparring chamber. Her lion haunches and taloned forelimbs tense beneath her powerful wings. Shift-blackened eyes frame the hard curve of her hooked beak. As she lowers her head, a single, sharp claw draws in and digs a narrow channel through the dirt floor. Three hundred pounds of muscle, feather and death stare down the privileged few gathered to challenge her.

A feline growl strains from her feathered maw.

Cloud's throat closes at the sight of her terrifying friend and mentor as she remembers to breathe. She forces a dry swallow and fills her lungs, trying to find calmness and slow her pounding heart though it continues to race. *It's an honour.* Cloud clings to the thought but instinct screams danger almost loud enough to override her still exterior and she's sure everyone can hear the pounding in her ears.

"Third-years," Hunter scans the semi-circle of students and settles his eyes on Cloud. "You will face our mentor, Master Sky. This is the first of three afternoons we will spend with her and focus on keeping our asses in one piece."

He adjusts his stance and ties on his scabbard and dulled training dagger. The surrounding students follow suit, unified by clicks and cinches in the dim light. As one of Sky's most advanced students, the young gryphon earned offers from several eyries to serve in the guard. Cloud suspects he only remains in Sky's Memphis Eyrie to torment her with his attention.

Hunter faces Sky as if he were made to take on the fully shifted gryphon. In a way, he is, since the infuriating jerk is her grandson.

Cloud keeps her eyes on him rather than let Sky's battle form rattle her. The other students watch Sky, their soft growls amplified by the rounded stone ceiling high above. Cloud anticipated today's lesson as much as anyone but once Sky shifted and her scent changed, apprehension ravaged her.

"When taking on a fully shifted gryphon, your priority is survival. All other goals are suicide."

Hunter turns and smiles earning a couple of nervous snickers because he's popular even when he isn't funny. Although this exercise challenges their psychological strength, many third year students receive near fatal wounds from even the most experienced and restrained Master. It takes centuries before a gryphon can shift beyond mere tail and wings on their human form into a fully-shifted beast armed with talon and claw and protected by a thick muscled body covered in feathers and fur.

Cloud feels Sky's pure black eyes focus on her though the absence of surrounding whites offers no clue as to where Sky looks. Sweat beads on her crawling skin, moistening her homespun clothes. Even thicker garments offer little protection from the chamber's chill.

"Master Sky will slash. She will growl. She will do everything but kill you.

"And she does not promise you won't be hurt."

His eyes settle on Cloud again and he winks, appearing oblivious to Sky who makes no sound as she circles around behind him.

Hunter's stupid sideways grin disarms her every time.

For a moment, she lets her mental guard down and smiles in return maybe because he looks so much like his brother. But he isn't Soar. That jerk hasn't spoken a word to her in three years. Didn't even say good-bye when she left for Sky's mountain.

Hunter sidesteps, just in time to disappear into Sky's shadow. The soundless predator pounces and consumes him in a blur of muscle and feathers.

Bloodlust ripples through the students, drawing them toward Hunter and Sky in the center sparring ring. Cloud inches away and eyes the exit then she catches sight of jerk number two.

Soar stands on one of the upper shelves above the tunnel, arms crossed, and watches his youngest sibling wriggle out from beneath Sky's massive body. Hunter jams his boots into her abdomen and shouts into the darkness as he pushes the giant gryphon off balance. Sky gracefully braces herself with her wings and keeps her beak out of the dirt but can't use her sharp talons on him with them sunk into the ground. Hunter twists up onto his feet and Sky faces him head on.

Hunter's lips snap back exposing teeth in threat then straighten in concentration. Sky doesn't give him time to move more than a foot. The beast's massive haunches twitch her forward and she pivots and stabs a clawed hind leg to his throat in a flash of sprayed dirt and filtered light that shouldn't be possible for something so large.

"Hunter..." Cloud breathes and her free hand moves to her own neck. The dirt beneath grabs at her feet and she stumbles on rubbery knees. She's taken on every challenge thrown at her but this one has nothing to do with her physical training. Sick fear, a stranger in her gut, moves in and begins to settle throughout her body.

The few glimpses she gets of Hunter show him not only embraced in Sky's talons but using his arms and legs to stay as close to her as he can. If she gets a hind foot between them she could rip him in half. Screeches and dust outside the sparring ring must be as intense within it as the chamber has filled with both.

Hunter's thick, pained voice cries out as the pair rolls then he digs his wooden dagger under Sky's massive wing. She shrieks, leans in Hunter's direction and drops the wing, giving him the opportunity to land a well-placed boot on her throat. The restrained blow shouldn't move her jaw but Sky reacts as if he'd put all his force behind it. Her clawed hind legs come up in defense and flick him away.

Hunter's head snaps back into the soft dirt before he can tuck it sideways and summersault over backwards. He's as smooth as Soar even when thrown and comes up in a crouch with his dagger drawn and his eyes on his target.

The three scratches marking his outer obliques aren't deep enough to be dangerous but each leaves a crimson stain on the waistband of his trousers.

Cloud doesn't realize she clutches her own scarred side until she feels the ridges of thickened skin through her tunic.

On the terrace above, Soar ignores her and watches Sky shake her feathers and prepare for her next student. His hands tighten around his biceps in response to Cloud's stare.

She scans the other shelves for her adopted sire, Master Talon, in the hopes he's come along but Soar is alone.

"Juniper," Hunter shouts as he stands and points at Sky. "Cloud."

She glares to see what the heck he wants but he tilts his head toward the center of the room and Sky in the main sparring ring.

Not yet, she moans.

Memories flow in dark currents around Cloud's weak knees. A small den lit by a fire. The warmth of home and family soothes her spirit. A female with dark hair lies prone before her. Her splayed wings bear the same unremarkable brown as Cloud's own feathers. A word reveals itself in Cloud's head: *Dame.* Dark feathered forms snuff out the fire then yield to a black, fully shifted gryphon pacing the tunnel outside the darkening den, its talons dripping blood. That female's black wings and fur were rare and she stares at the striding beast. The scent of an aggravated, fully shifted gryphon will never be forgotten and her nose twinges.

"Cloud," Hunter motions her forward.

Growing dust swallows the silver wall lights as she leaves the relative safety of the chamber's perimeter. Grit coats her throat and sticks in the layer of sweat between her palm and the handle of her small, wooden dagger.

Juniper's cry gets Cloud's attention and she whirls, ready to flee whatever danger she's found but the female rolls to her feet a dozen paces from Sky. Juniper allows a grin as she stalks forward, enjoying the thrill of battle. Cloud doesn't feel the lust for combat, only the nearness of death risen from the depths of her past. She embraced every task put to her, many in this very room, pushing herself to master every weapon and face every opponent no matter how obvious the mismatch.

The overwhelming power of bloodlust avoids her and the urge to flee chokes her veins and thoughts with equal amounts of ferocity. Her relief that Juniper walked away without injury isn't enough to replace her own dread she's next.

Sky dips her chin and prowls away, inviting Cloud forward.

She's just a naked gryphon, Cloud's unsure inner voice states. Naked? Definitely. Sky's human hands folded her tunic and trousers, leaving them in a neat pile. The same gentle hands set broken bones and bound wounds as her mouth once praised and encouraged. Now her talons flex beneath a foot-long curved beak, sharp enough to tear off a limb.

"Master," Cloud acknowledges but the tremor in her belly shakes the syllables through her lips.

Blood rushes her ears, spreading numbness to her mouth and she can't speak another word. Her words fade to a faint click in her throat. As Cloud steps into the invisible barrier marking the sparring ring no amount of heaving can pull sufficient oxygen into her lungs.

"Take position," Hunter's distant voice intrudes and Cloud complies. A single step spreads her feet but she doesn't really feel the handle of the wooden dagger as she pulls it from her thigh.

Sky rears up, a move she didn't make with Hunter, and releases a terrifying screech. With her wings spread in threat, she brandishes her claws and takes a step forward as brilliant blue sparks flare across her large feathers.

The jolt of Cloud's dagger landing on her own foot causes her to cry out, unaware she'd even dropped it and she slaps her hands to her ears to keep the echoes away. Blue sparks in Sky's wings flourish then fade and Cloud perceives the faint silver wall lights through the shadows around her as flickering warm yellow fire.

The thick dry musk of fully-shifted gryphon permeates her senses.

She no longer sees Sky or the chamber. The beautiful young dark-haired female lies dead, close enough to the fire to make the deep gold highlights in her hair shimmer. One year old Cloud holds back tears and clings to her dame. Fingers trace along flight feathers as she tries to rub away the deep bruises on her neck. No blood marks her body or pools on the floor.

The murderer's obsidian eyes flicker in the fire light. He nods to the black winged gryphon and it retreats down the tunnel as he draws a knife and turns on Cloud.

"No," Cloud drops her hands.

"No."

She runs from Sky and the chamber, terrified by the echoes of her pounding feet and the finality of death.

Soar grabs the stone terrace wall to keep from falling as Cloud's cries pierce his body. He regains his composure as the training continues below and hopes no one noticed him flinch while lit by Sky's brilliant blue threat display. He needs to follow, to release Cloud's soft, red hair from its knot and tangle his fingers in it.

He keeps a palm on the wall to stop himself. The last thing Cloud needs is to see him, the gryphon who dumped her cold the day she was accepted into Memphis. Three years without her hardened his heart.

What did you expect? Soar chides himself. *You had her then you shut her out.*

The fighting in the room below seems to go on for hours as Soar waits to set his plan in motion.

"Hey, brother," Hunter approaches through the tunnel leading up to the ledge. Soar stuffs his hands in his pockets before his youngest sibling can see the whitening knuckles. "We a go?"

"Yeah," Soar agrees. A go it is. If his cruelty three years earlier didn't count as hurting her then Soar's next move certainly will and he's an asshole for being here to pick up the pieces. Picking them up and using them.

"Look, Soar," Hunter bows then holds his chin up in submission. "You sure? I mean it isn't too late for me to stop this."

"Mm," Soar grunts with a shake of his head. Cloud's breakdown still chills him though indulging in conversation with his brother restores some warmth. "Things good back home?"

"Two births in the eyrie this year. You'd think our dame bore them herself she's so proud."

Soar laughs. Most females find a way to avoid going into season after a birth or two but their dame still wears out their sire every few years. Soar and Hunter's dame rules their birth eyrie in Oregon and is the sibling of Sire Lev, Cloud's adopted grand-sire.

"And she says next time you take off for your male dereliction of duty to come home and see her."

Of course she would. Males disappear for a few months every year to listen to the Earth, grow their treasure hordes and hunt. Females think it's laziness. Males are as solitary by nature as females are communal, even those who have sworn service to an eyrie like Soar has. And like Cloud hopes to although the coming hours will see that future taken from her.

"What happened to Cloud in there?" Soar asks though he knows damned well what it was.

"Beats me," Hunter shrugs then his chin drops. "You know Sky. She makes sure everyone loses their shit real good at least once."

Soar holds his tongue. While training in Memphis feels like a group thing, it's very personalized and Sky shows each gryphon in her charge exactly what their limits are.

What the gryphon does with the information, mastery or failure, is entirely up to them.

"Mine was a couple of years ago," Hunter goes on and Soar closes his eyes. "It was water—"

"Please," Soar holds up a hand to keep the words away. He wasn't in Oregon when Hunter and his twin snuck out. It was night and they somehow landed in the lake. Wind, the smaller of the two, had the presence of mind to draw her wings in and get them to shore but not before Hunter nearly drowned her in panic. The pair were eight and both had taken wing for the first time only a year before.

"Water," Hunter swallows and Soar drops his head back, a solid thud against the stone wall. "A night exercise, dark... water."

"Anyway," Hunter clears his throat. "The gryphon who's going to get her expelled is so mad his sire is sending a delegation to make sure our grand-dame handles things prop —"

"I don't want to know," Soar warns. Master Sky doesn't need help doing things properly but politics is politics and she'll have to put up with the so-called delegation. "And you're better off not knowing why."

"Right, right," Hunter answers as he jumps at Soar, gets him in a headlock and knocks him over. In a matter of seconds, Soar has his younger brother face down on the stone floor.

"You got a long way to go," Soar rolls off as the two catch their breath. "Make it happen, Hunter, and come to her den in an hour.

"Be pissed I'm there."

Chapter Two

Cloud chooses the most downstream bath and steps in. The day's lesson ended over an hour ago and the students have gathered for evening meal so she has the dim chamber to herself. The underground stream gurgles as it falls from pool to pool inside the sloping bath chamber. A different temperature fills each basin. Silver lights glow softly on the cavern walls.

As she unties her hair she shifts, drawing her wings in so her dirt falls in the water. Her human body is uncomfortable in the cold and she shivers by the time the water clears.

Water can't wash away the memories of Welch Peak. She rests, chin deep, in the icy water and gives in as her spirit numbs. She not only lost her dame at Welch Peak but she almost lost her adopted dame, Shadow, years later. Her fingers move up to her left ear and trace the jagged outline claimed by frostbite. She spent a week in a human hospital receiving treatment following Torrent's near fatal clawing of her stomach. The scars remind her of the pain that day caused Shadow. If Cloud had been tougher then Shadow wouldn't have watched her nearly die.

Now she has to dig deep into her pride to be a gryphon worthy of Shadow's guard.

Cloud rises to take wing, grabs a bar of rough homemade eyrie soap and drops back into the flow. She bought some human toiletries during her one trip to Memphis but they ran out more than two years before so she's at the mercy of the plain bars. At least this time of year they're scented with local wildflowers or honey.

Then there's Soar. Cloud went to his den five years earlier when she was twenty. As master of the Sire's royal guard, he was the most desirable male in the eyrie and sought after by the few single females living there. For Cloud, the master of Lev's guard was most likely to still be there when she finally earned her place in Shadow's guard and the fact Cloud had a crush on him didn't hurt either.

But his closed off attitude in public followed by his private dismissal broke her heart.

We had a thing, Cloud. We weren't a thing.

As much as she hated leaving home at least she didn't have to see Soar every day. If she can avoid running into him now, all the better.

Once satisfied the dirt is gone, Cloud steps from the pool and beats water from her feathers. The natural oils make sure they're practically dry as she pulls a tunic over her head and fastens it below her wings. Then she threads her tail through the gap in the rear of her trousers and pulls them up, securing the drawstring around her hips.

She's halfway up the tunnel before she remembers to brush her hair.

"Crap," Cloud sighs.

"Cloud," a male calls from up ahead and two members of Sky's own guard appear before her.

"Gryphons," she kneels but barely gets her knee down before each grabs an elbow. "What?"

"Silence."

The sharp male scent of their well worn armour clashes with the lingering perfumes of the female baths and these two gryphons could snap her in half if they wanted. She pulls her wings in under theirs and grabs at the stone floor with her toes to keep up.

They let her go ten feet from the opening to the eyrie's main chamber, tossing her toward the end of the tunnel.

Cloud turns and drops into a defensive position, knees bent and fists raised.

"Report to Master Sky in her den immediately."

"Am I in trouble?" Cloud straightens, chin high. Nobody gets kicked for blowing it in training. Mostly.

"A shame," one mutters as they brush past her.

"What's a—" she starts but their steely stares lock her question in her throat. The wave of looseness that jolts her stomach says she's in a lot of trouble.

Cloud takes a half-dozen deep breaths to quiet her pounding heart before entering the main chamber. Gryphons clean up from dinner as others squat or kneel on cushions around the perimeter or in clusters on the wide stone floor. The third-years' exuberant chatter fills the space. All wear traditional trousers and tunics, a light blend of cotton and wool woven by the students themselves.

Nobody gives her a second look.

Cloud walks silently through the tunnel to Sky's den. With her wings held still and careful steps she hopes to overhear any sound ahead but she passes uninterrupted by any noise other than the wisp of her feet on stone. Soar would have been to see Sky and his scent lingers wherever the tunnel steepens.

As she rounds the last turn, silver lights bid welcome and she enters the chamber to find Sky at her desk. Centuries of use have chipped the piece around the edges and worn the centre smooth. The graceful, curved, polished steel legs are the work of the intimidating Master and fight instructor seated in a modern, ergonomic office chair.

Master Sky epitomizes contradiction; former Dame and now combat trainer, blacksmith, master swordsman and the closest thing to dame and friend Cloud has since leaving home. She's also loving dame to several pairs of offspring including Soar and Hunter's sire. Cloud loves the eight-hundred year old female with all her heart.

But Cloud can't read her expression and drops to one knee, adding a bow for good measure.

"Master Sky," Cloud murmurs. "What happened today, I mean..."

She raises her chin as her eyes settle on the single item on the desk; a knife with a six inch blade and a jeweled handle. It can only be a ceremonial item since it appears to be made of gold, rendering it impractical for anything more than collecting dust.

The seconds still around them and a soft sweat breaks out beneath Cloud's clean tunic.

"Cloud," Sky says, her voice clear and unhurried. "I hoped you would volunteer an explanation. This knife should not be on my desk."

"Master," Cloud acknowledges although what she's uncertain. The knife has nothing to do with losing it at the sight of a fully feathered female.

Sky stands, pulling her mottled black and brown wings in tight as she steps clear of the chair then relaxes them as she moves around her desk. Her hands grip the rough edge as she rests her bottom on the corner and leaves the knife in view.

"Yes?" Sky tries.

Cloud looks helplessly up at her, completely confused.

"You are aware an item was stolen from Falcon last night."

"Master," Cloud nods again.

"Only half an hour ago I learned of its location and recovered it from your den," she gestures at the knife.

How in heck did it get in my den?

But there's no point in arguing. Cloud knows for certain she didn't accidentally pick it up and hide it. She's never seen it before. Sky found it in her den and any denial will just make her look like a liar *and* a thief.

And a coward.

Cloud sits hard on the stone floor as she understands what this means. Theft is one of the most shameful things one gryphon can do to another and if she's been brought before Sky then Sky believes she's guilty. Cloud's dream of becoming a ranger is over. There's nothing left for her here or at home for that matter. Her hands shake as she reaches to Sky for comfort but she draws them back. A thief will never join Dame Shadow's guard.

She'll never be trusted again.

Sky sinks to the floor and takes Cloud's trembling hands in her own.

"I admit you were reluctantly accepted into my program," Sky explains. Cloud looks past her at the knife before dropping her head. "Your unknown parentage and your youth. Due entirely to Talon and Lev's praise for your determination and hard work I took you in, certain you would wash yourself out in a matter of months.

"But instead you became one of my best students; first up in the morning and the last to retire. I have been deeply proud of you, Cloud, up until now.

"But my feelings cannot prevent me from dismissing you. Do you understand?"

"Master," Cloud chokes out. The harsh breath empties her lungs of all the air they hold.

"Stand," Sky orders as she gets up. She doesn't speak again until Cloud is on her feet. The stone under her no longer feels solid and she leans, catching her balance before widening her stance.

"Cloud, you are hereby expelled and will leave within the hour. You will not discuss the reason for your expulsion until you return to the Vancouver Island Eyrie. I will give you seven days to do so then your crime will become public knowledge."

Cloud nods, unable to manage the word 'Master,' and turns for the tunnel.

"Cloud," Sky says, her voice laced with the compassion she couldn't express before. "You have three months to prove you are more than what the stolen knife suggests. Return in three months. You will apologize. You will be punished.

"And maybe I can reinstate you as my student."

"We have broken a good gryphon, Soar." Sky leans on her desk, roughly pushing the gaudy knife away. "And her failure in the chamber... I pray she has the spirit to return and face me again."

Soar steps from a niche a dozen feet up the tunnel leading to his grand-dame's sleeping den. As he approaches her desk, he listens for Cloud but her footsteps have already faded.

"She didn't argue or fall apart," Sky continues, wings sagging with sadness.

"There's no other way," Soar says. And no chance for second thoughts. Sky has sworn Falcon to secrecy for seven days and now the knife Hunter took has been recovered there is no going back.

"I know," she sighs. "I don't doubt the importance of your quest."

"My favourite grand-dame," Soar sighs and hugs the old gryphon. "There will be no repercussions on you if I fail. Nobody in the Vancouver Island Eyrie knows what I'm doing and neither does Hunter."

"Yes."

"Her story has to hold up."

Soar lifts the knife from Sky's desk and twirls it in his palm.

"You know of Calgary's public efforts for recognition of democratic eyries by the Grand Council. Cooper, its leader, has gained friends in the Council and those friends could force our traditional eyries out. If Cloud doesn't believe her story she won't survive Cooper. Cloud will be sniffed out as a spy if her story has any cracks at all.

"Nearly every other gryphon we've sent into Calgary wound up dead."

Soar puts the knife down and leans on the desk.

"Soar... Does she know how you feel?" Sky puts her hand upon his back.

Soar shakes his head and moves away.

"The movement to destroy traditional eyries centers around Calgary. Cloud's birth eyrie at Welch Peak and the Vancouver Island Eyrie I serve have been devastated twice by rogues believed to be loyal to democratic eyries."

"I don't need a history lesson so you can avoid your feelings," Sky sighs. "Too many good gryphons have died over the years, both my kin and my friends."

"Lev thinks I'm taking some personal time after my visit here and he'll believe Cloud ran off in shame.

"I guess I better go after her," Soar says as he walks to the tunnel.

"Soar," Sky calls and he stops, certain she's about to tell him off. "She is a good choice for you. I'm curious why you haven't pursued her. Tell her. Tell her before..."

Before I send her to her death.

Damn, what do you tell your grand-dame who thought she knew everything about your personal life?

"Who says I haven't pursued her?" Soar remarks and Sky raises an eyebrow, demanding more. "If I asked she would have walked away from her dream to stay with me so I ended it. I hurt her, grand-dame, and when she learns what I did to her today she'll never speak to me again."

"Indeed," Sky mutters, her voice betraying both worry and anger. "In three months, Master Soar, you will assume the position of apology in my sparring chamber and I assure you, whichever pieces Cloud has left you with will be mine."

Chapter Three

Cloud's frustrated growl reaches Soar long before he gets to the covered opening to her den.

"No, no, no," she mutters then her voice fades as he takes a couple of noisy steps to get her attention. Even so upset, she should know better than to draw attention to herself.

Soar pushes past the curtain to find her kneeling amongst her scattered belongings. She spins, mouth half open, and whitens before returning to packing.

"Just when my day couldn't get any worse," she jams a handful of underwear into the bottom of her worn pack with such force her hand bursts through the bottom. "Do you have to stand so close?"

He stands all the way across her small den, maybe a dozen feet away, and isn't close at all. Cloud shakes her bag empty before lining the bottom with a shirt, carefully spreading it so the weight of her clothes will keep it in place over the hole.

Then she starts refilling the bag.

She's not over me, he realizes and all he wants to do is take back the last hour of her life but he can't. Cloud is his last chance to protect their home.

"Where are you going?" Soar asks.

"Not a word in three years and he pretends he cares where I'm going," she snaps. "If it's any of your darn business I'm going to spend a raunchy weekend in Memphis with your brother."

Soar modulates his voice so it won't penetrate the curtain to be overheard in the tunnel but it's hard. The idea she'd gloat about being with anyone else speaks to how angry she still is and if she means to lash back it's working.

"Even if I wasn't in Sky's den when she heard where Falcon's knife was you're still the worst liar I've ever met."

She shrugs as the pile of clothes around her gets smaller. "What the heck did you do to your hair?"

Soar ignores the bait since she knows damn well it's been short for years.

"You wouldn't have done it, Cloud."

"Of course I wouldn't have taken that royal *hatchling's* stupid knife," she says, her voice matching his tone for privacy.

"Then why didn't you tell Sky that?"

Cloud turns and looks at him like she's only just noticed him in the door.

"I let myself be set-up, Soar. My Master believes I stole because of my own stupidity. I was inattentive and brought failure on myself. Double failure, today of all days."

Beneath her jeans, her tail is already drawn in and she wrings a shirt she can pull over the light tunic she wears to travel.

"You know who set you up?"

"I am one hundred percent certain."

"And?"

He can't read her expression as she stands and drops the shirt on her bag. For a moment he thinks she's on to him already. Her anger with herself has turned into something feral and tenuous that could turn on him just as well as she could turn it inward. Damn it, even if she hadn't just been expelled for theft, her humiliation over her failure against Sky is more than enough to upset her.

He hasn't spoken this much to her in three years so her confusion about him can only add to her pain.

"Falcon," she says. "Royal jerk's been getting too touchy with the females and after he cornered me to experience his attentions I *accidentally* broke two of his fingers the next time Sky paired us."

"Damn it, Cloud. You should have gone to Sky," he hopes to sound like he's giving her a lecture although inside he's proud of her. Had Hunter known about Falcon? Soar's impressed with his kid brother. He couldn't have picked a better mark for the theft.

"Thinking back? Yeah, but at the time I felt he'd learned his lesson. Kept his hands to himself since then but the injury kept him from going on advanced maneuvers with Talon and he blames me.

"And why the interest in me, all of a sudden?"

"Well," Soar approaches, unsure what to expect from her. "I was—"

"You were what?" her voice shakes but at least she keeps it down. Soar pushes his wings forward, offering her comfort in their folds, but she takes a step away.

"I was wondering what Sky told you."

"She said if I could prove myself in three months I might be able to come back," Cloud doesn't retreat further, instead she steps in looking hurt, tired and fragile.

"Is that what you want?"

She drops her chin in a sharp nod then meets his stare.

"I have an assignment for you, Cloud. We can help each other out," his fingers touch just below her chin, tipping it up to his before finding his way around under her ear and toward the back of her neck. She'd let him touch her ear once and in those seconds he memorized every notch in its scarred, jagged edge.

Now she's close, too close, and he can't help himself. He avoids the scars but thumbs the lobe on his way by. "Hm?"

"Cloud? I missed you at—" Hunter stumbles to a stop at the sight of her so near his brother.

"Hunter," she says as she jumps clear of Soar.

"I just came to check on you," Hunter says but his light mood has turned to a scowl for his older sibling.

"I... uh," Cloud stammers. She has to remember Sky's instructions about keeping her mouth shut for a week. "I'm going away for a couple of days."

Jesus, the kid's a good actor. With his arms crossed he's the very image of the newly winged, angry, seven year old gryphon Soar recalls trying so hard to understand why his favourite brother is leaving and he can't go along. Hunter keeps his mouth shut and Soar recognizes the flush in Cloud's cheeks. She squirms inside as she comes up with a plausible explanation for Hunter.

"I'm meeting Talon for a night exercise."

Good try, Cloud, but he knows Talon isn't here.

The way Hunter's eyes roll to the ceiling shows he reacts more to the sight of Cloud and Soar than he pretends to be pissed. What had he seen? Soar had been reaching for the back of her neck like her lover would. Instinct made him seek the soft spots beneath her hair where his touch would calm her.

"You're a shitty liar, Cloud," Hunter blurts out. He's jealous and more attached to Cloud than he ever let on. "You're going somewhere with him."

"No—"

"He can't keep a female in his life for more than a month and when you figure out why *don't* come looking for me," Hunter's arms shake in spite of the firm hold he has on himself. "I'm sick of his hand-me-downs."

Hunter spins on his heel so fast he almost bolts into the wall as he storms from Cloud's den.

But Cloud turns on Soar before the curtain falls shut.

"A month?" she demands and smacks his wing aside as he tries to draw her near again. "I gave you two years. Let me correct that. I gave you two years of nights in your den when you were everything. Two years of you not having time for me during the day when everyone else was around and I bet not a single soul knew we'd ever been alone together."

"I didn't come here for you to take your problems out on me," Soar bites out to deflect the sting of her temper. "I need a gryphon for a job and you need to put a shine on your image."

Cloud's mouth snaps shut but the smolder in her gold flecked blue eyes promises danger, either to him or his heart and he doesn't give a shit which as long as it means she's going to come at him.

"Here," he holds out a ring with a key on it. "My van is fifty miles due north of the transition house and I'll be there the day after tomorrow. If you're not gryphon enough for what I have to offer, don't be there."

"You," she sputters.

Soar doesn't wait for an answer and drops the key on the stone floor before leaving to clear things up with Hunter.

As Soar steps from her den he hears the scrape of metal on stone as Cloud picks up the key.

Chapter Four

Cloud finds Soar's van nestled in the darkening Tennessee woods. She's seen it before; part camper, part van and more cramped than any den she's slept in and she isn't sure why he bothered to drive all the way here. While long, the flight from Vancouver Island can be done in a few days and without rest if one were up for punishment.

The van is old, as far as she's concerned, but it's clean and well maintained. Soar bought it new in 1970.

She doesn't bother going inside and has a restless night curled up in the nearby trees followed by half a dozen aborted trips home, each time returning to the key she left on the roof.

Her second night is spent on Soar's mattress above the cab with all the doors and windows open to keep his scent to a minimum. Even the breeze isn't enough to clear the air and it drives her out at dawn for another forty mile round trip back to the van.

Now she sits, tired and hungry on the roof, debating whether or not she will leave the key behind one last time and fly home. It's nearly dark and she expected him to turn up already.

She shoves the key in her pocket and jumps to the ground before stomping off to the matted down brush she slept on two nights earlier. There's no way she'll be waiting for Soar in his bed. Lesson learned.

As she beds down, he arrives from upwind, his feather light landing preceded by the rich aroma of deer. Cloud curls into a tighter ball to silence the holes in her stomach and her heart.

"Still here?" he asks like he doesn't give a crap. Whatever.

"What do you want, Soar?"

"Hungry?" He stops halfway between her and the van, a thick deer leg slung over each shoulder.

"No," Cloud sits but her stomach disagrees. The deep rumble rises to a whiny plea for food. One leg lands at her feet as Soar squats and starts in on his.

"You going to eat all that?" he asks.

Cloud found her old human-made folding knife in the trash at the Jasper Eyrie where she was reared. The chipped and dull blade sharpened up nicely. As long as she keeps the edge against meat and away from bone and hair it won't dull.

Each mouthful settles her stomach more than the last. With Soar's arrival, her decision to take on his assignment has been made. It would be even more shameful to run home right in front of him.

"What do you know about Calgary?" Soar asks.

Cloud reaches for her bag and pulls out her precious leather folder. It holds maps that once belonged to Shadow's brother, Condor. When Shadow learned of her interest in geography she insisted Cloud take them. She unfolds one of Canada and the US. Its curled edges are marked with Condor's tiny print and crude drawings of naked women, dragons and gryphons having sex in impossible positions.

"Besides what's on the map," he adds.

"Nothing," she doesn't take her eyes from the age-softened paper as her fingers skim the path from Tennessee to Calgary. Her uncanny and infallible sense of direction makes the map unnecessary once she's memorized the landmarks and incorporated the route into detail she remembers from other trips. Once she flies off, she can find the city with her eyes closed.

"Lev believes the rogues who attacked Welch Peak and our eyrie are associated with the Calgary Eyrie. It's a democratic eyrie run by a gryphon named Cooper. Doesn't use his gryphon name any more."

"Oh," Cloud raises her eyes from the map and considers what she might do with the gryphon who did so much harm.

"Forget it, Cloud," Soar tells her. "I doubt very much the trouble came from Calgary but Lev's insistence it did has caused a lot of tension in the Grand Council.

"The Council is deeply traditional but they are taking Cooper's side and that's bad news for us."

"I see," Cloud puts the map away.

"I need you to get inside Calgary and find out what Cooper has that gives him so much pull with the Council. After we decimated what Sire Lev claims was Cooper's guard at Welch Peak, Cooper started pushing for harsh sanctions for what he says is an unwarranted attack on a group of hunters simply gathering meat."

"Even though you think the rogue army wasn't his?"

"Yes," Soar admits. "He's using the situation to his advantage but I don't know why."

"That's bad," Cloud says and Soar nods.

"The Council could eliminate Shadow, in effect eliminating our eyrie."

"The Council's Will," Cloud hisses. No Shadow means no heir and the eyrie would die. The Will is the Council's private guard; gryphons sworn to a higher authority than a single eyrie.

"I'm not going to tell you any more about Cooper other than he owns a bar in downtown Calgary. Get noticed, find your way in and learn what you can. I have to be honest, Cloud. Every other gryphon I've sent in there is dead."

"But I've got nothing to lose," Cloud points out.

"Your situation sucks," Soar agrees. "I told Lev I was taking some personal time after my visit to Sky. What I didn't tell him was I would go into Calgary myself. I still will if you don't volunteer."

"I'm in," Cloud doesn't hesitate. She's temporarily blinded by the image of the moonlit map and can't make out Soar's expression in the shadows.

"What have you got you can use?"

"Honesty," she answers. Nobody but Lev, Talon and Shadow at home knows she's a royal gryphon. Not only can she tell when she's trusted but she can also push a gryphon into doing something he normally wouldn't. As long as even a small part of the gryphon considers what she wants, she can make that part so strong the gryphon will act. Shadow helped her refine the ability so the gryphon she influences doesn't feel a thing. Her magic should make the mission doable.

"Agreed," Soar sighs. "If you get to him he's going to check your story out and you won't leave alive if you're lying. Nobody back home knows what we're up to. If you don't come out they never will. If you're caught this can't come back on Lev."

"I understand," Cloud agrees. Since arriving at Sky's eyrie she hasn't paid much attention to politics, not that she ever did, and the imminent slow death of her own eyrie is something she has to stop.

Soar squats down beside the map and she leans away but not far enough to avoid the tingle of his body heat on her skin. She manages to take the handful of Canadian twenties he offers without touching him.

"I have a campsite here," he points to a spot east of Calgary. "Wyndham - Carseland. Whether you get what we need or not be there no later than two weeks from today.

"I'll fold the second bed down for you," Soar offers but it sounds more like an invitation.

What a jerk. She'd nearly kissed him back in her den and he still has her heart on a string. But she's wise to him now. Unless it's private, she doesn't exist and she deserves better.

"Don't bother," Cloud tosses him the key and puts her map away before curling up on the ground.

How can she sleep?

He can't. Winged, aroused and shrouded in blankets the smell of *her* - how can he? He could draw his wings in so his human side ignores her enchanting gryphon scent but he chooses to be tormented by it. They never slept together as humans so at least there would be safety from memories.

When Soar went after Hunter he'd been angry about the one month remark but by the time he found him, he realized it was true. He'd been shut off with every other female even in private. Except with Cloud. She filled his nights with emotional connection. She was happy with her life and adored Shadow and Talon. Her endless questions, posed in his dark den, were insightful and she didn't consider any answer complete until it contained a little piece of himself.

Soar liked the gryphon she saw inside him. During the day, however, the illusion failed and when she was accepted to Sky's program he stepped away, secluded in his shell. It didn't fit anymore and sure as hell wasn't comfortable but it was familiar and it was his. It was so different from anything he'd learned from Cloud he convinced himself he was wrong for her anyway. His only acknowledgement of her departure was a brief communication to Hunter to keep an eye on her.

Through a narrow gap in the curtains, Soar's shift-blackened eyes pick out every feather of her wing. She curls up beneath it with nothing but her feet sticking out. As the minutes pass, Soar's sensitive hearing detects her heart speeding up and she stretches before standing and flexing her wings.

She pulls her pack over her front and clips the belt behind before cinching the straps tight. Then she takes two steps toward him.

For Soar, keeping his heart and breathing as steady as sleep is easy, a skill all rangers have. It allows the enemy to get close and gives their supposedly dozing target the advantage of surprise. Except any half-smart attacker is wary of the trick and Soar's attacker gets a few steps closer, using her words for weapons.

"I doubt you're asleep," she whispers, her voice softer than the wind. "I want you to know..."

"Whatever, I guess. If I don't come home then remind Shadow how much I love her."

She dashes away and Soar loses sight of her after only a couple of steps though he hears the last ones she takes. Then all that remains of her is the brush of her wings through the warm Tennessee air until it too, fades.

Soar slides from his bunk above the cab and steps out the back door onto the soft long grass. She's easy to make out in the moonlight and he waits until she's completely gone.

"Tell her yourself, Cloud. If you're not out in two weeks then I'm going in after you."

Chapter Five

It's dusk when Cloud steps from an alley two blocks from Cooper's bar in downtown Calgary. To conserve energy, she took full advantage of the hot ground below and let the thermals carry her. The hours gave her time to accept her decision to take Soar's assignment and with acceptance came resolve. Whether she earns her way back into Sky's eyrie or not became irrelevant.

She sweats in the radiating heat to serve her Dame. The decision leaves her peaceful since service in any form protects her family.

Since all Council decisions are made in private, even learning the names of Cooper's allies in the Council can help.

Cloud's skin crawls with perspiration since her human body isn't as good with the heat as her gryphon form so she runs her fingers over her scalp to cool it only to have them get stuck in the knots. Maybe she should have found a secluded spot on the Bow River running through the city and bathed. Instead, she hid behind a foul metal bin to remove her tunic and pull on her bra and a sleeveless top. Otherwise she wears the same jeans she wore the last day at Sky's.

"Crap," she announces, getting the attention of a couple of drunk males. One whistles and blows her a kiss, which she automatically returns. When you don't know how to respond to a human then emulate them. She'd heard that once. In this case the male laughs and approaches, leering at her breasts. His friend pulls him away, apologizing.

I'm in so much trouble here.

She's an idiot when it comes to humans and an apologetic human is one she does not want to befriend.

A gryphon never apologizes.

The vibrant mix of noises flowing from the open doors to Cooper's gets louder as she approaches. Shouts and the smells of exhaust and human sweat mix with the lightness of her step since her wings are gone and disorient her further. Cloud spent a whopping twenty days of her twenty-six years in human places. A week in hospital, a day in Talon's rig and another ten days in a cabin on a Tofino beach. Then the trip to Memphis.

At least in the dark they can't see her ear. Cloud checks to make sure her hair covers it.

The sign above the double door flashes red neon. 'Cooper's' glows in handwriting cross-marked with diagonal lines to look like rope. To her right, human couples and gryphon males line up and she can't see much inside. The hallway makes a turn to the left and other than flashing lights there's nothing interesting other than a big male gryphon behind a window.

"Looking for someone, Cherry?"

Cloud startles at the loud voice. An immense bald gryphon male appears in front of her and she takes a step away, relaxing her knees and raising her hands. She quickly straightens up. He doesn't seem bothered by her defensive reaction and her magic says he's not mistrustful of her.

"Not really," Cloud answers. Her nervous hands recheck her ears as she realizes Cherry refers to her red hair. "No ... Bald?" she guesses at his name.

An enormous laugh shakes him.

"No cover charge for gryphon girls," he whispers as he leans around to inspect her bag. "Lie to me, Cherry. Tell me you don't have a weapon in there. Weapons aren't allowed inside."

"But I don't," she protests. The knife is in her back pocket.

"I'm Lawrence," he introduces himself as he leads her past the front of the line. "Take a seat at the bar. Get a drink."

"Thank you, Lawrence," she answers but he's already returned to the door. The gryphon under the coat check sign scrutinizes her then picks up a fat hardcover book.

The inside of the bar assaults her senses as much as the Calgary street. The music differs from the beautiful rich jazz she loved in Memphis. She heard country there too but the saxophone and sultry singer lit something in her spirit. The crazy lights and thumping bass in Cooper's make her stomach ache in a pleasant way. A night club, maybe? They'd passed one in Memphis but hadn't gone in. The boom, boom was similar.

Cloud's feet crunch on the loose floor and her nose wrinkles with the papery smell of sawdust beneath her feet. Bits of paper glow blue in the black lights like the white clothes on the patrons. On the far side, most of the stools sit empty and the wide, sunken dance floor surges with the beat. Tables surround the outside of the room. A set of stairs to her right leads down to another dance floor.

A large balcony rings the room. Winged gryphons, invisible to any humans, loiter at the railing in contrast to the wild goings on below. One male gestures behind him and two more approach the railing.

She swallows, wishing Lawrence was still with her. He's a good one to know. Making friends with the guard could get her in to places and keep her out of trouble. One of the three at the railing, short black hair and lighter golden wings flecked with ivory, nods her way and she reciprocates. Cloud resists the urge to bow in the presence of all the humans even though she has the feeling she should.

To this particular gryphon at least.

Even so, she dips one knee in respect. Another male brings him a drink on a tray and he disappears out of sight as Cloud is jostled from behind. A group of human females enters and several gryphon males move toward them. Some of the males also have their eyes on her. The gryphon patrons are mostly male which makes sense since females don't stray far from their eyrie. Cloud suspects she may be the only gryphon female in the noisy room.

She pretends to check out the surroundings as she keeps her eyes on two males who follow; a human and a gryphon. They don't head directly for her. Instead they work their way to the bar. The small wad of cash in her pocket should get her a drink and hopefully some food. She's thirsty and tired from the two-day flight.

The glossy wooden bar doesn't stick as she runs her fingers over the smooth surface. She expected it would with all the drinks flying around. The bottles sparkle in light shining up through the glass shelves. Cloud has time to read the labels of dozens of them before the male on the other side of the counter reaches her.

"Thirsty, Cherry?" The gryphon places a glass of water on a coloured cardboard square. His long sleeved white shirt says Cooper's on one side in the same script as the sign above the door.

"Did Lawrence tell you I was coming?"

"Are you a friend of Lawrence?" he answers with another question.

Cloud nods as she sips then puts all her money on the bar.

"Thank you."

"Water is free," he pushes it back with a laugh. "And anything else you want here. Gryphon girls don't pay."

"Okay."

"I'll have what she's having," the human gets to her first and takes a seat to her right. "And I'll buy her another."

"Prick," the bartender says so quietly only Cloud's gryphon ears can hear. Great, the human's a prick. She knows that term and appreciates the bartender's warning. Sky's eyrie had several of them as well; Falcon included.

The bartender puts down two more glasses of water and takes the man's twenty, giving him a handful of coins in return. By the time the prick figures out he just paid for two glasses of water the bartender is nowhere to be seen.

"Thank you," Cloud tells him. She pushes her empty away and picks up the second.

"Can't afford to buy the lady a drink?" The gryphon laughs. He takes the seat to her left and Cloud pulls her shoulders together since both insist upon leaning on her. They smell of sweat and liquor. The gryphon simply smells male while the human's unwelcome odor wrinkles her nose.

"I can afford my own drinks," she mutters.

"You don't have to," the human says and takes Cloud by the elbow but the gryphon gets an arm around her waist. Before she knows it she's been pulled over her stool and stands between them.

"Back off, little man," the gryphon says over Cloud's head. "This one isn't for you."

"The hell—" he argues as Cloud snaps her arm free of the human. Getting away from the gryphon proves tricky. She turns to face him so he can't hook his fingers around her middle otherwise she's trapped between his arm and her stool. The standoff only continues for a few more seconds.

"Come to my table," the gryphon orders and Cloud reaches around, digging her fingernails into his forearm.

"No," she insists but the big gryphon doesn't listen. His pupils dilate, swallowing his irises and moving on to the whites. Then a clutch of short brown feathers ripples up the sides of his neck and disappears behind his ears. As his bitter scent of aggression fills Cloud's nose, a patch of feathers appears in the V of his shirt.

The oblivious human gets a hand on her shoulder.

"Lawrence. Bar. Now," the bartender has a radio in one hand and holds the other at the males. "Easy gents. We'll all make sure the lady has a nice evening."

"You don't want to do this," Cloud tries, using her magic to influence the gryphon male but he has no intention of backing down and ignores her. She's stuck between two stupid, drunk males, both intent on taking her from the other.

"Lawrence," the bartender tries again and Cloud glances at the tunnel. Lawrence steps out, his white shirt shines in the black light, but with the swell of people leaving the dance floor for the tables he has no chance of stopping the gryphon before he shifts further and goes through Cloud to get to the human.

Much to her horror, the gryphon's front teeth merge and she knows he's out of control. The human chooses that moment to pull on her, setting the gryphon off. Cloud jams a thumb deep beneath the gryphon's collar bone and turns sideways to escape the hold the human has on her shoulders. As the gryphon makes his move she punches him in the chin, snapping his teeth together. He doesn't slow but his eyes lose focus.

Then she hooks one foot behind the human's knee and pulls, toppling him backwards as she follows through, bringing her knee up into the gryphon's stomach. As the air rushes from his lungs, Cloud steps clear and drives an elbow between his shoulders for good measure.

The two land in a passed out gryphon-on-top position.

Before Cloud can appreciate her handiwork, Lawrence has her around the waist and pulls her clear.

"You okay, Cherry?"

"Yeah," she says but the last thing she expected was to diffuse a fight. This one wouldn't have happened if she hadn't shown up.

"He's in some trouble when he wakes up," Lawrence mutters then looks up at the balcony. Several of the winged gryphons watch and Cloud's cheeks flush with the attention. "Get a foot up on them since you kicked their asses."

Cloud moves at his order. He's clearly the guard master and she's a guest so her response is quick and automatic. She puts one foot on the gryphon's back and raises her arms in victory.

"This one is going on the wall," he says as he takes a couple of pictures.

"Lawrence, trouble?" The male who nodded from the balcony arrives through a door by the bar so Cloud drops her arms and puts her foot down. His wings are gone and he wears a white Cooper's shirt.

"Yeah, Daniel," Lawrence explains. "One on break and my other two bouncers were tied up downstairs. She's quick. I don't think anyone noticed there was even a problem."

"Fortunately," Daniel approaches Cloud with a hand out. "I'm Daniel Cooper. I own the bar. What do your friends call you?"

Cloud looks at his palm and when she finds it empty she remembers to emulate and holds hers out. Her stiff fingers don't relax as he grasps them and bounces her arm up and down. Cooper leans forward over the bodies on the floor and keeps well out of reach.

"My friends here call me Cherry," she announces with her chin up. Cooper holds back a small burp with his closed mouth but it sounds more like a growl and Lawrence and the bartender drop their eyes.

"Lawrence," Cooper groans.

"Cherry from the eyrie," the bartender explains. "This your first time out? We didn't mean anything by it."

She suspects she's the target of some joke she doesn't understand.

"And what do folks who aren't your friends call you?" Cooper tries

"I suspect they also call me Cherry," she says with a glance at the bartender. "My red hair... I'm Cloud."

But Cooper seems done with her.

"Get him to the lockup until he's sober," he points at the prone gryphon. "I don't want him back here for a year and get the human a coffee and a cab.

"Provide Cloud with a quiet meal and a room. See that she's not disturbed until after noon tomorrow."

I'm in.

Chapter Six

Daniel Cooper places his palm over a smooth stone on his master bedroom wall. A small thunk buzzes his hand. Seconds later, he pushes the recessed door open and steps inside a cave-like chamber.

Uneven grey stone covers the unlit floor and walls. A tattered sleeping mat and a small wooden box rest at the far side of the otherwise empty room. Years earlier, over the course of two weeks, Cooper promised the Earth he'd protect the contents of the box with his life for inside is a relic so powerful it could bring an entire clan of dragonkin to its knees. In return, the Earth created the impervious box and the stone lock for the door. Both open only for him.

Cooper seals the door behind him and steps around the mat, careful not to touch it. He shared it for many years with his mate, a green dragonkin, before she was killed for stealing the relic away from its hiding place in the high Arctic. She bore their children on the mat and years later she took her last breath in the same place, a victim of a slow and vicious poison driven deep into her body by an arrow.

He thought he'd seen the last of the dragonkin for a while. The Grand Council knows he has the green dragonkin relic but he was certain they didn't know where it was hidden. That is until tonight, when a lone female gold dragonkin stepped into his bar and broke up a fight.

Two hundred years ago Cooper's grand-sire, Aledaar, found the gold dragonkin relic and used it to subjugate the entire clan. He retired as Sire to his eyrie and used his power over the golds to seize leadership of the Council. Over time he filled the Council's Will, their guard, with gold dragonkin. Each gold dragonkin succumbed to the gryphon and his magic trinket and was destined to follow his will.

Now Aledaar, Cooper's sire and younger sibling use the Council to drive out any dragonkin sympathizers and keep control of the Will. The threat of further atrocities keeps Cooper from refuting the Council's claims that Cooper himself has been decimating the traditional eyries. Those murders were ordered by Aledaar himself.

Now Cloud sleeps in an apartment a few floors below his own. He thought he saw the gold sparkle of her eyes from the upper balcony and was certain when he saw her up close. Cooper's time in possession of the green relic grants him the ability to tell dragonkin apart from ordinary gryphons. He can also draw upon their power of influence when he's near the green relic.

The half-breed descendants of rare dragons and gryphons are as misunderstood by the majority of gryphons as they were shunned as inferior by dragons.

If Cloud meant to destroy his eyrie or even bring him before the council it would have been with the Council's Will. Instead, she walked in alone and so painfully out of place that Cooper hesitated in gagging her and locking her up. Her quick move with the gryphon whose life she saved by stopping him gave Cooper pause that she could be dangerous but even then he offered her a room.

It only took Lawrence's resources a couple of hours to find out who she is; the adopted grand-daughter of Sire Lev of the Vancouver Island Eyrie, and before that she'd been raised as an orphan in Jasper.

Cooper shudders at the thought of his birthplace. If his sire, Sher, suspected she was dragonkin she'd have been raised by the Council and forced into the Will during her sixteenth year and if Lev knew he never would have let her out. Cloud would have been hidden and not sent off to train under Master Sky. Ranger training explains how she handled the drunk gryphon in the bar but not her mysterious absence from Sky's eyrie.

The only logical reason is nobody, including Cloud, knows she is dragonkin. She could be one of the few gold dragonkin not subjected to service in the Council's Will and her continued ignorance of her true bloodline will be the only thing protecting her from joining their ranks.

Cooper still has to be careful. Even though his attunement to the relic allows him to identify dragonkin by sight and his mate's tears protect him from their influence, Cloud's motives remain unclear. She could still order another gryphon to harm him.

According to the gryphon Lawrence stationed to listen in the room beside Cloud's, she laughed like a child playing with the shower, turning it off and on over and over until the pipes banged. Then she pulled off the bedspread, took wing and fell asleep on the floor. No TV, movie orders or phone calls like he expects from a gryphon familiar with the human world.

The small key in Cooper's pocket isn't the same size as the lock on the box but the lock shrinks to fit. When he opens the lid, a small ancient green dragon bone mounted on a gold bracelet illuminates the room with a brilliant emerald glow. His mate's eyes shone the same colour. It would lick over the whites, brightening with lust and he would kiss them with a consuming hunger as her small moans filled their den. Her breath would heat with pleasure, singeing his chest feathers then she would turn her head away before release cast flames from her mouth.

Cooper undresses, tosses his clothes aside and takes wing before kneeling by the open box.

"Eviscerate," he whispers as he fixes the bracelet around his wrist. He pictures her long blonde hair and smile and feels the true inner beauty of her kind. "My beautiful Lady

Eve. What do I do with this gold dragonkin? Kill her or protect her?"

Cooper curls up on the mat, comforted by the magic of his mate's kin and in a few breaths is asleep, waiting for an answer.

It's mid-morning when he puts the bracelet away and steps from the dark chamber. After showering, Cooper conceals a small handgun beneath his jacket, a knife around his calf and goes downstairs for breakfast.

In an hour, he'll find Lawrence and together they'll knock on Cloud's door and act on Lady Eve's advice.

Chapter Seven

The long flight to Calgary left Cloud feeling oddly out of shape; overworked in some areas and soft in others. When the clock says 10 am, she pushes the furniture to one end of the room and starts on a set of challenging exercises designed to change every muscle in her body into painful jelly. Then she runs through the set a second time, dripping sweat on the carpet and lingering on any moves that work muscles unused in flight.

The open curtains expose the streets far below where Calgarians move about in cars and on foot. She faces west toward home. The other side of the building looks east to the campground where Soar waits. He should be there by now and she has eleven days until she'll be there with him.

Then home with her head hung in shame although she can't be any more shamed than she is now. Every day she learns about this strange eyrie in the sky will earn back a little more of her lost pride.

Cloud puts her soiled clothes in the laundry bag as Lawrence instructed the night before. He explained that Cooper owned the building and the top four floors were restricted to gryphon residents. Her room sits on the second highest floor and the one above is off limits to everyone but Cooper and his guard. The stone of a mountain eyrie belongs to the Earth but this isn't stone so Cooper's ownership makes a small amount of sense. How he created it is beyond her.

She steps into the shower, squealing with surprise as cold water blasts her hot skin. She's barely towelled off and dressed in clean human clothes when three loud knocks on the door get her attention. Cloud freezes and concentrates on her surroundings. Only the shuffling of two large, unwinged males reaches her and after a moment the scents of Lawrence and Daniel Cooper ease in under the door.

"Cloud?" Lawrence calls. "Open the door, Cherry."

Cloud doesn't much mind the nickname since he explained it on the way to her room. She blushed like mad and he pretended not to notice.

Lawrence stands between her and Cooper when she figures out the locks and pulls the door open.

"May we come in?" Lawrence looks past her, directing her attention to the room and not the hallway.

"Of course," Cloud steps aside.

"Problem with the room, Cherry?" Lawrence asks. He strides toward the tumbled up furniture. Unlike the night before when the guard master wore black pants and a white shirt, he wears loose sweats and a short-sleeved T-shirt. Cooper, on the other hand, is better dressed in a grey suit, copper coloured shirt and a black tie.

"Um, I needed space for conditioning," Cloud says as she kneels to Cooper and then turns to bow to Lawrence.

"Why are all the pictures crooked?" Cooper asks so she turns again, amused by his laughter.

"I couldn't remember if they were all crooked or strai —" she starts but cold sharp steel presses against her throat as Lawrence somehow gets his elbow behind her back and under both of hers. It only takes a moment for Cloud to calm so she exhibits as little threat as possible.

Cooper hasn't moved other than releasing the smile from his face.

"Do not speak, Cherry," Lawrence whispers. "Daniel is going to ask you some questions. We know more than you think so don't take a chance by lying. If you speak of anyone but yourself I'll cut through your voice box and watch you bleed to death. Carpet is cheap and I'm very good at installing it."

Cloud raises her chin with respect though she's confused by the screwy instruction to talk only about herself. A frightened bead of sweat escapes down her spine and she's certain they can smell it. Maybe they think she's afraid she'll be caught lying but then she has a knife at her throat and that would scare anyone.

"Weapons?" Lawrence asks.

"Back pants pocket," Cloud replies and Lawrence's hold tightens enough to give her well worked shoulders a good stretch. She doesn't resist as Cooper feels one pocket then the other and removes the knife.

Then he feels her sides and around her bra before before lifting her shirt. Cloud tenses with her scars so exposed and Lawrence hisses. When the shirt drops, Cooper feels her legs and socks before stepping away.

"Is Cloud your real name?" Cooper asks.

"Yes."

"Tell me where your home eyrie is."

"Vancouver Island," she whispers, afraid to even swallow.

"Indeed. Is that your birth eyrie?"

"No, I was born at Welch Peak and raised in Jasper."

Cooper looks at Lawrence as he considers her answer.

"Your dame moved you?"

"I was the only survivor of the massacre," her voice deepens with bitterness, unable to completely shake the idea that Cooper was responsible. "I was raised by Tawny until Dame Shadow arrived and I left with her ten years ago."

Cooper turns aside and appears to study the furniture pile. The seconds pass and he opens the button of his jacket before tucking his fists in his pockets.

"Tawny passed a few years ago."

"I attended her blessing with a small delegation from Vancouver Island," Cloud says, her words no more than the movement of lips. The flight had been urgent and sad and Cloud struggled to keep up with Firn and Dove, dame and daughter in Shadow's guard. They arrived before the blessing was complete and Firn and Dove spoke at the climax of the ceremony, blessing Tawny's old spirit with magic protection for its passage to the heavens. Cloud didn't speak. As much as she wished to, doing so would have betrayed her royalty and the three positions at Tawny's shoulders were taken anyway.

It wasn't like her strongest magic was beneficial in any way; more like manipulative. What could she have said that didn't sound like a curse?

Cloud becomes aware of Lawrence's slow breathing in sync with hers.

"Tell me then," Cooper says. "What drove you from Vancouver Island to where you are now?"

"I left two and a half years ago for Master Sky's."

Cooper waits and doesn't ask any more.

"I left there six days ago and came here because I have nowhere else to go."

"Ah, I see. Describe the circumstances of your departure."

"I took an oath and will not discuss it for another day."

Lawrence stretches his thumb across Cloud's windpipe and presses the blade to her skin like he's about to slice through an apple. Cloud can't help it; certain he's going to kill her, her heart beats out of control and her knees shake.

"I accept death," she says with as much bravery as she can. "I will not further my shame by breaking my word."

"Let her go," Cooper orders and the knife disappears. Lawrence holds her up with one elbow and kneads her shoulders. He's good with his hands and the comfort of his touch pushes through the fear she suffered only minutes before. Now she understands it was a test, with grave consequences if she failed, but a test nonetheless.

"Good girl, Cherry," Lawrence says. There's no threat in his voice and Cloud is confused they both trust her. She hadn't been sure how they felt when they arrived but now there is no doubt.

As soon as her legs feel solid she moves to the small desk and leans on it.

"Did you commit a crime?" Lawrence asks. Cooper seems lost in his own thoughts and though he listens he's distant again like the night before.

"I didn't," Cloud says. "I refused a royal who felt he could touch me in any way he wanted."

"And he took revenge?"

Cloud shrugs since she's said too much.

"Perhaps you weren't the only one he assaulted," Lawrence speculates and Cloud's sharpened breath betrays her surprise at his choice of words. She'd convinced herself it was simply over-zealous flirting but the aggression with which Falcon treated her could easily be described as assault.

"We've all made decisions even knowing the personal cost would be high," Cooper sighs as he turns to the door. "Knowing what it cost you, would you do it again?"

"Yes," she admits.

"Then you learned something about yourself that most gryphons never get a chance to see. Lawrence, show Cherry where she can train without rearranging her suite."

The door eases shut behind him as the hydraulic arm takes its weight.

"They say you can tell one sparring chamber from another by the taste of its dirt," Cloud says and Lawrence laughs.

"You'll find no dirt in our gym. What you will find are several big gryphons who won't coddle you like your friends did."

Chapter Eight

Cloud has been in Calgary for a week and Cooper still isn't sure about her. She's done nothing to encourage his initial thought that she's a spy and other than being an innocent hick, or cherry from the eyrie, the only offensive thing she's done is work her ass off by volunteering to help with every little task she can find.

Lawrence, however, is quite taken with the young gold dragonkin. Not in a romantic way at all; Lawrence has been happily mated for decades. Happily means that, for now, both he and his female prefer to spend a large amount of time apart since their young became adults.

Cooper remains troubled by the fact Cloud is from Welch Peak. The eyrie was very sympathetic to dragonkin, as were Vancouver Island and a few others. One gold dragonkin in particular, Lord Fury, Master of the Council's Will, could be Cloud's sire and he must remain unaware of her existence. If Fury learns she survived it will only be a matter of time before he takes her before the Council. Cloud would be forced to wear Cooper's grand-sire's gold dragon necklace. She would be tortured with pain until she loses her will completely to the old gryphon. Aledaar's order to surrender all dragonkin can't be fought. Even Fury succumbed to the pain of refusal and turned his own son in.

With Cooper's grandsire Aledaar prone to dropping in accompanied by his dragonkin guard and all the pressure he's currently under from the Council, it could be only days before they arrive. Then again it could be months. Either way, he's running out of time.

For her own good, Cloud has to go.

Cooper is certain Cloud has never taken dragonkin form. The real threat of death from Lawrence would have caused any other dragonkin to shift into a much more dangerous form but not Cloud. Even a week of rough sparring with Lawrence and the guard failed to make her do any more than noticeably warm and occasionally let loose with a fierce growl that would leave an inexperienced fighter dripping shit down his tail.

His own Lady Eve fondly remembered the many times her own sire attempted to kill her and force her to take dragon form for the first time. In the end she shifted, severely wounding her very proud sire before she reigned her dragon side in.

Forcing a first shift on an oblivious dragonkin would be cruel and dangerous and frankly, not his job. He has mixed feelings about doing it for his own children.

Today, Cloud arrives at the gym first and is well into her workout with Lawrence when Cooper shows up with his laptop and phone. He plans to mix work with socializing then give Cloud the night off from the bar and spend the evening with her in his suite.

Lawrence understands why she needs to be somewhere safer. As much as Cooper's oldest friend likes having her around, Lawrence is one of a select few who appreciates the powerful nature of the green relic two floors up. He also knows the danger Cloud faces from the Council and the risk Calgary takes in harbouring her.

"Cherry," Lawrence breathes. Even after a round of exercises and nearly an hour sparring he won't get any closer to panting. "I don't suppose you're tired of hauling cases of beer up to the bar, are you?"

"What do you mean?" she asks. Cooper listens, eyes on the computer screen and coffee to his lips. Both Lawrence and Cloud are winged and dressed in traditional trousers. Cloud also wears a light tunic. The rest of his guard huddle around the room. Working nights in the bar downstairs makes the rough males perpetual latecomers. The late nights don't affect Cloud and even Lawrence's easy temper shows signs of wear from keeping up with Cloud's early mornings.

"Friends aren't always what they seem, little gryphon," he whispers and Cloud grunts a reply as she slips under his wing, landing an elbow in his kidney. "Sometimes it's in their best interest for you to do some damage to someone you care about."

"A good gryphon will always keep another from getting out of line," she paraphrases. The actual quote she would have learned in childhood is several paragraphs long.

"Put it into practice," Lawrence barks and Cloud takes a step back to assess Lawrence's change in stance from defense to challenge. "Enough dicking around. You want a shot at the guard you're going to fight me for it."

"How?"

Cooper's eyes narrow as the gold flashes in Cloud's eyes. The remainder of the guard takes notice as well. Although they can't see the change in her eyes their attention turns to the centre of the chamber where Cloud and Lawrence square off. The female is fearless. Even face to face with a gryphon nearly twice her size, she's ready to go before she's even heard the rules.

"Better me, Cherry. That's all. I want to feel a bone break. If it's mine, you're in. If it's yours, you're back to humping empties until I say you get another chance."

She doesn't answer as she brings her hands up. Only a tiny tremor and a dry swallow suggest a healthy caution. Lawrence's tail twitches, hinting at his coming attack but Cloud keeps hers still. It might be against her nature to harm another without cause.

She's headed for a rude awakening, Cooper decides as he moves to the edge of his seat. He's as caught up in anticipation as the rest of the room. As much as he avoids senseless violence, the gryphon in him is easily drawn to the prospect of an honest fight. Maybe that's why he owns a testosterone fueled gryphon bar.

"Yes, Master," she replies with a formal acknowledgement of Lawrence's status as head of the guard. A good gryphon never refuses her master's order, trusting he knows her limits better than she does.

Lawrence roars and charges, hands shifting to claws and immediately puts Cloud on the defensive. He's never shifted beyond wings and tail with her. She has little choice but to dodge and Cooper anticipates she'll turn in one direction or another, moving at the last possible moment without giving Lawrence time to follow but her move takes everyone by surprise.

Before Lawrence finishes his first step Cloud's heart stops, something bound to confuse those who don't know she's dragonkin. In order to prevent escalating the situation and for stealth she's gone silent, her circulatory system moves blood by the forces in her veins and arteries alone. As a result, her muscles flood with a constant supply of oxygen that boosts her strength and stamina.

She pounces straight at him.

Lawrence's knees are bent, feet placed far apart for leverage so she takes advantage of the gap and dives between, striking his thighs hard with the big bones of her wings before folding them and landing on the floor. The move almost gets her clear.

As she scrambles out of reach, Lawrence makes an ungraceful pivot. He doesn't bother grabbing for her. Instead he slams his booted foot down and just misses shattering her ankle. Cloud kicks to prevent being pinned from behind but Lawrence isn't going to bother with any traditional sparring tactic. That had never been part of the lesson plan he shared with Cooper the night before and the wild grin on his face shows he enjoyed her surprise move.

She gets to her hands and knees, still trying to stay out of reach, but she slows when she gets one foot underneath to stand.

It's all the advantage Lawrence needs.

Two and a half years of formal lessons from Master Sky never gave her a chance to experience the dirty tactics of the real world; predators and big males with the patience and desire to play with their opponent. Cooper tenses as he watches Lawrence's other boot come down on her trailing leg and the thud reverberates through the room. The bone holds but Cloud cries out as she rolls away.

Lawrence has her. His big arms loop under her wings, pinning her arms at awkward angles. The hold he has on one wrist will snap it when he increases the pressure. Cloud scratches at his head but her fingers only leave red lines on his sweaty skin and don't breach the surface.

"Surrender or I'll break it," he whispers but Cloud fights. With her weight on her good foot she dangles in his grip, face screwed up as she scrapes her heel down his shin. Lawrence knows what's coming and jerks her up a little higher so she can't stomp on his foot.

"Surrender, Cherry," Lawrence tries again and her forearm flexes.

"No," she whispers.

Then Cooper feels it. His skin tingles in response to her dragonkin influence. She's going to use it on Lawrence. Damn, if she doesn't know she's dragonkin then how the hell did she figure that out?

"You don't want to hurt me," Cloud growls, the strength of her influence makes Cooper's testicles quiver before they draw in for their own safety and he holds his coffee before him like a lame shield. Although he's not influenced by the words, he knows the power she wields over Lawrence.

For the briefest moment Lawrence struggles with the decision whether or not to let her go and Cooper realizes her magic is untrained and weak.

"You okay, Cherry?" Lawrence asks as he releases the hold on her arms and lowers her to the floor. He only sounds concerned. There's no hint of second thoughts for either challenging her or letting her go.

Cooper realizes he holds his cup too tight when the lid pops off. Black coffee slops over his thumb and makes a run down his wrist to soak the inside of his shirtsleeve. Lawrence has never backed down during a lesson and this time it looks like nothing more than a failure of character before the rest of the guard.

"I'm fine, Lawrence," Cloud holds her chin steady. Yeah, she isn't proud of what she's done but Cooper sighs in relief. If she knew she's dragonkin then she'd be proud of winning a battle of wills and avoiding a deadly decision but she isn't. Her lips press together with emotion as she lifts her chin and closes her eyes in respectful surrender. She knows she just made the guard master lose face in front of his rangers.

"Lawrence, a word," Cooper says with an appropriate amount of sternness but Lawrence flashes him a dirty look. Cloud flinches when Lawrence takes her wrist. He probes along the bones for damage before he moves on to her ankle.

"Lawrence," Cooper hisses as he kneels with the pair. "What the hell got in to you?"

"I didn't want to hurt her," Lawrence replies. He holds Cloud's calf and foot like a newborn and tests her ankle's range of motion.

"Bullshit"

Lawrence stops what he's doing as he understands what Cloud did. Without a word he puts her leg down and gives her chin a gentle nudge up.

"Bitches," he shouts as he strides to the far side of the room. The three heads muttering together snap around and the others nearby step clear. "You're not leaving the room until I've broken something."

Lawrence's rangers know better than to scatter.

"You don't need to see this," Cooper says as he helps Cloud to her feet. They stop long enough for him to slip his phone into his pocket and grab the laptop but the grunts and solid smacks of body blows fill the room before they're out the door.

Chapter Nine

Cooper insists on waiting in the hall while Cloud steps in to shower and change. Then she's going to his suite? Cloud limps across the room on an ankle that feels like the broken ribs from a year earlier except she has to walk on the angry bones.

If they were on to her she wouldn't see Lawrence coming and besides, the big bald male treats her like favoured kin, not a spy. And Cooper's unexpected warmth can be taken in more ways than one. Mostly though, Cloud figures she's not only in trouble for calling Lawrence off but Cooper's also figured out she's a royal gryphon and there's nothing she can do about any of it other than come clean.

"Oh, crap," Cloud pauses the hairbrush. Cooper's eyrie has no royal female. No Dame to sit at his side and bring life to this man-made eyrie in the sky, if such a thing is even possible. Could that be where things are headed?

Cloud pulls the shoulders of her shirt back to bring the front up higher and winces at the twinge in her swelling wrist. When she's sure nothing shows around the neckline she lets herself out.

Yet again Cooper's demeanour changes and this time he leans casually against the wall. With his jacket open and hands in his pockets he comes off as overconfident and

Cloud's more certain than ever that he's interested in her as Dame material even if it's just a business arrangement.

"Let me assist," Cooper offers her an elbow. Cloud reciprocates by holding hers out to him and he laughs, lacing his elbow over her hand. "Hold it."

"Okay," she's grateful for the support and it only takes a few limp-free pain-laced steps for her grip to tighten as she gets the weight off her ankle.

"How much trouble am I in?" Cloud asks. She might as well get right to the point. Maybe she can get out of having dinner with him.

"You've done something unconscionable?" His tone is light but there's a sternness that suggests maybe she has.

"Well, no," Cloud tries as Cooper presses the up button for the elevator. "Maybe, yes?"

"Which is it?"

The door slides closed behind them as Cloud hops around on one foot.

"It's not a big deal if you've already figured it out."

"I see," Cooper mutters as his arm relaxes. "We'll eat then we'll talk."

"Okay."

"Take a seat on the patio," Cooper instructs as they step from the elevator.

Patio is another new word and she hesitates, looking for something obvious or better yet something with a label but nothing she thinks could be a patio presents itself.

"Through the glass doors, Cloud," Cooper calls as he disappears. "There are some chairs. Put your foot up and I'll get you some ice."

The glass doors are more than thirty feet away on the other side of a huge room filled with dark colours and carved wood. Stone sculpture covers every surface. Although it doesn't feel much like a cave, Cloud can't get past the knowledge she's not in a real mountain. She makes three steps down and passes an immense sofa that would fit half a dozen winged gryphons before she slows, her eyes settling on a four foot tall drawing of a very familiar man.

With the patio and the doors forgotten, Cloud hobbles closer to the picture.

"It's you," she announces as Cooper approaches.

"You should sit," he says as his cold fingers take her elbow. In his other hand he holds a couple of ice bags.

"The hair is different," she compares. "And the jaw is a little small but it's you."

"Seems to have been the fashion then. The picture is fifty years old."

"Did you make it?"

"No," Cooper tugs and Cloud watches the picture as he leads her out into the heat and blinding light of August. Thunderheads stack up miles to the south and Cloud stops. Even up on the roof and so close to shelter, instinct kicks in warning her to keep her distance.

The soft pat of a palm on fabric draws her attention. Cooper sits on a bright red padded chair opposite an identically coloured lounge.

"Fifty years ago my life changed forever," he says. His voice starts out bright, reflecting the intense sun then darkens with the storm clouds that have already changed shape.

"Was a female involved?" Cloud immediately regrets her insensitivity but he doesn't seem to notice, instead taking too much time arranging the ice on her ankle and offering the smaller bag for her wrist. She can't help but hope he already has a female and dinner is just an attempt to make up for her injury.

"I knew right away that choosing her would force me into exile with my family. We'd already had a falling out over ideological differences, several in fact, and I was certain choosing her would bring me death or exile. I was exiled and I'm not yet sure that I still don't face death."

"I don't understand," Cloud says. Just because your sire doesn't like your mate is no reason to cast a child out.

Or kill them.

Cooper stands and takes a step toward her then his hands drop and he reaches for his buckle. Cloud's thick swallow hides not only discomfort but interest. She's seen plenty of naked gryphons, nudity in the eyrie is quite normal, but she's never seen a naked human. Then thoughts of naked gryphons remind her of Soar. The jerk disappeared from her life and turned up just in time to thrust her into this one.

Once the belt is free he opens the button and pulls his shirt clear. What the hell is he doing? Showing her all the goods before he asks her to mate with him?

The pants only drop a small amount and Cooper pulls the shirt up revealing a rough white scar just below his navel. The circle of tooth marks is a mating bite and Cloud can't help but relax. The position of Dame is already filled.

"She passed many years ago," Cooper says as he tucks his shirt in and does his pants back up. "I guess I needed to show you how deep my connection to her still is and how important my remaining family is to me. Her mark reminds me every day that choosing her was the right thing to do although the personal price I paid included her death.

"Do you remember when I asked you about the choice you made with the royal male at Master Sky's?"

"Daniel," an older woman interrupts, stepping through the glass doors to join them. Her light summer dress and bare feet reveal her skin and her age of probably six hundred gryphon years but she doesn't exactly smell like a gryphon. Cloud's speechless confusion allows for little more than accepting a glass of white wine. She smells more human than gryphon.

"This is Deirdre," Cooper introduces. "She cares for my suite and is kind enough to cook for me when I forget to look after myself. Cloud is Sire Lev's grand-daughter from Vancouver Island."

"Dear Cloud," Deirdre sighs as she squishes her bottom in next to Cloud's feet without putting any pressure on the ice against her ankle. "It is a pleasure to meet you."

Deirdre cocks her head aside waiting for Cloud to speak then laughs.

"Ask your question, Cloud. I'm certain you've not seen the likes of me."

With a nervous glance at Cooper, Cloud does.

"What are you?"

"She is direct, Daniel, and very young. Very pretty, too."

Cooper grunts as he sits back in his chair, content to let Deirdre tell her story.

"My gryphon parents conceived me in their human form and I was found abandoned in the woods as a babe, clinging to life. When I turned sixteen I ran away from my adopted human family. I would see things in the sky, winged men and women, sometimes just standing there on the street or in a park. We made a family trip here to Calgary and there were so many of the winged creatures. I knew nobody else could see them so I came here hoping for some sane answers. I asked the first one I found the same question you just asked me.

"When Daniel picked his wings up off the ground we talked a long time and figured out what I am.

"I am a gryphon, Cloud. I cannot shift and have a human life span but I can see you and my home is here."

"Wow," Cloud exclaims. "There must be—"

"More like me?"

Cloud nods and Deirdre adjusts the ice packs.

"Several. Daniel has a sense for these lost ones and finds a place for them with us.

"I shall have your meal prepared shortly, Daniel," Deirdre stands and then leans to Cooper to accept a kiss to her forehead.

"As I said," Cooper speaks again. "I had a falling out with my family over our differences and when I found Eve she was a proud warrior on a very dangerous quest. At first it seemed I was just a diversion to her as I could never be her match as a fighter but the more she explained her family's struggles the more I came to understand I was destined to help. We mated and parted ways and when I returned to my family and told them of her I was exiled as was my twin who took my side against my sire.

"He felt Eve and her kin were good for no more than service and certainly weren't good enough to mate with a common gryphon, much less a royal."

"You're royal?" Cloud whispers. "She was common?"

Cooper raises his eyebrows and tilts his head to the side as if to say it doesn't matter.

"After my exile I rebelled against everything gryphon. I embraced the human world but found I had little to offer so I did some research and hijacked an airplane. After it took off with me, my ransom and the passengers I went to the back of the plane—"

"And flew away!"

"Indeed," Cooper laughs. "I thought the Washington State wind ripped my wings off but they held and I made it to the ground near Snohomish. Then I went south through Mexico to South America where I changed the American currency to gold. After a small vacation, I returned to Calgary and started buying and selling houses, working my way up to ownership of this building and several others.

"The American authorities had their artist draw a picture of what the witnesses said I looked like so I tracked him down and commissioned the large picture you saw inside," Cooper snorts. "They noticed I had the same name as the hijacker but after they found no evidence I'd ever left Canada they took my interest in the picture to be simply amusement at the similarity and let me be."

Cloud doesn't understand half of what he said but she likes the big picture on the wall. Pasting such a ridiculously huge image of one's self so prominently is a very gryphon thing to do. She can appreciate something so pointlessly proud.

"Here you go," Deirdre announces as she backs through the curtains with a wide tray. It's laden with two covered plates and Deirdre places the whole thing on a nearby table before presenting Cloud with seared salmon, wild rice and barely cooked green beans.

"Thank you," Cloud nods as Deirdre serves Cooper and tops up his glass.

"Did you save some for yourself?" Cooper asks.

"I ate first," Deirdre burps and Cloud starts to giggle. Then she sobers at the sight of the storm clouds in the distance since they aren't so distant at all. In a few short minutes they've come much closer and beneath the contented sounds of their quiet eating she can make out the rumble of thunder.

"Is she safe here?" Cloud asks when she's sure Deirdre must be occupied deep inside Cooper's suite.

"Intuitive," Cooper answers between sips of wine. "No, she isn't and I would not have allowed you to see her if I didn't feel her secret is safe with you."

Yeah, Cloud feels his trust. In spite of his changes of mood and inconsistent attitude toward her, Cooper's trust has been solid since the day he and Lawrence questioned her in her room.

"Your mate," Cloud asks as she tries to understand him. "Was she a gryphon like Deirdre?"

Again the raised eyebrows. Cooper isn't giving up anything.

"Deirdre has an escape route and a safe place to hide, should the need arise."

But he's barely finished the sentence and Cloud is barely finished her dinner when he gets to the point.

"Tell me, Cloud, adopted granddaughter of Sire Lev and adopted daughter of Dame Shadow and Master Talon. Tell me how you stopped Lawrence from breaking your arm."

Cloud lowers her fork to her plate as her appetite for the last mouthful of wild rice and tender onions disappears.

"You already know," she says flatly.

"I want to hear you say it."

She rinses her mouth with the last of the wine before she speaks.

"I am a royal gryphon."

"'scuse me?" Cooper nearly chokes on what Cloud thought to be the contents of an empty mouth.

"I believe my dame was royal, Daniel, because I have magic. I can control gryphons," she tries to explain to Cooper's open mouth. "I shouldn't have embarrassed Lawrence like that I know but it just came out. He didn't *want* to hurt me and it just came out.

"And I know when I'm trusted. I feel you trust me and Lawrence does so please keep my secret. If I ever get back in to Sky's program the last thing I want are royals inviting me home to meet their Dame."

"My word," Cooper promises as he gets himself together. "In exchange for your word to keep Deirdre's secret is a fair trade."

In spite of being a little more together about Cloud's admission he's returned to being on edge. His relaxed hands ball and the muscles at his temples work in time with what must be urgent thoughts. Cooper puts his plate aside and approaches as his brow creases with the effort it takes to uncurl his fingers.

"Let's look, hm?" Cooper removes the ice and tenderly raises her ankle. Although the cold numbed it, fresh pain lances up toward her knee as he works the joint, testing it as Lawrence had. It didn't hurt then but Cloud was so amped up from the fight she didn't feel it or the wrist.

"Owe!" Cloud slams her hands down for stability, catching the fork handle in the process. Rice and onion launch up, bounce off her cheek and stick in her hair. Cooper probes along the bone.

"You may have a fracture," he says. "But I won't tell Lawrence. We'll let him believe your match ended in a stalemate."

"Okay," Cloud wheezes in a lungful as he puts her foot down and slides closer.

"I have children. Did you know?"

Cloud shakes her head and draws back as he reaches for her face.

"Hold still, I'll get that out. You remind me very much of my daughter; always taking the brunt of any disagreement with her brother.

"I've patched up many of her injuries over the years. She's as tough a fighter as her dame. My son lives far from here but she still comes by, sometimes just to let me clean her up."

Cooper's love for his daughter comes through in his voice. He's a very different gryphon when he talks about his family than when he talks of anything else. The lines of worry grow deeper, as does his voice and Cloud can't help but smile. The tenderness she always receives from her adopted parents is as touching as Cooper's and she couldn't miss them more. She leaves him to his silence as he picks food from her hair.

"We should go in."

Rain patters around them, staining the concrete tiles and red chairs with dark spots and Cloud starts at a crack of thunder. She's been oblivious to the darkening of the sky and the flashes of lightning.

"Are you homesick?" Cooper asks. The great long sofa is as comfortable as it looks and Cloud stretches out, her stomach full, relieved to be away from the storm.

"More than I ever thought possible," she says. Four days to Soar is both an eternity and far too soon.

"Perhaps you worry they won't believe you?"

"They will," Cloud says but her shame can only reflect poorly on the Vancouver Island Eyrie and her Sire and Dame.

"They must miss you terribly," Cooper adds.

"I hadn't thought—"

Cooper's phone rings, interrupting her, and he excuses himself to the other room to answer. As he speaks to the person on the other end Cloud leans back and closes her eyes, hoping he didn't notice the guilt gnawing at her resolve. By the time Cooper returns she no longer cares about him or his secrets.

All she wants to do is go home.

Chapter Ten

Cloud hasn't bothered to check in.

Soar grips the wheel like it's responsible for his week in human camper hell. Granted, he'd never demanded or arranged an update but still. She left him there listening to dogs that won't stop barking because they don't like his bigger predator presence.

And the little kids.

And the big kids.

And every time there's a happy couple it only reminds him how dumping Cloud was the shittiest thing he's done to anyone in a long time. It's second only to getting her expelled and right up there with sending her into Calgary. The pair in the campsite next to his can't screw quietly enough for his gryphon hearing and all he can think of is Cloud.

Tell me about your day, Soar.

He still whispers his answer to the question she asked every time she came to his den. Sometimes following a rough exchange of dominance and urgent sex. Other times they'd simply nuzzle each others throats in gentle surrender before he brought up her leg and took her standing just inside his den.

Tell me about your day, Soar.

She'd whisper as her breath grew tight and she accepted him; both his presence deep inside her and the piece of his spirit he would share as he answered her question.

His answers don't mean the same without her to hear them, particularly when he's alone in his Cloud scented campervan. She's never going to care enough to ask again. If he's learned anything about her it's that her compassion and forgiveness are always ready and genuinely offered but he's going to make sure she keeps her distance until she knows all his crimes against her.

Even then he's certain to be the exception; the one asshole she'll never forgive.

As he drives west to Calgary he passes several terrific thunderstorms. One travels directly over the highway, flooding the road with heavy rain then battering him with wind and hail. The electrical interference chops apart the weather forecast. Soar gives up on the radio and turns it off, assuming the parade of severe weather would continue.

No matter.

The skies over Calgary are clear for the moment so it's safe for a quick fly around. Lawrence and the guard won't let anyone airborne within a thousand feet in any direction but Soar doesn't have to get that close to check out Cooper's penthouse. If there's no sign of her outside then Soar will head to the bar for a drink and some gossip from the regulars.

A pretty red-haired female in Cooper's will be noticed by every male in town.

It's late Friday afternoon and the downtown core still hasn't purged itself of workers so it takes nearly half an hour to find a large enough parking spot two blocks from Cooper's. Nobody notices Soar's shirtless form step out onto the sidewalk and down an alley. In this heat, he doesn't stand out. Once out of sight he takes wing and returns, invisible to human eyes, and climbs the ladder to the roof of his van.

After waiting for a break in traffic to allow for the brief drop as his wings take the air, Soar dashes across the roof, fills his wings and beats higher. He turns to take a path between two buildings and gains altitude as he passes over the Bow River then circles, careful to keep both his distance from Cooper's and his eyes on the patio.

He doesn't need to circle long to spot her.

Just as Soar gets high enough to see the penthouse in the distance he swears as Cooper tucks his shirt in and does his pants up. Cloud can't tear her gaze from his zipper to look Cooper in the eye.

Soar drops as jealousy weighs him down and he forgets to move his wings, falling thirty or forty feet before he gets them going and rises. An older female joins Cooper and Cloud but Soar hardly notices. Instead he calculates the odds of getting past the two big guards Cloud can't see on the roof. He'd love to drag that stupid female home by her ear. What the hell is she thinking and how far has she gone with Cooper to spy on him?

It's Soar's own fault and he keeps watching, punishing himself with the sight of them drinking wine and talking while they eat. Cooper slides over to Cloud and takes her leg up on his lap. Cloud startles as he starts to rub it then moves closer, cupping her cheek in his hand.

Soar has seen enough. He drops around to the alley where he took wing and shifts to human form before returning to his van to retrieve a shirt. The walk to Cooper's is a blur and he doesn't recognize the gryphon in Lawrence's usual place at the door. That could make things harder. If he's going to get a swing at Cooper for putting his hands on Cloud he'll have to keep his mouth shut until he knows where the big, bald bouncer is.

The bar is quieter than usual but Soar usually frequents it later in the night when any bad gryphon behaviour is hidden by the crush of bodies. The music is a little quieter and the clientele is a mix of business people with empty glasses and young women who arrived early and will look bored until the place fills up.

There are also the gryphon tables. Humans steer clear of the rough assortment of big 'men' who never dance and only get up to use the restroom. For the moment, Soar avoids them as well. If Seth behind the bar can't tell him anything the gryphon tables will be his next stop.

"I'm looking for a red-head," Soar says as he takes the seat right in front of Seth.

"I'm not a pimp," the bartender replies but the answer comes a little quickly even for Seth. "Are you drinking from the local menu tonight, George?"

Yeah, Soar bites his tongue. Human place, human names and the local menu is for gryphons. Since this is a work visit, Soar knows he better keep it brief, polite, and semi-sober.

Seth leans to look at Soar's shoulder and makes sure the mark of Lev's guard is hidden beneath his short sleeve. Soar isn't stupid enough to march in displaying that. As long as he respects the bar as neutral territory he'll get somewhat neutral answers.

"I guess it's the reserve tonight, Seth," Soar says as he drops a fifty on the polished wood. "My boss's grand-daughter is missing and I'm keeping an eye out for her."

Seth doesn't answer as he pushes a nearly full glass of home-made eighty proof 'reserve' across the bar.

"You gonna make me say it?" Soar asks but Seth only stares in reply. *Christ.* "With honey."

Seth chuckles as he digs around under the counter for a little bear shaped bottle and squirts in a couple of tablespoons before adding a pair of red plastic stir sticks.

"I think your drink is starting to become popular. I gotta get a bottle of this sweet stuff every year or two now."

Soar toasts Seth and makes his way to the gryphon tables. The bartender knows something about Cloud, no denying that, but his reaction is more in line with protecting Cooper's privacy than warning Soar off.

The opportunities for gossip at the gryphon tables aren't promising. He has a choice between half-drunk and will-get-his-talons-all-over-anything so he chooses the latter, God help him. If he sidled in next to anyone other than one of these two he'd be outside fighting within the hour.

"Rabbit," Soar tries to sound friendly but the older gryphon scowls as Soar sits. Then he brightens when he sees who it is.

"Well, what is it you want Soar? And where is that pretty friend of yours? Talon?"

Soar snorts as he draws in a mouthful of the reserve. The honey makes it palatable and within a few seconds Soar feels the burning shape of his insides. He leans deep into his chair, tips his head back and lets the very hard liquor have its way with him.

"Ah, drinking alone?" Rabbit keeps going. "You didn't call him the morning after?"

"Nope," Soar answers. If he's going to learn anything from Rabid, or Rabbit as Soar chooses to call him, he has to play along.

"Ha!"

It's been too long since Soar has been out drinking and he eases his glass down as the deeper kick of Seth's reserve rampages through his system.

"Seth says if he has to toss you out again you won't be allowed back in," the waitress mutters as she slides another reserve across the table. "Ever."

"Thanks, Miss," Soar answers, careful with every syllable before he elbows Rabbit who can't get his eyes off her breasts. Seth knows this trip isn't purely social and by now Lawrence does as well and maybe even Cooper. "Anyway, Rabbit, I'm looking for a red-head. One in particular. She's kin to my Sire and she's missing."

"Red-head, you say," Rabbit uses the excuse to shove his chair a little closer. "The only one I seen here arrived about a week ago. Don't know her right name. Everyone calls her Cherry."

If Rabbit refers to Cloud the only thing stopping Soar from starting a fight with the old bastard is that he can barely make out his drink a foot in front of him. At first Soar thinks it's been topped up but then he realizes the first one is empty and he's into the second. What the hell? Soar crushes his eyes shut and stares even harder at the glass and he could swear the level is even lower.

"She busted up a fight between a big gryph and a stupid horny human," Rabbit continues like he hasn't noticed Soar's trouble keeping track of his drinks. "Been working in the bar every night since, except tonight."

"Oh?" Soar slaps Rabbit's hand off his thigh.

"Rumour is she took Lawrence on, neither ones come down yet and from what I hear Lawrence didn't win. She's a sweet one alright. I'd love to get behind her, push her tail aside and find out if that hair is as soft and red underneath—"

"Wath yer mouf," Soar slurs but Rabbit just laughs. Both Soar's drinks are gone and what little motor control he has left takes heavy advantage of the chair to stay upright. He doesn't feel any drunker than he should but the memory lapses from just the past hour prove there was more than just honey in the reserve. Either Seth made sure Soar will co-operate or he needs to get far away from Rabbit while he still can.

"This way, George," Soar tumbles from his seat and looks up to see Lawrence, his white shirt glows blue in the black lights. "You've got a meeting."

"And it's Rabid, asshole," Rabbit mutters as a boot makes sure Soar doesn't give them any trouble.

Chapter Eleven

It wasn't the first call from Lawrence that bothered Cooper.

Master Soar arrived in the bar downstairs to ask questions about Cloud. Didn't seem like a big deal, in fact it could help get her on her way home. He wants to see Soar and orders Lawrence to bring him up.

As he returned from that call, Cloud curled up on the couch, groaning for a moment as she figured out her good ankle shouldn't rest on the bad one. She only had a couple of glasses of wine and probably hasn't drunk a thing before.

Now that she's passed out he remembers something about dragonkin being unable to hold their liquor but then he's seen a few drink Lawrence under the table over the years so it could just be a combination of the big meal, the injuries and relief that she's decided to go home. In any case, Cooper finds a blanket and turns out the light before helping Deirdre with the dishes.

Outside, the lightning becomes more frequent and the sway of the building in the strong winds becomes noticeable. Even with the patio doors closed and the heavy curtains drawn the rumble of thunder can be felt in every surface he touches.

The second call starts out as a problem and evolves into a nightmare.

Lawrence reports Soar passed out after two drinks, a victim of a suspected drugging by Rabid. The idiot had been banned more than once for going after females for an intimate interaction to which they would never consent and males for whatever they have in their wallet and their secrets. Soar, as master of Lev's personal guard, is riddled with good ones. Now Rabid is detained in a back room and Soar woke up swinging. He's under guard on the floor below Cloud's room and Cooper's night just keeps getting longer.

"Move Rabid downstairs until his eyrie can—"

The shudder of a high pitched report of thunder freezes Cooper's words behind his lips. The electrical discharge that causes it isn't natural at all.

"Lawrence," he whispers as he hears half a dozen more. Likely ten miles out, far enough away to be clear of the thunder cell overhead. The closing of a dragonkin portal is unmistakable to anyone who knows what to listen for. It opens silently, a dangerous hole in the sky, and snaps shut with such force it would kill whomever didn't exit promptly. Dragonkin can travel great distances through the use of their portals and so many closing at once can only mean Cooper's grandsire comes accompanied by more muscle than needed for a social call.

Tonight they've given up waiting for him to surrender the green relic and have come for him.

"Aledaar," Lawrence says and Deirdre drops her towel. She steps from the kitchen and Lawrence knows she'll be clear of the building in minutes. She doesn't even stop to accept a fatherly kiss goodnight and Cooper worries for her already.

"They won't come directly to your suite in this storm," Lawrence's voice flattens as he switches from bouncer to guard master. "I'll delay him in the bar as long as I can."

"Do it," Cooper hangs up, sure he has no more than fifteen minutes to convince the little gold dragonkin on his sofa to leave. Aledaar and his guard will fly in low, as clear of the storm as they can, and enter through the bar. They won't come prepared with human clothes so they'll stay invisible and winged and use the freight entrance rather than marching in wearing red leather armour like some Vegas act.

"Cloud," Lawrence shouts and she sits with a start, her blanket falling to the floor. "Come with me. I'll put you in a spare room tonight. Deirdre's room is next door if you need anything. If you're ready to go home tomorrow I'll have your things brought up and you can leave right from the roof and spare your ankle."

Cooper begins with a lie to get her near the green relic and as they make their way down the hall he's struck with a plan to both protect it from Aledaar and get Cloud away before she's discovered.

"Okay," Cloud turns aside to yawn as Cooper leads her to his own room.

She hesitates in the doorway. Cooper's jacket rests on the big bed beside a stack of his fresh laundry but he can't afford to wait. It's his room and she knows it.

"I need to show you something," Cooper tries and she tries a step before using the wall for support. "In here. I'll show you my secret."

He rests his hand on the stone panel and pushes the door open as soon as the lock releases. By the time he kneels at the box Cloud stands at the opening to the private chamber. His small key opens the lock and green light fills the chamber.

"Look," Cooper instructs. She's curious and when he's this close to the relic he has as much control over its magic as if he were wearing it. Cooper's influence could rival that of Master Fury and possibly even Aledaar himself when he uses the gold relic. "You want to look."

"Oh, yes," Cloud breathes and licks her lips as she inches closer. She no longer notices how much her ankle hurts. The gold dragonkin feels the pull of the green relic.

"Come, don't touch," he adds as she kneels beside him with her hands reaching for the relic. In the green light her red hair appears nearly black.

"No, no," Cloud says to one hand as she pulls it back with the other. Cooper feels a little sick from his use of the relic's magic and because using it to manipulate anyone is something he finds fundamentally wrong.

"You won't remember coming in here," he pushes the magic as hard as he can and rocks with nausea, swallowing to keep his dinner in place.

"No," she says again but she speaks to her hand. Her knuckles whiten as one fights the other over the relic. It's a sign her magic is strong and Cooper keeps up his mental assault.

"You want to go home but I asked you to stay as my companion on your terms. I kissed you and you know I want more but you trust I'll respect your terms."

Cloud uses both hands to touch her lips with the memory of a kiss that never happened.

"Who is Soar to you?" Cooper needs the false memory to fit or it won't last.

"Lover," she whispers.

"And why did you come here?"

"To spy," she says. Although he suspected that sort of deception all along it pains him to hear it from the young dragonkin. She continues though, easing his concerns about her handlers. "Lev thinks you attacked his eyrie and mine at Welch Peak but Soar thinks there's something else going on. I trust you, Daniel. I don't believe you'd ever hurt us."

Bless her. Cooper wants to pull her out and end this twisting of her memories but he's running out of time.

"I took a phone call and you, you nosey gryphon, listened in. Soar came here to spy," Cooper lies. "We caught him and he's confined one floor down from yours. You're scared we'll hurt him. When you leave my suite you won't remember admitting you're a spy or the green treasure before you, will you, you nosey gryphon? You'll grab your things so it looks like you were never here. You'll free him and escape up the south stairs from the roof out of sight from my patio. You'll never escape through the bar."

At least the last part is true.

"Yes," she says as a promise to forget. If the Will spots the gold glow of her eyes they will take her.

Cooper seizes her left hand and presses it to his, the key in between.

He whispers in the old words as a thin line of saliva leaves the corner of Cloud's mouth and her eyes roll up, hiding the glow of gold to be replaced with deeply green-tinted whites. Cooper passes control of the box and the stone lock on the door to her and only her. Unless Cooper dies or asks for the key back she won't remember it at all. Cloud is now the master of the relic and nobody will ever get to it but her.

"Leave," he commands. She's out of his apartment and running down the hall by the time Cooper has the box locked and the chamber door closed. Her uneven steps make him wince at the pain she must be in, running on a fractured ankle. He staggers to his bathroom to throw up then goes to wait before the picture of himself for his grand-sire Aledaar to take him into custody. If he's lucky he won't die in front of the giant sketch. Lady Eve's tears protect him from the Will influencing him into surrendering the relic but that doesn't mean they have nothing to use against him.

They have his daughter, Flay, who serves the Will but not due to any gold relic influence. She's a green dragonkin and immune to Aledaar's gold relic but she's in love with a gold dragonkin, the son of Master Fury, and her loyalty to the Will protects the lives of both her mate and Cooper.

The hand-drawn man behind the glass doesn't look much younger than he does now and Cooper tries to mimic the slight smug smile. Happier times, rebellion and the rush of running head-long into the future with a beautiful mate at his side and armed with nothing but grand and honourable ideals.

Tonight, those ideals and the hope Cloud proves as brave and resourceful as she seems are all he has.

Chapter Twelve

Soar drops his aching and disheveled body on the bed. He's locked in what appears to be one of Cooper's 'rooms' on the floors high above the bar. Why he's imprisoned and not dead is only a mystery if he's stupid enough to believe Cloud hasn't been caught. He gets up and bangs on the door.

"Why the hell am I in here?"

"Master Soar," the voice in the hall says. "Shut the hell up."

He has some recollection of his bruised face in the mirror before he woke up on the bathroom floor, his stomach churning undigested reserve and honey.

Shit.

He should have known better than to close his eyes when Rabbit was near. Bastard must have slipped him something. Soar's knuckles hurt but other than sore muscles from a struggle and the shiner he hasn't been roughed up by Cooper's guard. Maybe he just got out of hand and they locked him up for his own good.

Maybe he got lucky and neither he nor Cloud have been busted for spying. Another wave of nausea hits and he finds himself banging on the door again. This time he hears a familiar voice but she doesn't make any sense so Soar dismisses her strange command as a remnant of the booze and drugging.

"You're so tired," Cloud growls, her voice strains like she carries both big males on her back. "You want to sleep."

Then there's the sound of their two large bodies going down as one drops to the floor and the other hits the wall before sliding down to join the first.

"Crap, crap, crap," she mutters and Soar hears movement outside and another thud as one body rolls over. The first three keys she tries don't work and Soar has time to cross his arms, pissed with jealousy over what he saw on the roof and hopes it comes off as disapproval over how she's chosen to handle her assignment.

"Soar," she pushes her way in and goes straight to him. His anger only lasts for a moment as she hobbles in and throws her arms around his shoulders. Soar gets his around her and her old pack just in time for her to push away with one hand.

"You shouldn't have come," she insists. Her swollen wrist is shoved protectively between her breasts. With her good hand, Cloud grabs his elbow and stands on one foot. "Honestly, you nosey gryphon and how much have you had to drink?"

Her nose wrinkles.

"At least I wasn't on the roof drinking and making out with Cooper."

Cloud's cheeks blossom as her eyes pop wide open and she puts her fingers to her lips. Then she jumps as a massive roar of thunder rattles the building.

"Wasn't," she says and Soar doesn't have to see her blush deepen to know she's lying. He saw the two of them on the roof. "We have to leave. I was doing fine until you showed up and started asking questions."

I was? He could have been. Damned if he can't remember it.

"I know exactly what's going on here, Soar," she spins and heads for the door. "And if you want to stay here and be punished for it feel free. I'm leaving. This is my mission and I'll say when you debrief me."

"Damn it. Wait, Cloud. Hold the door."

Soar hauls both unconscious guards into the room and breaks into an angry reserve-scented sweat with the effort.

Then he kicks one in the thigh.

"That the one who hurt you?"

"No," she hisses. "That was Lawrence teaching me a lesson I'd never learn from you or Sky."

"And that is?"

"Don't test me, Soar," she shoves her pack in his hands and he loosens the straps to put it on. "I'll knock you out and carry you home if I have to."

She's right. If Cloud figured out what Cooper is up to and Soar was snooping around they can't waste any time. He gets an arm around her waist and starts to take her down the hall but she pulls him in the other direction.

"Stairs," she orders. "We go up. There's cameras in the elevators and the stairwells but we're just a few flights from the top and the door to the roof and will be gone by the time they send anyone."

"Cloud," Soar tries, pushing her against the wall. She tries to resist but her pulse peaks in her neck giving away just how much her body still listens to him. "Please tell me where he kissed you."

The gold flecks in her eyes flash and he expects a harsh reply to rub his face in it.

"I don't..." she replies. "I mean, he kissed me and asked me to stay with him as his companion on my own terms. I know he wants more than that but he'll respect my terms."

"Where?"

"Maybe," she tries then she starts to repeat herself as the elevator bell rings. "He kissed me and—"

"Move," Soar has her in his arms and through the door into the stairwell as the elevator door slides open.

"I get it," Soar hisses as he hauls Cloud up the stairs. At this point she'd take the sore ankle over the painful grip he has around her. "He kissed you and gave you a come-on speech and you claim you don't remember where."

"Of course I remember," she insists but the truth is she doesn't. The only two males she ever kissed were a human when she was a kid and the big half-drunk male who carries her up the stairs.

"Then where, Cloud?" he demands as they pause on the second to last landing. A blast of wind rattles the door above them. "This is insane. The storm will rip our feathers off as we're cooked by lightning."

"No other way," she rubs at her side where his fingers dug in and thinks of Cooper jumping off an airplane. "We'll be fine."

"Where," he demands again. The desperation in his voice is more than sensible concern for flying away in a thunderstorm.

"You're jealous," she says and he looks away before taking her in his arms for the last push up the stairs. Darn, she should be sensitive about it considering how much she wants him to say anything to acknowledge what they were but when she opens her mouth she's anything but. "'We had a thing, Cloud. We weren't a thing,' you said then you didn't speak to me again so don't act like you give a darn who's mouth I stick my tongue in.

"I chose you because winning your heart would be hard and I shouldn't have been surprised you blew me off."

"Take wing," Soar orders. He already has his shirt off and binds her pack to his chest. Her only treasure, Condor's maps, are in it and Soar knows. Any other gryphon would leave the bag behind but he understands how important it is to her and she's embarrassed by her cruel outburst.

Cold wet wind forces its way under the heavy steel door.

"Soar," she pulls her shirt off and stuffs it down the front of her pants but can't get the hook on her bra without turning her wrist. "What I said right now. I needed to say it. I'm just as hurt as the day you sent me away."

He turns her to the door and opens the hooks then slides the straps from her shoulders. She adds the bra to the bulge in the front of her pants.

"Be scared. Going out in that is the stupidest thing I've ever done," he whispers and slips his arms around her waist. "I couldn't have stopped myself from begging you to stay and you would have given up everything to do it."

She gets her hands on the door and feels every large missile of rainwater crash into her palms like the door isn't there at all.

"We're going out," Soar orders. "Stay low and get to the ground as fast as you can. My van is two blocks away south, south east. If we get separated meet me there."

The rumbling outside increases from all directions at once as the warmth of Soar's lips touches her just under the ear. He gives her some space as she takes wing, crowding the small concrete cubicle with more feathers. Voices several floors below tell her Cooper's guard is close behind.

"Open the door, Cloud."

She shoves but it won't move against the press of wind. Soar's hands join hers as the wind lets up its assault just long enough for them to get it open.

The wind changes direction tearing the door from their hands. Cloud tries to pull her wings in tight but the heart of the storm drops on them. The deafening roar buries Soar's shout then the tornado takes her. As she spins, she can see him fly to the side, mercilessly pressed against the wall beside the door. For half a minute there's nothing but blackness, pain and shattering glass.

Chapter Thirteen

Something larger and more violent than a knock on the door heralds Aledaar's approach.

A brutal outburst from the thunderhead above rocks the building as the windows break from a massive drop in air pressure. Cooper's ears pop as he drops to the floor then the pressure equalizes when his apartment door bursts open.

The heavy curtains keep any inward falling glass near the frames and Cooper knows only a tornado could have taken the windows out. As he pulls himself to his feet, he turns to the door to face his grand-sire.

Lord Fury, Master of the Council's Will, leads the group. The gold dragonkin barely clears the opening both in height and the width of his shoulders. Considering the nearly identical red hair and the matching shape of their eyes, there is only one dragonkin who can be Cloud's sire and it's Lord Fury, the walking death before him.

Behind him stands Aledaar, leader of the Grand Council. His human form is covered in an expensive suit and he would have been carried by one of the dragonkin through a portal from the Russian Arctic to Calgary.

As they take position on the other side of the sofa they are flanked by Fury's son Con and Con's mate, Cooper's own daughter, Lady Flay. The message is clear. Both Cooper and

Flay have no choice but to comply and Cooper will. He would never put his child in a position of acting against her own sire even though he knows she'll protect the green relic with her life as her dame had.

"Danie—"

Lawrence.

Two guards, one a gryphon and one a gold dragonkin, flank Cooper's guard master. Judging by the bruising, Lawrence stalled them a little too long. The gryphon who interrupted Lawrence with a firm right fist is Torrent, Cooper's younger sibling and the bastard who'd been more than happy to lead the devastating raids on Vancouver Island and Welch Peak. Talon's alleged ass-kicking back at Welch Peak left Torrent with a gash on his lip that makes his smile positively menacing.

The last member of the Will stays by the door. She's young and scared and can't be any more than sixteen. If she were much younger then she wouldn't have survived the trial of Aledaar's gold relic. Instead of guarding the door, her eyes dart back and forth between her wings and Lord Fury. Damn, it may only be weeks since her sire tried to kill her in order to force her into full dragon form for the first time and it's clear by her attention on her leather wings the novelty of not having feathers still effects her.

"I'm quite certain the relic is here," Aledaar says. He doesn't address Cooper by his gryphon name. Nobody does. As an exile, he no longer has one.

Cooper looks at his daughter. She's as fearless and loving as her dame, Lady Eve. Although she stands with her head high like any proud member of the Will, she chews her bottom lip with worry. Conflagration, Lord Fury's son and her beloved, glances at her. He knows as much as Cooper how Aledaar's blackmail of the only green dragonkin in the Will hurts her. Her co-operation ensures Cooper's life as his co-operation now ensures hers.

"It is, grand-sire."

Aledaar's long white hair dampens his lapels. He's nearly nine hundred but his mind is as sharp as any young gryphon's and he can be as cruel and playful with his quarry as any hunter.

"Let's go then," Torrent stomps toward Cooper. He wears the red of the Will although he's never been a good enough ranger to meet Fury's expectations.

Cooper doesn't argue and leads Torrent to the master bedroom.

"Fury," Aledaar tilts his head toward Lawrence. "See he regrets his bad manners."

As they enter the room, Cooper winces at Lawrence's grunt.

"Open it," Aledaar orders.

With a sigh, Cooper places his hand on the stone panel.

"Well?"

Cooper does it again but nothing happens. He tries to contain his relief that passing control of the door to Cloud worked.

"It won't open," Cooper shrugs. Sparks fly before his eyes from a blow to the back of his head then in them as his forehead strikes the door. When he gets his eyes open he still stands but his vision is tinted red with the blood trailing towards his lips.

"Again," Torrent hisses but he doesn't wait for Cooper to move. Instead he twists Cooper's wrist, driving him to his knees as the bones groan. Cooper crawls closer to the stone door to ease the pain but Torrent only forces Cooper's elbow forward, wrenching his shoulder and tearing the tendons in his wrist.

"Damn it, exile," Torrent kicks, doubling Cooper over and breaking a rib. He abandons Cooper's arm and instead boots him again. The knot in Cooper's thigh makes him cry out in spite of his desire to remain silent for Flay's sake.

"Tell me how it opens," Aledaar demands.

"It won't open for years," Cooper gasps but he's silenced by his broken ribs and pounding head.

"We shall see," Aledaar strides from the bedroom leaving Cooper alone with Torrent. "We bring him alive, Torrent. Do not disobey me."

Chapter Fourteen

"Cloud!"

The same wall of debris and wind that tears Cloud from Soar's arms pins him down so he can do nothing more than watch as it takes her. By the time it releases him, his lungs are empty and the entire roof rattles under golf-ball sized hail. As he rolls into the doorway to avoid the shattering hail stones, the noise from the tornado fades to be replaced by the music of running water.

"Cloud," he gasps and as his hearing returns, the splashing changes into the distinct sounds of shattering glass from Cooper's building and those around it.

"I will find you, Cloud," he swears. The hail yields to the dark of night and falling rain. The storm knocked the power out and other than a frozen ice-blue after-image from another burst of fork lightning there is nothing to see. "If I ever have you in my arms again... just give me a chance to make it up to you."

Soar shifts his eyes to gryphon sharpness, allowing him to use even the smallest amount of light. The cascade of glass continues, broken only by a few cries for help but none from Cloud. Most sensible Friday night drinkers should be holed up in Cooper's or any of the other street level bars.

Once he drops from the edge, Soar stays as far from the buildings as he can. The strong winds suck jagged chunks free of the buildings and into his path. The chatter of tiny pieces of broken glass on intact windows accentuates explosions of larger sheets as they land below. As Soar gets his bearings, he figures his van may not have escaped the tornado.

Damn, she could be anywhere and he circles one building after another, scanning every balcony and hole for her until he reaches the Bow River where the devastation stops. He can only hope the wind didn't drop Cloud in the water.

Soar follows the tornado's path back toward the downtown core and there, six stories up amongst the fluttering of curtains freed from their apartment windows, he spots movement inconsistent with the rest of the damage. As he gets closer he sees long flight feathers protruding through the bars of a balcony railing and a bare foot, no, a hand, as still as the windblown feathers are disturbed.

"Cloud," he calls. Magic hides his gryphon form and disguises his voice as something humans will dismiss as uninteresting background noise.

He alights on the patio ledge and grabs hold of the rail. Cloud's naked form sprawls over flimsy furniture and planters. As he tosses furniture aside, she moans and his heart leaps with hope the tornado left her with enough life to save.

A human doctor might see her shaking and drawn in limbs as a convulsion or evidence of head trauma but the seasoned soldier in Soar identifies something very different - battle stress - and in a gryphon her age it could very easily turn deadly.

Cloud's flushed and swollen throat tries to protect her body from the absolute terror of the storm. White circles surround the dark centres of her eyes and she's scared almost to death. Unless he can settle her in the next few minutes there will be nothing he can do but watch her slip away in the dim light of the storm.

In the field, a group of fighting gryphons will step in for another in this kind of shape using everything at their disposal to bring the traumatized gryphon back to reality, calming their body and mind to reverse the condition humans call shock.

Gryphons call it death because without help, that's where Cloud is headed.

"Cloud, little gryphon," Soar soothes as he gets a large striped cushion off her. "You're okay, Cloud. All over, eh?"

As long as he doesn't make a big deal out of it and remains calm she has a chance but damn it, she's been carried three blocks by a tornado and thrown into a pile of planters. Soar turns his head aside so she can't see the moment where his confident mask fails.

Her stubborn limbs don't make it easy to untangle her from the other debris and other than an alarming asymmetry of her upper torso she hasn't received even a scratch. He read somewhere about a tornado destroying a house, leaving the kitchen table and an unfinished puzzle intact. They're an unfinished puzzle alright, Soar and Cloud, and he hopes forgiveness hides somewhere in the pieces.

He checks for broken bones, every touch sweet and soft as he caresses her tense muscles the way he used to. Soar doesn't see the body that used to drive him wild, only *her* and the chance he may never see her that way again. He knows her body as well as his own and after a minute her shallow breaths deepen and she swallows.

"There," he tries. "I've got you, Cloud."

"Pants!" she shouts and tries to cover up but her left arm doesn't come down with the right. Soar's running out of time. She can't draw her wings in to increase her blood pressure until he relocates her shoulder and he can't do that without hurting her and making things worse.

"Alright, little gryphon. We'll find you some pants. Indoors first, okay?"

Soar gathers her in his arms and holds the base of her left wing, reaching around behind his back with his left hand and immobilizing it as best he can so no movement pulls at her shoulder. His other arm takes her just below her butt.

"Easy," he stands and waits only long enough for her to inhale again then he sits on the rail, swings his legs over and drops, taking air as gently as he can and gliding toward his van.

Cloud clings, her fingernails sink in wherever they find purchase on his skin.

"Remember what you used to ask?" Soar whispers over the wheeze of wind and chatter of breaking glass. He flares his wings so their descent and landing will be gentle. "You always pushed me for that one word answer, elegant you called it, and I have it. One word that tells you everything. One word on which the rest of my days hinge."

Tell me about your day, Soar.

A rough tremor shakes through her. She draws in sharply and doesn't exhale though she tries to grunt past the blockage in her throat. Half a mile later he touches down and her muscles relax. With her head drawn back, her breathing eases. Soar keeps her bare feet from the ground as he finds the key and opens up. A slush of hail and broken glass covers the toes of his boots.

Once inside, he draws his own wings in and wastes no time in setting her shoulder. It's tricky without someone to hold her wing so he improvises. After wedging her in at the table, he ties the wing up before putting her hand on his shoulder, locking her elbow and feeling the dislocated joint. He snaps it back in place.

Cloud screams, a good sign, though no less alarming than the silence he listened to all the way to the ground. After lowering her arm and bending it gently across her stomach, he holds it still. The rest of the job is up to her.

On his knees at her side, Soar holds her shoulder as she continues to shriek. Her throat rattles with the discharge of phlegm, which combined with swelling, choked her. The sound breaks and she swallows.

"Draw your wings in, Cloud," Soar coaxes. "Please, little gryphon, please."

Soar keeps her upper arm pinned to her side so her shoulder doesn't dislocate again and she growls and tries to fight him. Elbows in is not a comfortable position for shifting but it's better than the alternative of relocating the joint again.

Another cry breaks free as Cloud does what he asks. Her large flight muscles soften and narrow then become rigid and he has to hold her tighter to protect her shoulder as the big bones draw down and in and the feathers start to fade.

"Fucker!" she hollers, presumably at him, and Soar would laugh if she wasn't in so much pain. He's never heard a curse stronger than 'crap' pass her lips and hopefully never will if this is what it takes to make her swear.

A solid fist bashes the camper door as the last flight feathers disappear.

"Police, everything alright in there?"

"It's open," Soar hollers. "We need help!"

He doesn't need them thinking he hurt the naked female seated at his table.

The two police officers, a man and a woman, don't need a second invitation. A piece of glass that must be the size of a building hits the ground on the opposite side of the camper and the two pile in even as the camper still rocks in the explosion.

"What do you need?" the female gets her bearings first and shoves her partner aside.

"On my buddy's balcony a few stories up watching the lightning," Soar rambles like he's overwhelmed. "The wind sucked her out found her a block away."

"Pants," Cloud moans. "The wind took my pants."

"Yeah, baby," Soar whispers.

Another teeth-rattling crash shakes the camper. Little missiles pit the aluminum surface and there's a snap as a window cracks. Soar's grief for his beloved second home will have to wait.

"Spare keys in the visor," Soar says to the male who gives a curt nod and heads to the front. He'd done a good job of keeping his eyes where they should be but Soar's girl is naked and the cop is, well, male. "Hold her still. I relocated her shoulder and gotta get the table out of the way."

The female officer smells sweet with light floral perfume and cold rain as she presses past and replaces Soar's hands with her own. As the campervan eases into gear, Soar envisions the old thing riding on rims within a block considering the layer of glass crunching under the tires.

"Hey, sweetheart," the cop says to Cloud as Soar takes the table apart and props it up so it can't fall. "What's your name?"

"Ch... Ch... Cherry Cooper," she mumbles.

Damn you, Cooper. I hope you told her what that means. Then Soar decides he'll skin any gryphon who had that kind of talk with her.

"That's pretty. Is Cherry short for something? Charlene?"

Cloud looks at the police officer in confusion then calms when she see's Soar. He grabs her a t-shirt and a pair of his sweats along with the first aid kit.

"And who's your friend?"

"Master Soar," Cloud answers and Soar winces.

"It's George, Ma'am," Soar says. "George Noble."

"Hi, George. How many stories up?"

"Six," Soar answers as he rolls up the shirt to get the sleeve on her injured arm first. That way he can get it over her head and other arm without aggravating her shoulder.

"You rode a tornado six stories, Cherry," the cop's voice suggests she ignores Cloud's confusion though her pointed look at Soar is laced with concern.

"We're clear of the debris," the other officer announces as they get Cloud to her feet for the pants and Soar sets up the second bed, pulling it out where the table had been.

The officer's hands quickly trace around Cloud's body, then rest on her palm where she times Cloud's heart. She retrieves a flashlight and peers into her eyes then puts it away. Finally her hands feel her scalp and she looks at her fingers when she's done.

"Cherry needs to be seen at the hospital," the female says. "A possible broken ankle, a deep contusion on her wrist.

I can't see any sign of head trauma or internal bleeding but then I'm not a doctor."

"Agreed," Soar says though he won't be taking her anywhere. "You guys are going to be busy. I'll call for an ambulance but there's folks in more need than her."

"It took my pants, Soar," Cloud tries and they get her settled in the corner with a pillow supporting her elbow. The female officer briefly inspects Soar then nods and they run back towards the debris field. The van sits only a couple of blocks from the broken buildings and Cloud startles every time a piece of glass falls. Even the click of the door after the police leave bothers her.

Soar turns off the lights to give them some privacy as another course of thunder crushes its way over the city.

"Soar?" she calls.

"Here, little gryphon," Soar elevates her leg up on his and she grabs a fist-full of his wet shirt. Cloud pulls so hard a button pops.

"Remember when you first came to Vancouver Island?" he asks. With one hand he takes a large elastic bandage from the first-aid kit as the other feels her ankle for the break or dislocation. She walked on it before the tornado but that doesn't mean it wasn't battered further. Cloud ignores the prodding so he wraps it up, not too tight in case it's still swelling.

"A few weeks after you first moved to Vancouver Island there was a thunderstorm and it wasn't until you didn't show up for evening meal when we noticed you'd left. Talon and I looked for you for hours as the storm went on and on."

"Yeah," she shivers. Soar moves beside her and she curls up into his shoulder then he covers them both with a spare blanket. Other than the warmth of blood still pooled around her neck she's cold enough to make him shiver.

"I found you on that rocky point a few miles north. Your chair, you called it. A perfect stone shelf. You'd been sitting there watching the storm like you summoned it yourself and you fell asleep. The next time there was a thunderstorm

Shadow practically tied you up to keep you in so you put your hands on the wall so you could feel the thunder.

"She let you sneak out when it was over and you went right to your chair. I always wondered what you were thinking, out there alone."

Soar uses his left hand to feel up and down her back for more damage. The human-sized flight muscles are all tender, in fact they're painful, and he figures the wind tried to take her wing. She's lucky she only dislocated her shoulder since setting a dislocated wing is nearly impossible for a single gryphon.

"I could see the whole world from up there, Soar," Cloud moans as he gives up on checking her back. The damage doesn't much matter right now anyway since she won't be flying again until he gets her home to Firn and Dove for healing.

"Nothing will hurt Shadow as long as I can fly there and watch for trouble but now I can't fly."

Cloud's legs twitch as another button pops on Soar's shirt.

What is he supposed to say to that? Every gryphon in the eyrie feels the same way about Shadow but Cloud doesn't need to hear that even the children and the old can do a better job of protecting their Dame than she can.

This is why he can't keep a female in his life for more than a month. He's either so mute they think he's a complete asshole or he opens his mouth and makes them feel like shit. Only Cloud ever had the ability to expand his detached and insensitive vocabulary into something that could be considered sensitive.

Soar gives up on talking and does the only other thing he can think of. His hand goes to her stomach, low over her womb like only her lover would, and she hisses at the intrusion.

"Let me do this, Cloud. No strings, no sex. Just reassurance. Later, if you want Lev and Talon to run me off for a while or forever just say so."

Cloud's eyes bore into him and for a moment he's sure she can see the mark each of his misdeeds has left upon his spirit. Then, with a swallow, she does something he doesn't expect.

Her chin comes up in submission.

"I'm in trouble, aren't I? It's death."

"Yes, little gryphon," Soar brings his lips to her neck before opening and placing his teeth on her throat in acceptance of her surrender. A momentary sharp ache in his front teeth accompanied by a change in her scent brings a growl to his throat. It's early yet, so early she probably isn't aware, but she's going into season. The reason for the growl is unclear. They're unmated so he should only feel the need to stay out of her grouchy way but all his teeth want is to mark her then follow through with a thorough attempt at knocking her up.

Shit, gonna be a rough couple of days ignoring that.

"Cloud," Soar gets a hold of himself.

"Do it... t," she stutters and Soar starts by simply placing his lips on hers. His thumb moves between them, unsealing the kiss and drawing the tip of her tongue out to meet his before he goes back to stroking her belly. Afterplay, it used to be, and would often lead to foreplay. Beneath the thin soft layer of fat all females have she's grown strong and her muscles work as he deepens the kiss and she shifts beside him.

Cloud squeals at another round of thunder so near the lightning's white glare has barely disappeared but Soar doesn't back down. She warms and he uses his thumb to tease her tongue as he works her jaw and throat. He's also unbearably aroused. The first touch of their lips sent his own lightning to his groin and now his cock thickens, throbbing hard each time she squirms with fear; even harder each time she squirms with pleasure.

He isn't aware she's released his shirt until her good hand finds the button on his jeans. Cloud's fingers fumble at the clasp before driving down behind seeking something solid.

"No," Soar orders. Hadn't she heard him? No sex even though suffering until his erection subsides might kill him.

"But—"

"I will not repeat myself." Soar won't because he can't. If she persists at all he'll give in, mark her and God willing become her mate. Either the scent of her season is already more powerful or he's just more susceptible. "There will be no more than this until we've had a chance to talk about us."

"Crap," Cloud moans but she removes her hand and Soar resumes the kiss with small pecks to her lips and jaw, tasting each inch of her warming skin.

Minutes later, she doesn't startle at the thunder and Soar draws back, satisfied she's doing better and relieved the torment of kissing an aroused Cloud can start to fade.

"Field medicine one-oh-one?" Cloud asks. The tremors are gone from her voice and she tucks her head under his chin and yawns. For humans, sleep might be a bad thing after such a trauma but for a gryphon it means they're in the clear.

"Yeah, little gryphon," Soar sighs. A single gasp, equal parts relief and the remaining reserve in his system, promises to pull him under with her. Just to make sure they get some rest, he pulls Cloud up to one end of the bed and using his arm as her pillow, consumes her smaller body in his embrace. Even though his clothes are still damp the heat between them is perfect.

With a final sigh, Cloud's chest rises and falls smoothly in sleep.

It takes Soar a little longer.

He has her back but it's only a matter of time before she finds out he had her expelled from Sky's. If she was still awake he would tell her, Soar decides, so he feels like less of a jerk but he knows he probably wouldn't. He has Cloud in his arms and he won't give her up again if he can help it. When the time is right to tell her, he will.

"Tell me about your day, Soar," Cloud asks, her voice softer than the rain.

He never thought he'd hear those words from her again and his heart aches with his betrayal. Even with what's happened to her she thinks of him, the undeserving sod that he is.

He hopes she's gone back to sleep but her eyes remain open and she expects the answer he promised.

"Forgive."

She sleeps in spite of the diminishing storm and rising noise of voices and vehicles. Soar slips from her side and behind the wheel to drive them a few miles west. When he can no longer stand the distance from her, he pulls over and returns to her side.

Chapter Fifteen

"What?" Cloud demands as she keeps brushing.

The half-open door to the tiny camper bathroom opens a little more revealing Soar, arms crossed and very unhappy. The black eye doesn't help him look nice and honestly, as long as he's going to look at her like that she doesn't care how he got it. As his scowl deepens his muscles flex drawing her eyes down. He wears nothing but his jeans and the toothbrush slows as he shifts his weight, tightening his abs. Maybe he should pass on the hairbrush as well since the wild spiky look goes well with the angry flash of his eyes.

Darn, he looks good. Not missing any workouts, that's for sure.

In addition to his apparent attitude he smells particularly aggressive and male and incredibly like Soar.

"What?" he snaps as her eyes drop below his buckle.

"You haff no idea how bat my human mouf tastes in ta norning," Cloud resumes eye contact and lifts her chin to keep the foam in.

"So you stuck my toothbrush in it?"

"I not hoffling alla way ta nine," Cloud holds her bad ankle up then spits in the tiny sink. "Hobbling."

Soar slams the bathroom door, shutting her in, so Cloud finishes washing up before rattling the handle though she makes no real attempt to open it.

"Soar?" she calls then rattles the handle again, this time feigning alarm. "Soar? Help!"

There's no sound from the front of the camper other than a pan landing on the stove. Why the heck is he so touchy?

It's PMS for sure.

Shadow once explained that for human females there was one week a month when everyone, particularly males, did their best to antagonize her. Cloud had been skeptical *everyone* could be so organized considering there were so many females having PMS at all different times until Talon tried to help out.

"It was all my fault," Talon had said. "I kicked the chamberpot at her on purpose when my arms were full and I couldn't see she left it in the middle of the den."

Then he stomped off and Shadow raised her eyebrows. *See?*

Cloud didn't, not right away, until the sound of laughter from every other male in the great chamber reached her. She knew. Each and every one of them, Talon included, was trying to annoy Shadow.

And now, based on her experience, Soar is a classic case. She doesn't need a room full of males to confirm it.

Cloud picks up Soar's comb. It's troubling she doesn't remember Cooper kissing her even though she can say with absolute certainty it happened. After going through their evening piece by piece the only time she doesn't really remember is when they were in his room. Going in there, yes. Running from his suite, yes, but nothing in between. She carefully runs the comb over her scalp and no tender spot presents itself. It could simply be emotional trauma from the night before but then why didn't she remember it before the tornado got her?

With her eyes closed, Cloud tries to remember. If she closed them for the kiss that could be why she doesn't have a visual recollection. Her fingers brush her lips and the familiar touch tingles but fails to stir a memory. Were her lips open? Were Cooper's? She relaxes her mouth and lets the tip of her finger slip in place of his tongue but all she remembers is the taste of Soar and his kiss.

"What are you doing?"

"He kissed me," Cloud says, pulling her hand down. She'd been so wrapped up in imagining a kiss with Soar she didn't hear the door.

"Just stop it, Cloud. He didn't. You're a bad liar and all you're doing is digging yourself in deeper."

"Jealous much?" She asks as the door slams shut again but then she's sorry. Might be better to let it drop. All they need to do is put up with each other for a day or two for the drive home. Just because she understands why he broke it off doesn't mean there's any reason to pursue what they had. For a few minutes the night before they had it again and her heart can't afford to hope.

Soar hunches over his phone and hides it with his shoulder when she gets out of the bathroom and she has to squish past him to turn the sausages. Once his thumbs stop tapping he tucks it in his back pocket and pulls on a clean shirt.

Darn.

This shirt, like the one he wore the previous evening is a long sleeved, ribbed T with buttons running down to mid chest. Sexy, particularly when he pushes the sleeves up showing off dark hair matching the ones peeking out from the buttoned opening.

Cloud gives her head a shake.

"Your pocket is buzzing," Cloud points out but Soar only grunts as he dumps two spoons of instant coffee into a small mug next to an empty one for her. He knows she prefers hot water. "It's buzzing again."

Soar tips his head to the ceiling and mutters something she can't make out.

Then his phone starts ringing.

"Shit... hey, Talon," Soar puts the phone to his ear. "Yeah, I got the messages. I just needed some privacy to reply."

Cloud moves the sausages to drain on a folded paper towel and starts breaking eggs into the pan then pours hot water into their mugs. Once she sets the kettle down and turns off the gas burner, Soar takes her elbow and edges closer. Her skin warms as he noses her hair. For a moment she enjoys their strange domestic scene.

"No, buddy," Soar says. "Cloud is with me. I found her last night at Cooper's."

"No," Cloud mouths and Soar pulls her into his shoulder to quiet her. If Soar wasn't so close, Cloud's shaky knees would drop her to the floor. She is far from ready to face her family.

"I don't know," Soar sighs. "I'm not sure what she wants. She was caught in the tornado and something about Lawrence—"

Soar holds the phone at arms length as it emits several loud creative sentences involving Talon's skyblade and Soar's ass.

"No, I'm not bringing her straight home."

Cloud is as surprised as Talon's silence suggests he is with Soar's refusal. Even though both males are guard masters, Talon is her adopted sire and his say is absolute when it comes to Cloud. With the exception of Shadow's say, in most cases.

"She's embarrassed and upset," Soar continues and Cloud turns to face him, her surprise continuing. Maybe the big, heartless idiot really knows how he hurt her. Maybe his request for forgiveness is based on an honest understanding of her feelings.

She still isn't certain of his.

"And she's still asleep—"

Soar sighs as his free hand reaches around Cloud and grips the waistband of her borrowed sweats. After a moment of listening to Talon go on Soar gently pushes her head to his shoulder and rests his chin in her hair.

"Of course she didn't do it, my friend. Stealing simply isn't in her," Soar talks over Talon until he shuts up and lets Soar finish. "Cloud is the grand-daughter of my Sire and the daughter of my best friend and my Dame. Whether she returns home now or later she will understand I won't be far away.

"I don't envy your task, my friend," Soar finishes. "Convincing Shadow that Sky doesn't need her help isn't going to be easy."

Shadow and Sky?

"What's going on with Shadow?" Cloud demands the moment Soar disconnects the call. Something is up and she feels a little sick her beloved Dame might have done something very, very stupid.

"Sit," Soar orders before he picks her up and dumps her on the pull-out bed. "Silence."

Cloud glares at him but she holds her tongue. If she isn't convinced his answer will come faster if she's quiet she's going to lose it on him. Soar turns away and starts serving breakfast.

"Soar?"

A single snap of his fingers is followed by him giving her the hand; a palm pointed right at her face.

Cloud takes back any thought she had about his brief outburst of sensitivity when he spoke to Talon. She shifts her position, gets to her knees and gives him the growl that made Lawrence think twice.

What the hell was that?

Whatever just came from Cloud sent Soar's testicles somewhere up around his kidneys. He ignores the burn of hot coffee as it coats the niche between his thumb and first finger and the mug rattles against the counter as he sets it down. The vibration of broken glass on the roof ceases and trails into a small cascade of the shattered glass falling to the ground outside.

Can't a gryphon get a break? Even a sip of coffee between ass-reamings because that's what he just wrapped up with Talon and exactly what's coming from Cloud.

Soar chews his lip as he turns to face her and takes a step back. Her eyes have shifted to complete blackness and she menaces him with her teeth.

"You will not do that again," Soar says. "Sit down and close your mouth, gryphon."

Not little gryphon either. She is way out of line. He's the damn guard master and she's the disgraced trainee.

To his astonishment, she does, sticking her bandaged ankle before her. Troubling, however, is the disobedient scowl remaining on her lips and not so much for the insubordination it represents. Soar tugs the front of his shirt down to hide the stirring of arousal their bickering causes. It shouldn't be happening to him but it is, verbal foreplay leading up to the hunt and each aggressively dominating the other and submitting before...

"Dame Shadow heard you were expelled and she assumed you would come home," Soar says. "Which you obviously didn't. She took off with half her guard for Memphis to find out who framed you because she doesn't believe a word of it."

"But—"

"I said silence," Soar instructs and puts his coffee under his nose to mask the sweet scent of her season. "She has a six hour head start on Talon who has taken the remainder of her guard and several of Sire Lev's to catch her."

"But—"

"I know. He won't talk her out of it."

"She can't," Cloud moans.

"I know," Soar agrees but Cloud is on her knees again.

"I mean she *can't*," Cloud shouts.

"I know," Soar raises his voice. God, does he know.

"Because she's—"

"I *know*."

"Pregnant."

Soar lets her outburst sit. He can only imagine Talon's anxiety. The flight to Memphis is far too long for her to make without risking the children but he knows Talon. If he can't stop her then he'll carry her, ten times that far if he has to.

"Immobilize my shoulder so I can shift," Cloud insists. "I'll stop her."

Soar drops to the bed. "No, little gryphon."

"Please?"

"No. We both know you're not able to fly anywhere no matter what I do."

"I can," she whines but the trembling from the night before starts again and Soar takes her good hand to still it. Cloud clenches her fist but it doesn't help so Soar presses it to his lips.

"Even if you could, we aren't stepping outside. There are at least two members of the Council's Will circling above the city and not a single gryphon in sight."

"The Will," Cloud gasps. Soar helps her back into her corner and brings her plate.

"If they're here then something serious is going on. Since you were one of the last gryphons with Cooper last night it's best we get hundreds of miles away from here as quietly as possible."

Cloud drops her chin in defeat.

"Talon will find her and the guard with her is likely carrying her. I can guarantee she won't fly a single kilometre on her own, okay?"

With a snittle, Cloud spears a sausage in the middle. She doesn't even try for the knife. It's either bad manners or her left wrist is too sore.

"Any idea why the Will is here?" Soar asks. "That was your mission after all."

"Nope."

Great.

"He wouldn't hurt us, Soar. I'm certain of it. Whatever he has going on with the Council... I'm not sure he has any control over it."

Soar grunts as he takes his breakfast. His appetite hasn't broken through the reserve hangover but he's certain if he gets hungry he'll be unnecessarily susceptible to an arousing argument with her.

"Why?" Is the only thing he can think to ask.

"He figured out who I am and where I'm from right away. All of it. You'd think if he had a hate on for Welch Peak or Shadow's eyrie then he and Lawrence wouldn't have spent the last week running off males and treating me like their own offspring."

He risks a glance at her but she's too absorbed in her meal to notice.

"He has children you know."

"I didn't," Soar's knife ratchets across his plate sending a fried egg over the edge and onto the blanket. That's one hell of a surprise. Not much is known about Cooper. Even his home eyrie isn't much discussed and nobody knows the reason he abandoned it. Some figure ambition and the strange loner was unwilling to wait for the passing of his parents or openly wish for the passing of his sibling, the rightful heir, who disappeared about the same time Cooper left Jasper. Any other rumours were more wild speculation for the personal gain of the one telling the tale and most of the stories he heard came from Rabbit.

Yes, the asshole had drugged him, but his penchant for booze meant he spent lots of time in bars collecting useful gossip.

"He was exiled from his home over his choice of female, can you imagine?"

"No," but it sounds more like choking. That's the last reason Soar expected.

"Mm, he took her knowing he would never see his family again."

She looks guilty. The set of her mouth matches her down-turned eyes. Lord, maybe the time she spent with Cooper was too long given that she feels she's betraying his personal life.

"Did he tell you which eyrie he's from?"

"Does it matter?"

"Yes, maybe it will help you figure out how he ties into the Council. Could be a detail you think isn't important?"

Soar takes her empty plate and passes her the mug of hot water. It's cooled some so he tries his coffee.

"Does he look like anyone you know?"

"Other than the massive self portrait in his suite? No."

"Seriously?" Soar laughs. Arrogant bugger. For a moment Soar likes the prick but only for a moment. The blank look staring at him over the mug says she doesn't understand what he's getting at.

"You know Aledaar is the head of the Council, right? And Sire Sher of Jasper is his son."

"Yes," she shrugs then she shudders. At least the trembling has stopped. "So Torrent is Aledaar's grand-son, big deal."

Torrent was never punished for nearly killing Talon's sister and bringing Cloud to the brink of death. Not to mention how he snatched Shadow, twice, and if the rumours were true an alliance between Torrent and Cooper caused the raids on Lev's eyrie and Welch Peak. That is if you asked Lev.

Now Cloud says he was exiled. Such a split wouldn't put Cooper in league with his younger brother and means Soar can only guess what ties Cooper to the Council.

"Cloud," Soar tries as gently as he can. "Cooper is the firstborn son of Sire Sher and Dame Arden. He is Torrent's older sibling."

He moves to take her mug before it spills.

Cloud pushes her plate aside and looks up, eyes focused far away at the sky.

"He took me to his room," Cloud says and Soar bites his tongue hoping she won't torment him further with the kiss bullshit. "I remember going in there then nothing clear until I left. The words he kissed me come so easily but when I try and remember it..."

"What happens, little gryphon," Soar asks. Her eyes lose focus and she swallows before bringing her fingers to her lips.

"All I see is green."

God, she must have hit her head.

Chapter Sixteen

Miserable female.

All Cloud does is talk.

They drove west after breakfast and she was silent for all of ten minutes. Probably while he ran into the gas station to pay for the fill up and buy her a stack of magazines and top ten paperbacks. At least in the gas station he didn't have to listen to her.

It doesn't matter she's in season and it drives him nuts. Soar is quite certain she's as annoyed as he is which makes his desire for her even worse. Some of Talon and Shadow's pre-mating arguments were as stupid as they were intense. The best ones preceded one of them chasing the other from the eyrie for exactly what Soar knows he should avoid with Cloud.

His miserable female.

In spite of his understanding he can't ignore his hormones. Hormones he shouldn't have for her considering they haven't completed the Ritual of Exchange where he offers her his bite. If she accepts by biting him in return then she would offer her tears. The simple act of touching them will bind them permanently. Soar would remember if that ever happened and considering neither bears the other's mark he's sure.

The other thing he worries about is their tail.

Not any gryphon tail; the one concerning him, actually two, wear red leather armour and are occasionally visible high above. They can only be members of the Council's Will, possibly the same two he saw in Calgary. It's rumoured many of them are dragonkin, a mix of dragon and gryphon, and the dangerous enforcers are the last thing anyone wants to run into. One for sure is dragonkin, Soar's good friend Conflagration, and who gives a gryphon kid a name like that anyway? The name made sense when Soar learned what Con really is.

Cloud hasn't noticed the pair and it seems whatever went on at Cooper's the night before follows them. Soar hopes the Will has lost interest since he hasn't seen them in a couple of hours.

With a sigh, Cloud drops the last magazine on the floor with the others. The female reads like a demon, tearing through three paperbacks while tormenting him with a running summary of their plots, reading passages and exclaiming 'is that even possible' while turning the book sideways to reread a sex scene to herself. Then she told him about each article and shoved nearly every picture in his face. With the death of the last page Soar hopes he'll get some peace.

"So," she announces. "What else you got?"

She looks so vulnerable all bandaged up and dressed in his clothes until she opens her tormenting mouth; the same one in which she stuck his toothbrush.

Soar turns to glare at her but the sun chooses that moment to pound in, lighting up her red hair and making the gold in her eyes sparkle like fire. It also shines off the metal clip holding the bandage on her leg. Okay, the bad leg on his dash is somewhat acceptable. It's covered at least and should be elevated but when her other bare foot joins it he nearly pulls over.

"Will you get your feet off the dash?"

"Jerk," she mutters and slides her foot down, catching the latch holding the glove box shut and popping it open. "Ah ha."

Soar tosses his hands up in surrender. Between the dazzling smile, beautifully framed face and her genuine pleasure with her discovery, he's hopelessly proud she likes something of his.

His good mood is short lived. It takes her twenty minutes to tire of quizzing him on the maintenance manual. Then she moves in on the insurance papers.

"Pleasure use?"

Soar keeps his mouth shut.

"Pardon?" She demands although she knows damn well he didn't say a word.

"It means I'm not using the vehicle for work."

"Oh."

Silence.

Thank you.

"So," Cloud starts and hides a smile as Soar flinches. Who knew encouraging PMS in a male could be so much fun? Once she figured out the only way to fight his irritating behaviour was with her own his PMS was much easier to deal with. It's like displaying dominance without going through the work of chasing him down, catching him and stopping just short of killing him. "If you were taking something somewhere for Sire Lev would it be work?"

"Yes," Soar snaps, emphasized by a pop of his jaw so she responds by putting her feet up.

"Hm."

Instead of relaxing in the quiet she grants, his fingers tighten on the wheel and his fists roll back and forth around it. Then one hand drops to his crotch again and tugs at the denim seam as he shifts his hips.

"You know," Cloud says, doing her best to sound like a big know-it-all. "Talon's truck has three foot pedals, not two like yours and his hand stick is so much bigger. He touches it all the time."

"Do you know anything about driving?"

"Lots, I've been watching you all day."

"Get your feet off the damn dash," Soar growls so Cloud counts to ten before she puts her feet back on the floor.

"So if you're taking me home because Talon said so isn't that work?"

"No."

"Oh."

Soar exits right off the highway but Cloud misses the sign and an opportunity to engage him in talk about it.

"I'm hungry," she announces.

"I can't imagine why," Soar answers and speeds up.

"We haven't stopped in hours," Cloud whines and likes the response. Soar's pupils dilate and he glares at her as the whites nearly disappear. A chill spreads down her spine and centres deep in her belly as she turns her back on him, getting the growl she hoped for.

Traffic thickens as Soar drives north across the Fraser River and into Mission. Cloud knows this part of the province well and doesn't need her maps to tell her where she is. Annoying Soar helped her ignore Welch Peak as it passed them to the south an hour before. The empty caverns are usually far from her thoughts but thinking of Torrent earlier in the day makes her feel the dead eyrie's presence in her own internal map.

Some things, like the location of her birth eyrie, can be ignored but it always feels near. Welch Peak is a big red X attached to her with an unbreakable tether.

"So if I'm not work then am I pleasure?"

Soar doesn't answer and instead picks up speed. The campervan struggles with the rural roads and Cloud doesn't like how it leans in the turns and threatens to skitter wide through the corners.

"Am I work or pleasure?"

"Will you just shut up?"

"Argh," Cloud growls and starts to put her new magazines and books away. Shadow will enjoy them when they get home and afterwards they will be passed around among the residing gryphons until their edges are ragged and the pages start to come out.

Soar pulls onto a dirt road and Cloud yelps as everything in the camper, gryphons included, jumps about. She's already stiff from sitting all day and the bouncing pushes sharp pain through the muscles down the left side of her back. Fortunately most items are either seatbelted in or secured in the locked cupboards.

The crazy male's laugh pops goosebumps over Cloud's skin and she braces her good foot against the dash.

Trees on either side narrow in and a final turn points them directly at the late day sun.

"Shit," Soar swears and grabs for his sunglasses. They hit another bump, knocking them out of his reach.

"I'll get it," Cloud says and unbuckles. She played with her visor enough, or more than enough judging by how much it bothered Soar, and knows precisely how it works. She's more than a little angry he doesn't notice not only her quick response but also how observant she's been with the workings of the van.

As she pulls the visor down, Soar shouts in surprise first at her nearness then again as the spare keys hit him square in the crotch.

"Ayee, female!"

"Got it," she yells again as her good hand dives for the keys.

Soar takes one hand off the wheel and seizes her wrist. She's held in place practically on top of him. With her breasts in his face it's a miracle he can see but maybe he can't. Soar slows and Cloud turns to look out the front window to see why.

The dirt road has widened into a dead end barely roomy enough for them to turn around.

"What do you think you're doing, little gryphon?"

He doesn't let up his grip as they stop and Cloud's shoulder presses on him so she can keep her balance. Leaning over with her weight on her one leg isn't as easy as it should be considering the campervan rocks as they come to a stop.

"I was just grabbing the—"

"Penis?" Soar demands and Cloud feels her cheeks darken.

"No," she gasps. Granted, annoying him has been fun but that's it. The physical attraction has more to do with spending the day alone and so very close to the only male she ever wanted.

"You were," Soar turns and she can feel his hot breath on her cheek. His warmth spreads over her skin and settles between her thighs. She's trapped and vulnerable to the big male who proves his dominance by holding her wrist.

"Keys," Cloud says and realizes where the keys are. She would have to bury her hand deep between his legs to get them. "Oh no."

She manages a thick swallow and looks down and blushes even harder at the serious erection inches from her fingers. A flush of tiny deep brown feathers bursts to the surface of his skin around his collar and fades leaving behind his delicious male scent.

"Then explain why we've been arguing," Soar hisses then he forces her chin up with his nose. The tingle of his lips on her throat has her moaning.

"You have PMS," she whispers and finds herself in her seat as his laugh fills the cab.

"You've got to be kidding me."

"Shadow said to expect it when—"

"You're in season."

"I," she struggles to her feet as Soar stomps to the back of the camper.

"You know," he growls. "The worst part is I'm acting like your mate. I shouldn't care if you're in season and all I can think about is getting under your tail. I drove us down here..."

Soar presses his palms to his eyes as he gets his heavy breathing under control and Cloud inches toward the door.

"But I think I got a handle on it. If you want me out of here just say so. I'll stay nearby until Lev gets someone out here for you then I'll give you some space."

"But I'm not," Cloud argues. How long has it been since she was last in season? Years. Far longer than normal but she and Shadow attributed it to her intense training delaying things like with a human.

"How could you not know?" Soar braces his forearms up against the bathroom door and rests his head against one. "You're twenty six. How could you not know?"

Cloud's good hand covers her mouth in an attempt to keep the tremble from her lips. How can the jerk who dumped her make her feel so young with a single question?

"The last time was when I was in the hospital after Welch Peak," she explains. There's no point in going anywhere but home. He's right. She's in season and he shouldn't care but he does. Soar isn't himself and his obvious interest in her makes him do things he shouldn't. Sometimes she hates understanding people. It would be a whole lot easier to lash out at him when his frustration makes him do it to her. "And once a couple of years before."

"Cloud, I shouldn't have put it like that," Soar says. "I haven't been decent to you. Let's go home."

"You don't want me?"

"I never said that, little gryphon."

"Then why are we leaving?"

There's something going on with him that runs deeper than fighting the urge to mate.

"Am I not the kind of gryphon who should be a dame?" Cloud demands. The light changes as her eyes shift to black.

"I suppose I'm not," she admits though she still struggles with her temper. "I'm trained to fight, not nurture."

"Damn it, Cloud," Soar bashes his forehead on his arms. "I've never seen a dame who isn't good with her children. Doesn't matter how big a bitch she is to everyone else but that's not all I want. My female must be able to protect my young with as much force as I can."

He turns to Cloud and places one hand on the wall. The other scratches nervous circles around his stomach. Cloud holds her tongue, afraid of ruining the moment by opening her mouth. It's the closest they've ever come to discussing their relationship.

"I want you, Cloud," he admits. "Everything else aside; you being in season, how I'm reacting to it, forget all of it. Even without the tension between us I want you so this is how it's going to happen.

"If any part of you doesn't want me now, timing or if I blew my chances with you two and a half years ago or if there's anyone else then take your seat and buckle up. I take you home and we talk later when I've cooled off.

"If you want to mate with me and become my female today, if you want everything I have to offer including all the shit that comes with it then step outside and try to hide from me. I guarantee I'll hunt you down and when I find you, I'll take you and you'll make me the proudest gryphon on the continent."

He doesn't drop his eyes and neither does Cloud. She's never seen him so exposed. Even the night before when he asked for her forgiveness, not even the night in his den when she never said it was her first time and he didn't ask. Soar had been horrified with himself then; more for assuming she was the kind of female who dropped in for casual encounters in male dens than for not taking his time.

"Soar," she breathes but his stare doesn't soften. Whatever she does she needs to face him. Turning her back on this big predatory male will push him into deciding for her.

"I forgive you, Soar," Cloud says. "But it doesn't mean a thing unless you've forgiven yourself."

She backs up a step, careful on her ankle, and runs. Once the door slams behind her she leans on it and assesses the terrain, the direction of the wind and where the trees offer the best cover.

She limps away at right angles to the direction of the wind. The tree cover isn't the best. The obvious thing would be to run downwind where the tree cover is denser and her scent won't carry him straight to her.

The thrill of being hunted lasts only for a moment. It's cooler and darker in the trees and the realization she's prey spurs her on.

Chapter Seventeen

Soar feels the snap of metal on metal through the camper's frame. He wasn't certain what to expect from Cloud; either to take a seat or step outside and isn't prepared for either. With a deep breath, he lets his eyes close and his head fall back as he tunes out the sounds she makes.

She isn't going to waste any time getting away but he waits and when he opens his eyes the outline of sunshine on the floor has moved. Hunting her down will be a challenge. She's injured so he needs to keep some control but she's also clever and well trained. Anticipation of her surprises gets him going. The preamble to regular gryphon sex involves an exchange of dominance; each defeating the other and each exhibiting trust in their partner by allowing them to see them submissive.

It's very different when the female is in season as he was told by his sire many years earlier.

Soar must defeat her and prove he's worthy of siring her children each and every time. Not only that, but he'll bear her mark when it's all over and everyone will know she belongs to him.

After everything he's done to her he has a lot to make up for. The Ritual of Exchange and their first season together need to be perfect.

As he pulls his shirt off he laughs at the idea of him and children but the thought of Cloud swollen with his offspring is both amazing and alarming at the same time. It's also completely arousing. He's never considered the idea with any other female. Only Cloud.

Once his favourite shoes are off and safely tucked away he takes the top sheet from the bed above the cab and ties it around his waist. Not sexy, but at least he can keep his hands free. When she takes wing he'll need it to support the weight.

Soar locks up and pockets his keys.

As much as he spent most of his seventy-five years simply enjoying females, never successful in any long-term arrangement, he always remembers the tales his parents would tell of their mating. His sire had claimed his dame when she was in season. They didn't conceive then but the ten days his sire spent seeing to her every comfort as she laid in were remembered with such love they caught the imagination of their rough son, Soar.

Yeah, as big a dick-head as Soar can be to the gryphons in his life the idea of being everything to the right female is something he's always wanted.

What he can see of the sky above is clear of the pair of Will guards who'd followed them the first half of the journey. Heavy branches overhead cover most of the campervan roof and unless anyone is flying directly overhead it will be hard to tell Soar's vehicle from another.

Soar circles the van, inspecting the ground and surrounding brush for evidence of her passage, and spots several snapped stems leading off toward some thinner ground cover. The wind blows north toward denser brush and he decides her path west is a ruse. Instead of following her he goes north, careful to avoid breaking branches or disturbing anything. If he leaves no trail she'll have a hard time tracking him should she return to the camper.

Once in the brush and trees, he finds they aren't as thick as they appeared. He can smell her mixed with the scents from the camper and moves further away to avoid confusing it with any fresh scent. It doesn't really help. He's been so immersed in Cloud she seems to cling to his skin and hair and he can't take a breath without it containing a hint of her.

Fifty feet from the van Soar stops and turns in a complete circle to make sure he's alone then drops to a vulnerable position on the ground. He crawls several feet before he finds the mixture of Cloud and freshly broken branches. She's been through here and Soar calculates how long she's been alone and how quickly she can move.

Damn it, he hadn't watched the time. He has a good idea how fast she can move on the ankle from the night before but will it be any better from rest or stiff from being stationary?

Before he can decide, the snap of wood on stone reaches him from no more than thirty feet away. Still on hands and knees, Soar's head snaps up and he moves sideways into denser brush affording him better cover then bobs his head around in the direction of the sound.

There, just past a pair of trees he spots her. The shirt he put on her the night before stands out low to the ground.

Maybe her ankle hurts more than he thought if she settled down to hide. Maybe it made her clumsy as well since he heard her.

Soar gets lower to the ground and prowls, each foot and handfall placed with absolute consideration of the brush and maintaining silence. Instead of a direct approach, he goes wide around to the right to flank Cloud as he gets a better view. Her hiding spot is excellent and other than a few glimpses of the shirt, he can't see enough to know if he's been spotted. Even listening doesn't help. She's absolutely silent. Soar has seen it before during a stressful sparring match. The little gryphon somehow controls her heart so well only her breathing gives her away and if she's been working with Master Sky then Cloud could be a very quiet adversary.

Just north of her position he picks up another small sound. Not the crack of a branch but the soft rustle of something softer on bark. Curious. It isn't the shuffling he expects from a frightened gryphon.

The new sound comes from further away, just the slip of fabric on a branch and his eyes snap up.

If he wasn't hunting her he'd whistle in appreciation. Right above the spot where he'd gone to the ground to smell for her he can see her leg twenty feet up a tree. The trunk hides her body and he can only see her knee. Even with one arm and one leg the female can climb.

Soar decides to move in on the empty shirt to draw her out. With his eyes on it he ignores her in the tree and creeps forward, remaining concealed behind the trunks.

Cloud keeps her heart and breathing silent as she watches Soar stalk the shirt she left hidden in the tight knot of trees. She's still downwind of him and his attention is on the decoy. As he circles, he comes close to her.

Very close, in fact.

Had Soar continued much longer he would have crawled right over her and that wouldn't have been too bad at all. He's powerful and sure as he moves behind another tree. Each muscle forces more of his scent from his skin and Cloud resists the urge to squirm her naked body on the ground in appreciation of her male. God, he's gorgeous; sleek and strong and hunting *her*. Everything she wished for when she committed to going to his den five years earlier is finally going to happen.

He's right too, she grudgingly admitted to herself as she ran from the campervan, ducked into the trees and headed north to set her trap. Cloud is in season but she is also about to claim her male. Another female in her position would let the male hunt and prove himself but for Cloud there is some pride involved. He dumped her like she was nothing important then rudely sent her off to Calgary.

She's no match for him with her injuries and damn well knows it. Whether she simply runs to be caught right away or gives him a little showing up and runs to be caught after doesn't matter. The result will be the same.

Once Soar has a small lead she mirrors his movements, holding her good arm out for balance and taking every step with him. No part of her shadow or scent reaches Soar. Her strides don't have to be longer to catch up. Soar's path isn't straight since he works to stay hidden from the shirt in the trees and her direct route allows her to quickly gain ground.

He pauses and looks a little further toward the sweatpants in the tree. Cloud had tossed them up intending them to be her diversion since they were easiest to remove then when she found the nest of trees she struggled out of the shirt and hid it there before moving further down wind.

He discovered them out of order but it works to her advantage because now she's behind him, quiet, invisible and about to strike.

But he stops short of the trees and she realizes he thinks she's in the one further ahead. Her chance is almost gone so she holds her breath and seizes his throat with her good hand.

Cloud's fingers take control, digging in around his windpipe as she gets close behind but not close enough to touch him and give away her body position.

"Cloud?" Soar hisses, his voice rising to a squeak.

Her eyes drop closed and she grazes his shoulder with her teeth to demonstrate her dominance. Then she licks at him before nipping at his skin. Soar doesn't try and turn on her.

"God damn, Cloud," he shudders then forces a dry swallow down past her hand. "God damn."

She laughs, enjoying her victory. As her hand slides up to cup his jaw she lets her forehead rest on the base of his neck. Always comfort the prey after the capture. Each of them savours the intense thrill. Cloud's exposed nipples brush against his damp skin as he recovers. His scent changes to predator, working her heart a little harder as their roles reverse.

"This is my first hunt," Cloud admits. She should have told him she was a virgin five years earlier and the least she can do is tell him she's never done this before. "There's been nobody but you, Soar."

She resists as Soar takes her hand and pulls it around him but he insists with his grip so she let him. His chest swells with pride then she feels the length of his thickening cock through denim.

"It feels like I've been like this since I sent you away, little gryphon," Soar groans and in spite of her apprehension at becoming prey she explores, dragging her palm up and squeezing his shaft. Soar's fingers tremble over hers as he feels her feeling him. "Waiting for you to come home, praying you would understand why I couldn't hold you back."

He looks up and laughs, a chesty rumble, at the sight of the sweatpants in the tree above. Then he drops a hand to her bare thigh. "Are you naked?"

At that moment the balance of power shifts. Cloud perceives the ground cover and trees have thinned immeasurably and without the benefit of clothing she's completely exposed.

She hooks her good ankle over Soar's shin and pulls at the same time she pushes his back sending him stumbling forward.

Her next few steps jumble and blur as she escapes.

Soar's growl forces a fearful sweat from her skin and she runs, ankle and shoulder numbed by adrenaline as she bounds north and away. Cloud's vision narrows, everything goes to shades of grey. The only objects in clear focus are ones in motion. Leaves and branches move in the wind, tree trunks she passes, even her sling covered arm and glimpses of her white knees as she plummets through the forest.

Soar's breathing roars behind her. He doesn't try and move quietly, not like before. She's turned her back and his inner hunter has reacted, determined to bring her down.

Cloud dodges a tree as she tries to stay on level ground but in her panic she hasn't looked far enough ahead and clutches her arm to her side as she tumbles to a stop just short of a small cliff. The drop is too far to try in human form.

Soar crashes only a few feet behind her and she scrambles up but he seizes her from behind. Both his arms circle her around the waist, stopping her from driving headlong into a tree so thick she couldn't get her own arms around it.

She shrieks in pure, shrill terror and Soar roars in victory as she thrashes her legs and grabs for the tree as if it could save her.

"Little gryphon," Soar growls, barely human and she knows his teeth have shifted into sharp points to mark her. "You're mine."

Then he bites, scoring the surface of her skin where her neck and shoulder meet and Cloud cries out again, this time in surprise and pleasure. The initial burn of saliva driving under her skin is worse than she imagined but almost as quickly one hand releases her. Soar grasps the back of her neck and finds the spots that will comfort her. At the same time he withdraws his teeth and nuzzles the wound with his lips and tongue, soothing the sting as her terror slips away.

"My little gryphon," he croons, pulling away only long enough to speak.

"Soar," she breaths as her eyes roll up. She feels his tongue work every tooth mark, connecting each part of his bite with the deep ache in her belly. When her legs weaken with fading adrenaline Soar lowers them both to their knees.

"Steady," he instructs and she spreads her knees for balance. The soft, damp forest floor cools them. God, there are still spots before her eyes as the heaviness passes from her limbs. The pain down her back peaks then numbs and she can imagine the scrape from her fall at the cliff top or perhaps she's only aggravated the injury from the tornado. No time for it now. Soon she'll lay in and have ten days to recover.

Cloud decides it's mostly cuts and scrapes as the heat from Soar's body both soothes and warms them.

"Are you naked?" She asks as he presses the head of his erection against her ass.

"Hold your shoulder still," Soar says and she does. He helps, his left hand holding her elbow still. "Take wing with me."

It's then she understands the purpose of the sheet he had tied around his hips.

"Don't hesitate," he orders and the feel of his heart slowing with the accompanying drop in blood pressure triggers her own shift.

Cloud moans under the weight of her wings. The flight muscles down her back protest the change and she holds her breath as they tear further.

As soon as the big bones are solid Soar grabs her left wing. Cloud concentrates on the feel of her longer female tail extending. It rests between his legs and twitches at his calves revealing discomfort she can't hide.

"I know, little gryphon," he whispers. She holds her shoulder tight to her body as Soar folds the wing and binds her in the sheet, two corners tied around her waist and the other two under her arm.

With the pain eased, she's ready.

"Please," she begs.

Soar lifts one knee, planting his foot then lifts her leg and places her thigh on his. Her season is the only time he will ever take her from behind. The combination of where his cock hits her and the placement of her tail will trigger ovulation which, according to Shadow, is the most un-be-God-damn-leivable painful thing ever.

As he pulls her tail aside she pushes closer.

"Still," he orders and she does. He holds her with one arm as he strokes himself once, twice then tugs her closer seeking her moist entry.

As Soar chins the sheet from his mark he slides his cock halfway inside her and the forest spins around them. Then again, he seats himself deeply and for a moment Cloud's body rebels against the unnatural intrusion from behind but then he moves, hardening further with each thrust. He eases up only a little as he presses her winged back to his chest and she gasps as he finds the right spot deep inside. Soar's other hand reaches around, pressing firmly low on her belly and increasing the pleasure.

Cloud angles her good wing forward and out of his way as Soar beats his in the small clearing, their power rocking them together.

He whispers in the old words of the males. The complete language escapes her but she knows some of the words. *Earth, dame, fertility.*

Children.

Soar's fevered voice matches the intensity of their movements then fades to a whisper as if he were overcome by the moment before building again.

Mark him, Cloud thinks to herself and throws her head back. She can only reach a spot high on his neck, plainly visible to anyone and she hesitates. He'd been so private about them before but it's like he knows what she thinks.

"There, so everyone can see," Soar's ragged voice flames with the same passion building in her. "Hurry."

Cloud's teeth ache as they sharpen and she feels herself stir to orgasm. Soar nears release as well as he thrusts repeatedly, deep and hard.

As she feels herself slip over the edge she bites him just below the ear.

Her own cry explodes as Soar thrusts home one final time. An all consuming orgasm takes them both at once, shattering the stillness of the forest. Soar holds her as Cloud's muffled whimpers replace his roar, she licks at his wound, driving her saliva deep inside and soothing the terrible sting.

The last waves of climax echo between them as Soar withdraws then he's before her, opening the sheet and pushing the sling aside to reveal her adornment. Interlocking scales pattern the gold, their edges not rounded but pointed instead and curving under. Soar takes her hand and after layering their fingers together they touch it together.

"So amazing, Soar," Cloud murmurs. Smooth cool metal runs under their palms as they stroke down over her breast then rough as they explore back up. Soar adjusts the sheet, binds her wing tight to her body and places the knots so she doesn't have to lie on them.

As he lays her down in the cool brush, Cloud tucks her head into his chest and he wraps an arm around her, cradling her close. His other goes to her stomach, low over her womb.

After a few rough breaths the world becomes solid. He watches her expectantly.

"Little gryphon," Soar whispers and she manages a smile before the first un-be-God-damn-leivable cramp hits. Painful at first, then just a pleasant ache and Cloud bursts into tears, just as unable to cope with the gentle discomfort as she would have been with the pain.

The moment is too much.

Soar strokes her belly to ease her pain with his touch and watches her tears fall. Before the first drops from her skin, his tongue catches it then follows it to the source. He kisses her eye dry as another burst of fresh tears pours forth.

"I know," he whispers. "It hurts."

"No, it doesn't," Cloud hiccups as her breathing settles. She opens her dry eyes and watches her mate. Soar's lips are still damp with her tears. "Nothing could have prepared me for how good and whole I would feel now."

"Me too, little gryphon. Me too."

They lay together as the sweat dries from their skin. Cloud's damaged flight muscles hurt far more than the weak pleasurable cramps throbbing deep inside. In ten days she'll try and shift. If she can't then she's expecting their twins. In the meantime, Soar will give her everything.

Chapter Eighteen

It was deep night when Soar returned to the camper for blankets and his daggers. By dawn he'd hunted for her breakfast. Her tears hadn't caused him pain like what Talon described after mating with Shadow but her magic was protective and her tears had made Talon's bones unbreakable.

Painful indeed.

Soar knows Cloud's magic is in trust and although she hasn't yet admitted to being a royal gryphon he feels her trust in him. With each meal he brings her and each night he remains awake at her side her trust in him grows. Part of him is proud she's pleased with his care. The other part of him feels worse. He dreads what it will be like when her trust disappears and that moment will come when she finds out her expulsion from Sky's was entirely his selfish doing.

In three days Cloud will try and shift. Although neither has said it he knows what a delicate thing gryphon conception is. Cloud has been battered and injured and the chances are faint but he stays awake and hunts and guards her in the vain hope it will be enough to overcome her physical condition. There is nothing more he can do. When a female is lying in she is never relocated and in fact the only time he allows her to walk from the place they mated and the shelter he built is so she has some privacy to toilet.

This morning he follows a bear, not to kill since they could never eat a whole bear in three days but because he suspects she's looking for something very, very good. Something Soar wants first.

In spite of Soar's excellent care, Cloud deteriorates each day and he suspects her pride won't allow her to admit how much she hurts.

He's already found a lake with trout and a few spots for rabbit. They had venison the first day and Cloud had been ravenous but each day since then her appetite retreats as the dark circles under her eyes advance.

In three days he'll take her home to be healed and until then he'll keep her comfortable.

Soar watches the bear from a spot on a rock. She's beautiful and brown, not old enough for cubs but fat and healthy. Through his shift blackened eyes he watches her prize. The bee nest is active. Nestled in a fallen tree, its occupants fly in and out, constantly busy.

The bear complicates his task.

Since he first left his birth eyrie in Oregon, Soar can't pass a bee nest without satisfying his sweet tooth and if his mouth wasn't watering already he'd still brave their little stingers for what they can do for his mate. Soar has been stung so many times over the years he's quite immune to their medicinal effects.

With a sigh, Soar stands. He brought with him a couple of plastic zipper bags from the campervan and needs to beat the bear to the nest. Once he steps from his ledge he glides. He flares his wings as he slices silently toward her. Even armoured for protection, Soar's natural claws won't match her strength or thick fur. His only options are surprise and size if he wants to bully her away. She's only twenty feet from the hive when he lands before her. With a roar, Soar extends his wings.

She pauses and licks her lips. He's never sure how another big predator will perceive him. Prey animals scatter since they instinctively react to his presence but a big hunter like this takes the time to think. When she doesn't move, Soar takes a step toward her and rattles his wings. He can't allow himself to show any submission or the bear will either attack or go around, whatever it takes to claim the hive.

This one sits back on her butt.

He takes another step and she shakes her head then with a snort she turns and retreats, thinking twice about her snack.

Soar doesn't bother to chase her. His mate will wake soon and he doesn't want to miss the shine of the sun on her hair as the dawn light finds its way into her shelter.

The bees trail into and out of an opening in the old tree and Soar quickly removes a chunk of the dried and rotten trunk to expose the warm comb and release an angry swarm. His wings beat, stirring the air in an attempt to confuse them but many find purchase on his legs and head and he curses as their stingers penetrate his skin. Once he fills the larger bag with dripping sweet honeycomb he scoops up a dozen bees into the other. When it's nearly zipped shut he puts his lips to the opening to blow air in and earns a sting from one that does not want to treat Cloud. He seals the bag and turns to see the bear patiently waiting her turn.

Soar offers a respectful nod to the fellow predator and takes off, one hand full with the warm, heavy bag of honeycomb and the other vibrating with a dozen angry bees.

He pauses to retrieve the rabbits he gathered then returns to find Cloud limping back to their small nest.

"I couldn't wait," she smiles, a little sheepish knowing he won't approve but she really couldn't if she went by herself.

"I have something for you, little gryphon," Soar holds the zipper bags behind him, out of sight, and she leans to see. "Uh uh. You're always impatient for surprises."

She laughs but her voice is throaty and weak and it's more than just morning roughness. Soar doesn't look too closely at her shape, afraid she's lost weight.

With her good elbow in hand, Soar helps her kneel then she drops her butt to her heels and shifts sideways, partly seated with the weight off her ankle. It's nearly the same size now as her good one though he can't tell if there's been any improvement in the bad wrist since it's wrapped up in the sheet supporting her wing.

"Close your eyes," Soar orders and Cloud does though they pop right open, holding his with her full attention. "I'll go get a blindfold, little gryphon, but I can't promise you'll enjoy it as much."

Cloud harumpfs and this time she keeps them closed. He puts the bees on the ground between them and opens the honey covered bag. It had been overfilled and the golden liquid leaked out, coating its already sticky surface. Doesn't matter. If the venom helps he'll carry her to the lake to bathe before settling her in for the night.

"Open your mouth," he whispers. Her lips still hold their pink colour and they flush darker so he kisses her as he coats a finger in honey.

"Mm, Soar," she breathes and pinches her eyes shut even tighter to be good and earn it. "More."

He traces honey over her bottom lip and a large drop runs down her chin. It's followed by her tongue and a small gasp of surprise. Before he can get more her lips seal around his finger and draw it in.

Soar's groin tightens as she sucks it clean and he joins her, licking up what her tongue missed and occupying her mouth while he breaks off a large piece of comb. Once it's between his teeth he presses it to her lips. She accepts, chewing happily as a small amount of honey leaks past her lips.

"Wow," she sighs and opens her eyes. Cloud spots the plastic bag and hooks her finger in.

Soar knows what's coming and closes his eyes but doesn't open his mouth.

Cloud's sticky mouth covers his and Soar decides as soon as she's well he's going to see how much honey she'll let him use.

"Naughty, naughty gryphon," she tisks and instead of offering the honey to eat she strokes her fingers over his neck and follows with her mouth.

"Fuck, yeah," Soar moans as her lips stick to her mark just under his ear. "So not fair."

Yeah, there won't be sex for three more days and if she keeps this up it will be a sticky, uncomfortable wait in his black leather armour.

She shuts him up with honey covered fingers in his mouth, sliding them in and out as his tongue curls around.

"Good breakfast," she whispers, tracing around his mark with her mouth. "You are the best mate ever and I will tear anyone who argues to pieces."

Her gentle praise as she nudges his chin higher fills him with pride so deep nothing will ever match it.

"I have something else," he swallows as he gets control and Cloud lets him go as if sensing more sexual play will only heighten his frustration.

When he picks up the other bag she leans away and looks at him with alarm.

"Field medicine, Cloud," he explains. Her lips unstick with a pop as she starts to speak then she closes her mouth as she gets closer to the bees. She's curious as she studies them and is careful to keep her distance. The bees do the same, clustering on the far side of the bag to stay as far from her as possible. Funny things.

"Oh my gosh," she exclaims. Up close she can see the holes their stingers made in his skin.

"The price of collecting them, I'm afraid," Soar admits with a sideways smile. She laughs but her concern doesn't fade. "The venom is good for pain and enough will help you rest. I'm a menace to these little guys and their venom doesn't bother me anymore."

"How many times have you been stung?"

"Today or in my lifetime?"

"Forget I asked," she shakes her head.

"Okay," Soar unties the sheet and she holds still. Her shiver isn't from the chill of having it removed. Cloud's heart and breathing speed up and a little colour drains from her cheeks. The extra pain she's in with her wing unsupported will be temporary. He drops the sheet and opens the bag enough to remove a little squirming bee from it.

"But," she protests. "Isn't it dangerous for the babies?"

It's the first time either one has dared mention the possibility of success. Cloud believes they've conceived and he doesn't want to ruin it for her.

"Why do you think I have three younger sets of siblings?" Soar asks. "My sire always treats my dame to ease the pains. Swears by it."

"Does it hurt? I've never got a sting."

"No worse than my kiss," Soar teases.

"I thought so," she scolds but she hides her nervousness.

"Lean on me."

Cloud does and he feels she got stickier than he thought. With his arm around her and her left wing in his left hand, he moves it enough to get under it and presses the bee to her skin. It's disobedient and he has to drag it over her skin several times before it stings her then he drops it aside and leaves its little venom sack pumping.

"Ow."

"We'll start with three."

"Oh."

Soar quickly wrangles two more and stings her several inches above and below the first. She doesn't comment and gets heavy as her breathing slows.

"How's that?"

Cloud giggles then hiccups.

"That was fasht," she slurs and starts laughing.

"You're a pretty cheap date, little gryphon," Soar hurries to rewrap her wing before she falls over. Euphoria isn't unheard of when gryphons are treated with venom but he's never seen it. Her half-open eyes blink once and she dozes as Soar lowers her down. She doesn't stir when he positions her on her good side and covers her up. For the past week she's been the most sleepy awake person he's ever seen and now that she's relaxed he can as well.

As Soar leaves the sheltered nest the sky darkens and he looks up just in time to see two red armoured gryphons disappear past the tree tops.

"Oh, shit," he hisses. They head toward his campervan and Soar runs after them as he checks his weapons. He's no match for two members of the Will, possibly dragonkin, who with their mere words could make him stand on his head and bark like a dog.

Soar stumbles to a stop as he enters the clearing. He knows the lone dragonkin and the other is nowhere to be seen.

"Conflagration," Soar drops to a respectful knee. Over the past few years the two have become friends, frequently drinking together at Cooper's, but today Soar wears the black leather of Sire Lev's guard and Con wears the Will's reds. This is business. Although Con is Cloud's age, he acts for the Grand Council and any slight to his authority insults the Council.

"Master Soar," Con acknowledges. He's in his gryphon form. Once, Con drunkenly admitted to being dragonkin and followed it up with a brief and even drunker shift. Soar doesn't remember much about it other than the smooth leather of his wings and the gold tint of his skin.

And the black eye he received for calling Con a bald gryphon just before Con fell over laughing in agreement.

"Where is your friend?" Soar demands as he gets to his feet.

"Keeping a respectful distance."

"And your business?" Soar wants to get the Will away from his female.

"I felt it better to see you alone considering our relationship," Con admits. "But you already know I'm not here for drinks."

Soar acknowledges with a terse nod. With his head turned he can listen for any noise coming from Cloud's direction.

"I will be brief, Master Soar," Con starts. "Daniel Cooper was taken into custody a week ago, the night Calgary was hit by the tornado. He has something that belongs to the Council and Aledaar has tired of Cooper's games. Cooper was involved with a female. She disappeared and I am here to take her before the Council for questioning."

"She's laying in, Con," Soar growls. "I'm sure even your orders don't include disturbing her."

"The matter isn't urgent," Con appears bored but Soar's experienced eyes detect tension. "And even if it were we would not disturb the female you acknowledge is involved with Cooper."

Shit. Keep your cool, Soar.

"You've told me nothing we don't already know. Cloud, adopted grand-daughter of Sire Lev was expelled from Sky's program for theft and sought refuge in Calgary, apparently too ashamed to return home. The morning after the tornado the local media lit up with a report of Cherry Cooper who was pulled from a six story balcony and survived. Her companion, George Noble, my gryphon friend, assisted two Calgary Police Officers by getting them clear of the falling glass.

"Then Cherry and George disappeared and the Police Chief would very much like to thank them."

This time Soar keeps his mouth shut. The red armoured gryphon or dragonkin or whatever accompanied Con remains absent.

"Cloud was reared in Jasper as an orphan and is the only known survivor of the atrocity at Welch Peak, yes?"

What is Con doing? Soar feels pressure in his throat and knows it's Con's influence as the dragonkin tries to make Soar talk.

"Yes," Soar agrees but only because there is no point in lying. The realization he could have said no suggests Con might not be trying very hard. Perhaps courtesy to his friend?

"When she didn't arrive on Vancouver Island we checked in Memphis. We ran in to Dame Shadow and had a brief chat."

Bastards, Soar decides. Interrogating a pregnant female.

"She is very concerned for Cloud and volunteered all she knew in the hopes it would help us find her.

"Shadow spoke with several gryphons in Memphis including your youngest sibling, Hunter. He told her he knew nothing of the expulsion but when she said he was lying he admitted to stealing the knife and hiding it in her den. He claimed your female had spurned him one too many times and he wanted revenge.

"He said he acted alone, also a lie, and refused to speak further. Your youngest sibling spends his days apologizing in the sparring chamber."

Damn, brave gryphon. Soar never promised his brother he wouldn't get in trouble for helping with his plan and knows the kid will do whatever he has to in loyalty to Soar. Hunter could be on his hands and knees suffering under the weight of his wings for weeks and that's mild considering some of the things Sky has done. She's taken a gryphon's flight feathers for less, grounding the criminal for a year or more until they grew back.

"The Will spoke privately with Hunter," Con says and Soar goes cold. It's only a matter of time before Cloud finds out what he's done and that time is very short if Con keeps talking. "He admitted he framed Cloud on your order, Master Soar."

Then it happens. The bottom falls out of Soar's heart ripping Cloud's trust out with it. She listens and he's brought to the ground. Soar clutches at his chest part in relief the moment has finally come and part in pain not for himself, but for her.

"What is your involvement with Daniel Cooper?" Con asks and the scratching of tiny invisible claws to his throat returns.

"None," Soar says. He can't allow himself to whisper no matter how weak his voice is. He explains to both Con and Cloud. "Lev believes Cooper is responsible for the atrocities. I wasn't so sure and had to know. My eyrie is at stake, Con. I sent Cloud there to give me ears on the inside. If she didn't have a cover story she believed she'd be dead."

He struggles to his feet, somehow heavier since the absence of her trust weighs more than its beautiful presence.

"And besides you and Hunter, who else was aware of this?" Con continues to push his influence.

"Nobody," Soar lies, soaked in too much guilt to be surprised he's defied Con. Nobody will go after Sky for her part. The shame of Soar's plan is his to bear alone.

"Alright," Con nods. "Cloud will go before the council and I suspect they will need nothing more than for her to verify your story."

Con runs toward the dirt road and launches himself skyward. The beat of his wings fades as Soar returns to his mate.

Chapter Nineteen

"Soar?"

Cloud doesn't have to ask who landed behind her but if she doesn't speak then he'll just put her breakfast down and leave again for the sky above. He hasn't complained about the silent hours she spends by the fire watching the flames and the glowing coals. Three days alone with him so achingly near has been as hard on her as she imagines it's been on him.

Soar's betrayal was the last thing she remembered before waking in the camper. He washed the honey from her skin before leaving to guard from outside. Only once did he try and talk to her and she wandered into the trees to pee rather than listen. She forgave him and was ready to listen but something in the way he couldn't yet meet her eyes told her he still needed to punish himself. Otherwise, Cloud has stayed put to give him no cause to worry for her.

The scents of rabbit blood and raw trout turn her stomach with more power than the day before and she shivers, a deep full body tremble that hit late last night and worsened since she heard him get up to hunt. She made it into the trees to throw up then to the fire to try and warm.

"Cloud," he sounds humbled but he comes.

Her vision ripples and she clamps her eyes shut before trying again. Soar settles his weight on the ground and lays the food out before her. And he's out of arms reach. What the heck does he think she's going to do? Strangle him with one hand? Cloud no longer hurts over what happened in Sky's mountain. She had to believe she'd been expelled or Cooper would have seen right through her.

"You look rough," Soar says, his eyes tighten in concern. Yesterday she had no trouble hiding the headache and iffy stomach especially since he avoided her but today it's much, much worse. Not to mention she thinks he gave her bad bees or something. She can't see where he stung her but the itch makes her crazy. At least the pain in her shoulder remains illusive.

"Stomach bad," she mutters as her hand covers it.

"Yeah?" For a moment the playful gryphon with whom she mated returns. Soar looks at her stomach then his face falls.

"I'm injured, Soar. Sick," Cloud mutters. She drops her eyes to the rabbit then when her stomach fails she turns to the van to throw up. He exhausted himself caring for her but even that isn't enough. She's not healthy dame material and hasn't been since the day she got hurt. She tries a smile but her teeth chatter. The fire fails to ease her fever.

"Yeah," he moves the meat aside and shuffles closer. Then he tips her chin up and kisses her forehead. "Damn, your warm."

"Must have caught something at Cooper's."

Soar feels her cheeks then her throat. She shivers when he lifts her good arm to feel under her adornment.

"How long have you kept quiet about this?" He accuses but before she can answer he runs to the van, returning with a small towel. After soaking it in water from one of the bottles he filled while hunting he wipes down every bit of skin he can. The coolness fades and she imagines steam rising around them.

"Soar, I'm not angry."

"No?"

"Look, there's something I should have told you before we mated and I would have, I swear, if I knew things would get this serious. It all happened so fast."

"You're royal," Soar says as he lifts her chin again.

Cloud looks at her mark, high on his neck as he dabs around the one on hers with the cold cloth.

"How did you know?"

"Talon told me," he admits. "The first time you came to my den... after, you know. I confessed to him. He's your sire and it's my duty to be respectful and have a conversation about you."

Males, she sighs. *Can't use a chamber pot without having a conversation about it. And then they call it 'you know' with the female in question even though 'you know' hurt like hell at first and wasn't over until he took them both to heaven.*

It also explains Soar's black eye the following day. At the time Cloud figured somebody got lucky sparring with him. She'd been pretty naive about males when she was twenty. Maybe she still is.

"What did he tell you?" If Talon told Soar everything it will make this so much easier. Maybe.

"He hit me for not speaking with him first, for starters," Soar says. "He said you know when you're trusted and you wouldn't have gone near me if I didn't trust you. Or if you didn't trust me. He said to keep it quiet. If word got out we had an unmated royal in the eyrie you'd have unwanted visitors. He said you wanted your training taken seriously because you want to be a ranger, not a Dame."

"All true," Cloud shivers. She drips water and sweat and the cool breeze through the trees goes right through her.

"He made me swear I wouldn't hold you back, Cloud. That's why I dropped you. If you wanted me half as much as I wanted you and I handled it so badly. If I'd only said something...

"I found where you hid your dinner last night," Soar interrupts himself as he holds the cloth on her forehead. He's right. She'd have given up on her dream for a male, the last thing she thought she wanted, but for this male she'd give up everything.

"Yeah, what else did Talon say?"

"That was it."

Soar pushes her lids up further and Cloud winces at the extra light streaming in.

"Badly bloodshot, you been crying?"

"I don't cry."

"You did," he whispers and kisses the tip of her nose.

Soar unties the make-shift sling and immobilizes her wing with one hand as he keeps her steady with the other.

"Look, you're going to draw your wings in and I'm going to carry you home."

"Not yet," Cloud moans. The feeling in her legs fades and she isn't so sure she has the focus to shift. She no longer detects the rabbit smell although the little body sits next to them and the movement of the living forest comes to her in bits and pieces. "There's more to my magic than trust, Soar, and I think it'll cost me yours."

He barely looks up as he explores her torn muscles. The smell of infection reaches her nose as air gets under her wing. Infection and something far nastier she'd once scented from a sealed trunk in Master Sky's den. She turns aside and he forgets about what's under her wing as he holds her still. Yellow bile from her empty stomach pools in the grass.

"Wings," he insists. "Now."

"Wait, I can make gryphons do things, Soar. With my magic I can make them."

"Uh huh."

Cloud's lips tingle and she sags.

"Have you ever used it on me?"

He rubs the back of her neck with the towel.

"Our first time. I wanted you to be the one and you wouldn't have if you didn't want it too. You just needed a little nudge."

"We'll talk about that later, Cloud," he mumbles in a pinched voice. Cloud's shame deepens as his trust in her weakens then fails.

"It's my fault," he shakes his head. The admission, however, doesn't bring back any of his trust in her. "Oh damn, Cloud."

Through her blurring vision, Cloud can see he holds something long in his hand. Two? Three? Might be one in her double vision.

"Feathers, Cloud," he moans. "You're losing flight feathers."

But something above catches her eye. Gold and green lights wrapped in shadow appear above the trees.

"Pretty," she murmurs as everything goes black.

"Huh?" Soar asks.

Lost flight feathers are far from pretty. A gryphon can lose one but three on one wing could ground her and if the others are just as close to falling out then she isn't safe airborne on her own. Not that she's in any shape for flying; her left wing is three-quarters the size it should be and the remaining feathers have lost their sheen.

But it's too late for an answer. Cloud's unconscious body weighs him down and three gryphons wearing the blood red leathers of the Council's Will alight next to the campervan. Beneath his feathers, Con hides his dragonkin form.

Soar doesn't know the others.

I don't have time for this.

The big red-haired one in front can only be Fury, Master of the Council's Will. If seen alone one could mistake Fury for being squat but he's over seven feet tall so squat makes him as broad as a truck. Con stands to his right and a female Soar doesn't know is to his left. Her long blonde hair, severely drawn back from her symmetrical features and full lips make Soar think she has it in for him. Fury's wild red beard and unkempt hair glitter with gold and silver ornaments. His double-bladed axe must weigh sixty pounds.

He's the gryphon the Will sends if you're in deep, deep trouble and that isn't what Con suggested three days earlier.

"Master Fury," Soar bows as deeply as he can considering he clutches Cloud in his lap.

"Gryphon," Fury nods then he turns to Cloud. "Is this the female?"

Con nods.

"She's injured," Fury says as he kneels and reaches to touch Cloud.

Soar turns away with his mate and growls; his body instinctively protecting her while his mind tries to tell him to submit. Her fever has to be more than a hundred and five and Soar sweats under his wings from holding her. With effort, he turns and allows Fury to touch Cloud's forehead.

"We escaped Calgary during a thunder—"

"I'm aware," Fury inhales, his nose nearly on Cloud's shoulder then he pries one of her eyes open. Even in a few minutes they are more red than before. "This is a dragonkin sickness."

"The only dragon she's been around is Con and he never got close to her."

"Dragonkin," Fury corrects. "There are no dragons around here. Show me the injury."

"Damn it."

Fury should let Soar take her to the river to deal with the fever. Instead he removes the sling.

"Bees?" Fury asks as he peers under her wing. He looks Soar over. A fresh set of stings from the morning's foraging cover both his arms.

"Field medicine," Soar explains but Fury should know that already. Soar gets a glimpse of the three boils that are more like black pus filled blisters. Each two inches mass throbs exactly where he'd administered the venom.

"The venom reacts with her blood and creates toxins," Fury draws a knife. "The toxins are killing her."

"No!" Soar tries to grab her.

"You want me to help her," Fury's voice stops Soar. Of course he wants her helped and in spite of Fury's strong will, Soar forces himself to allow Fury to use the knife. The boils rupture with a hiss. Toxins squirt onto the grass leaving it blackened and smoking.

"Tell my sibling we're coming," Fury tells Con. Con bows and disappears up into the trees.

"Wait, coming where?" Soar demands. "I have to bring the fever down."

Soar grabs Cloud and pulls his arm back, shocked by the painful sting her fever causes his palm. Why doesn't she burn Fury?

"She needs more heat, not less, Master Soar. If she were healthy she could withstand a sting but she isn't and has three. My sister can treat this and if you're coming with us then you have a minute to get your gear on or be left behind."

Soar can't fight or argue because he can't heal her. He wants to turn and protest but he's already pulling on his leather trousers as his body moves without instruction from his mind. As he laces up his tunic and straps on his knives he wonders if all mated males are so completely dopey.

"I will bear Cloud through the portal," Fury says as Soar ties the last knot on his armour. "Flay will carry you."

"Who?" Soar turns as the female nods.

She's carrying me?

"Where are we going?"

"Skyfall, Master Soar," Fury stands proudly. Cloud is small in his arms. Even from across the remains of their campfire Soar feels the heat of her fever. "You shall be a guest of the Dragonkin."

"I hope our *guest* is delicious," Flay comments as she looks Soar over. Is she flirting or does she plan on eating him?

Maybe both.

141

Flay and Fury turn and take off and Fury's shout booms out ahead. Soar, speechless again, beats away from the clearing in pursuit.

Stories Soar remembers of Skyfall, the dragonkin city, place it on every continent. Other than Con, who never went beyond proving his drunken admission of being a dragonkin with a drunker albeit brief shift to dragonkin form, Soar knows nothing of them at all.

Except the Council's Will is full of them and you can't resist their command, even if it's to slice your own throat open.

Then Soar defied Con, hadn't he? He knew Con's will should have forced a truthful answer and he outright lied to him. Instead of admitting Sky's complicity he denied involvement of anyone but Hunter.

When they cross the lake where Soar caught the trout, Flay and Fury glide and shift with the crackle sound of crunching cellophane. Their instant change increases Soar's unease as the morning gets even further from anything he can control. The realization that Cloud's illness needs more than a dip in the lake frustrates him. Fury's flight feathers merge and turn from brown to a deep, scaly gold. Flay's change to gray-green and her skin takes on a decidedly green hue. Her tail narrows and grows by half again in length while Fury's only becomes thicker. Their speed doubles, making them even harder to chase.

Cloud's breath hitches, ragged and heavy, and the new urgency of Fury's flight tells Soar she's in deep trouble. There was no time to grasp anything more than disappointment at her magic manipulation of him and now he could lose her. One minute a confession of seduction and lies and the next weakening gasps for air.

A bolt of lightning staggers down a kilometer ahead and sparks a rough glowing oval directly in their path. A few seconds later another appears a few hundred yards beyond.

Fury drives on with Cloud and as Soar fights to keep up, Flay blocks his path.

"Stay back," she yells and he has to pull up short to avoid knocking her from the sky. "The next portal is mine. We can't follow through Fury's."

She stays in his path, forcing him up, and with a crack of thunder the first portal collapses behind Fury. Cloud disappears.

"We're next," she calls and takes off for the second portal. With more agility than a gryphon can pull off, the green dragonkin flies up over him, her stomach to the sun. "Tuck your wings in."

Soar doesn't question and he's bound from behind by her awesome strength and he couldn't fight free if he tried. Flay's arms bind his wings and her legs wrap around his thighs. The pointy moulded breasts of her red armour dig in to the base of his wings. She sized him up as a passenger, not a date.

Flay dives and with a cry that chills his blood, they hit the portal.

Chapter Twenty

Flay releases Soar as the electric boom of the portal's collapse behind them stops battering his senses. The thick air stinks of acrid, cold campfire and tints everything in a brown haze. As he gets his bearings and glides after Flay, he orients himself between the light brown ceiling above and the darker ground below.

"There," Flay points and they descend through a massive chamber. A stoney bridge stretches over a hundred meters across a steep sided mountain valley. Thick, dim air obscures the far ends of the gaping cavern. Square buildings at either end of the span cover the slopes beneath the semi-solid barrier that protects the city from above.

He follows Flay's arm to see Fury, Cloud in his arms, on foot approaching a dwelling at one end of the bridge. The door opens revealing a shifted dragonkin female outlined in the flames that fill her chamber.

Soar runs, unable to decide if flight or feet will be faster. His attempts at each only hinder the other.

He's only a few steps from the door when Fury emerges alone. The heavy stone slams shut. As Fury steps aside two things happen at once. The edges of the door fuse with the wall and Soar slams up against a now unremarkable block of stone.

"Cloud!"

The futile thuds of his palms turn into frantic scratching as he seeks the edges of the door.

"Master Soar," Fury places a palm on Soar's shoulder. "She is perfectly safe."

"You bastard," Soar mutters as he steps back hoping a broader view of the wall will give him a hint as to the location of the opening.

"Lady Tempest is dragonkin and completely able to tolerate the heat."

"Who, the woman who took my female?"

"No, Master Soar," Fury straightens up in a fair approximation of gryphon pride but on the big dragonkin the pose is no more than an insulting display of arrogance. "Lady Tempest is your dragonkin mate and I know this because I am her sire."

Soar's feet tangle as he turns to Fury. He doesn't even try to stay up as he falls back against the wall.

"I named her Tempest and believed her dead at her dame's side. She is a Lady now, since she has no dame.

"This is a good day, Soar," Fury continues as he walks to the bridge. "I have my daughter and Conflagration has his sister. A very good day."

The sway of Fury's axe and swagger of his tail irritate Soar then his eyes fall to Cloud's flight feathers, still in his hand. God, it's nonsense of course but Fury's tangled mass of red hair is indistinguishable from Cloud's when she was younger and her magic influenced him just like a dragonkin member of the Will.

Shit. The most dangerous being he's ever run in to sired his mate.

This isn't a good day at all.

"My daughter was a virgin when she came to you," Fury states.

Soar says something insightful like 'uh.' If Talon hit him he can only imagine what Cloud's sire might have to say.

The pair sit on a couple of old upholstered chairs outside Fury's home, another door in the stone wall like the one into which Cloud disappeared. Soar still can't get his head around the name Tempest.

They are on the opposite side of the bridge perhaps a hundred yards from where it connects with the rough street paralleling this side of the canyon. On either side, rows and rows of similar doors front upon stone roads that terrace one above the other. Only the bridge connects both sides of Skyfall, the dragonkin city.

Few dragonkin move about considering the size of the city. Some shuffle or walk but none hurry. All struggle with the current of heavy depression that Soar witnessed in many neighbourhoods over the years. The word slum succinctly describes Skyfall. The shabby, deserted stone hovels hold a few slumped and beaten down dragonkin, nothing like the great and powerful city he imagined. It only needs wrecks on flats and gangs of youth out to ensure their law holds superior over all others.

Maybe this conversation with Fury would be less strange if Con and Flay weren't present but then they don't seem to listen. The human formed pair, Con in jeans and Flay in a little green dress, embrace on a loveseat. Her loose hair lends some softness to the sharp good looks Soar saw back at the campsite. Flay dozes in Con's arms as he plays with her chin and strokes her cheeks with his lips.

"They all are," Fury continues. "She chose you and you didn't stand a chance like poor Con here."

Con interrupts his caresses to give Fury the finger.

"Dragonkin females are like that. Tempest's adornment? Just means you've completed the gryphon ritual. Dragonkin males don't waste their gold on a female."

Soar puffs his lips and exhales. He thought the same thing as he tried to figure out how and why Cloud, or Lady Tempest, became his. Her flight feathers rest across his legs and he smooths them out but they're soft and unruly and prefer to curl up and tangle under his fingers and behave more like his unsettled confusion.

Fury still wears his reds and adjusts himself before reaching down past his chair for a bottle of whiskey. He breaks the seal and passes it to Soar for a long pull before helping himself and passing it to Con.

"Portalling makes Flay sleepy," Fury explains with a small amount of disgust.

"Makes Con horny," Con mumbles.

"Being near your female makes any male horny," Fury laughs. Flay doesn't stir and Con extends his middle finger to his sire for a second time. "To think, Master Soar, Lady Tempest was reared in Jasper under the nose of Aledaar's own son.

"Tempest won't be in there for hours. Our best healer cares for her," Fury continues and waves the bottle at the other end of the bridge before he passes the whiskey around again. Soar needs his nerves soothed and the smooth liquid grants him enough patience to wait without annoying anyone. "You must be a competent ranger for a dragonkin female to choose you."

The burn keeps Soar from laughing. Cloud's years in Memphis have made her the one who's competent.

"You find the idea amusing?" Fury asks. "Then you've never fought her in her dragonkin form."

The hand holding the half-empty whiskey bottle shifts from human to something Soar has never seen. Fury's fingers thicken and lengthen as his entire forearm takes on a deep gold hue. The nails become claws and leave scratches in the glass as they lengthen. It's unnerving to see Fury with one arm a foot longer and twice as thick as the other. Gold scales the size of a man's thumbnail overlap all the way up into his armour. The scale tips curl under, some so long they turn up, just like Cloud's adornment.

"Yes, imagine facing that. Dragonkin do not have to grow old to fully shift."

Nauseating. Not the idea Cloud can do it but the sight of Fury with one arm completely shifted into a large scale covered talon proves how very dangerous the dragonkin could be.

"You doubt Lord Fury, Master Soar?" Fury asks. The talon shifts again, returning to the form of a human hand but the dragonkin lord speaks in challenge.

"No, Lord Fury," Soar says and sets Cloud's feathers aside. "I don't doubt you at all. If anyone has the capacity to shift my world, it's her."

With a tilt of his head toward the stone wall that hides his mate, Soar says exactly whom he does not doubt.

Chapter Twenty-One

"Lady Tempest?" A female speaks.

Cloud stretches on the warm stone beneath her with no recollection of drawing her wings in or undressing. Her heavy and tired muscles bear more than the understanding she and Soar haven't conceived. The dangerously hot air should burn as she breathes but it doesn't.

The voice echoes the name she heard over and over before she woke through the crack of thunder and the rush of wind. She remembers Soar's arms around her then she was swallowed by the lightning hole in the sky.

"Lady Tempest?"

A hand touches Cloud's shoulder and she sits with a start, drawing her knees up to cover herself in a gesture of human modesty.

"Oh my gosh," she gasps. The older female has leathery gold wings and wears a long sleeveless tunic. Her bare legs and feet are tinted with the same dirt that dusts the stone floor. Only slightly alarming are the gold scales that run in a band past her ears and down her neck before disappearing into her clothing.

Cloud swallows and her mouth goes dry at the sight of the female's eyes. They glow like gold fire and not just her eyeballs. If she turned her head the luminous disks would appear to float above her heat reddened cheeks.

"My name is Cloud," she manages before she blurts out. "What are you?"

"I am dragonkin like you, Lady Tempest," the female takes a seat by Cloud's legs. Up close, the glowing disks become translucent then disappear revealing the violent gold flecks that ripple and weave over her irises.

"I do not have much time with you, Lady Tempest. The room is cooling and they expect the door to open and for you to emerge."

"Who?" Cloud stammers.

How many more of them are out there?

"Your male waits with your sire. You are in Skyfall, the dragonkin city."

"My sire is dead," she says but the female waves her silent.

"Your babies are fine, Lady Tempest."

Cloud's jaw drops as her hands slip between her thighs and over her stomach.

"Dragonkin are not plagued with the inability to shift when they have conceived. Our females go into season at the worst possible time. Your season was triggered by your injuries.

"You don't trust me and you shouldn't nor anyone else out there. Keep your mouth shut and continue to be overwhelmed. Don't let them find out you're pregnant, not even your male."

"But—"

"No.

"Your sire will take you before the gryphon Grand Council. Aledaar will put a powerful relic around your neck. The pain will be immeasurable but your pregnancy has altered you enough you will be immune. When it's over follow their orders and escape when you can.

"Aledaar uses the relic to control our kin but he won't control you. You will truly be a free dragonkin and only a free dragonkin can kill him. He must be wearing the relic when he dies and your kin will be freed.

"If they find out you're pregnant before you wear the relic then you'll be imprisoned until your young are born. He'll claim your will and that of your children when they are strong enough to survive. If he finds out when you're free then he can still claim them.

"Do you understand? You must be free from Aledaar."

Cloud only understands she's telling the truth. The female talks nonsense but it's the truth.

"How do you know this?" Cloud demands as a large square tears into the stone.

The gold winged dragonkin rests her hand in the centre of it.

"Because," she smiles with hope although her voice betrays great sadness. "I'm the only free dragonkin and I'm imprisoned here, in our fallen city. My own kin have no choice but to kill me if I portal outside, such is the will of Aledaar.

"Now, I'll see if I can find something for you to wear."

With a nod, she pushes the stone door open. Other than a slight rumble with the movement there is no hint of a hinge and it seems one edge of the door connected to the edge of the wall facilitates its weightless swing. Through the opening, Cloud is able to see an immense cavern. On the other side stone buildings appear stacked in rows upon each other.

A crack of thunder reverberates over everything and Cloud scoots backward until her skin presses against hot stone.

"Here," the female says when she returns. She doesn't appear bothered by the noise outside. "Someone has portalled in. If you cross the city you must use the bridge. You don't want to be hit by a portal when it grounds."

She still doesn't make any sense. All Cloud wants is to get to Soar if he's indeed waiting for her outside.

The tunic and trousers she's given are definitely gryphon, right down to the secure hand-stitched double hems and bone buttons closing the tunic at the waist beneath the wing openings.

Before she's even finished knotting the drawstring of the trousers, she's on her feet. The female's hand guides Cloud to the door. Vertigo hits and leaves her swaying as she grasps the size of the chamber. It must be a mile long, the sky browned but visible through the strange translucent ceiling. The stacked buildings on the other side are several hundred feet away.

Soar picks up his pace halfway across the bridge. He's dwarfed by the gold-winged dragonkin male at his side. The dragonkin's massive axe swings at his side and he wears the reds of the Council's Will. It's enough to make Cloud turn and run back to the warm room but the female still holds her.

Sire?

His red hair is not so different from Cloud's when she doesn't keep it up. With a hand on Soar's back, the dragonkin whispers and Soar nods before approaching Cloud alone.

"You may shift as you like," the female says when Soar is within earshot. "Fly every day to get your strength back."

Then she's gone, leaving Soar alone with Cloud as she nears the male.

"Little gryphon," Soar says and arches his wings forward to draw her close. His eyes follow the silhouette of her shoulders against the stone behind her instead of her wings. For a moment he looks sad. Cloud assumes it's since he doesn't know a pregnant dragonkin can shift. Then he smiles. "You're okay."

The deeper she sinks into his wings the more his gryphon smell wins out over the scent of shifted dragonkin. As she folds in his embrace she doesn't see him. Instead the broad smile of a raven haired female looms before her. The cavern disappears to be replaced with fire-lit stone walls and the smell of the scene she imagines makes her heart lurch. It's the room where she was born, the same room where Torrent nearly killed her. Gryphon and dragonkin mingle, confusing her senses as the deep laughter of a male comes from within her vision and outside of it.

"Cloud?"

Soar's tight embrace brings her back to the present as the male's laughter fades to a delighted chuckle. The scene stretches and thins and her birth dame's dark eyes become lighter as they are replaced with her mate's.

The older female kneels before Cloud's sire. He doesn't acknowledge her when she extends her arms, palms and wrists up.

"Lady Tempest has not conceived, Lord Fury," she says.

"Thank you," Fury touches her wrists without drawing his eyes from Cloud.

Cloud's anguished yelp is muffled in Soar's shoulder. At least she's spared lying to him.

"I heard that name, Tempest," she whispers. Anything she can do to avoid admitting the female told her anything is for the better. That path only leads to telling lies and until she decides how much of the story is true it's better to live with whatever Soar and this Lord Fury have to say. "I heard it when the lightning took me from our campsite and the voice, I remember it, too."

"Yes," Soar smiles but there's an edge to his charm as he does his best to reassure her. Soar doesn't like this place and neither does Cloud. The tension in his muscles matches hers and she knows if he'd listened in on what the female had to say he'd agree with her.

Keep your mouth shut, Cloud.

"We are in Skyfall, the dragonkin city."

Cloud's eyes wander to Lord Fury.

"Not yet," Soar insists. "Look at me. Your sire is here as is your brother."

"Oh," Cloud exclaims. A dark haired male waits with a blonde at the other end of the bridge. His gold wings stand out next to the dusky green of hers.

"They are very happy to have found you," Soar continues. "But that is Lord Fury's story to share. Tempest was the name you were given at birth. Your dragonkin name."

"I don't want to be here, Soar," Cloud whispers, her voice tuned so only he can hear her. "I want to go home now."

"Lady Tempest," Fury calls.

Soar kisses her eyes and turns her to face her sire.

"Lady Tempest, come to me, child."

Cloud shoots an angry glance at Soar not because she's angry at him but because she wants him to know she's angry. She hasn't been a child for ten years and her bristling at the slight isn't missed by Fury. He chuckles, causing the ornaments in his overgrown beard to sway with his enormous axe.

"Come," he extends a hand.

Cloud's resistance slips away and she feels what can only be described as an *urge* to comply. She would have if she didn't feel forced. Her instincts tell her to fight. Her will is hers and she won't surrender it.

"Lady Tempest," Fury growls. "Kneel before your sire."

"Back off," Cloud replies.

"Cloud," Soar hisses.

She doesn't like what Fury's doing. The burn in her throat means he's using the magic Cloud thought was royal. There is nothing royal about it and experiencing her own trick turned against her confirms what Soar said is true.

Cloud is dragonkin and this male is her sire.

"Back off," she repeats and shoves her magic at him as hard as she can. Fury's smile stiffens as he shuffles one foot back a few inches. Then he struggles forward a step as if he's fighting a stiff wind.

"Here," Fury demands again and this time the pressure in her throat is painful.

Cloud says nothing, unable to speak. Is this what it was like for Soar when she went to his den? When she told him he wanted to have her and pushed like Fury does now?

"When I learned you were raised in Jasper I hoped you would choose better than this," Fury loosens the axe at his waist. His teeth lengthen and the gold glow of his eyes deepens so she cannot see the whites. The tilt of his head tells her Fury can only be disappointed with Soar.

"You," she growls but her voice chokes off as the burn in her throat deepens.

"And what do you have to say about this?" Fury demands, shaking a finger at Soar. "I never would have let you mate with a *gryphon!*"

"Lord Fury," Cloud finds her voice.

"It's sire," Fury replies. His voice sounds rough with the same irritation Cloud feels in her throat. "And you will kneel."

"Mind your manners," Cloud says with more volume than before. Soar is her choice and the big scaly gold dragonkin is just going to have to deal with it.

"Cloud," Soar warns a second time.

"I will not hear that name in my city again, gryphon," Fury spits. "This is no place for gryphon names or gryphons."

Fury's fingers lengthen and the gold of his scales deepens until it shimmers in the diffused amber light from above. He draws his axe and Cloud steps before Soar. The words imply threat but his actions bring it to life. The axe is placed lovingly on the ground and Fury's fiery eyes flare brighter.

"Do you have something to say to me, Lady Tempest?" Fury demands.

"Get behind me," Soar tries but his voice is too loud in her head like her hearing has increased in sensitivity a hundred fold.

It only takes a second for Fury to shuck off his red boots then his armour falls away leaving him naked. Thick scales hide his entire hairless body and he hunches forward, forcing his genitals to hide back in the protection of his thighs. His toes curl and lengthen as the balls of his feet widen and the feet themselves almost triple in length. They look like dog feet with the heel off the ground. No sooner does Cloud digest what's happened to his legs than her breath comes to a stuttering stop.

This isn't any influence of Fury's which has caused it.

Fury is half again his size. Wings that could shatter Cloud and Soar flat in a single stroke are pulled in tight for attack. The joints at the ends of the big flight bones are topped in four inch serrated claws. Matching claws adorn each of the long thin bones running from that joint to the lower edge of his wings.

Smoke pours from his nose and he smiles, revealing canines as thick as Cloud's forearms.

"Oh, oh," Cloud pants and pushes herself into Soar. Her vision sharpens on Fury and she's only aware of Soar's presence as a cooling body behind her. Other than Fury, Cloud's precious mate is the only other being she perceives in the enormous cavern.

"He ishhn wortty of Lor Furee chyl," Fury menaces. As his tongue forces the mangled words between his teeth saliva drips at his big scaled feet. Foul smoke rises from the thick drops. The rumble of his voice sets Cloud's bones aching and Fury advances on the pair.

"I don't care what you think," Cloud spits in reply. Her tongue is hot and heavy in her mouth, unwieldy, and at first she thinks it's fear that takes her words but it isn't. It's bigger and her jaw has lengthened to match. Fury's own snout makes his face and head unrecognizable. His nostrils are big enough for her to stick her fists in.

"Kill him," Fury's words set her off. She's already tried influencing him into backing down and Fury hasn't listened.

There is pain everywhere for only a moment as heat and power surge through her limbs.

Soar shouts behind Cloud as she drops into a crouch. The noise she makes is very much like the growl she gave in Soar's camper. It comes from deep inside.

As she strides toward Fury she starts at the sight of a second pair of gold scaled dragonkin claws reaching ahead.

Cloud tries to grab them but instead the dragonkin hands reach instead as her own. There's a fleeting concern for her clothes, too small now that she's as large as her sire, but there is little time to care. Fury moves faster than she thought possible for such a bulky body and his flaming gold eyes are set on Soar.

Oh, crap.

Oh, shit.

If Fury's transformation didn't have Soar ready to take Cloud and flee, Cloud's certainly has. Her borrowed tunic and trousers are in shreds at their feet. The gold adornment that once only covered her breasts has spread and joined with her natural scales that now cover her body. Her tail is as wide at is base as her backside which itself is impressive in size.

"Soar, get back," Con shouts and Cloud turns her massive gold head enough to look behind her. Before Soar can tell Con to fuck off, Cloud's tail swings to the side, knocking Soar through the air.

It's going to take a lot more than a slug from Cloud's ass to dissuade him, even with her four times his size and armed with all sorts of sharp edges. Before Con gets a chance to interfere, Soar is on his feet and leaps to her back, straddling her wide hips and trying desperately to get his arms around her. She's too big, however, and he has to cling below her wings. The tips of her scales grasp his leathers giving him some friction but they also dig in at his knees where there is a gap between his boots and trousers.

Cloud bucks, momentarily distracted from Fury who continues to antagonize her with his growls and posture. Fury gets on his hind legs and stands straight enough to expose himself. His smooth penis is recessed in a protective fold but the fact he'd show it is primal and insulting and has Soar ready to go after Fury himself.

I'll kill you and keep my gear intact, is what the rude display says. The arrogance is astonishing even from what Soar knows about the dragon lord.

Con and Flay crash into Soar as a single rough ball of gold and green leather, adding Soar's feathers to the mix as they tumble to the ground. The moment he's off Cloud she strikes at Fury. First, he feels the vibration of her charge then a flash of light accompanie a burst of flame but he can't tell which one of the gold dragonkin did it. As Fury and Cloud merge into their own tangle, Soar can't tell them apart.

"Get off," Soar grunts and strikes at Con. His first instinct is to go after Con and to not disrespect his female but Flay's right to his gut silences his protests even through his armour.

"Got him?" Con asks.

"Yes, love," Flay replies as she shifts her weight to keep Soar down. Con gets to his knees in time to see Cloud and Flay tumble from the bridge and into the chasm below.

"Settle down," Flay orders.

"I'd tear you apart if you weren't such a—"

"Female?"

"Bitch," Soar snaps but Flay laughs.

"You'd do well to pay attention like my Conflagration, you idiot gryphon."

"Fuck you," Soar gets the heel of his palm under her chin and pushes but the blonde doesn't budge.

"Look," Con breathes.

Flay doesn't release her grip but shifts enough to allow Soar to see. Either Cloud or Fury flies up past the dwellings on the far side of the city with the other in pursuit.

"Pay attention," Flay slaps Soar and this time he uses both hands on her. A violent shove gets her off but she knees him in the belly to keep him down, rolls him over and immobilizes him from behind. "This is a rare opportunity. One day my Con will have the honour of doing this for our children."

"What, kill them?"

"No, release their dragons and you will do the same for your own young."

"Jesus," Soar sighs. There's nothing he can do but wait for the outcome. Even in dragonkin form Flay is stronger and he can't help Cloud if she breaks his ribs.

"See?" Con says. "My sister is all dragon now. Fury is simply trying to stay alive until she gets control of herself."

What he says looks true. The two gold dragons make a tight turn at one end of the chamber. Now he can see the trailing dragon is slightly smaller. She's clearly pissed off, her roar echoes down from the semi-solid roof and she shoots another round of sticky burning fire at Fury. As she pursues, she passes through the smoke and flames that trail him.

"Maybe she'll kill the bastard," Flay prays and Con takes his eyes from the fight long enough to shoot her a dirty look. She shrugs. "Maybe. She's as strong as her sire. I was barely fourteen when my sire released my dragon. Lady Tempest is twice that age and fully grown."

"Yes," Con murmurs in awe of the display. He's not the only one. The streets on either side of the chasm are lined with small clusters of upturned faces. "She is strong but young. My sire can hold this form much longer and this will end either when she returns to dragonkin form or defeats him."

"Lord Fury would prefer injury," Flay explains and Cloud interrupts with a screech. Fury dodges and by some luck she anticipates and moves beneath him. All four of her talons are poised to strike. For a moment, Fury looks down at his daughter and almost smiles.

"To be injured or killed," Con clarifies. "Will make him most proud of his child."

Then the moment passes. Cloud rolls, belly up, and Fury readies his own talons in defense. Soar had his doubts that Fury wasn't trying to harm her but no longer. Fury is able to occupy three of her four sets of claws as he dives away. Her hold is strong and Fury cannot shake her grip. As they plummet below, her one free rear leg slashes deeply into Fury's belly just below his ribs and Soar can't tell if it's the confusion of their entanglement or if she sunk the full six inches of her rear claws deep inside him.

There are shouts from both sides of the city and Soar finds himself on his feet, Flay's weight gone. The scent of blood travels quickly to them as Cloud and Fury crash down, narrowly missing the bridge.

"Get Lord Fury's sibling," Con orders and with a nod, Flay runs off.

Soar doesn't wait for any more bullshit orders from Con or his bitch female. Each step toward the precipice is an agony. The dragonkin on the far side of the *hole* in the middle of the city can see what has happened below. They point and exclaim amongst themselves but Soar can't afford to spare them a glance.

When he's only a few steps from the edge near the bridge, his vision fills with gold and red and the rush of leather wings. The wash as Cloud bursts up from below brings Soar to a stop. She's nearly dragonkin, her scales and claws are gone, but she's still a foot taller than Soar and clutches her naked human-formed sire to her.

"Help," she cries. There's barely room between Soar and the ledge but she finds a toe-hold in the narrow space and lands, almost immediately returning to her gryphon size. The only difference is her wings are the thin gold leather of a dragonkin. Her feathers are gone.

"Got him," Soar grunts as he takes Fury's weight in his arms.

"I didn't," Cloud gasps. "I couldn't…"

Her voice fails as she drops to her knees. Then Con is there and together he and Soar bear the big male to the warm stone room from which Cloud stepped only minutes before.

Chapter Twenty-Two

"Beautiful female," Soar whispers as a brownish dawn finally lightens Skyfall.

Cloud hasn't spoken much since Soar returned to her side. She cried out when the stone door sealed Fury and the healer in and had to be forced into the trousers Flay shoved into his hands.

Their half finished meal from the night before sits nearby. She was only interested in the food until Con and Flay left them alone. Even Flay's explanation of Fury's actions and releasing her dragon failed to get her attention although she relaxed when Fury's sibling announced he was healing and would see them in the morning.

Cloud's beautiful adornment covers her breasts even in dragonkin form and other than her gold wings the only change is two strips of soft scales that run from behind her ears, beneath her adornment and disappear into her trousers.

"Please say something," Soar asks. She shifts in his arms then squirms upward on their sleeping mat to meet him nose to nose.

"I was thinking," she starts.

No shit. You've been thinking all night, but Soar keeps his mouth shut. He's been thinking as well but more about how they're going to get home than about life with a dragonkin. Life will happen, getting home may not.

"Do you still want me like this?"

"It's different," Soar explains. "I don't feel any urge to hunt but I'm as attracted to you as ever."

"Same, but this," she sits and stretches her wings. "And what I turned into."

"Your dragon kicks ass," Soar says. Inside he prays she doesn't notice his insensitive old self who doesn't consider the feelings of the shaken female at his side. There are better words he could use to describe the great gold mass of scale and flame who impressed and scared the hell out of him at the same time. Who made him need to be a better male to show his gratitude for winning *her*. "And you're still as beautiful outside as in."

She accepts his touch under her chin then he gets bolder, anxious to demonstrate his acceptance. Under her gryphon scent is another that is different from that of a shifted gold dragonkin and only noticeable when he wets her skin with his tongue. It's a little darker, rich, ancient and dangerous, but her natural sweetness still floats above it and fills his senses. Her dragon scent should scare him but he's driven to exhibit power to match the deep oily tang that hovers over her damp skin.

"Soar," Cloud moans and pushes him aside but not to push him away. Her lips find his mating bite, red and swollen in his gryphon form, and she seals her mouth around it. With each soft suckle of the circle of ridges Soar tenses until he throws her back, nestling his erection in her belly and claiming the mark he left on her shoulder.

"Little gryphon," he growls into her flesh. "No hunt needed. Just the smell of you and I'm yours."

"Are you sure? My dragon, I couldn't control her. I could have killed my sire when I met him. She was so angry, I could barely keep her from killing you for slowing her down even though she came out to protect you. She forgot everything but going after him."

"Cloud—"

"No. Don't, Soar," Cloud's voice hitches, making her shrink beneath him. She forces her hands between them and he groans, expecting them to slide down inside his trousers but they go down hers instead, cradling her womb. "One day, Soar, we'll have children and you'll have to try and kill them or someone they love to turn them like he did to me. Are you ready for that? I'm not. I didn't want that.

"All I could do was watch as I turned into a monster."

Soar slides to her side. Cloud's wings are spread beneath her, their span wider than her feathered wings. He's lucky. Even after his betrayals her trust in him has returned. The precious gift is something he'll never squander again.

"Cloud," Soar unties her drawstring and eases her trousers down to expose her trembling hands.

"Soar."

"One day," he pushes her fingers aside with his lips and inhales the warmth of her belly. Under his breath, the small hairs stiffen and rise to meet his kiss. "There will be children and I will not fail to raise them as gryphons and as dragonkin. I'm proud you chose me, Cloud."

Beyond their half open stone door is the rasp of booted feet on the dusty stone road out front. Leather and a hint of Flay's perfume seep in before the sounds stop.

"Master Soar? Lady Tempest?"

Soar groans. Another hour with Cloud would be nice but it's time for the promised chat with Fury and trip north to face the Grand Council. Lady Flay's voice sets Soar on edge. It's sweet and kind and he can't decide why she annoys him so much other than she talks to him like he's some sort of drivel who will never understand his role as the mate of a dragonkin. He may not, for now, but love and loyalty to Cloud will make sure he figures it out and he doesn't need the green skinned Lady Flay to help him with that.

"Come," Soar helps Cloud to her feet. Before she can turn to the door he seizes her by the back of the neck. He only has to work his fingers a bit for her to relax and settle into the safety of his wings. Cloud's lips part under his thumb and he tastes her as they succumb to the memory of their honey kiss a few days before.

"Lady Tempest?"

Impatient bitch.

Flay is alone, pointy red breasts ready to give Soar another unpleasant trip through her portal since he assumes he'll have to ride with her. She's done everything possible to be annoying and he can't see her passing on another chance. As far as he can tell, mainly from the occasional ragged electrical discharge and the constant smell of ozone, portalling is the only way in or out.

"Join us on the bridge," Flay says. If doing what she says gets them away sooner then Soar has no real reason to complain.

Cloud presses her brows together as she watches Flay walk ahead. With a hand on her adornment, Cloud nudges Soar and nods toward Flay to ask her question.

"I am gryphon, Cloud," he explains. "Your brother, Conflagration, is not."

"Lady Tempest," Flay says. "Had you chosen a dragonkin to be yours you would not have to wear *his* gold."

"Have to?" Soar asks but Flay keeps walking as if she hadn't repeated what he just said. Flay makes it sound like Cloud has to wear some smelly old sleeping mat.

Con and Fury wait on the bridge and Cloud nestles in under Soar's wing as she pulls her own in to fit. Other than the five of them, nobody else has come to see them off in fact both sides of the city are completely deserted.

"Tempest," Fury greets his daughter but barely gives Soar a glance. Soar doesn't care. The less he has to talk to Fury the better. "I will portal you from Skyfall myself."

"Sire," Con says. "You are not completely well."

"Well enough to carry my daughter, Conflagration, and I trust no other."

Something bothers Soar about Con's agreement that Fury is well enough to carry her. It's nothing he can explain other than the words came too easily from both.

Cloud steps from Soar's side. Her dragonkin tail is long, thin, brushes the ground, and covered in the same soft scales as her stomach. Sexy as fuck. She approaches Fury then drops to her knees, offering her raised wrists in submission as the healer did the day before.

"Sire, my Lord Fury," Cloud says. Her submission is genuine.

"Rise, Tempest," Fury brushes his fingertips over her wrists. Soar can't help but shudder as he touches her with his sharp nails. "You were in Calgary with Cooper, were you not?"

"Yes," Cloud gets to her feet.

"Cooper has stolen something rare from the Council, a bracelet with a brilliant green stone, do you recall seeing such a thing?"

"No."

"Your male had you expelled and sent you there."

"The master of my Sire's guard is not required to tell me the details of an assignment," Cloud raises her chin and speaks with such conviction that Soar's heart swells to feel her so proud of him. "Had he not done everything in his power to ensure our success and the safety of my eyrie he would not deserve to be the master of Sire Lev's guard. I would gladly have him sacrifice my pride a thousand times for those who love me."

Then she backs up a step, placing herself between Soar and Fury. Soar doesn't speak to stop her possessive display as he did the day before.

"What did you learn about Cooper?" Fury asks.

"I spent most of my time with Lawrence and the guard. Cooper is an exile," Cloud says. "He invited me to stay longer but then he caught Soar spying and we fled."

"And that's all?"

Cloud's terse nod is marked by a swell of pink around her ears. She left out the bullshit kiss which is fine with him.

Damn, maybe she's outright lying. She hadn't been evasive the morning they left Calgary but Soar had been ignoring his own needs so much he would have missed any sign of her not telling the truth. The nervousness doesn't fade and she fidgets, fisting the sides of her trousers as Fury considers.

"There is no need for you to go before the Council," Fury decides with a nod to Con. "Go ahead and inform them."

Con steps from the bridge and catches the air. He rises quickly, following one side of the gash through the city then turns at the far end to race along the other. He's barely straightened from the turn when thunder rends the air behind them and Cloud clutches at Soar. His toes pivot beneath him as she turns them both toward Con's portal. Soar saw a few portals the day before but this is the first she's witnessed and the thunder so soon after the tornado could bother her.

A hole the size of a house appears in the air high above the chasm below and only feet from the stone mountain wall marking the far end of the city.

"We, we," Cloud pants as she crushes into Soar.

"Yes," Soar whispers. They'll be next through the lightening hole in the sky.

"Oh."

Con races for the portal and tucks his wings in at the last moment. The portal stretches vertically and closes with a bang as its bottom connects with the ground. A cloud of dust and rock erupts from the chasm as the portal's power discharges into the earth. The bridge shakes as the explosion of thunder rolls over them then softens as it reaches the other end of the chamber. When the echo returns it isn't strong enough to shake the bridge although Cloud still trembles.

"I can't do that."

"Not yet," Fury is almost kind but there's a coldness about him. Soar won't have ease until he gets Cloud away from her sire. He pushes the thought aside. It's no way to think of her kin. "Perhaps you could introduce me to the kind gryphons who welcomed you to their home?"

"Yes," she agrees then Flay has Soar's arm and shoves him from the bridge.

"Fly, gryphon," Flay orders and Cloud squeals as Fury wraps her in his arms and takes wing.

Flay dawdles, allowing Fury and Cloud to get ahead, then takes the turn at the far end of the city. This time Soar feels the dragonkin charge their portals. The small feathers at the base of his wings stand on end and his skin burns first as Fury's portal cracks open then Flay's just above it. As they speed up and pass over the bridge, Flay grabs him from behind. Soar can't help but struggle in her grip and she squeezes him too hard in response.

Ahead, Cloud's wide eyes meet his from over Fury's shoulder. Then it's over. Fury's portal snaps shut, silencing Cloud's frightened cry.

The last thing Soar sees as they enter Flay's portal are Cloud's gryphon flight feathers where they lay abandoned outside Fury's home.

"Damn it," Soar sputters as he crashes into a tree.

The night blackened sky looms heavy above and he has to be close to home. The warm salt air of the Pacific Ocean washes over his skin and mixes with familiar scents of cedar and Douglas Fir.

"Flay?"

Where the hell did she go?

Soar rights himself as his eyes adjust to the moonlight. Flay glides overhead. Her wings glow in the dim light, at least from below. From above she'd be invisible.

"Where are they?"

"Must be nearby," Flay answers.

"Nobody is nearby," Soar says and goes higher to be sure. "Where the hell did he take her?"

"Give me a minute."

A minute is all she's going to get. His female is missing, no scent or sight of her, and it's unlikely for either Flay or Fury to have messed up their navigation. As the seconds pass, Soar pushes his gryphon hearing making it as sensitive as possible. There's nothing but the movement of the forest and the small lives of creatures below, both the night animals seeking safety or prey in the dark and the others waiting sleepily for daylight.

"Master Soar," Flay calls.

She's even higher and several hundred meters away. Her voice carries high above the crash of heavy, black swells on the rocky tree-lined shore. It softens as she picks up speed and heads for the open ocean.

"You will never truly have her," Flay shouts. "They won't let you."

"Flay," Soar curses as he turns to follow. No misguided dragonkin can be blamed for his missing mate. The green dragonkin helped Fury take her.

"You know why I don't like you?"

"Wait," Soar calls though his muscles ache for oxygen. Flay is fast and he can't overcome her lead.

"Because… " her words are taken by the rupture of the sky and lost to the broken echo of her thunder reflected by the surface of the Pacific.

"Flay!"

There is no hope of catching up. Even if he had the head start the green dragonkin slices the air with no effort at all and would already have passed him.

For a moment he loses sight of her against the black hole that is her portal then it snaps shut, grounding into the salt of the ocean. When the sound passes the only evidence of her portal is a glowing green disk of phosphorescence, little creatures glowing with anger in the wind tossed ocean.

God damn it.

Fury didn't buy Cloud's tale and took her to the council so Soar can't interfere. Soar has only been to the Council once in the years he's served Lev. It's a long haul with little game or warmth and he has little choice but to make the trip. If what Flay said is true then Lord Fury isn't going to make life with Cloud easy.

Chapter Twenty-Three

As the violence of the portal passes, the intense and bitter cold touches Cloud everywhere Fury's arms don't.

"Where are we?"

The aurora borealis lights the sky and twisting ribbons of green and gold compete with the vast night blackened star field above. Snow and ice below reflect the colour of the northern lights instead of the blue-white of the moon.

This isn't the humid summertime warmth of Vancouver Island.

"Will you fly?"

"Where are we?" Cloud demands then Fury drops her. "Hey!"

"Lady Tempest," Fury says. "I understand it is traditional for a gryphon sire to force his child to take wing for the first time so I'm surprised you protest."

She has no choice but to fill her dragonkin wings with the icy Arctic air.

Fury flies on toward a glacier smoothed mountain. Several pairs of winged gryphons or dragonkin circle one end. There is no hint of dawn or sunset in any direction and even if there were she wouldn't know which it is until her internal compass figures which way is which.

"Is this a dragonkin place?"

"My Lady Tempest," Fury explains. "This place is what the humans call Bolshevik Island."

"You said we were going to Vancouver Island," Cloud calls out. Bolshevik Island, the home of the Grand Council, is far north of continental Russia and as cold and remote as a gryphon can get.

Flay and Soar aren't with them and nothing else of note is near except for Fury and the Council's mountain. Fury's sibling, the healer, had been right. Cloud will go before Aledaar to face something far worse than turning into a dragon to kill her sire.

"I only said you would not go before the Council regarding Cooper, nothing more. Come, Tempest. Lady Flay has arrived with Master Soar only an hour flight from here. By the time they arrive we will have finished our business and can take you home."

Liar.

If Fury really meant for their business to be brief then he should have said something before they left Skyfall. Now she's alone, pregnant, and knotted with more homesickness than at any other moment since she moved to Memphis. The healer's exact words to Cloud are forgotten under the weight of her resolve to get through Aledaar's trial and escape. Her powerful dragonkin sire must bear a deep humiliation, his pride long spent after taking Con to Aledaar for the pain that will be Cloud's.

Soar hid his disappointment at their failed mating well, showing only tenderness and relief that she came through her injuries and the bee poisoning but he deserves the truth. There has been too much deception from both of them and now she's the one who will need forgiveness.

She also hasn't had time to get to know her brother, Conflagration, or his female, Flay. Both seem held back on the opposite side of a gap in *something* Cloud doesn't understand, Lady Flay in particular. She is older than Cloud and Con but still under the age of sixty and compared to the long lives of gryphons, and presumably dragonkin, is very young indeed.

"Our benefactor, My Generous Sire Aledaar, holds in trust a rare relic of the gold dragons. Once a dragonkin has called her dragon for the first time she is honoured by Aledaar and allowed to wear the relic as a symbol of her acceptance into adulthood."

"Fury, I want Soar to be here with me," Cloud tries and gives up on gliding after him. With a few strong beats of her wings she has to open them wide to brake before flying past him.

"Wow."

"Yes," he laughs. "My daughter has found her true wings. Only an hour, Tempest, then you both will have some time to understand where you have come from and what is ahead.

"Many years ago our kind was despised by the gryphons. They called us half breeds and worse things and we were hunted and killed. Aledaar is our champion and has given us safety. He's restored our honour in exchange for our loyalty."

A pair of red leathered members of the Will circle and greet Fury before returning to their rounds. Even in gryphon form their eyes glow like his and hers though she hasn't seen them herself to know for certain.

Most activity around the Council's mountain takes place at one end and Fury leads her to the other.

"We have direct access to Aledaar here," Fury explains as they alight on a broad ledge. Instead of a door, a tunnel leads in at a steep angle to the right so close to the stone side of the mountain the wall must be paper thin in places. From anywhere but the opening it would be invisible.

Cloud looks back the way they came and the sky is empty. Even her shifted dragonkin eyes are unable to spot Soar and Flay against the green lights on the horizon.

"It will be dawn soon, Tempest," Fury whispers and takes her elbow. The only thing that keeps her from pulling away is a numbing acceptance that she has no choice. Without a map to plan her flight and no knowledge of how to portal she could be lost for days without food - if she can outrun Fury.

No, this is her chance to be free not only for herself but also for her children she hasn't had time to think about and for everyone else she loves.

"Sire," she murmurs. "I am more than proud to stand at your side and take my place as a dragonkin."

Fury's rough beard tickles her nose as he places a scratchy kiss above her eyes.

"You are nervous."

"I've been a dragonkin a whole day," Cloud allows. She can't even identify with her new name. Fury is a stranger, unwelcome in his touch or his tone. "Yesterday I was a gryphon."

"A dying gryphon," he tugs her through the tunnel. "A dying gryphon who would be a corpse now if I hadn't arrived when I did. Your male has a long way to go to earn any respect from me."

"But—"

"You will be silent. You will kneel before Aledaar and take your place as my daughter."

Dark stone walls hurl past and Cloud doesn't say more. Ahead, there are raised voices, all male. Could the healer have lied to get her to go along without a fight? Her second thoughts are stripped away as Fury drags her forward into a small, well lit chamber. The walls are perfectly flat although they are porous giving away their composition of cold rock. Too many silver lights give the illusion of daylight inside.

The backless gold chair before her holds an old gryphon male. Low arm rests leave room for his large dark brown wings. Long white hair flows down his back.

Cloud blinks away the sudden brightness and submits to Fury's hand on her shoulder.

"My Generous Sire Aledaar," Fury intones as if uttering the name of the most powerful gryphon on the planet is its own reward.

"Ah, Lord Fury," Aledaar rises. His long red robes drape round his feet as he turns, their colour only broken up by a heavy gold chain around his neck. Dangling at its lowest point is a section of a dragon jaw bone the length of Cloud's forearm. Several large molars are firmly embedded in the bone itself and the entire piece glows with a fierceness much brighter than the eyes of the dragonkin in the room.

"Conflagration told me the news. Your daughter was found safe and would come pay her respects."

Fury nods and extends his hands, wrist up to Aledaar, so Cloud does the same. Aledaar doesn't touch Fury as she's come to expect. Instead, his hands remain folded on his stomach. The dragonkin around him, including Con, give the old male room.

Cloud can't take her eyes from the relic he wears. It's clearly magic, anything that glows on its own must be, and her mouth dries as Aledaar comes closer. For a moment she thinks of Cooper and his kiss.

"My Generous Sire, this is my daughter, Lady Tempest."

"Well," Aledaar says as he inspects Cloud. Wings, eyes, teeth, and even her offered wrists don't escape his hungry gaze. It's more like she's a prize than anything else and her value will be decided before she has a chance to speak.

"Lady Tempest," Aledaar's smile doesn't reach his eyes and he presses his hands tighter to his body and away from her. "The gift of your loyalty will be repaid by mine, I promise."

"My Generous Sire Aledaar," Cloud answers the way Fury had. "I am proud to—"

Cloud's head snaps back, wrenched by a big hand tangled in her hair then she looks up into a face she only sees in nightmares. Torrent's misshapen leer fills her vision and her hands grab hold of his tunic.

"Cloud," he hisses as his other hand clamps down on her mouth, silencing any protest.

174

"Torrent," Aledaar barks. Her mouth is freed though the fingers in her hair continue to twist until they break whole strands. "Lady Tempest."

Aledaar unlocks the heavy clasp behind his neck. It parts with a thunk and Cloud loses sight of the alluring glow as Aledaar leans down. Then, without touching her, the chain is draped over her shoulders. At first there's warmth at her belly in response to the relic's presence then as the clasp closes under Torrent's fist the heat begins to burn.

The moment Aledaar drops its full weight to her shoulders, the burn inside her flares even brighter. The building pressure is the only thing that keeps the chain from fracturing bone. As it is, the weight seeds deep bruises.

"Unh," she moans as her hands fall, dead at her sides, and the room dims with the rising fire in her stomach. At her side, Fury growls and Cloud is unable to look since Torrent's grip prevents it.

"Fury, you will see she is not disturbed and inform me when this spectacle has ended."

The disgust Aledaar hid before he placed the necklace around Cloud's neck is now as powerful as the burn she can't fight. The room before her ripples in the heat pouring from her mouth and her limp body can only dangle as Torrent lifts her from the ground. Only Cloud's boneless wing-tips reach the stone floor.

"One day, little bitch," Torrent promises, each word accented with a shake that cramps her muscles and sends pain through every nerve in her body. "One day I will be the master of the relic you wear. I will send you home to kill every gryphon you love and you will live out your life as my broken plaything."

The loose, painful knots in Cloud cohere and force thick burning acid past her lips to sting her neck and chin. Flames and smoke erupt as the fiery pitch ignites in the air and small globules explode, flinging tiny burning bombs at the stone ceiling twenty feet above.

"Until then," Torrent drops her. "I will have to get by with the satisfaction of how much you suffer."

Cloud folds up, landing hard on the stone. Her head falls against Fury as she comes to rest on her side facing the chamber door. Torrent strides from the room, shadowed by the remaining dragonkin. They are replaced by Lady Flay. Con doesn't raise his head as he passes her.

"I had no choice but to leave Soar behind, Tempest," Flay whispers as she gets to her knees. "They'll kill him if he interferes with their plans for you."

Any last hope Soar will come for Cloud sears inside her throat.

Together with Fury, Flay straightens Cloud's wings and draws her hair away from the burning mess that continues to block her throat and leak from her nose and mouth. At least on her side with her head tilted and her mouth toward the floor, she can breathe between episodes of vomiting.

"Daughter," Fury strokes Cloud's cheek. "When you were nearly a year old I took you from the eyrie to Skyfall for your naming. Your dame stayed behind with Con. When I brought you home, it was Con's turn and I made the journey a second time with him tucked in my arms.

"Upon our return, all life had been taken from Welch Peak. My female and my daughter were dead. I was told there were no survivors so I returned to Skyfall with my small son and my grief. Your dame was Lily and Con carries her dark hair and eyes.

"She had royal blood, Tempest. She knew the weather and could control it to an extent.

"When Con was fifteen I released his dragon and brought him here with the same lie I told you. The relic you wear will steal your will as it took mine. There was no choice but to bring you here. The pain of fighting Aledaar's will is worse than what you now face. The only relief is to submit.

"There is no hope for our kin, Tempest. Only shame and eventually death."

Understanding why Fury betrayed her doesn't mean much. Not now. Not at all. If Cloud could speak she would send him away.

"Lady Flay, you are charged with her care and training —"

Fury's voice breaks and for several minutes there is nothing but the painful gurgling in Cloud's throat. The silence ends with a joint wrenching convulsion that brings another burst of sticky fire.

"As is the custom, Lord Fury," Flay nods as her hand finds Cloud's shoulder to steady her tremors. "As the female closest in age it is my honour."

"How long, Flay?"

The drink the green dragonkin puts to Tempest's lips is cool and sweet and from the first sip it eases the terrible rawness in her throat. Flay cradles her like a baby, her ministrations a blur of holding Tempest's weak body on the chamber pot and wiping her chin with scraps of cloth that were alight by the time they were tossed aside.

It's a cruel rebirth for the naive young gryphon who once believed her biggest problem was how many weeks she'd spend on hands and knees apologizing to Master Sky. Now that life is a memory, blackened through the filter of fire and pain brought on by the relic.

"Five days, Tempest," Flay sways side to side and tucks Tempest's head against her neck. "If you hadn't fought so damned hard it would have been over in two."

"Yeah."

Until she has a chance to safely resist Aledaar she won't know if it was worth it. Although she harboured the deepest wish the healer was right, she couldn't bring herself to give in, not until the relic broke her.

"Sit her up."

Tempest clings to Flay in response to Aledaar's voice. He must have heard the pains and vomiting had stopped. There's nothing to do but comply and she does her best but Flay still has to hold her upright. She pulls Tempest's hair out of the way and Aledaar removes the relic before replacing it around his own neck.

Through the haze of puffy eyes and exhaustion, Tempest makes out Fury's red hair and brilliant gold eyes floating at Aledaar's shoulder. Nice of her sire to come by now when it's all over.

"Lady Tempest," Aledaar says. "You shall never disobey me or give harm to me or any of my kin. The pain you experienced will be your punishment should you ever resist my will."

"Yes, My Generous Sire Aledaar," Tempest coughs but she refuses to collapse. Her throat feels full of glass. Though she wishes to stare the old gryphon down, her eyes drop to his feet in submission as her hands rise, wrists up. She can only hold the position for a few seconds before her elbows sag and her arms fold in over her adornment.

"You will tell me about Cooper's green relic," Aledaar orders.

"What green relic?" Tempest says.

"Were you ever alone with him?"

"No," she lies.

There is no pain from her disobedience. She's still numbed by the humiliation of surrender to the gold relic but even that shouldn't stop the punishment for lying. For good measure, though, she eyes Aledaar's gold relic and cringes against Flay.

You pinfeathered excuse for a Sire. You don't own me.

She hides her relief with a couple of sharp coughs to the side. If she had the strength to take up Flay's dagger and open Aledaar from testicles to throat she would.

"Very well. Master Soar waits for you at the main entrance. Lady Flay will see you cleaned up and dressed appropriately.

"He will leave, Lady Tempest, or he will die."

"How 'bout now?" Soar demands of the two dragonkin assholes who haven't let him past the main entrance to the Council's mountain for a day and a half. Yesterday things had become physical more than once, mostly on Soar's part, and the dragonkin had let their dragons out just enough to overpower him into exhaustion before tossing him out onto the stoop.

"No," is the one word answer. It comes in stereo from the stoic bookends on either side of the tunnel mouth, the same two who were present when Soar arrived after a four day flight. He asked the same question many times of another pair who guarded the opening during the night.

He's been offered food and drink since any visitor is offered the necessities upon arrival but nothing more. No explanation of the delay. No acknowledgement they know who he's talking about. No confirmation she's even here.

Just no.

Soar turns his back on them and faces the frozen Russian landscape. There's nothing to see out there either. Rock and ice disappear into the low cloud that began to blanket everything just after dawn.

If Fury took Cloud back to Skyfall then why doesn't someone just come out and tell him he's wasting his time? A gryphon can only retie his armour so many times to cover up his desperate vigil. Nothing short of needing the only female he'll ever touch could ever humble him like this.

Again there are the sounds of more than just the guard at the entrance but Soar doesn't bother to turn. Patrols in and out and nobody, not even gryphons he's known for years, pay him any mind.

"Soar?"

Finally someone has come to see him, some old bureaucrat by the sounds of it, and when he turns she is as much a stranger as the raw and defeated voice that said his name.

"Cloud?"

His female seems barely able to stand on her own, the weight of the soft, red floor-length robes could be enough to pull her to the floor. It isn't that she's unsteady, since she is able to walk past the two dragonkin at the door.

Instead, the past five days have drawn the life from her.

Cloud's eyes have sunk into bruised circles, broken blood vessels are clearly visible around her eyes and one eyeball is mostly blood red, showing only a brave patch of white at the inner corner. The lustre is gone from her hair. Then there is the peeling red blistering skin around her mouth and down her neck. Her hands are invisible in the long trumpet sleeves of the robe but they are clasped low over her belly and appear to move, scratching at her skin. How the hell far down do the burns go?

"It's Lady Tempest," she corrects as she stops, only six feet away.

Soar works the corner of his lower lip in his teeth and tilts his head to say he hears her but he won't be calling her *that*.

"Are you alright?"

"Ah," she tries a weak laugh then has to clear her devastated throat to continue. "I've been to Skyfall twice since Fury brought me here. The bee poisoning was far worse than we thought. In the end the only hope was to encourage my body to purge the toxins."

One shaking hand comes up and waves past her chin before disappearing into the red folds with the other. After seeing what happened to the grass when Fury ruptured the boils, Soar understands what happened to her skin.

"I'm only a few minutes away by portal if needed."

"Damn it," Soar says. "I didn't know about the bees, I swear. Your suffering is entirely my fault."

"Nothing for it."

Tempest's bruised eyes hold Soar's until his guilt is too much and he has no choice but to look away. He did that to her, almost killed her, and maybe more than once. All the love and bravery inside his little gryphon was almost taken and he has nobody to blame but himself.

"It's time for you to leave, Soar," she rasps and her red eye swells with pink tears as she works to get the words out.

"I will wait here for you."

"It's time for you to leave, alone."

"Cloud," Soar insists. "Not alone. Together."

"We've been mated since I came to your den five years ago, did you know that?" She pauses. "Perhaps an error on my part. Inexperience. Maybe even a lack of options. You were the best choice given the unattached males in my life."

"You don't mean that," Soar lowers his voice to a whisper and looks past the guards and into the entrance for evidence of anyone listening and sees only the bitch Flay, waiting.

"We had a thing, Soar," she turns his own words on him. "We were never a thing. We had a thing, ten beautiful hormone and instinct driven days geared entirely toward reproduction."

"She tell you to say that?"

"Look at me, Soar," Cloud orders. He does and just looking at the damage to her face is all the blame he needs for her condition. "Am I lying?"

Soar studies her ears, the throat where it isn't burnt. His heart sinks a little further with each square inch of perfect, gentle whiteness. No telltale pink betrays a terrible lie.

"No," his voice breaks as he looks away, hoping to find something that doesn't tear him up inside even if it's the walls but she's so close. The ragged passage of air through her throat takes what he did to ease her suffering from the dislocated shoulder and makes it into something unforgivable.

"Let me make it simple. I do not wish to have a life with you. Get it? When I'm in season again I will seek you out, but there is no chance of anything more.

"You are not compatible with what I am."

Soar doubles over like he's been slugged. Trust lays beneath her cold words but somehow it isn't enough to keep her.

"Tell Dame Shadow my sire survived Welch Peak and I will see her soon. If you claim me as your mate to Shadow and Talon I will deny it. Better they think you found some obedient little thing while you were away than nearly killed me in your haste to spare me the dignity of bearing my own pain.

"We had a thing, Soar," Cloud turns and head high, keeps talking as she sweeps past the guards. "That's all we ever had."

Flay doesn't spare him a glance as she falls in behind Cloud.

"Lady Tempest," Soar whispers. She isn't Cloud any more. His brother was right. He can't keep a female in his life for more than a month and Cloud has figured out why.

He always screws it up.

"As you wish, Tempest."

There's no sound behind him as he steps from the ledge to take the air under his wings.

Chapter Twenty-Four

"You get used to the burn," Flay says.

Her hands are magic. Both massage the portalling muscles up beneath Tempest's wings. Most of the energy comes from the sky and earth, it only needs a dragonkin trigger, a spark from the tight, thin muscles. The burn isn't so bad, though. It's the horrible fatigue that does her in. The warmth of their turn around point on the California coast would put her to sleep on its own anyway only it would take a little longer.

Flay gets dozy after portalling which is a blessing. So far Tempest has been able to hide the outright killer sleepiness that is worse every time they go anywhere. She figures it's the pregnancy and won't get better for a while. At least with Flay asleep, Tempest can rest with her.

The green dragonkin has been Tempest's mentor and friend for three months since she recovered in her arms from the abuses of Aledaar's relic. Then only hours later she was back in Flay's arms, holding back tears. If tears would have helped wash away the memory of watching Soar's heart break she'd have let them loose and only Flay's constant whispering she'd done the right thing gave her any solace at all. The only blessing to the relic's torment was the ability to hide her lies. She first noticed how easy it had become with the lie to

Aledaar. After that, hiding the lie to Soar was easy even though it was impossibly hard.

"Are you sure?" Tempest asks. The burn is a little nasty and she hasn't completed a portal yet without wanting to find a rough tree on which to scratch her back.

"Yeah, sure," Flay laughs. "Well, no."

"Thought so."

"You've been quiet lately."

"Thinking about Soar," Tempest admits. Her arms are tucked in, hands out of sight on her belly. During the past few weeks the firmness has started to protrude, she thinks, and it won't be long before she can't hide it, much less get her red leather trousers fastened. Her breasts no longer fit comfortably into her sculpted leather chest piece. Soon she'll run away, but not yet.

"Thought so."

"How do you do it, Flay? You don't see Con at all unless you're away from the Council with him. I feel like I cut my spirit out when I sent Soar away."

Flay's fingers continue to work, sending sparks up Tempest's big flight bones as the swollen muscles relax.

"My loyalty to the Council is not from Aledaar's relic," Flay starts. "I know you've been wondering. When I chose Conflagration I knew about the relic and Aledaar. Con promised it would be okay but it wasn't. As soon as Fury found out he brought me before Aledaar and told me how it was going to be."

Flay's strong fingers stop their work and she drops to Tempest's side, curls up around her bent knee and helps herself to a piece of Tempest's jerky.

"There would be no physical torment for me if I told Aledaar to stick it up his boney feathered ass."

"Flay!"

"It's true!"

For a moment they giggle at the irreverence of the remark then Tempest's brow crosses with concern for her friend.

"There's Conflagration's life, for one," Flay begins to list the reason's she can't disobey Aledaar.

"And?"

"My sire's."

"Oh," Tempest isn't sure she's heard it all. Flay plays with the hem of Tempest's tunic, eyes down, mouth a troubled red line.

"He's in the Council's dungeon at the moment," she says.

"Oh, Flay."

"He has some time. The law says four full moons when the prisoner does not resist then his life is forfeit if Aledaar so chooses. That's only a week away."

"What are you going to do?"

"My sire would be angry if I did anything stupid to save him. I know, Tempest. I know if I told you anything you could be forced to turn on me."

The idea doesn't hold with the truth but Flay doesn't know Tempest is free, free of Aledaar and his will and immune to any order Aledaar could give except the ones with consequences for Soar.

"Come on, let's go back," Flay bounces to her feet. "I want to spend some time with Con."

"But don't we stay the night?" Tempest is tired enough with one night's rest. Another so soon is going to be exhausting. "It's beautiful and warm and smell the ocean, Flay."

"No, I want Con then my own sleeping mat."

Without waiting, Flay runs and dives from the hill they prepared for the night.

Tempest has no choice but to follow and races through Flay's wake to catch up. The warm sunset lightens the red of Flay's armour as it brings out the gold in her hair and Tempest's wings.

Tempest's own red armour is nearly the same size as Flay's and she'd been put in it as soon as she recovered from the relic. Accompanying the leathers are knee high boots which lace up the front, a dagger at her hip and a short, curved boot knife designed for slicing open the laces. The boots slide off anyway so it isn't more than a quaint addition like the leather helmets they left behind. They did wear their modern wrap around safety glasses. No dragonkin would be seen on the wing without them.

"To the Council," Flay shouts.

With a powerful tensing of the muscles in her back, Tempest generates her charge. She's still drained from their earlier trip and Flay is nearly to her portal by the time Tempest has enough energy to spark hers. It runs up over the tops of her wings and she uses their entire span like a large radar dish, focusing her energy and placing the seed for her portal far ahead.

"You okay?" Flay calls.

"Brilliant," Tempest answers as her portal finally cracks open. Each beat of her leathery wings brings her closer and she sags, fighting to stay alert.

The shattering lightning strike of Flay's portal closing jars Tempest awake long enough to fly straight then her own portal has her and spits her out the other side.

"Shit, Tempest," Flay shouts. "Where are you going?"

There is nothing but white and blue ahead and no sign of the Council's mountain. Tempest shakes her head in confusion. How could they both have gone so far off course?

"Turn around. It's the other way."

"O-ay," she answers. Mouth troubles.

There it is. The mountain looms ahead.

Tempest laughs and follows after Flay but after a few beats of her wings the confusion settles into an uneasy knot. Flay banks to the left and come to think of it the ground does as well. Whatever. Tempest eases over in the same direction and stalls, dropping like a stone. The winter-blue sky flips past over and over and she grabs at it to hold it still.

"Oh hell, Tempest," Flay's lips mutter by her ear and the tumbling slows as the horizon levels out before them. "Damn it. Oh, fuck."

Tempest reaches up and tries to smooth the worry from Flay's face. Instead she jabs a finger in her eye.

"Let me talk when we get in," Flay orders. "You portalled six times today, not twice, understand?"

"Fuck sex times? Oh, sorry." It's the first time Tempest remembers swearing ever and it's embarrassing. Horrifying, actually.

"Oh shit, yes," the cursing continues and Tempest snorts. Flay's bad mouth is worse than usual.

"Flay? Oh, no."

The main entrance comes up awful fast and Tempest gets her hands out again, this time to spare herself a painful face plant into the mountain.

"Easy," Flay whispers.

The red armoured guards whisk past then the tunnel walls move just as quickly. A drunken right and then a left bring them closer to the den the two females share.

"Lady Flay?"

"My Lord Fury."

"Hi," Tempest says from over Flay's shoulder and remembers her instructions. Given the filter between her brain and mouth is off it's better to do what Flay said and keep quiet.

"What the hell is going on?"

Flay tries to kneel for him but Tempest can't hold herself up and the two fall sideways into the wall.

"Lord Fury," Flay says.

Even in her shaky state, Tempest can tell Flay is nervous. It only takes Fury a few steps to close the distance between them.

"I was teaching Tempest the danger of portalling too many times and pushing herself too far."

"And?" Mistrust comes off Fury in waves but that's nothing new when it comes to how he feels about Flay.

"She portalled six times. I wanted her to experience the symptoms and we're going to our den so I can show her how to recover."

"Indeed. Are you sure she isn't drunk?

Fury doesn't wait for an answer and takes Tempest firmly by the back of the neck. He studies one eye then the other then gets under her wing and probes the spent muscles.

"What were you thinking, Flay?" He's angry but he helps pull Tempest up a little higher before she can slip from Flay's grip. "She's drained. The light in her eyes is almost gone."

"We discussed her symptoms between portals and she started and ended at almost the same place so she never appeared anywhere alone," Flay lies. "This is a lesson she cannot learn from a simple talk."

Fury shakes his head so vehemently he appears to shiver.

"If anyone sees her like this, Flay, it isn't you who will be punished."

"Thank you, my Lord Fury," Flay sighs then as quickly as Fury storms away, the two females are off again down the long tunnel to the female dragonkin dens. Fortunately, their route is deserted and Tempest does her best to hinder their progress as little as possible. The further they go, the harder it is to do more than keep her feet from tangling with Flay's.

Tempest understands Fury's threat. The one to be punished can only be Flay's imprisoned sire.

Once in their den, Flay kicks the mat aside and leans Tempest against the opposite wall. She stands to pull her armour free before stripping Tempest down to adornment, scale and skin.

"You need heat," she says.

Tempest expected heat.

Flay leans forward, arching her spine like she's going to throw up. She does, after a fashion, except it's the nasty acid dragonkin keep in their version of a gall bladder. As it comes up she ignites it with a charge originating in the same muscles she uses to portal.

In seconds, flame chars at the rock. A second burst circles the hot centre she made and evens out the cool spots.

"Up you get," Flay tugs her up then as they lay down she arranges their wings to keep the heat in. "That's it."

Flay breathes hard, forcing more heat through her skin and filling their gold and green leather cocoon in warmth.

"You're pregnant," Flay whispers.

"Yes."

"You're free, aren't you? Aledaar doesn't control you."

"Yes," Tempest agrees. She's at Flay's mercy whether her secret is kept or not.

"There are things Con and I don't talk about. There are herbs I take to stay out of season. It would kill him to have to turn children in like Fury did to you. He doesn't ask and I don't tell. There are things I don't say because he can't hear them and things he doesn't ask because he can't bear the answer.

"Aledaar ordered my dame murdered because she believed the green dragonkin should remain free. My sire and I still believe in freedom and not just because she wanted it but because it's right.

"My twin is with my kind, where my sire and I should be, but my choice of mate and my sire's situation keep us here. Nobody knows where the green dragonkin are but me and Aledaar is convinced they're in hiding."

"What do we do?" Tempest asks. The intense heat makes her skin crawl as the muscles beneath drink it in.

"I'm making you too warm, forcing your body to draw out the last of your reserves. You'll feel great for about an hour and you'll manage a portal but then you're going to crash far worse than before.

"When you're better, Tempest, you'll leave and you won't be going alone."

For Daniel Cooper, the days and nights since he was taken from Calgary have been nothing but blackness and just enough protein to keep his gryphon form from freezing. It's been months since his capture but the exact number of days until the fourth full moon won't be known until the answer is zero.

Then it will be over.

Even Torrent's intermittent company, with his boots and fists and nothing Cooper's chained and weakened body can do to fight back, is a break from the cold wait for the end.

"Sshhh."

The whisper outside his cell door is sharp, quiet and female.

Although Cooper's sense of time is off, his internal clock says tonight's dinner was early and the female outside the door is here far too soon to have brought him another meal. Also, his keepers are male.

"Try that one."

Another whisper as the familiar rattle of keys is followed by the reluctant movement of the lock's inner workings. It would be better if it was Torrent. It's more likely these females have come to see he is tidied up for his last day.

"Sire?" Luminous green dragonkin eyes appear one at a time past the edge of the door. The light soothes his eyes. His daughter is foolish to risk a trip to the dungeon and he tells her as much.

"Flay, you shouldn't be here."

"Neither should you, sire," she answers as a second pair of dragonkin eyes appears next to hers. These are gold although not brilliant like Flay's eyes. Their glow has all the dullness of a spent penny.

"Flay?" Cooper tries. The presence of a gold with his daughter is bad news and can only mean Aledaar is up to something.

"This is Lady Tempest," Flay explains. "Daughter of Lord Fury and a free dragonkin, sire."

"Oh, no," Cooper moans. Cloud, grand-daughter of Sire Lev, the Cherry from the Eyrie and the key to his safe room in Calgary and the box holding the green relic, is here.

Either Aledaar has the green relic already or it is only a matter of time until the memory block Cooper forced on the young gold dragonkin fails and she hands it over.

"Sire," Flay's warm hand cups his cheek as she kneels then she offers him her wrists. "You worry so. Lady tempest is pregnant. Aledaar couldn't take her will and she has to leave soon. So do you I might add, so…"

"Daniel Cooper?" Tempest asks. "Daniel is your sire?"

"Yes," Flay fiddles with the metal collar that attaches Cooper's chain to the wall. "Open the bag."

"But how did you get here?"

"Aledaar took me into custody the day of the tornado, Lady Tempest," Cooper says as the heavy metal collar and chain fall away.

"Aledaar has several large delegations in the main chamber," Flay explains. "They want his help settling a bloody territory dispute and nearly all the Will is needed to keep the peace. We couldn't have planned a better turn of luck to break you out."

Flay helps him to his feet and sets to undressing him. After months of cold spray downs and rough, black prison wear the touch of friendly hands is freedom. To see the sky again, even if it is so near the stench of Aledaar's Grand Council, will be heavenly.

"Wait, Flay." Tempest steadies him. The days and nights chained to the floor have left Cooper nearly unable to stand. The only way he could straighten up was to lay on the stone floor.

Flay works his tail through the hole in the back of his trousers. It's unlikely anyone but Con and Cooper would notice the tension she carries as she works faster, even roughly, to get the trousers up and fastened.

"You've lost a lot of weight," Flay observes as the waist slides down a few inches before it stops. "I was worried these would be too small."

"You're putting me in Will reds aren't you."

"And I am feathered if you hadn't noticed. My dragonkin wings will attract too much attention."

"Flay, are you coming with us?" Tempest asks.

She nods once and turns Cooper so Tempest can fasten one side of his tunic while she gets the other. Cooper has been clumsy and cold for too long to even dress himself.

"You only have enough energy to portal yourself, Tempest," Flay answers. "I will bear my sire."

"What about Con?"

Warm sheepskin slips over Cooper's head and Flay fusses to make sure his ears are covered. Then the tight squeeze of a leather helmet.

"Aledaar will not harm or threaten him until he knows where I am and then he will use Con as leverage. Let's hope that's at a time of our choosing."

Flay stuffs some jerky into Cooper's hands and he chews while bored footsteps echo past the closed door and away, down the long tunnel outside.

"Calgary?" Flay asks.

"No," Cooper thinks. "I doubt it's safe and that's the first place they'll look for us.

"It's time we made some friends, Flay. We are going to see the one gryphon who hates me as much as Aledaar."

"Oh, shit, sire," Flay says then she shrugs. "We'll probably be imprisoned together down here within ten minutes anyway so I guess it doesn't matter where we go."

She knows exactly what he has in mind.

"Lady Tempest," Cooper says. "We are taking you home. Sire Lev is fair. He will hear me out and perhaps grant us sanctuary."

With a destination in mind, Flay opens the door just enough to set her ear to the opening and listen.

"We can't use the main entrance without passing through Aledaar's self-serving gathering. The only other way is through Aledaar's private chamber," Flay says. "It should be empty."

"Lead the way."

Cooper hadn't been conscious for his trip into the dungeon, Torrent saw to that, and isn't surprised to find he was in one of the cells nearest the guard station. With Aledaar's security needs upstairs, the station is empty and they hurry up a set of broad stone steps then through a dark hallway that parallels the rear of the main chamber. The thick wall hides their footsteps.

A single gryphon approaches, dressed in the Will's reds. His eyes target Tempest in the lead with Flay, still in gryphon form. Cooper takes up the rear and gets a hand before his face to hide his rough beard.

"Dragonkin," the gryphon spits and Tempest bows.

Even in Aledaar's Will, led by Fury himself, there is prejudice.

They slow as they reach Aledaar's private chamber. A shadow moves in the entrance and the room isn't empty. There is a snort and satisfied sigh.

Torrent, Flay mouths.

We can't wait for him to leave, Tempest says.

No, they can't. Judging by the faded gold of Tempest's eyes, her body has been deeply stressed and she's close to collapsing in fatigue.

Wait, Tempest orders.

No, Cooper argues but she runs off, doubling back down the long tunnel. If his recollections of the Council chambers hold then she's headed for the main chamber and will pass through the proceedings, dragonkin and gryphons.

Eat, sire, Flay presses more meat into his hands. *She will clear the way, if she has to walk out the front door she will do so. It's you and I who must leave in secret.*

Flay, Cooper complains but she's right and he lets her push him further to the darkest part of the tunnel. Long minutes pass before Torrent's shadow is joined by another.

"My Generous Sire Torrent," Tempest kneels.

No, Flay holds Cooper back. *She knows what she's doing.*

Cooper thinks Tempest's words are purely to insult Torrent, that is until he speaks.

"My dirty little pet," Torrent croons his approval. "Have you come to submit to me?"

"My Generous Sire Torrent," she says again. "My Generous Sire Aledaar wishes you join him."

"Stand, bitch," he hisses and Tempest gets to her feet, hands raised and head down. "Do not refuse me my pleasures."

Tempest grunts as Torrent's hand falls squarely on the side of her head. For a moment Cooper doesn't care what the price will be for stepping in. His younger sibling not only assumes the title of the leader of the Grand Council but has also singled Tempest out for abuse.

"My Generous Sire Aledaar wishes you to join him," Tempest repeats as she lowers her arms. "And I do not wish to be struck again."

Torrent swings, this time the back of his hand meets solidly with Tempest's cheek hard enough to knock her sideways. At the same moment, the low voices of several gryphons approach from behind at the opposite end of the tunnel.

Now, Flay orders. *Like we belong here.*

They form up side by side as Torrent turns.

"You will wait here, Lady Tempest, and when I return we will discuss your lack of respect."

Torrent stomps out and seconds later Flay and Cooper stride into Aledaar's chamber. Tempest cups her cheek and in the lit room Cooper can no longer make out the glow of that eye. The blows cost much of her remaining energy.

"Let's go," she turns before he can say anything and Flay shoves him toward the tunnel hidden in the curtains behind Aledaar's great chair.

"Tempest," Flay whispers as they break into a run. "When you arrive, head for the ground. I don't trust your wings."

"Okay."

"How long—"

Cooper starts but Flay silences him with a sharp pull on his elbow. The air around them cools as they reach the opening to the outside.

"Since I arrived, Daniel Cooper," Tempest stops at the opening and the three of them scan the sky. "I do not fear him."

"Go," Flay hisses when they find the dark skies empty. "Quickly."

Chapter Twenty-Five

Soar wakes, stumbling from his den.

Talon's 'move your ass, buddy, we got shit' shook him out of bed.

"I have Shadow," Talon's voice leads Soar to the main chamber. "Lev is with us and sent most of his guard to the family dens to protect the children. The rest are here with you."

"A little more information would be nice," Soar grumbles.

"Tundra," Talon says as he hauls Soar to the big gryphon's side.

"Master Soar," Tundra nods. "We have a delegation from the Council. Two gryphons and a dragon-thingy."

Oh, Lord. It's either bad news about Cloud or some other kind of trouble from the Council. Either way it's serious.

"What do they want?" Soar asks. He double checks his weapons although they won't do much good against a dragonkin.

"An audience with Lev," Tundra's massive shoulders rise and fall in a single shrug. "They have been provided hospitality in the chamber at the entrance."

Soar hopes Talon was too busy to notice that Tundra smells of Feather, Talon's sister, although Talon would have his hands full if he tried to run Tundra off, mostly with angry objections from Feather.

"Crossbows," Soar orders. "You and two others. On the dragonkin. He can't control the three of you at once and if he tries to turn any of you, hit him in the throat."

"Master?"

"That's the way it goes, Tundra. Everything you've heard about them is true and they're dragonkin, not thingies."

Tundra grabs two others who are already armed with crossbows and takes another crossbow from a third.

"Let's go," Soar orders and the four enter the tunnel leading to the main entrance.

The creak of their black armour fills the tunnel with soft echoes. Without an order or conscious thought, they fall in step to mask their numbers from the listening ears of the waiting delegation. Two rangers wait on either side of the door to the chamber ahead. Both face their visitors and Soar is pleased. It's what he would have done considering they don't know if the delegation is friendly or is hiding their true intentions.

Soar steps in first, followed by Tundra, and the others form up behind, one on each side. The crossbows come up as they take aim at the dragonkin.

Where is the other gryphon? There's only one but there are two shifted dragonkin. One gold and the other is the green one, Flay.

Nice.

All three wear the reds of the Will and smell of ice and snow, not the rain and Pacific Coast fall outside. The gryphon is a little on the skinny side for a member of the Will.

"I am Master Soar," Soar nods as he introduces himself. "State your business, Lady Flay, and the names of your companions."

"Soar," it isn't Flay who speaks. The gold dragonkin turns but does not approach and Soar locks his emotions down as she removes her wrap-around glasses and helmet.

It's Cloud, healthier than she was when they last spoke. Her skin has recovered from the burns and the bruising around her eyes is gone but she's weary. Soar hides a smile of smug satisfaction that she isn't looking her best.

The feather-winged male remains still, content to let the dragonkin speak.

"It's me, Tempest," she says. "Can we please speak with Sire Lev?"

"Well," Soar rolls his eyes as he considers. "No."

Tempest frowns and turns to Flay. The green presses her lips together and tilts her head at Soar.

"Please," Tempest tries. "There's, um, a relic and Aledaar…"

Her voice sinks to a whisper as her leathery right wing draws in then droops, tip down on the floor.

"I m… mean—"

Soar gives up, turns on his heel and stomps through the cross-bow carrying guard and toward the door. Whatever she has planned can wait until she has the respect to not waste his time.

"Damn it, Tempest," Flay growls, setting his hair on edge. "Tell him or I'll kick you where you don't have scales."

Soar gets a hand out and grabs the stone opening as he wills himself to stop and not walk away from whatever Cloud has become.

"Yes, *Tempest*," he hisses as he turns. "Tell me why every dame in the eyrie is getting ready to flee with her children, why Dame Shadow is under guard and why I'm down here dealing with you."

In his hurry to dress, he tied his trousers too tight and they rub uncomfortably around his tail. He takes two steps closer, adjusting the fastening as Tempest's jaw works.

"I," she mutters but it sounds more like 'A.'

The nearer Soar gets the more uncomfortable she looks and he's good with that. She needs to know that crawling back will be the worst trip of her life.

"Am p..." she swallows, two, three, four times and her right wing extends in a series of jerky pulses as Flay moves to her. The soft gold scaly leather of Tempest's wing stretches impossibly thin as the long bones align then hyperextend, pulling the wingtip up. "Am pregnant."

The wing stops and so does Soar, just a breath away from touching his nose to the beads of sweat on her forehead. He'd expected anything from her, including a shameful apology.

Anything but this.

"What?" At first her admission does nothing to ease his anger with her but as the seconds drag on he needs to hear an explanation more than he needs to speak his piece.

"Aa," this time the swallowing doesn't stop and the right wing starts to beat. Flay gets her arms around Tempest before she knocks herself over.

"Sshhh, Tempest," Flay whispers. "Don't try and talk, you'll get through this. Relax."

"Bees," Tempest shouts as the wing calms and falls. "Bees."

"Tempest," Soar tries. For the moment the only thing that matters is there is something very wrong with his pregnant female. "I swear I didn't know the bees would hurt you."

"Bees," she repeats as the swallowing resumes.

"She portalled too many times today," Flay explains. "She was drained before we left and the pregnancy prevents her from getting her energy back quickly."

"I don't understand," Soar says, angry with Flay. Whatever the bitch did to Tempest might have hurt his children. Behind him, Tundra and the other gryphons are silent. Yeah, guys, this is the mate I wouldn't name.

"Your babies are fine, Soar," Flay whispers and offers a smile. "Tempest can think, but everything else is misfiring.

We've all been through it. She hid her condition as long as she could but when I figured it out we fled."

"Figured it out," Soar echoes as Flay grabs his wrist and places his fingers on the subtle firmness of Tempest's belly. Even through her blood red armour it's there now that he knows to look for it.

"This, you dumb gryphon."

"Ah, fuck," Soar says mainly to himself. Flay is right. He's a dumb gryphon for standing there asking questions and not putting his mate first. "Come here, Tempest."

But she doesn't move. Her pulse picks up as she tries to resist the inviting pull of his wings. Misfiring, Flay said. Tempest could stand on her head instead of taking a single step so he surrounds her with his arms and wings and Flay is smart enough to get clear.

"She needs to be comfortable to rest and recover," Flay says.

"Food?"

"There is too much risk of choking. She can eat when her motor control returns."

"We're gonna talk, Tempest," Soar says. He doesn't care who hears. Ignoring her in public hurt her and he won't do it again. "Just the way you like until we're clear about everything. Then you're not leaving my side even if I have to take on the whole damn Will to keep you, understand?"

"Bees," she whispers as Soar tucks her head under his chin.

"Yeah, bees."

"Master Soar," the male next to Flay speaks. He kneels, then in a very dragonkin way he bows and offers his wrists up in submission.

"I am Daniel Cooper," he says as the helmet and glasses come off. "I am grateful for the hospitality we have received. I ask to meet with Sire Lev and agree to any conditions you name in order to do so.

"My relationship with the Council is not what it seems, nor is Aledaar and his relationship with the dragonkin. Allow me to explain to Sire Lev, please, Master Soar."

Cooper is gaunt and unshaven. With his head uncovered, a fading yellow bruise stands out in the space between one eye and his beard.

"Master Soar," Flay kneels at Cooper's side. "Daniel Cooper is my sire and was a prisoner of Aledaar until we freed him tonight. The Council will consider us criminals and we ask for sanctuary, if Sire Lev would be so generous as to consider it."

She stands and reaches through the tangle of Tempest and Soar's arms and wings to feel her pulse and stroke her hair from her face.

"We will leave if you request it, Master Soar," Cooper adds. "We have no wish to bring trouble here."

"Shit," Soar shakes his head. A decision like this isn't his call and Lev needs to address it as soon as possible. "Tundra, disarm Daniel Cooper and escort him to Sire Lev. He is a guest until Lev decides otherwise."

"Master," Tundra acknowledges. He's a good gryphon and hands off his crossbow before pushing the others' weapons to the ground. Then he helps Cooper to his feet and removes the dagger and boot knife from his belt.

"This way, Daniel Cooper," Tundra says. "And welcome to Vancouver Island."

"Thank you," Cooper nods to Soar and takes his place surrounded by the three rangers as they leave for the main chamber.

"Will you carry her?" Flay asks.

Soar gathers Tempest in his arms. She's like rubber and cooler than he expects.

"Don't fight me, Tempest," Flay whispers and places a hand on Tempest's head. "Sleep."

Soar's skin tingles with the power of Flay's will and Tempest forces her heavy lids up. She studies Soar, his eyes, his mouth, then draws a deep breath before her lashes fall.

"You used your will on her, didn't you?"

"My sire can feel dragonkin will too, a gift from his gryphon mating with my dame," Flay explains. "You can resist it, can't you?"

"Yes," Soar doesn't know what to do with Tempest besides hold her. His last attempt at treating her was a disaster.

"I was unkind to you, Master Soar, when we were at Skyfall. I was jealous. My male and the rest of his kind are slaves to Aledaar. He has a powerful magic, an old dragon bone, that he uses to subjugate the golds. Tempest suffered for days until he broke her spirit but he does not control her. The pregnancy prevented it.

"Until today, I thought Con would never be free but now we have a chance.

"I have come to love this young female. We are kin, she and I, as you and I are. I do hope you won't hold my mistreatment of you against me or my sire."

"I don't know what to say, Flay," Soar rocks side to side with the gentle sway of holding an infant. "I accept your words."

"Thank you. You should join Lev and my sire. Cooper is very weak and will need rest as Tempest does. Come."

Damn, he feels silly now that Flay guides him toward the tunnel.

"It isn't my intention to interfere or be a nuisance," Flay says as they make the climb to the main chamber. "She is my charge, a young dragonkin in need of a mentor. I will stay with her as long as she needs me and remain nearby after that. You will probably want me around to deliver your young unless you know another midwife who is fireproof."

"I—"

They are interrupted by a rush of gryphons coming the other way. Talon and Shadow lead and Soar rolls Tempest a little closer to hide her face.

"Talon," Shadow gasps. "Oh my God, what are they? Dragons?"

"Later," Talon hisses and picks Shadow up. With four months to go in her year long pregnancy, she's awkward on her feet and still insists on doing everything for herself. Lately it's been easier for Talon to deal with her stubbornness by packing her around and bearing her complaints.

"But wait," Shadow strains to look over Talon's shoulder. He adjusts his hold to keep her white feathered wings from bashing everyone around her.

Soar and Talon pass each other, back to back, in the narrowest part of the tunnel, Talon protects Shadow from the dragonkin and Soar shields Tempest from their eyes.

Not ready to explain Tempest and me to them, not yet.

"Ward the entrance, remember?" Talon growls over Shadow's struggles.

"But I want to meet the dragons!"

Flay laughs, an easy music that is welcome in the wake of Talon's panic. If Lev ordered Shadow to use her precious energy to put up a protective barrier at the entrance then whatever Cooper conveyed in only a few minutes is dire.

"Does she need warmth, Lady Flay?" Soar asks.

"I can provide it if you feel she will be more comfortable."

"Please. I know I have a lot to learn about her."

"I am at your disposal, Soar," she whispers as they step into the main chamber. "As I am sure my sire is as well."

Lev and Cooper kneel together at the far side. A small fire has been lit and Cooper warms his hands between mouthfuls of meat. Firn, Sire Lev's companion of the past decade, sits nearby with her hands on Cooper. She pays particular attention to his wrist and interrupts her scowl only to ask questions about it.

"Over here," Flay gestures to a deserted section of the chamber then holds a hand up to keep Soar away. She leans forward and with a wet retch, coughs up a mouthful of something Soar is sure he couldn't produce. It ignites with a loud snap and she spits fire at the ground. There are several shouts from behind, the last and loudest from Lev telling everyone to stand the hell down.

Heat radiates from the floor and Flay turns. She coughs once, releasing a small cloud of sparks and black smoke then runs her tongue around her mouth and spits out a wad of flame.

"That's, um," Soar watches as her sticky spit burns itself out.

"I know," Flay says. "Really fucking cool, right?"

She sits on the hot rock and holds her hands to Soar who curls Tempest up beside her. With Tempest's head on Flay's thigh, Soar steps back. His feet are already too warm even through his boots.

"You'll want to keep the heat in, yes?" Firn says.

"Thank you," Flay helps lay the blanket out and tuck it in.

"Are you Lady Flay? I am Firn of Sire Lev's guard."

"My dame spoke of you when I was small."

"I am honoured," Firn nods. One side of her mouth smiles. The other does a fair imitation in spite of the scars from defending the eyrie from the attack decades before that claimed Shadow's dame. "A dragonkin's friendship is a true treasure and I miss Lady Eviscerate dearly. Come, Master Soar. Sire Lev wishes you to join him."

Talon waits with Lev and Cooper, Shadow nestled into Talon's side. Her eyes don't leave the dragonkin and she looks ready to burst with questions. She knows better though. The thick tension around Lev tells Soar things are very, very bad. Shadow's yawn is echoed by Cooper.

Soar tries to not look at Tempest, his female, finally home after far too long away. Whatever shit happened at the Council will never happen again. He'll make sure she understands there is no better place for her than at his side.

"Master Soar," Lev acknowledges as Soar kneels, completing their circle around the fire. "Is the gold dragonkin okay?"

"Lady Tempest's part in their journey has been tiring. She is in Lady Flay's care."

"Good. Then there are plans to make. Daniel Cooper has an item we must recover from Calgary then we shall take on Aledaar himself."

Chapter Twenty-Six

Seriously? How did I get my foot in the chamber pot?

Tempest woke alone in an unfamiliar den with only the scent of Flay for company. Her red armour lies stacked to the side and she wears only her adornment and trousers. After falling asleep in Soar's arms, she found herself here and staggering into the chamber pot. The next ten minutes were spent using it without knocking it over and fastening the trousers she doesn't remember putting on.

Although she didn't expect to spend the night with Soar, waking without him is a disappointment.

With a sigh, she leans over and hits the back of one knee with her fist to get it going, then the other. Several blows later she's moving but not so sure she can stop. Maybe Soar is just busy but her heart is heavy with the thought she may have done too good a job of dumping him

The tunnel is thick with the scents of breakfast and as she nears the main chamber her stomach rumbles. Venison, fresh baked hardbread and stewed fruit make her mouth water. Tempest hasn't had a breakfast like that since the morning she left for Sky's eyrie.

Upon entering the main chamber, her own footsteps are the only sound. Tempest doesn't really care. Leather or feather, it doesn't matter what her wings are made of. Her face hasn't changed and she's still the adopted grand-daughter of the Sire, not that she ever made her parentage mean anything in her own home.

As Tempest proceeds, she tries to adjust her path and aim for the kitchen but her legs don't cooperate and she marches on, straight for the tunnel to the main entrance.

"Tempest?"

Soar!

It's good she doesn't have to look to see who called her. She can't steer or stop and hopes someone blocks her way before she walks right out and plops into the ocean below the salt-whitened eyrie entrance. She didn't float very well as a gryphon and doesn't want to find out if dragonkin can swim.

"Tempest, wait," Soar grabs her elbow. He doesn't pull, instead he gets in front and digs his feet in as her legs continue driving toward the exit.

"Please," he whispers.

Tempest's arms respond and she rests them on his bare chest. The needle-like quills of his chest feathers dig into her palms and must be pricking him as well.

"Stop, don't leave me."

Her legs finally submit after she's pushed him half-way across the chamber. His words and tone of voice do what her brain couldn't. Soar doesn't command. Although his plea is subtle, it's there and Tempest's heart gives in, desperate to promise she never will.

"Bees."

Crap. Mouth still doesn't work right.

"Where are you going?" Soar demands then takes her elbows and holds her close. He only wears his black leather trousers and a single dagger and is wrapped in the cloy of his heavy armour. His soft, long flight feathers fold behind her. "Never mind. I know you still can't talk properly.

"I will say this once," he raises his voice enough for it to carry to the farthest corners of the chamber. "And I want to be absolutely clear."

Tempest's eyes dash from side to side. Everyone looks at Soar holding the gold dragonkin. Near a small fire, Lev sits with Cooper, Flay, Talon and Shadow. Soar called her from that direction and five sets of eyes, one fiery green, watch.

"I screwed up," he says. "Bad.

"I kept you secret and I turned on you when you left for Sky's. Then I took advantage of my brother's trust to have you expelled and used you to do the one thing I couldn't... get into Cooper's eyrie with an air tight cover story. Only you didn't know it was a story and I took away the only future you wanted.

"I've been yours for six years, Tempest, since you first came to my den and I've been a shameful excuse for a mate. I wouldn't acknowledge you, I abandoned you and I used you.

"And then I poisoned you and if the dragonkin hadn't come I would have killed you."

There's the sound of a scuffle by Lev's fire. A squeal of delight from Shadow follows Lev's cursing.

Soar glances at them and drops to his knees. The only thing stopping Lev from charging between them is Flay. She isn't afraid to get in front of the angry Sire.

"My Lady Tempest," Soar rests his hands on the waist of her trousers and waits for any sign of objection.

Tempest has none.

It's been months since his touch and years before that. She takes his head in her hands and strokes the hair at his temples.

"I'm so very, very sorry," he whispers though not quiet enough for his apology to be private, "I don't care who knows. Your spirit is my weakness, Tempest, and my greatest pride. You carry my children and I swear I will not mess things up again."

His lips nuzzle her belly.

"I love you, Tempest," Soar breathes, warming her skin with his words. "You deserve better than what I've been."

"Bees," Tempest says. It takes every ounce of concentration to speak slow over-articulated words. "I love you."

Soar gets to his feet as a flash of brilliant green leather blocks Lev from his sight.

Shit.

"Master Soar," Lev growls. "You will come with me now."

"No," Flay insists. "Sire Lev, I cannot allow you to antagonize Tempest's dragon. Her hold on her is tenuous at best and right now she is weakened. She nearly killed her sire just a few months ago when he drew her dragon out."

"I see," Lev says.

Soar shudders inside. He's not only admitted to mistreating Lev's grand-daughter but to claiming her as his mate without even speaking to her sire or grand-sire first. Talon is just as angry and the only thing holding him back is that he has to prevent Shadow from jumping in.

She's ecstatic.

"Sire Lev," Flay drops her wings then kneels. The female has good sense. Nobody stands up to Lev without following up with speedy submission and an explanation.

"Lady Tempest, Soar's female, you know her as Cloud. I am certain she has no objection if I speak for her.

"She understands why Soar had her expelled. She is proud for her part in what came next. As he said, she is pregnant and that is the only thing that prevented her from becoming Aledaar's servant. My sire told you last night she is free and the only one who can kill Aledaar and free her kin.

"Lady Tempest is the daughter of Lord Fury, Master of the Council's Will and the sibling of my mate, Conflagration. She is my beloved kin."

Tempest raises her chin, bumping Soar with her nose. This close, her auburn lashes catch the light.

His hold around her tightens as he works the back of her neck with his hand to relax her.

"Sire Lev," Tempest gasps. Damned if a little affection hasn't given her back her words. "Please don't be angry with my Soar. If he hadn't done everything to make my mission to Calgary a success he would not deserve to be the master of your guard. We have made friends and uncovered the truth about Aledaar and the gold dragonkin.

"We have hope."

She turns, a little clumsily, and Soar keeps his hand on her neck.

"The healer in Skyfall told me of Aledaar and the relic. She said there would be pain and there was. I went before Aledaar thinking no further ahead than getting through it, hiding my pregnancy and coming home.

"It took five days for him to break me."

"Damn it," Soar mutters. The torture of the relic caused the bruising around her eyes and the burns. There was no bullshit relapse.

"Soar waited for me. I was cruel and sent him away because they would have killed him. Yesterday Lady Flay learned my secret and we freed her sire and came here."

"Wait, my friend," Lev says to Cooper then rubs his eyes. "First thing is first.

"Master Talon, Hunter spent two months on his hands and knees apologizing for his part in Soar's plan. Contact Master Sky and have him sent here so the loyal young gryphon might be considered for Dame Shadow's guard."

"Sire," Talon grumbles. He still looks pissed at Soar.

"Second," Lev continues. "We will arrange a family den for Master Soar and Lady Tempest.

"Third, Lady Flay, should I ever do something so stupid as to go after a female dragonkin's mate you have my permission to knock me flat in order to stop me."

"Sire," Flay nods.

Sire Lev rubs at his cheek. Soar knows the big, blonde gryphon is putting together all the pieces. Every bit of information he's heard since Tempest arrived the night before is sorted. There will be no indecision.

"Fourth?" Shadow says. "Lady Flay said Cloud, um, Tempest has a dragon."

"She did," Lev looks at the ceiling. So does Talon. Both know what she wants, as does Soar, and he's nervous about it too. Shadow has held her curiosity back and can't wait any longer.

"I would very much like to see it."

No, Tempest shakes her head and Flay nods in agreement.

"Dame Shadow," Flay explains. "Tempest and her dragon are still getting to know each other. It takes years for a dragonkin and her dragon to learn to trust and respect each other."

"Awe," Shadow sighs, unable to hide her disappointment.

"I know my dragon well," Flay adds. "She is very sweet and good tempered. She is not bothered by a room full of strangers and would be honoured to meet you."

"Yes?" Shadow asks Talon but even as she gets more excited she steps behind his wing in case Flay spits fire again.

"Sire," Cooper speaks. "My daughter would not offer unless Dame Shadow will be as safe with her dragon as she is with her."

Flay gets a hand on Cooper's shoulder and kicks her boots off.

"I have seen her dragon fight, Sire," Cooper says. "I know what she is capable of when threatened. There is no danger here."

"Yes," Lev sighs. Soar suspects there is more to this demonstration than simply pleasing Shadow.

Flay's leather chest piece drops to the floor with her boots then her trousers. The strips of soft green scales that run down her neck hug the outer curve of her breasts before fading just past her navel. She kneels and places her hands on the ground. Beneath her lengthening wings, her back broadens as she begins to shift.

"Oh," Shadow exclaims. The circle around Flay feels very small and everyone takes a few steps away to give her space. Where Tempest's claws were a deep brown, Flay's are a brilliant dark green. Her scales thicken, spread down her limbs and cover her snout and with a snort, Flay bows.

It is a much more peaceful scene than Tempest's attack on Fury.

"Talon?" Shadow peers around him.

"Come," Cooper holds a hand to Shadow and kneels beside Flay's heavy head. Flay lowers the lids that cover her gold eyes, the only part of her body that isn't green. "I will introduce you."

Shadow steps around Talon. He stays near and neither Flay nor Cooper seem bothered by his protective presence. Trust must learn to go both ways.

Tempest radiates her trust for Soar. He hopes he's worthy and that she feels his trust in her.

Cooper supports Shadow as she gets to the floor.

"Here," he says as he places her palm on Flay's nose. "Don't move your hand. Dragon scales are so rough you could scrape your skin off."

"Okay," Shadow swallows. "She is so warm."

"Yes."

Flay raises her head and turns to Cooper before returning her gaze to Shadow.

"You have given us sanctuary, Dame Shadow," Cooper says. "Welcomed us to your home and even though you know what we are and the danger we bring, you welcomed us as your friends. Lady Flay would like to share her scent with you so all green dragonkin know your kindness. This dragon is very fond of you."

"Really?" Shadow lightens her touch and strokes Flay in spite of Cooper's warning. Her fingertips rasp gently on her scales. "Your daughter is so beautiful. I don't understand how anyone could fail the dragonkin.

"I'm ashamed, Sire, that one greedy gryphon could bring so much pain. Lady Flay, you are always welcome here. You need only arrive and you will be shown comfort and friendship."

"Yes," Lev agrees.

Flay raises her head and rests her cheek against Shadow's large belly then a single tear runs from her eye. She moves just enough to scuff Shadow's wet skin.

"Oh!" Shadow exclaims.

"You felt a spark?" Cooper asks.

Shadow nods and holds Flay's head close.

"She will protect you with her life, Dame Shadow. It is a very rare gift."

Daniel Cooper leaves Flay content in Dame Shadow's arms. He's spent too much time on his knees in the Grand Council's dungeons to remain on the ground. A long soak in the warm eyrie baths followed by a shave and fresh clothing eased the chill and pain of captivity. It also gave him respite from Firn who, while a good healer, was vocal in her disgust that Torrent had kept his arm broken.

"Sire Lev," he says. "As I stated yesterday there is a complication to retrieving the green relic and I wanted Lady Tempest with us before I explained."

"There's another relic?" Tempest asks.

When she arrived in Calgary she seemed lost and incomplete. Even the day before when they stole from Bolshevik Island there was something missing from her as if he were watching a partial reflection. Today, in Soar's arms, she is whole and content. The pair comfort each other in a way that fills Cooper with memories of his Lady Eve.

"Indeed. What do you remember about the night of the tornado?"

Tempest looks at Soar with a measurable amount of discomfort.

"We talked, I remember, and you asked me to stay with you," her fingers brush her lip and Soar lets out a soft growl.

Then he turns his chilly stare on Cooper.

"But your phone rang and I overheard you caught Soar snooping so I found him. I dealt with his guards and we escaped from the roof."

"That memory isn't accurate, Tempest," Cooper explains. "When I am near the green relic I have the will of a dragonkin. The relic is in my trust and I would never use it to bind a dragonkin's will to mine as Aledaar has but my prolonged nearness to it has given me some dragonkin gifts.

"That night, I used the relic to replace your memories so you wouldn't remember what I really did."

"And what did you really do, *my friend*," Soar voice thickens with danger. "Make it quick."

"Lady Tempest," Cooper says. "It is time I asked you to return my key."

The effect on Tempest is subtle. She eases against Soar and rests her fingers on his lips, then hers.

"You didn't kiss me," she says to Cooper.

"Told you so," Soar growls.

"You lured me to your room. You said it was a guest room and I could leave from your balcony the next morning —"

"Damn it," Soar barks.

"Easy," Lev says but Soar is far from easy. He shields Tempest within one feathery wing and rests his free hand on his dagger. Flay opens her large eyes as Lev gets an arm in front of Soar. Shadow works a patch of soft scales behind Flay's ear openings and the dragon is content not to get involved.

"Hear the whole story, Soar."

"There's a stone on the wall," Tempest says. "When you put your hand on it a door opened. By the time I got to it you'd opened a box and the room was full of green light. The relic…"

"Yes," Cooper adds. "I asked you about Soar and why you'd come to Calgary. Then I transferred the magic that opens the door and the box to you and used the relic's will to make you forget. I planted the false memory of a kiss and told you to flee.

"I cannot recover the relic, Sire Lev. Lady Tempest is the only one who can get in the room and unlock the box. I gave her the magic and made sure she wouldn't remember. She spent months with Aledaar and Lord Fury. The only one who could give Aledaar power over the greens was right there the whole time."

"You cannot go, Daniel Cooper," Tempest says. "They will only imprison you again."

"What do you suggest, Tempest?" Lev asks.

"Nobody has to know he gave me the power to open both the door and the box. I also suspect we need the relic's magic to return control to Daniel Cooper."

"You are clever, young dragonkin," Cooper smiles.

"Too clever," Soar says. "I will accompany her."

"That isn't the plan," Lev says. "We need friends at our side to take on Aledaar. As we decided you will go with Lady Flay as my proxy to bring as many of her kin from hiding as you can. Daniel Cooper remains here. Firn will not budge on her orders for his recovery. Talon will be here and I will seek out as much support as I can from the eyries who once questioned Aledaar's leadership.

"Tempest will go alone."

Chapter Twenty-Seven

Flay opts for traditional eyrie clothing when she returns to her dragonkin form and holds Shadow's hand until Tempest tells everyone she needs more sleep.

"My den," Soar orders and hands Tempest off to Flay and Shadow. "She knows the way."

"She will not be pleased if you insist she remain here," Lev says when the three females are gone. White, gold and green, there isn't a common gryphon among them yet they've become very close in a short period of time. "Tempest knew she'd face Aledaar since you were in Skyfall."

"I know."

"It's been a hard lesson for Talon to learn. Shadow has a duty to all who live here and there will be times it will put her in danger."

"Shadow isn't—"

"We're not talking about Shadow," Talon interrupts. "Tempest faced danger in Calgary. You put her there. Then she went to Aledaar alone. I expect that loyalty from Shadow's guard, as Lev expects it from you and the rest of his guard.

"We have never asked a thing of Tempest. Never given her an order or asked more of her than we felt she should give yet she is more generous and loyal than we ever expected."

"She is a good dragonkin," Cooper sighs.

"She would refuse to be considered for the guard," Soar snaps but being right about it feels empty. Even one-upping Talon makes him feel like a shit when it used to be satisfying. Tempest is Soar's now and he doubts she'll consider Shadow's guard any time soon. At some point Tempest's loyalty became a competition between Soar and Talon. It happened so quietly nobody noticed until it was over and it no longer mattered.

"Shadow's mark on Tempest's shoulder wouldn't allow her to pose as a member of the Will yet she serves as if she were born with it," Soar tries to soften his victory.

"You're probably right, my friend," Talon concedes.

So much has changed for Tempest in the past few months that Soar worries he doesn't really know her at all anymore. His only certainty is that he needs her.

"It's been a long night," Lev says. "Get out of my sight for a while, Soar."

"Sire," he acknowledges. "If you'll excuse me."

There will be private words later but for now there's time for some quiet before Soar leaves with Flay. He intends to spend it at Tempest's side.

"Master Soar," Cooper calls and Soar stops. "I'm sure Flay had this talk with Tempest… make sure she turns her head aside."

"What?"

"You mean *when* and I understand it'll help her recovery."

Shit, can everyone butt out?

"Later," Soar mutters through his teeth though getting his little dragonkin alone in his den is a fine idea. By the time he reaches the tunnel Lev's laughter is ramping up for a second round.

Soar's den is quiet and he stands in the tunnel waiting for any sound from the other side of the curtain that covers the opening. When nothing comes, he steps in to find Tempest alone. The scents of Flay and Shadow are nearly gone.

"Lady Tempest," he says and she smiles.

Soar's assessment only takes a moment. Her mouth is symmetrical and not half-sagging like the night before. Her head tilts like she's about to have a shy moment and it's all for him.

Thank God.

She's slow but she approaches with sure steps. Soar doesn't want to break the spell by even breathing. The dream of her in his den has been stolen every morning for the past three years and now it's here. Her sweetness, the brush of her adornment against her skin and the tiny creaks of her leather wings as she moves strike deep. Soar's aroused response fuses memories of this moment to his heart and releases a possessive growl.

"Touch me," Tempest says as her hands take his hips, at first for balance then to explore. She grasps the handle of his dagger then places a palm on the hard plane of his stomach.

Soar's struggle to be gentle ends when her rough grip cups his erection.

"Touch me," she whispers. Her other hand grasps at the fastening for his trousers.

With one hand he seizes the back of her head, twisting through her hair while he claims her mouth under his. Against his wrist, the scales on her neck become rough and as her mouth opens in submission she exhales hot air. A shiver moves over him, traveling the length of his body and hardening him further against her hand.

"Good," she murmurs.

"Better than good," Soar groans as she bites at his lower lip. Her teeth are damned sharp and the sting as she breaks his skin nearly pushes him over the edge. Then her long tail twists around his thigh, drawing him in even closer.

He lets her take control of the kiss, nibbling, sucking, as he unties her trousers with one hand. As they fall he gets a foot up to push them down as she slides her tail free. The skin beneath her adornment is soft and with each breath her dark dragonkin musk strengthens. Soar's hips move without waiting for his instruction, grinding his cock against her skin.

"I missed you," she moans as his own trousers sink to his thighs, his dagger clattering to the floor.

Every informative word Flay shared with Tempest over the past few months flashes through Tempest's mind. The precarious jumble of memories of their conversation and the hard instincts of the moment become an intense rush of action. Flay's words were mostly warnings about keeping it safe for her relatively fragile gryphon lover but after seeing how Soar responded to her longer and sharper canines she will do as she pleases.

Tempest's tail finds it's way around Soar's leg, just beneath his barely exposed ass as his knees lock, fusing them in place. Then he pushes his wings wide behind him, bracing them against the wall on either side of the door.

"Here," he groans. "Right here."

She can't agree more and slides her nails around his back and scratches him with approval. Other than his back to the door instead of hers, they stand in their favourite place to make love.

"Don't make me wait," Tempest breathes. The words come easy now but a wave of weakness warns she'll need rest again soon.

Soar's bruising fingers release her ass as he pulls one leg up, cradling her knee over his elbow.

"Now," she barks and as his cock finds her entrance, she seals her lips on her bite-mark under his ear, driving a shout from his lips. Tempest's other foot comes off the ground as he takes all her weight in his arms then lowers her as he thrusts.

"Tem…" a deep shudder silences Soar and for a moment nothing moves.

"Yes, my love," she moans. "I need this."

"God," Soar gasps as he digs his heels in. By simply shifting his weight he buries himself inside her again and again. Each time he fills her, her spirit heals and the long agony of their separation is driven further away.

As soon as she links her hands behind his neck Soar keeps his pace steady. He knows her signals. Each move is timed exactly right and she's on the road to release. All he has to do is hold out until she gets there.

"My gryphon," Tempest whispers and licks at the wound on his lip. Her skin hardens as if shifting to scale and each movement courses pleasure over the entire surface. As she nears her peak, her throat stiffens and something Flay said comes to mind but she doesn't remember what and pushes the memory aside.

Soar senses her impending release and welcomes his and for a moment Tempest's breathing is blocked, her orgasm seeming connected with whatever is going on in her throat. Her growl clears it as Soar swears and grabs her chin, pushing her head away.

As his knees fail, they sink to the ground in an explosion of ecstasy and fire. Tempest's legs lock around Soar's hips, binding him in place as she rides out the last of his powerful orgasm.

"Oh, shit," Soar moans as he rocks back on his butt and kicks them clear of the doorway.

Over the smell of slightly singed feathers coming from the ridge of his wing is the stink of burning fabric. Tempest's laughter masks a shout of 'fire' from the tunnel and they roll clear of the burning curtain just in time to avoid setting Soar's singed wing alight.

"Oops," she giggles.

Soar scrambles to find her trousers before the eyrie gryphons arrive with chamber pots of sea water.

"Damn it, damn it," he curses as he grabs for a pair of his to put on her. Tempest's are lost under the mound of burning curtains. It isn't a simple fire. The heavy fabric immolates with a throat full of very flammable thick, dragonkin acid.

"You alright?" Tempest can't make out who shouts from the hall.

"Hell, yeah," Soar's satisfied grin makes her heart pound. "My fucking God I set you on fire."

"Stay back," another voice outside hollers.

"Tell me about your day, Soar," she asks as Soar pulls the sleeping mat into the farthest corner from the door and nestles Tempest in his lap.

"My day?"

"Yes," she yawns.

"Didn't waste any time did you?" Talon's voice reaches them through the smoke.

"Piss off, Talon," Soar mutters.

Tempest's cheeks redden and Soar wraps his fingers over her blush. Dark grey human silhouettes appear and disappear as loads of water are dumped on the burning curtain. Human form protects their wings from the fire but their efforts only add steam to the smoke and the fire burns on as merrily as before.

"I learned something today, Tempest," Soar says. "I learned that when you have nothing to fight for then you have nothing worth fighting for.

"I don't want you to go to Calgary. I don't want you to ever leave the eyrie again or my den for that matter but keeping you here would turn you into someone other than the female I fell in love with and would make me someone neither one of us would like."

"I don't want to go either," she says, unable to hide her fear. To be separated again so soon threatens to tear away the small measure of security she's found.

"If we do nothing," Soar rests a hand on her stomach and lets his voice fade with the stillness of their moment. In spite of the hustle at the door, nothing intrudes.

Tempest is the female who will fight for his children as hard as he will. She's everything he's ever wanted and with each wrapped in the scent of the other it's a proud moment for him to share his small family with everyone in the eyrie.

"If we do nothing then these little dragonkin have no future except service under Aledaar and I won't stand for that."

"No," Tempest turns to watch the fire. The remains the water won't extinguish are scooped into the pots and hurried to the main entrance. "I won't either."

Chapter Twenty-Eight

Three days after Soar departs with Flay, Tempest portals to Calgary. Flay took him only a few hours after the fire. The portal route was complicated, she explained, seeding new portals before even passing through the one before them and hopping through their route to the green dragonkin hiding place.

The unique discharge of the final portal not only had to be timed right, but also had to have the correct electrical field to verify she is a friend.

They won't talk if I get it wrong. Flay said. *We'll be dead.*

Here's to getting it right.

There's been no word since.

No gryphons guard Cooper's building and the sky above is empty except for a helicopter tracing the Bow River. November settles over the city with cold temperatures, bare trees and deep snow. Ice lines the river shore. Weak noon light only brings grey to the newly reclad buildings that had been stripped of their glass the previous summer.

Cooper's balcony appears intact. The red-cushioned furniture Tempest and Cooper sat on is gone. At first she thinks the pieces have been put away but it's more likely they were stolen by the tornado.

Nothing to do but try and get in. A grab and go will be ideal.

Tempest alights on the snow covered cement patio and studies the windows. The sliding door is open a finger's width and the heavy curtains are torn behind the glass, evidence some windows were broken by the storm and replaced. Someone has been looking after things since Cooper was taken.

A large pack strapped to her front covers much of the red leather including her altered trousers. Shadow called it maternity armour and wondered how she would look fighting in them.

Talon said 'no.'

Tempest slides the door open enough to pass then she yawns, a deep full body gasp for air. The warm room hits her hard with drowsiness that dulls her senses and muffles her ears in the feel of good warm wool.

"Darn," she mutters. It isn't a good time to lose her senses.

The room is somewhat intact. Several of Cooper's sculptures have been knocked over. One lies broken on the floor and another rests on one end of the sofa. The portrait of Cooper still hangs although it's off kilter. Otherwise slivers of day stab through the curtain and a single bulb in the kitchen casts more shadow than light.

Tempest goes straight for Cooper's bedroom. He warned it will be safer for her to bring the box with the relic still inside but just in case she has a key and a handkerchief sized piece of thin leather to handle it.

A few steps into the hall she receives her only warning she isn't alone. A large, un-winged gryphon appears from behind and clamps a hand over her mouth as the other holds a cold steel knife to her throat.

"The rules, Cherry," Lawrence hisses. "Remember the rules. Talk about anyone but yourself and you're dead."

Tempest lets herself go limp in his arms, daring a small nod. How could she have let the big male get behind her unnoticed? The answer is simple. She's plain old tired and her smell and hearing were the first to go.

"The last dragonkin here left me unconscious on the floor for two solid days. Will sons of bitches. They took Cooper and killed a number of his guard."

No wonder Lawrence is cautious but even that isn't enough to explain the flatness of his voice nor the tremble in his hands. Although she doesn't speak, Tempest tests his will by pushing hers into him. The force of it slamming back into her takes the light from the room and all sensation from under foot.

"Wake up, Cherry," Lawrence whispers. She must have passed out because the view has changed although his hold on her hasn't. With the wall at his back, she has no leverage and cannot push away or turn to attack. He's also not acting of his own accord. Flay never discussed what it meant when another's will was so effectively closed but Tempest can guess.

Lawrence has been influenced by a dragonkin but she doesn't know to what end.

It could be as simple as allowing access to the suite to whomever gave him the order or he may have been told to defend the place with his life.

"Don't make me wait."

"I am Lady Tempest, daughter of Lord Fury, Master of the Council's Will."

"And?" Lawrence snaps.

"I'm here for the box."

"Nobody can get the box," Lawrence argues and the knife presses harder against Tempest's skin. "The Will, they tore the walls apart, nothing but stone underneath. Not even light getting in there."

"I am free, Lawrence," Tempest hurries. Sweat beads on Lawrence's skin and he allows her to grasp the arm holding the knife. He paces and her legs dangle and bash his shins. "Before he was taken, Cooper gave me access to the door on the fourth full moon. In three days."

The simple plan surprises her but it could work. Tempest will get the rest she needs to portal out and if Lawrence buys it he won't force her to open the door now.

"Lies," he growls.

"Master Soar and I," her voice squeaks. Speaking presses her voice box against the blade. "I'm pregnant. Aledaar does not control me and he never will."

Tempest stumbles as Lawrence drops her. She takes a defensive position once out of his reach and draws her dagger.

"I do not wish to fight," she says, holding to the rule to only talk about herself. She's too weary to take Lawrence on by force.

"Lady Tempest," Lawrence nods. He blinks, several times, processing her story. Tempest is now certain. He's been programmed and she'll have to be very, very careful. "Three days?"

"I'm to deliver the box," she improvises. "There are six places I can leave it depending on the time. I don't know any more than that."

Better not dig myself in with details.

"Three days," he swallows as he puts his knife away.

"Yes," she sheaths her blade and turns for Cooper's room.

Lawrence didn't exaggerate when he said it had been torn apart. Drywall covers the floor and the backs of the chamber's wall stones are visible. Even the metal studs have been torn away in places.

"I cannot sleep in this dust," Tempest says.

"I'll clean," Lawrence seems to have composed himself or at least integrated Tempest's plan into his orders. He won't interfere, for now.

"Gryphon."
Too loud.

Soar lost count of the portals at four. Each successive concussion battered him further until he fell unconscious and it took less than a minute from when the first one popped open until the blessed black silence. Now his head splits and some asshole keeps shouting. It's one hell of a hangover and the room is damn hot. The heat comes up through the stone beneath him so he is far underground.

"Uh," Soar retches and clamps his mouth shut before he can shame himself by throwing up. The only feathers he hears moving are his own and their rustling is drowned out by the shifting of many pairs of leather wings. Either he's in the hands of the council or they made it to the green dragonkin stronghold.

"It still smells like a gold," a female speaks. "We should kill it. We should have done it three days ago."

Voices around mutter their agreement. Soar feels fear and anger in this group of dragonkin. Although the Will might not like him much they certainly wouldn't be afraid of a lone gryphon.

"*It* is a he," the first voice again followed by more shaking. "Gryphon."

"I am Master Soar of the Vancouver Island Eyrie," Soar opens his eyes. He's surrounded by green dragonkin, all young and clustered together in three distinct knots around the room. The one squatting before him has Flay's long blonde hair and looks a lot like Daniel Cooper. He wears brown armour, as do the others, and two oversized brass handled daggers are strapped to his thighs. In spite of the surrounding mob, Soar likes this dragonkin if only for his choice in weapons.

"I am Fire," the green announces. "What is your business with my sibling?"

"Daniel Cooper sent us," Soar says. Everything around him doubles as he sits and it takes every effort to kneel and offer his wrists to Fire. "Lady Flay has his letter."

"I have read it," Fire stands. "However she is only just waking. The passage was very hard on her and considering she hauled you all the way here it's a miracle you made it to the ledge before she collapsed. Tell me why you smell of gold dragonkin."

Soar falls back on his ass as Fire's will infiltrates his senses. Now isn't a good time to learn he's only resistant when weakened, not immune. It's easier to repeat the words Cooper gave him than to completely fight Fire's will and make some shit up.

"My female, Lady Tempest, is a free gold dragonkin. She is the keeper of the key to the green dragonkin relic and Daniel Cooper has sent her to retrieve it. We gather forces to move against Aledaar and ask the green dragonkin to assist. Aledaar still seeks the green relic for himself."

"The very words in my sire's letter."

"He resists," the female behind Soar argues. "Mated to a gold! We cannot trust him."

"We will not kill him," Fire orders. "At least not until I am able to speak with Lady Flay."

Shit.

"Should your story bear up, Master Soar, you may live. Bring him."

Fire strides from the chamber and several green dragonkin haul Soar to his feet.

They disappear one at a time through a crack in the wall. Soar has to turn sideways to get through and even then it's a snug fit. It seems the dragonkin are more flexible where their large bones connect and even with a firm shove from the mouthy female, Soar's passage lacks their silent grace.

"Stick to the left," she says. The annoying, flat tapping of her nails on a drawn blade echoes to him from stone walls.

The chamber itself feels as spacious as Skyfall but his sharpened gryphon sight can make out the other wall only twenty feet to his right. All sound is swallowed above and below in the immense crevasse.

"The ledge is very narrow," she croons then Soar stumbles as she boots him in the butt. Soar turns and finds nothing under his left foot and her hand on his shoulder to steady his balance. She's striking, now that he gets a good look at her, though the short black hair appears to have been chopped with a knife it lays in elegant curves at her cheek bones. "Should you fall, there is no room to fly. Your only chance is to portal before you die at the bottom."

Soar growls and doesn't bother pointing out he's a gryphon and can't portal. The female's satisfied laughter adds the emphasis.

"Female," Fire calls from up ahead. "Do you wish to demonstrate?"

She grunts and puts her knife away before turning Soar around and pushing him ahead. The shelf becomes even slimmer and he's forced to turn sideways since his wings won't fold in as close as dragonkin wings do. There is no way to walk forward and stay upright.

"I wanted to push you off the ledge but *no*," she mutters, dragging the word no into a masterful three syllable sentiment. Is every green dragonkin female going to dislike him on sight? Not that he cares, except when one wants to shove him into a bottomless pit.

Soar turns his attention to the ledge only a few inches from his toes as he shuffles sideways. Nobody volunteers to go after him and portal him to safety if he falls.

A gryphon is never afraid of heights but at seventy-six years old Soar sure as hell knows when to be cautious.

It's common sense, he decides. *Not fear.*

"We had to haul you down here. Whoa!"

The dragonkin ahead is gone and so is the ledge for that matter. The obnoxious female has him by the tail.

"This way."

Another push and he's in a broad tunnel. Fresher air coats him in the smells of leather and food. Why couldn't they have just dumped him here? The dryness in his mouth isn't from the heat. It remains and even his iffy stomach doesn't object to the idea of a drink.

"In here," she says and Soar steps into a large chamber. It lacks the breeze that cooled the tunnel but the food smell is strongest.

"Master Soar," Fire calls and in the dark he spots the green embracing his sister, Lady Flay.

A clay mug of tepid water is shoved in Soar's hand and he kneels with Flay and Fire. Smoked meat and hard crackers are laid out and Fire nods that Soar should eat. Flay has already started. Before the first morsel reaches his lips his senses are overwhelmed by the charred coating of hot peppers underlaid with vodka. The pieces are so infused with flavour that Soar can only guess what it was when it had fur.

"You read our sire's letter?" Flay speaks around a mouthful.

"Indeed," Fire answers. "It is time, then?"

"Mm."

The spiced meat stings his mouth and his eyes water as he shakes his head to try and knock the burn loose. Soar drinks to soothe his fiery tongue rather than to quench his thirst.

"It's good," he mutters but his voice fades to the same horse whisper he got from his first ever taste of Seth's reserve.

"It is," Flay agrees and offers him a smile. Her water is untouched.

"Eat," Fire pats his sibling's hand as he excuses himself.

Soar expected more of a conversation between the two but after only a few ambiguous words some sort of plan is in motion.

"That one," Flay tips her head at the female who followed him along the ledge. Fire stops to whisper in her ear. The female grins at Soar, chilling him in spite of the spicy food and the warm room. "Is heir to the rule of the green dragonkin though it is my sibling who leads in this place. I do not know her name nor the names of most of these dragonkin. They fear that if Aledaar gets the relic he will punish all who assist us. That old gryphon has even robbed them of who they are.

"Our great city, Ochre's Honour, has fallen to sadness and surrender. Lord Ochre founded the cavern-city hundreds of years ago and his dragonkin worked hard until it rivaled Skyfall in its beauty. We lived there when I was small and I remember the daylight through the ceiling and the brilliant robes of the dragonkin. Nobody wore armour then unless it was called for. When Fire and I passed our fifth year my dame, Lady Eviscerate, and my sire decided to move. It was safer for Ochre's Honour to have the relic somewhere else.

"A few years later we returned to leave her bones with those of our ancestors. It was the last time the dragonkin who chose to leave were allowed to return. There are many dragonkin bones waiting to go home.

"Since then the elders remain and the young come here. Our elders are prisoners and the young grow up in this dark hole. Only a few of us on the outside know where Ochre's Honour is.

"The only truth we have is one day we will have a chance to stop Aledaar. If he didn't control the golds, we would simply kill him for attempting to take the green relic but with them forced to fight at his side there will be much loss of life. Now that we have a way to kill Aledaar and free our gold kin, the balance of power can shift to us."

The way to kill Aledaar is Tempest. Soar's love will be in Calgary, alone and facing who knows what as she attempts to bring the box to Cooper. Even now she could be back in the hands of the Will. She'd be alive but only so Aledaar could claim Soar's children as his servants. His only comfort is Tempest will never give up.

"These young," Flay continues. "Have never seen a gryphon. Gryphons are feared because of Aledaar."

"So what happens next?" Soar asks.

"Ochre's Honour."

The dark haired female slips out the cavern door after Fire and Flay gives Soar a soft elbow.

"Hurry it up, Soar," she says. "The next leg of the journey will be much easier."

Damn, he thought the green dragonkin lives were somewhat normal and never imagined their people would be as broken up and depressed as the golds. The abject shame of Skyfall was haunting and the greens are no different.

"Flay," Fire calls and they move across the cramped floor to the tunnel. The fear he'd heard earlier in the young dragonkin voices is now blessed with a small amount of hope. The chamber goes quiet as the dozen pairs of dragonkin eyes watch.

"Wait," Fire says, blocking Soar from leaving behind Flay. "Flay will show her the way. Might want to stand clear."

If there's going to be fire then Soar will stand as far back as they tell him plus a few extra steps out of the way.

The female faces Flay and both spread their wings in what appears to be threat, neither taking her eyes from the other. For nearly a minute they negotiate their positions as the air charges, standing Soar's chest feathers on end. The heat they create stings his exposed skin and he gets a hand up to limit the dryness it causes his eyes. The subtle glow of green smoke forms a fist-sized sphere between them. Just when it takes solid form, Flay cries out. The ball slams into the other female, sending her spinning.

She stays on her feet and coughs as the green smoke clears.

"Ready," Flay claims. Her cheer sounds forced, however, and she straightens her armour before binding her hair back with a length of leather cord.

"So we won't get knocked around so much this time?"

"No," Fire mutters as he braids his own hair but he won't look at Soar. Something is up, he's just not certain what. A young male steps forward to pass Soar his weapons and not just the daggers. Several smaller blades Soar kept concealed deep in his armour appear to have also been liberated from him during his stupor. These are secured as quickly as the daggers. The smirk on the mouthy female's face suggests she might have had a hand in fleecing him.

"Master Soar," Flay holds out a hand and he follows her down another hall to a broad ledge. "A moment, it is safest if the portal is seeded before we jump."

Not only is a portal at the bottom the only way to escape a fall it's also the only way out. Great.

"Now!"

Soar's lungs are knocked flat as he tumbles from the ledge in the arms of the black haired female. Far below the crack of a portal opening bounces up the crevasse and goes right through them, shaking bone and muscle as if they were no more solid than the air around them.

"Flay!" he gasps. *Bitch.* God damned dragonkin. Is she too tired from the last trip for a passenger? The chasm walls charge past and the heat builds as they plummet deeper into the earth. All he can do is hold still and press his head into the female to keep his ears from being scraped off.

For a split second they're embraced by the plasma green edge of the portal then with a bang they're free, tumbling in the cool salty mist of the West Coast.

"What the hell?" Soar demands as the female lets him go.

She doesn't listen and circles through thick fog until she finds a rock outcrop on which to land. Soar follows and charges at the female the moment his feet hit the ground.

"Wait," she holds her hands up and takes a step back. *Yeah. Believe it, female. This gryphon is not pleased.*

For the second time he's been dumped off at home. It wasn't the way to Ochre's Honour that Flay taught her. It was the way here.

"Please," she tries again and cowers though not from him. Wind makes the massive trees groan and ache against each other and her head whips around as she tries to assess the sound.

"Understand, Master Soar," she gasps, eyes everywhere but on him. "We planned this before you woke. Had you gone to Ochre's Honour you'd be killed without question, Flay and Fire too for bringing you, and you would never get a chance to ask my sire for help."

Soar turns his back on her to hide his feelings. He's a gryphon and an envoy to speak for Sire Lev himself, not some beast looking for trouble, but here he is back on the Island with a young green dragonkin who, it appears, has never been out of the underground fissure from which they just portalled.

"What is your name," Soar asks as he faces her. She still gazes at the trees then spins at the sound of a loud breaker, smashing the rock shore nearby.

"My n… name?"

"Yes," he softens. One green dragonkin to help is better than none.

Godspeed, Lady Flay.

"Agony," she breathes then a broad smile breaks across her features. "Agony."

Soar bows as she tosses her hands up.

"Agony!" her shrill voices pierces through the trees and up into the dense fog. "I am Agony!"

How long has it been since she was allowed to use her name?

"I am Agony," she says again. "Heir to the rule of Ochre's Honour. We can only wait for Lady Flay to return. If my kin won't send help I will bring the other young dragonkin here.

"What is that?" she asks. Another winter wave hits the shore, driven by the wet wind that knocks great drops from the trees.

"The ocean."

"Ah," she sighs and takes a step toward it. She's overwhelmed with the outside world as much as Tempest still is.

"I will show you the ocean, Agony, Heir to the rule of Ochre's Honour, then I will introduce you to Sire Lev and we will wait for Lady Flay."

There is nothing else to do but wait for Flay and Tempest.

Chapter Twenty-Nine

"Lady Tempest," Lawrence lets himself into Cooper's apartment. His clean white Cooper's shirt glows under the full black apron he wears when hauling stock around. "The full moon is only hours away."

"Yes, Lawrence," Tempest replies.

That it is and she's running out of time.

Her late dinner consists of canned soup and stale crackers, all that's left in Daniel Cooper's barren kitchen. Tempest wears a mid-calf length dress she borrowed from Deirdre's room and a thick pair of socks. Even with the patio doors locked tight against the cold it still sneaks across the floor and since she's in human form her feet don't stay warm.

Something is very wrong with Lawrence. He's agitated one moment and overly friendly the next. Then he leaves her alone for hours with firm instructions to not leave the apartment followed by companionship setting every nerve she has on edge.

"Not 'til dawn," she continues. "But I will start trying the lock after midnight."

Lawrence is an awkward solid object blocking the door. The heavy silver rings he wears make dull clicks as they knock together and have been for days since he can't stop wringing his hands.

"Why Tempest?"

"Pardon?"

"Why did they name you Tempest?"

"Um," she wipes the corners of her mouth with a half-piece of paper towel. "Well, my dame was a royal gryphon and her magic was with the weather. I guess they thought I'd have a similar magic but my dragonkin blood is too strong, I suppose. Other than a fondness for storms…"

She shrugs. Lawrence seems to believe the lie. She can't tell any longer if he trusts her. He doesn't trust anything and turns toward a blank patch of wall. In profile it's clear his chest heaves though not in time with his noisy breathing.

"Take me," he grunts.

"I can't promise Daniel Cooper will be there," she shields her discomfort with him behind a sip of water. "I'm to leave the box if it's deserted."

Lawrence glowers and doesn't try to hide the stink of threat. He's become a dangerous gryphon, driven by whomever tampered with his actions. The small tremors of his hands only still when he resumes tangling his fingers. A menacing growl comes through Lawrence's stiff lips and Tempest does her best to return a smile in spite of his fused tooth plates.

"But I understand you serve him best at his side," Tempest tries to ignore the posturing. His cheeks flush but it fades as he gets some control of himself.

"Yes," he turns and stomps back to the door. "I'll return by midnight."

"Okay, Lawrence."

The thuds of his booted feet track down the hall, followed a minute later by the hum of the elevator. Once it disappears, she waits for silence.

Tempest keeps her eyes and ears pointed in the direction of the elevator, alert for any sign of its return, and goes straight to Cooper's room. The living room clock chimes ten and she squeaks as the bells batter her sensitive gryphon hearing.

Once the ringing clears and she's satisfied she's still alone on the tower's top floor she pulls the dress over her head then lays out her armour. Then she stands on each foot with the other to step out of the socks. With the key and leather piece in hand, she inspects the tall opening. Bless Lawrence for being so thorough. He spent nearly an hour vacuuming every corner of the room so there would be no dust for his pregnant guest to inhale. Now there is no chance of dusty prints or disruptions around the door perimeter betraying her early entry to the room.

She palms the stone plate to disengage the lock and waits for any sign she's been heard.

Then she pushes the door open and strides in.

With purpose, she reminds herself. *In and out like you were never here.*

The box rests on the corner of a worn sleeping mat. In Tempest's memory, the room glows green with the power of the relic. It isn't much larger than her palm. Such a small thing hides unimaginable power. The days of agony under Aledaar's gold relic give her a good idea what this one is capable of except this one isn't the monster its gold companion has become.

The key is long enough to go half way through the box and the lock is far too small to fit but as she touches it to the small hole it expands enough to allow the tip of the key to pass. Before a single flash of green can enter the room, the lid opens and the piece of leather covers the bracelet.

Tempest scoops it up and folds it deep inside the leather while making the packet as thin as possible. As she snaps the box shut the hum of the rising elevator reaches through the open chamber door.

"Oh, crap," she hisses and gets to her feet. Lawrence hasn't been gone very long.

There's no handle on the outside of the stone door with which to pull it closed and her fingertips scrabble at the edge before finding purchase. The door thuds shut at the same moment the elevator comes to a stop.

Tempest tucks the leather packet in the lining of her red leather chest piece. It will be uncomfortable but with it concealed between her breasts at least there won't be a bulge. She returns the key to the thigh pouch on her trousers. Then she pulls Cooper's bathrobe over her bare skin and draws several slow breaths to ease the furious pounding of her heart.

Lawrence lets himself into the apartment as she goes to the bedroom door and turns toward Cooper's private bathroom. She starts walking so he can catch her moving in that direction and avoid giving him any clue she's already been inside the stone room.

"Lady Tempest."

"Goodness, Lawrence," she turns and clutches the robe shut. She can be excused for not hearing him with human ears and the sight of Lawrence winged and dressed for battle is enough to set her pulse pounding again.

"Door," he points at the stone panel she just closed. "Door."

He can't have been gone more than ten minutes and he's returned in full armour. The deep grey chest piece, leggings and helmet draw the colour from his blue eyes, leaving them flat and cold. His fingerless gloves are made of the same thicker and shinier black leather as his knee-high boots. A single, heavy blade rests down the centre of Lawrence's back. It lays still until the nervous twitch of his tail sets it swinging, the jeweled handle moving with it.

Even the soft brown of Lawrence's brows and feathers brings no warmth to him.

"I was going to shower and get a bit of sleep."

"Try the door."

"Not until I'm armoured, Lawrence," she sighs. "Because we're not waiting around for a second before we go."

"Dress then," he says while his fingers work. The urgent rattling of his silver rings troubles her and he exhibits far more agitation than usual. The tendons in his neck swell until the sharp vibration of his grinding teeth sends a shiver over her body. "But then the door."

"Alright," she concedes.

Tempest gathers up her armour and steps sideways to the bathroom since it looks like he isn't going to leave. Feathers flush the sides of his neck before he tilts his head roughly to the side and releases a single gunshot pop of the vertebrae.

"Alright, Lawrence."

Once the door shuts, she sheds the robe and shifts to dragonkin form. The bathroom is so spacious that she could bathe winged and she has more than once.

As she threads her long tail through the slit in the rear of her red leather trousers she draws them up and adjusts the fastenings. Where they once tied neatly below her navel they now ride up a little higher and tie on either side over her hips. As she fusses with the relic hidden in the front of the chest piece, Lawrence bangs on the door.

No comment accompanies the thunks and when they stop the clatter of his rings resumes just a few feet away.

Once she's satisfied the small, precious packet is concealed, she steps out and pushes past Lawrence to sit and get the rest of her gear on.

"Where are we taking it?"

"I won't say, Lawrence," Tempest says, chin up in careful submission. "What if they grab us before we portal?"

He grunts then grasps his grey leather helmet in both big hands as a moan of pain escapes. Whatever he's allowing her to do goes against his programming.

"Okay," she sighs as she pulls her backpack on over her stomach. With the top open she can drop the box inside the moment she's back in the stone room.

Lawrence steps aside and stays close as Tempest places her palm on the stone. With a thud the door opens and she steps in, looking around as if she's never seen inside.

"Ah," she says as she snatches the box up and drops it in her bag.

"Run," Lawrence barks and pulls her from the room before she can close the stone door. Pictures mounted in the hallway are sent flying by their wings as they tear across the heavy carpet. Breaking glass and splintering wooden frames mark their passage.

He pulls the sliding door aside with enough force to jam it open then pulls her into the cold and sends her reeling over the ledge into the Calgary winter night.

Lawrence urges her even faster as they rise and turn south to cross the Bow, the silent channel of dark, running water slashes through the snow. Clear black sky surrounds their flight as he hurtles forward.

"Do it," he shouts.

And Tempest does.

She lights the burn in her back muscles to seed a portal to Welch Peak. It will be deserted and she can use her dragonkin speed to escape Lawrence and make a second portal home. He must want the relic but if that was all he wanted then why didn't he grab it and disable her before she could let her dragon out? The only answer is he wants Cooper as well. As far as Lawrence knows, only Daniel can access the box and he'll take the chance he might be waiting at their destination. She needs a quick getaway on the other side of the portal.

The electric tightness in her body eases as the invisible seed forms a kilometre ahead, just south of the last city lights, though the burn remains. The homes below can't deal with the explosive discharge and she's been taught to avoid it if at all possible.

The portal opens with a snap, its green rim expanding from the fist sized seed to a torn hole much broader than the span of her wings.

"Beneath me," she shouts to Lawrence and he has the sense to draw his wings in so as not to interfere with her flight. Even though her arms don't reach all the way around his bulk and the pack, he's heavy, but not unmanageable. Tempest glides to the portal opening without losing much height.

Just as she readies to transition the portal and drop Lawrence, he wriggles to turn in her arms. Tempest fights to keep their course straight and avoid a fatal contact with the edge of the portal but with her attention split between keeping them alive and Lawrence getting in the pack she doesn't notice what he's really doing until it's too late.

Tempest's wings fall limp as Lawrence gets a hand on her throat.

"Don't struggle," he warns but she does. The skin around her neck burns as he wraps a fine silver chain around it. Before she can get her hands up to fight him, her body becomes heavy in his arms and he takes their weight on his wings. The portal seems suspended upside down before her eyes and everything goes black as it slams shut.

"Don't move, Cherry, unless you want to be unconscious again."

Welch Peak lies ahead, its profile clearly visible from the bare ledge on which Lawrence deposited her. She rocks slightly as he takes the box from her pack.

"The chain around your neck is a gift from Aledaar," he whispers, voice deep with shame. "If you move you'll pass out again.

"No Cooper? No matter. Aledaar will make sure he comes of his own accord."

Lawrence stands.

Tempest can't even move her eyes to look up at him. Her heart and lungs work but nothing else.

"Only a gryphon can remove the chain. It will disable any dragonkin."

"Lawrence," she tries but the moonlit clouds heaped up around Welch Peak fade as her own breath becomes a dull buzz and the chain around her neck threatens to claim her consciousness.

"I hope Aledaar kills me when he's finished with me, Cherry. I really do. The pain is too much to fight. Tell Daniel my spirit is loyal but my will is gone. I'll make sure you're found, I promise."

His feet drag across the broken rock surface then he's gone, wings beating hard as he disappears north-west into the night.

"Lawrence," Tempest whispers a final time as his figure grows smaller, just a dark shape against the deep, silver clouds.

Soar.

Commotion in the main chamber wakes Cooper. Even in his den, the vibration of voices conveys excitement and not a small amount of anxiety. The arrival of nearly fifty green dragonkin the night before, both the young from their deep cave and warriors from Ochre's Honour, packs the Vancouver Island Eyrie to capacity. They are sufficiently guarded so Dame Shadow removed her wards, allowing her to recover some of her energy.

New and familiar dragonkin faces bring back many memories of his own Lady Eve, both of the good times and of her lingering, painful death. The presence of both his children, Fire and Lady Flay, and their eagerness to fight also unlocks even older recollections of Eve, his sweet, brave fighter.

In spite of the excitement, tension grows as the hours pass without word from Lady Tempest.

"The Will."

The words echo down the hall and through the heavy curtain that seals Cooper in his den. He staggers in a one-footed hop while he hurries to dress. It ends in a rough collision with the wall before he's able to get his tail and other foot into his trousers. Then he pulls his tunic on as he hurries through the tunnel.

"Bring her," Soar says as Cooper enters the main chamber. Tundra, of Shadow's guard, takes Fire and the pair disappear into the tunnel leading to the main entrance.

Green dragonkin line the walls, mixing with Lev and Shadow's black armoured guard. Their bodies cast heavy lines through the space as only half the silver lights are lit and the main chamber is still dim for night. It isn't Shadow that Soar has sent for if Tundra is headed out. She's gone and each tunnel surrounding the main chamber is guarded by an equal number of dragonkin and gryphons to keep her location secret. Cooper steps through the guard at the opening to his tunnel.

Almost immediately, Lev turns on his heel and with a snap of his fingers points at Cooper. His blonde hair is tangled from sleep though he's fully armoured and armed including the two long skyblades crossed between his shoulders.

"You, out."

With a nod, Cooper steps back but lingers close enough to see what's going on. When he turns, Lev and Talon are gone from the center of the chamber and stand near the tunnel to the entrance, blending in with the rest of the guard. Whomever Tundra escorts in will have her back to Lev as she faces Soar by a small fire in the center of the chamber.

It only takes a moment for Tundra and Fire to return. They're imposing, striding in, wings arrogantly flared, on either side of a smaller gold dragonkin, a female, he supposes. Only her gold wings and glimpses of her red armour are visible behind Tundra as the three move to the centre of the room and stop ten feet from Soar.

"Welcome," Soar speaks.

As the two guarding the female step aside, her eyes widen as she takes in the room. Cooper looks to see what has alarmed her and finds nearly a dozen crossbows trained on her.

"Oh," she sighs and her breathing settles into tight gasps for air.

Cooper's stomach knots with disgust at Aledaar sending such a young gold dragonkin to face a room packed with heavily armed and extremely seasoned fighters. This dragonkin guarded Cooper's apartment door when Aledaar came for him. If she's stupid enough to try and influence Soar she might very well find herself the recipient of a dozen crossbow bolts. Youth makes her no less dangerous. In fact, her tenuous control of her dragon makes her even more so.

"Sire Lev," she drops to her knees but doesn't offer her wrists, the pose carefully chosen to show respect but not submission. She's uncomfortable showing gryphon style respect and her hands clutch the knee of her red leather armour for lack of anything better to do. "I am Torch of the Council's Will and I ask your assistance in relaying a message."

Soar nods toward Lev but to Torch it must look like he's urging her to continue.

"Sire Lev," she rises but Soar raises a hand.

"I am Master Soar of Sire Lev's guard," Soar says.

"I will speak only with Sire Lev," she's firm but her thin voice rises more like it's a question.

Then Cooper feels the tingle of her influence as she tries to push Soar into taking her to Lev but she won't get anywhere with him. He's immune to her influence and she didn't actually tell him to do anything. Damn, maybe she's just being careful and she's smarter than she looks. If she had ordered Soar the crossbows may have gone off.

Soar's smile broadens and he raises the hand again. When he lowers it the crossbows drop.

"Your influence will not work on me. You may try working your way around the room with it but I doubt you would be allowed."

She swallows, the click in her throat echoes through the room.

"Torch, you may trust Sire Lev will hear your entire message."

"I," she pauses then starts again, lowering her voice. "I am to ask Sire Lev to deliver a message to the exile Daniel Cooper."

Cooper's brows rise with curiosity. *Why would Aledaar think Lev knows where I am?* The question doesn't linger as he realizes the answer. Since Flay and Tempest disappeared with him then Aledaar must believe Lev has heard from Tempest.

"Please, continue," Soar encourages.

"The message for Daniel Cooper is this. The courier from Calgary is in the custody of the Council."

How Soar takes the news without revealing his terror for Tempest is a miracle. Cooper has to steady himself on the wall as he's rocked by the revelation. Not just that Aledaar has the relic but that he has Lady Tempest.

"I shall see it done, Torch," Soar promises as he approaches the gold. She seems to have recovered at least a little from her fear though her lips still curl in quick, nervous smiles. "Now, on behalf of my Sire, please pass along our deepest respects to My Generous Sire Aledaar. Are you sufficiently rested for your return?"

"Yes," she sounds surprised with his courtesy.

"Are you certain?" Soar tries. "You are welcome to rest in safety should you require it."

What is Soar doing? The sooner Torch is gone and they can deal with the loss of Tempest and the relic the better.

"Thank you, Master Soar," she kneels one last time. "I will relay your respects and your hospitality upon my return."

"Safe journey, Torch," Soar nods.

She turns and Tundra takes position at her side to escort her from the eyrie. Once they are out of sight, Cooper steps from his tunnel in time to see Soar drop to his knees. Soar's hands cover his own mouth to ensure his silence and Cooper is tempted to screech in rage on his behalf.

"Hey, buddy," Talon pulls Soar to his feet and the two hurry to Lev, beating Cooper there by only seconds.

"We move now," Soar insists but Lev shakes his head.

"You know she won't be harmed, Soar," Cooper says softly. "Aledaar will want—"

"I know what he'll damned well want."

Soar's children.

"And we will move soon, my friend," Lev assures. "But we will not rush. Whether Aledaar has forced Tempest to open the box or not is moot. If he hasn't then it's only a matter of time and while our friends are here and in Ochre's Honour they are still clear of his reach. This could simply be a ploy to draw us out."

"Sire Lev," Fire interrupts. "When we are certain the messenger has portalled away I will go to Calgary and investigate my sire's home for any evidence to support Torch's claim."

"Torch believed what she said," Shadow's voice rings from the far end of the chamber. "But that does not make it true."

"You," Talon glares at his female. "Should have been a fuck of a long way down the tunnel."

Shadow crosses her arms and pouts, causing Talon to hide his grin of surrender to his mate's charm. Flay is quick to return to Shadow's side and casts Talon a look of 'I had no idea she came out here' in spite of the fact she ordered herself to hide with Shadow. Again, Cooper is struck with his daughter's beauty. With her hair down, Flay looks nearly the same age as Eve was when Cooper first met her.

"Fire," Lev says. It's increasingly difficult to talk as the activity in the main chamber increases in volume and urgency. "Please, bring us what news you can. In the meantime we will prepare to depart. We cannot discount a move on this eyrie so between Shadow's wards and the dragonkin and gryphons left behind, my gryphons will be well protected and we should have sufficient force to take on Aledaar.

"I know most of the Council would never consent to his treatment of the dragonkin without the threat of befalling the same tragedy Torrent set upon this place and Welch Peak and I suspect when we make our move many of his loyalists among the Council will withdraw.

"Our attack is justified and our only enemy will be the Will. We need only give Tempest her chance to take Aledaar's life and the conflict will be over."

"Soar," Fire nods. "I will return within the hour, my friend."

Then he disappears through the crush around the main tunnel.

Cooper stays back, allowing the gryphons and dragonkin to prepare. The eyrie females hurry to provide dried meat and the packets are tucked away in black and brown armour then the departing warriors pair up. Each gryphon is matched with a dragonkin for transportation then half the chamber is emptied to allow the dragonkin to share the rendezvous location among them.

They plan to meet several hours flight from Bolshevik Island. Far enough away they won't be spotted by Will patrols and the crash of the portals will not be heard and close enough to fly in with sufficient energy to fight. Flay goes over the location of the hidden entrance to Aledaar's chamber then Lev, Soar and Talon withdraw to a corner to modify their assault plans considering they now involve freeing Tempest from the dungeon. It's a huge complication and Lev decides to bring six more, three gryphon and three dragonkin, to allow for a dedicated team for that task.

"Soar!" Fire runs in and skids to a stop on the smooth stone floor, head snapping side to side looking for him.

"Soar," he says again and draws him close as Talon and Cooper join them. The chamber becomes quiet and Shadow watches from under Talon's reassuring wing.

"Your apartment is deserted," Fire speaks to Cooper before turning his attention to Soar. "The patio door is open as is that of the stone chamber. The box is gone. There is no sign of Lady Tempest, though there are signs of a struggle."

Shadow folds herself in Talon's wings, her face torn with worry. His lips whisper through her hair as he mutters soft words of encouragement. Though Cooper can't make them out, Talon's tone and loving kindness are enough to ease Cooper's own fear.

"My friend," Lev says softly as he lifts Soar's chin. "We leave."

Chapter Thirty

Inky?

Tempest imagines she sighs since actually doing it will put her under again. The sky is definitely more inky than oily. Through the first hour after dusk she could have sworn it was absolutely oily but as more cold minutes passed she surrendered to the idea of inky. Her second night on the mountain ledge would have found her gryphon form frost-bitten and frozen but as a dragonkin she is surprisingly tolerant of the below zero cold.

Maybe Lawrence never got a chance to fulfill his promise she'd be found before he was taken by the Will.

"Hey!"

Tempest resists the urge to startle at the distant female voice and focuses ahead to where it came from. Dawn wakes the sky behind her and in the distance a flying being speeds toward her and continues to shout.

"Lady Tempest?"

When the female comes close enough, Tempest recognizes it's a green dragonkin dressed in heavy brown armour. Short dark hair peeks out from beneath her helmet, curving up over the edge either naturally or from the wind.

"Oh, no," the female whispers. She smells of the Vancouver Island Eyrie so Soar must have succeeded in enlisting the help of the green dragonkin. "No, no, no, no, no."

Then she reaches for Tempest's throat, fingers extended not in threat but to feel for life. Tempest's alarm isn't that the green might harm her. If she touches the chain then she'll be stuck paralyzed on the stone shelf, slumped over Tempest and waiting for help right there with her.

"Stop," Tempest exhales, barely forming the words with her stiff lips and the green stays her hand.

"Lady Tempest?" she tries again.

"Necklace... no... gryphon only."

The inky sky thickens to oily as consciousness threatens to flee. Stars blur and slide, doubling and tripling with uneasy speed and where the sky is dark it takes on a sickly sheen. When Tempest's vision is again clear the green leans close, studying the chain.

"Ach," Agony's lips draw back in disgust and a sharp shudder rattles her wings as she studies the chain. "I am Agony. We received word you were here and I have come. A gryphon, then? Where the hell am I supposed to get a gryphon?"

As she stands, she turns and her right wing trails over Tempest's shoulder.

"Uhn," Agony gasps as her right side collapses and she stumbles to the ledge. Her limp right wing tangles around her right leg as she lurches even closer to going over.

No, Tempest wills Agony to get control of her lurching two-step.

"Wow," Agony groans as she drops to her knees then falls backward onto her brown armoured butt. "Just wow."

With a heavy shake of her wings, she is back on her feet. The first rays of dawn light behind Tempest bring out the highlights of Agony's deep green leather wings and she stares, fascinated with the gold thread embroidering Agony's heavy belt. Dainty flowers and vines are revealed as the light strengthens. Agony stretches her wings and draws them in, over and over, until the right moves as well as the left.

"Don't. Move."

She turns and points at Tempest. The order is made with such authority Tempest believes she has a choice in the matter and is almost willing to try.

Agony's belt holds two heavy daggers, the gold embroidery covers not only the sheathes but also the straps securing them to her thighs.

The green releases a shrill cry and dives backwards from the ledge. In the silence that follows, Tempest hears the rhythmic beats of her wings as she rises somewhere out of sight and flies away.

By the time the sun hits the top of Welch Peak, a male's shout followed by a rapid stream of insistent curses approaches from the south.

"Female," he shouts and under the brush of Agony's wings on air, leather rubs leather. The male grunts and it becomes clear Agony struggles with him. Feathers rustle then a brown winged gryphon tumbles past.

Hunter?

"What the hell is the matter with you?" Hunter gets to his feet. With only a glance at Tempest he takes an aggressive step toward Agony then two steps back. "You, you, *dragon*."

Agony hisses and a palm sized gob of burning phlegm lands with a splat between Hunter's feet.

"Hey!"

"I am dragonkin, not dragon," Agony spits again. This time Hunter steps sideways to avoid it sticking to his shin. "I am Agony, heir to the rule of Oehre's Honour and you will obey me, *gryphon*, or I'll pull out your feathers and find me someone else."

"That just makes total sense," Hunter mutters. He remains crouched. With his hands spread, he's wary but he hasn't bothered with his daggers. Although Agony is loud and spits fire, Hunter faces her with justifiable caution rather than aggression. It's just like him to be curious about her and the fact she's pretty gives her more leeway with him than Hunter would ever admit.

"Just take the necklace off her and get on your way."

"Is that all? Why don't you rob her yourself? Crazy *dragonkin*. I want no part of robbing a member of the Will."

A third sticky burning ball, larger than the first two, flies at Hunter and the scramble of movement to avoid it is followed by a sigh of concession. With a grunt, he drops on his knees beside Tempest.

"Shit, Cloud?"

"This is Lady Tempest," Agony explains with a large amount of patience. Her words slow as if she were explaining it to a child.

"No," Hunter disagrees. "Why can't you take it off her?"

"It's paralyzed her and me too if I touch it. It won't hurt you."

"You sure?"

The flat sound of a smack on Hunter's leather helmet is his answer.

"Cloud?" Hunter tries as he gives her shoulder a gentle shake. Then his cold fingertips touch her neck as he unwraps the chain. "It's just silver."

The moment Tempest is free of the dark jewelry she draws a sharp breath and straightens her limbs, reveling in the deep and painful full body stretch. Then Hunter gets a hand behind her shoulder and helps her sit.

"Hunter, Agony, thank you."

"Do you know this gryphon, Lady Tempest?"

"Of course she knows me," Hunter spits. "She's my..."

His voice fades and his brow settles into a pained scowl. The events at Sky's eyrie remain far in the past for Tempest but for Hunter it was many weeks of apology on his hands and knees and who knows what else Sky put him through to make amends for framing Tempest for theft. He wears the same anguished frown as when he thought she chose Soar over him. At the time she'd been so caught up in her own personal humiliation she didn't give much thought as to why Hunter was hurt. Hunter's pain gives way to sadness then quickly turns to hope. *Darn.*

"I'm," Tempest takes Hunter's hand and tries again. "I'm his sibling's female."

Hunter's face falls then he forces a smile.

"This is Master Soar's brother?" Agony asks then she laughs. "Of all the gryphons I could have found."

"Found? You kidnapped me."

Hunter digs through his pockets and finds a large packet of dried meat. There's silence for a few minutes as Tempest chews, careful not to bite her tongue as the weakness from the chain fades and her coordination returns.

"Hunter, I found my sire. He wasn't over there in Welch Peak when my dame died. Nor was my sibling," she shakes her wings. "As you can see he isn't gryphon. Tempest is the name I was born with. Did they say why Lev sent for you?"

Hunter shakes his head since he's still recovering from the news about Tempest and Soar.

"I guess we'll fill you in when we get there."

"We need to go," Agony says. "How long have you been here?"

"Night before last," Tempest says around the last slice of dried meat.

"Two nights up here? But you're pregnant for gosh sakes," Agony exclaims.

Tempest gives her a warning glare, desperate to avoid dumping any more bad news on Hunter but the gryphon brightens.

"Really?"

"Yeah, Hunter."

"What's that?" Agony interrupts and grabs Hunter's left wrist, twisting it so she can look all the way around.

"A watch," Hunter gives Tempest a what the hell look. "It tells the time."

"You don't just *know* what time it is? Gryphons are so *hopeless*." Agony casts Tempest a what the hell look. Tempest can't help but laugh.

"Bring the chain, Hunter. Maybe we can use it."

She holds a hand to each of them and together they pull her to her feet.

"Agony, I would be deeply in your debt if you would portal Hunter the rest of the way to the eyrie."

"What? Portal?" Hunter asks.

"Just do what she says," Tempest says. "I'm anxious to see Soar."

"Wait," Agony puts a hand on Tempest's elbow. "Aledaar's messenger said the courier had been captured so Soar and the others have departed for Bolshevik Island. We believed it could only be you in custody."

"Darn," Tempest drops her chin, more than disappointed. "Lawrence, Cooper's guard master, took the box from me and put the chain around my neck before he left me here. He's the courier Aledaar has. The box is gone."

"They left right away," the green says. "We thought Aledaar had you. Then there was another messenger, a gryphon, who said you were here."

"I'll have to hurry to catch up," Tempest rushes through the words in the hopes that giving them speed will get her to Soar faster. "They'll waste time trying to find me. I have to get there before I lose my chance to kill Aledaar."

"Cloud?" Hunter interrupts. "You're worrying me."

Agony continues as if he isn't even there. "Nobody knows where their meeting place is but them. You'd waste energy searching and probably be caught by the Will and locked up or worse yet Lev will make the attack and you won't be there to do your part."

"Why are you dressed like the Will?" Hunter pushes. His head snaps back and forth between Tempest and Agony, impatient with them both. Soar wouldn't have put up with being left behind in a conversation like this although his aggravation would be as tangible as Hunter's. Then Tempest notices he holds her hand and has been since Agony said Soar is gone. Not in a romantic way at all either since his fingers aren't intertwined with hers. He's stepped up to protect her in her male's absence.

"You're being foolish, Lady Tempest," Agony insists. "But I think you're right. Their attack on Bolshevik is based on the belief you're there. We need to consult with Lord Render. He's in charge of the eyrie guard for the time being."

Who is Lord Render? Must be one of the green dragonkin Soar found to help.

"Will one of you tell me what is going on?" Hunter demands.

"I will," Agony says then with a running dive, she's off and airborne.

"Do what she says," Tempest reassures. The poor gryphon is nervous. He's gone from getting snatched out of the sky to voluntarily going with his kidnapper.

"I am happy for you and Soar," Hunter whispers. "I came to care for you at Sky's even though I always felt your spirit belonged to him."

"I'm grateful to have you, Hunter."

Tempest takes off, wings a little stiff, and Hunter has no trouble keeping up. The bright sun is at their backs as they fly in the direction of Welch Peak.

"Oh," Hunter exclaims as Agony's portal cracks open. Tempest's lights the sky half a kilometer further on.

"Fly toward it," Tempest suggests and he changes direction only to be caught in Agony's grip. Hunter shouts until his protests are swallowed by her closing portal.

Tempest flies on to hers but she isn't going home, not quite yet. Nobody can know the relic is safe and she can't take it home. Cooper will sense its presence.

Cold, salty mist greets Tempest as her portal discharges into the Pacific Ocean. She gains altitude and circles until she's certain she's alone. Far below, her chair, her place of solitude, bravely faces the ocean. The natural rock formation waits sixty feet above the surf.

Tempest dives then brakes with a stiff snap of her wings to alight on the small platform. It only takes a moment to fish the small packet out from between her breasts and slip it into a deep crevasse in the rock. Her arm sinks into the stone, swallowed up to her shoulder, before she is satisfied the relic will neither come out or slide in further out of reach.

If something happens to her then the thing will eventually fall into the ocean and that will keep the green dragonkin free.

The wind and waves still long enough for her to whisper a quiet wish before she speeds south, undeterred by her growing fatigue.

The eyrie entrance is busy.

Agony, Hunter, Tundra and an enormous older green dragonkin circle along with several others and Tempest moves to meet them. No words are exchanged in the open and she follows the direction of the big green's sternly pointed finger to the water line where the salt-whitened gap in the stone is hidden by a few defiant trees. The prevailing winds have shaped them so only branches facing away from the water remain.

"Lord Render," Agony kneels and Tempest follows her lead. If Agony is heir to the rule of a dragonkin city and has to kneel to him then there is no doubt Tempest should as well. After a moment, Hunter imitates them though he places himself close enough to Tempest to make it clear he's looking after her.

"Agony," Render says. "Stand my dear and introduce us."

"Lord Render," she nods once all three are on their feet again. "Lady Tempest, daughter of Lord Fury, Master of the Council's Will, and Hunter who is the sibling of Master Soar."

"Fury?" Hunter gasps. "He's a dragon... kin?"

"Sshhh," Agony hisses at Hunter before she finishes. "Lord Render is my dame's sibling. She rules Ochre's Honour."

"We are pleased with your safe return, Lady Tempest, and on behalf of Sire Lev, welcome to the Vancouver Island Eyrie, Hunter."

Hunter nods, open mouthed, and Tempest replies.

"Lord Render," she says as the foursome makes its way to the heart of the eyrie. "I must leave for Bolshevik immediately."

"I do not believe Sire Lev will delay his assault for any longer than needed," he agrees. "And things are more grave than you think."

"Oh?"

They enter the main chamber and Tempest seeks out Shadow and Flay. The pair huddle together by a small fire with Cooper and Firn's daughter, Dove. Dove, like her dame, is a royal gryphon gifted with healing magic and the reason for her to stay behind among such a heavy guard of gryphons and green dragonkin can only be because they expect trouble. Dragonkin, gryphons and their equipment clutter the chamber and a mix of morning meal and unfamiliar spicy smells makes Tempest's stomach rumble.

"Tempest?" Shadow clings to Flay's elbow as she's pulled to her feet and Tempest holds a hand to them to stay put.

"What has happened, Lord Render?"

"Young Torch of the Council's Will returned not a half hour ago. I had half a mind to imprison the child here until the matter with Aledaar is settled. I'm quite certain she is deeply scared and will be of no use to Aledaar when we attack. She can't be more than sixteen summers and will only be killed in the bloodshed. Such innocence—"

"Lord Render," Tempest interrupts.

"Alright," he re-orders his thoughts. "At midnight on Bolshevik Island and every twelve hours after that, Aledaar will order two gold dragonkin to fight to the death until such time as he receives the key to the box."

"You can't take him the key," Shadow says. In spite of Tempest's request for a moment with Render, Shadow and

Cooper have joined them. "To subjugate the green dragonkin is beyond even consideration."

"Dame Shadow," Tempest takes her hands. "Our loved ones move to attack Aledaar because they think I'm there. I must surrender. If I don't then my kin will die at each other's hands, that is certain, and we will lose our chance to free them. They might kill Aledaar but that only means Torrent will take the relic and things there will carry on as they do now."

Shadow pulls her hands free and crosses her arms, fiercely hugging herself between her adornment covered breasts and her belly. As her lower lip begins to tremble, Tempest kisses the tips of her own fingers and touches them to Shadow's mouth to still it.

"I have never asked for a thing," Tempest whispers as she embraces Shadow to hide the shaking of her own hands. "My only wish has been to serve you. To feel your love and to return it a hundred fold. I would be ashamed to be your daughter if I stood by and let lives be taken when I could have fought. When I could have saved even one.

"I'm scared, Shadow, beyond any fear I've ever felt and all I need to get through it without the burden of disobeying you is your pride and your blessing that I do this thing."

"Tempest," Shadow says. Even considering her size, she holds a fierce and powerful bravery in her heart that is an example to all she serves. "I would go in your place, if I could. Come, we'll see to your preparations then I need to rest. Talon's gonna kill me if I can't put up half decent wards."

Tempest laughs, an action that clears her clouding eyes.

"Hunter," Agony says as Shadow and Flay lead Tempest away. "Show Lord Render the chain."

Soar departs Vancouver Island at sunset and arrives in the dark Russian Arctic.

The long hours since darken further, both the sky and the deep worry he feels for Tempest and the coming battle.

Forty gryphons and dragonkin hide in a cold, deep crevasse three hours from Bolshevik Island. Their quarters are cramped and invisible from the gap above but Lev doesn't plan on keeping them there any longer than he has to. Once satisfied their portals hadn't attracted the curious, he sent a single gryphon to fly in close to the ground to assess the activity around the Island.

Until he returns, there is nothing to do but wait which is something Soar isn't good at or happy with. His thoughts are of Tempest and his children and his short temper is worse than usual considering what he's heard about Torrent and how he singled her out for mistreatment. The bastard has it coming and it will be a race between Talon and Soar to see who gets the privilege. The honour will likely be Talon's since Soar and his team of six will go to the dungeon to free Tempest but that doesn't mean Soar won't do his damnedest to get to Torrent first.

Lev will take the bulk of their forces, including Soar's six, in through the front door while Talon and a small group attempt to secure Aledaar after entering the secret passage that leads directly to his chamber.

"One coming in from the south," Talon whispers from twenty feet above.

South?

Soar scrambles to his feet and joins Talon at a small gap in the rock. The gryphon they sent ahead went north to Bolshevik. Anyone coming in from the south is going to be a problem.

As they watch the lone flier approach, the gryphons and dragonkin below fall silent. The seconds tick and after a minute it's clear whoever it is doesn't wear red. The leather is lighter, nearly the same colour as her wings and she's close enough now to see she's female.

"Lev," Soar hisses and the Sire joins them. "One female gold dragonkin."

Lev points at Soar then up and Soar doesn't hesitate to stand alone on the bare rock hilltop. If Lev said hide then Soar would have but they've hidden long enough and he doesn't welcome a return to the tense monotony of the crevasse.

She alights no further than twenty feet away. The gold is unarmed and Soar nods in recognition. He doesn't know her name but he knows who she is.

This female saved Tempest's life back at Skyfall when Soar had nearly killed her with bee venom. She was never introduced and was barely acknowledged by the dragonkin in the city.

"Master Soar," she kneels and holds the position of submission. "I am Lord Fury's sibling."

So much for a name.

"And you found me how?" He doesn't bother with politeness and won't acknowledge there are any more of them than him. If she's not Tempest then she's not free.

"Daniel Cooper sent you here," she states then she smiles. "This place is special to him. It served him and Lady Eviscerate well as a sanctuary many times. I guessed that if Cooper is involved with you then this was a good place to start."

"That doesn't make me feel any better about how you —"

"Lady Spite," Lev says from behind Soar. The Sire steps into the open and is quickly followed by Talon. Soar tries to help Talon get between Lev and the female but Lev firmly pushes them aside. "Stand, my dear friend."

"I have not heard my name spoken in many years, Lev," Spite says but her eyes sparkle with pleasure. Then she shakes a scolding finger. "You risk the wrath of the mighty Aledaar by letting it pass your lips."

"I'll take that chance," Lev laughs. His big hands take Spite's and pull her up before he swallows her in his embrace. "Firn is here."

"I'm pleased to see her again," Spite says. "My heart has ached since I heard of your eyrie's losses. It has been too many years. We must get below and talk. I believe you will want to get on with your task right away and I will join you."

The four disappear back down into the rock. It's unnerving that Spite could even guess what Lev and the others are doing hiding so near to Bolshevik Island. The renewal of acquaintances delays learning the purpose of her visit and although the mood lightens it is quickly replaced with concern.

"Sire Lev," Spite begins as they settle into a corner with Talon, Soar and Firn. "Just a short while ago Lord Fury was recalled to the council by the news that Lady Tempest has surrendered to Aledaar."

"We knew that she'd been captured," Soar says.

"She surrendered minutes before the messenger came for Fury."

Soar glances at Talon and Lev as he rakes his fingers through his hair. Whatever happened to Tempest didn't happen the way they thought but Soar tries to express his version anyway.

"She was captured more than a day ago," he states. The words tumble from his lips, giving away his concern and confusion.

"The gryphon Lawrence acted under the influence of Lord Fury and took the relic from her some time after they left Calgary," Spite explains. "It is he who was captured. When Aledaar found the box sealed he threatened to pit the gold dragonkin against each other in fights to the death until he received the key. Tempest must have heard you thought she was already at Bolshevik and surrendered."

"Damn it," Soar growls.

"Spite," Lev whispers. "You know they will kill you for leaving Skyfall."

"That is my choice, Lev," the gold dragonkin gives her head a determined shake. "I hid in Skyfall because it is the only place Aledaar's order for my capture cannot be carried out. One can only leave voluntarily. I have been there long enough to hear of the death of my mate, to learn my young daughter did not survive Aledaar's trial. My son was killed in Aledaar's service. Some gryphons in the Will feel the dragonkin are expendable and the treachery of their prejudice has taken my family.

"Master Soar," she takes his hands and continues. "I am a free dragonkin, protected from enslavement by my unborn children as Tempest was protected by yours. I will not sit idly by and watch them taken from you. Aledaar will die either by my hand or by Tempest's. I'm not going in case she fails. My intention is to take Aledaar's life if it's the very last thing I do."

Her warm hands squeeze the chill from Soar's cold limbs.

"Tempest will fight to do the same," Soar says.

"I hope so. This task is too important for either of us to have hurt feelings for getting to Aledaar second."

Lev gives a low whistle as the room bursts in to quiet action. Only the sounds of their breathing and the shuffle of metal, feather and leather give any hint of their departure.

"Aledaar knows you have plans with the green dragonkin," Spite says. "He's certain you will move against him, considering he believes he's in possession of the relic. Entrance to Bolshevik will not be easy."

"If they expect us then portalling in close will give us the benefit of surprise over the stealth of being spotted half an hour away," Soar nods to Fire, his transportation.

"Agreed," Lev leaves the crevasse first. The rest depart silently behind him and cluster in the monotonous Arctic wind. There is no fear among the gryphons and dragonkin. Under the green fire of the northern lights, the dragonkin appear nearly as black as the brown winged gryphons. "Portal in right on top of them. There will be blood shed today. Your courage honours our gold dragonkin friends. Let's see them free."

Chapter Thirty-One

Tempest portals to the very spot where she arrived with Fury when she first came to Bolshevik Island. At that moment just as with this one she's deeply aware of the emptiness in her immediate future. Aledaar's trial waited for her then and now she faces one of another sort. She has nothing but her wits with which to get through the next few hours.

It's only an hour to Aledaar's deadline and the frigid dark coats the world in all directions. The Council's mountain is only a few kilometers ahead and the Will's patrols are double their usual size.

It makes sense.

Torch, Aledaar's messenger, couldn't have missed the large number of green dragonkin preparing for battle alongside Lev's gryphons. She understands how Torch felt when she walked into the main chamber of the Vancouver Island Eyrie when it was packed full of warriors. Tempest feels the same way, inadequately prepared to stand alone against Aledaar and the Will.

Her black prisoner's garb was Daniel Cooper's idea and doesn't do much against the cold. She won't be out in the chill for long if the large number of Will guard headed her way is any indication. Black is the colour of both surrender and incarceration and Tempest expects both will come quickly. After that, she can only hope to stall Aledaar until Soar gives her a chance to kill the old Generous Sire. She'll never get close enough on her own.

Several short lengths of the horrible silver chain hide in the sleeve seams of her tunic. The ends are tightly wrapped in a scrap of black cloth so she can safely grip them to pull them out yet they are small enough they shouldn't be detected when she's searched. In tests that Flay volunteered for, a three inch piece was sufficient to disable a dragonkin and rendered her so clumsy she was safer clinging to the floor. The rest of the chain is ground into grit and pressed into the seams of the patch-pockets of her trousers as if it were no more than lint. A small amount of dust will prevent a dragonkin from making a full shift although getting her hands in the stuff to toss it on someone will limit Tempest as well.

A small, old key hangs on a chain around her neck. Even the tiny weight makes her feel top heavy. The key is close in appearance and size to the one Cooper always carried and used more out of habit than for any other reason.

Lawrence believes it's the key that opens the box, Cooper explained as he strung it around her neck. *Not the hand that holds the key.*

As she flies, the key rests against the inside of her tunic and occasionally shifts against the skin of her upper arm. Tiny jolts of cold from the frozen, tarnished brass bring back a little alertness. A day and a half of rest on a mountain next to Welch Peak did a lot of good but the two portals that got her home then to Bolshevik have left her nearly exhausted.

The northern aurora is Tempest's only companion as she circles. In addition to the green and gold ribbons of light, a streak of bloody crimson hangs directly above. A single member of the Will removes himself from the group and approaches. While Tempest recognizes her brother, Con, the lights in the north eastern sky redden.

"Tempest," Con matches her speed and paces her slow circle over the frozen snow. All she knows of her brother is filtered through Flay's love for the gold. He's been cool and distant with Tempest and unlike Fury who's obvious about it when he shows detachment, Con has been completely disinterested in knowing his sister. At least Fury tried to show her affection if only once or twice.

Maybe it's just easier for him than getting to know me and losing me again. Maybe it's easier for me to let him.

"Conflagration," she answers. "I have come to meet Aledaar's demands."

Con turns away.

"You shouldn't have," he whispers. "We can't help you, Tempest. Whatever you think you're going to do here will end in the destruction of the green dragonkin and your death."

"I understand."

"You don't," he barks and for a moment there's a glimpse of their dame, angered and scared, in a fire lit chamber when Tempest was very small. Tempest can't look away as the memory of the cries of slaughter echo about her ears. "I'm happy to die here, fighting at Aledaar's order, if it means my Lady Flay remains free. You will give Aledaar the one thing he needs to enslave her and his power over me prevents me from doing anything about it."

"What if I—"

"What if you what?" Con tilts his head toward the Council's mountain. "Stop him? You're naive and foolish."

"Con," Tempest completes her last circle and glides toward Bolshevik Island. "You don't speak for everyone here."

Fatigue fuels second thoughts and she considers fleeing. The next few beats of her wings barely keep her level and she might not remain high enough to make the entrance. Heck, she doesn't even have the energy to portal away.

It's impossible to tell if his silence indicates concession or continued disagreement.

"Perhaps you're right," Tempest admits.

Soar's scent is long gone from her skin after the days apart. The warmth of the fire she started in his den faded leaving her with nothing but bravery with which to face

Aledaar. Even the ten days they spent alone in the cool, fragrant forest after mating are so distant that Tempest's only proof is their growing young hidden in her shameful black clothes.

For them, she decides. That responsibility is enough. *Not for Con or Flay or even for myself. Not for all the dragonkin but just for two.*

Tempest's thoughts keep her from noticing the six members of the Will as they take their places around her, above, below, on either side and in front and behind. She's watched from all directions and there is nowhere to go but forward in the small box of airspace they've left her.

There is no further chance to talk to Con, to reassure him Flay is safe or even to reassure herself that anyone she left behind will be protected and she isn't certain he wants to hear. Shadow's wards and the heavy presence of gryphon and dragonkin guard should be enough.

She isn't restrained when they land at the main entrance, nor is she spoken to. Her guard steers her forward, completely surrounding her as they did in the air. Con lingers behind, leaving her alone with the large gryphons. They press in against her as the tunnel narrows for the last forty feet to the Council's main chamber.

A sharp pain in her left thigh sends her stumbling. No hand moves to steady her and as she extends her arms to catch her balance they are slapped down. When she recovers her footing and presses her hand to the muscle there is no stickiness of blood on the fabric but the deep tenderness hints at a painful bruise. The gryphon to her left looks straight ahead.

They emerge into the empty main chamber.

Normally at least a few members of the Grand Council are present regardless of the time but tonight it's empty. She could force the guards to free her but five would teach her silence before she could influence a second. They cross the chamber in formation, avoiding the sacred space at its center. One doesn't step into the center of the room unless blood will be spilled on the stone floor. Then they walk under the gold and red drapes hanging from the ceiling and covering large sections of the walls. The fabric is as still as the room is empty.

Tempest closes her eyes for a moment. Her heartbeat, like those of the gryphons around her, is swallowed in the heavy crimson curtains along with the solid thuds of their boots. She silences her heart and doesn't give a damn if it's seen as threat. The last thing she wants is her courage to be silenced by the big empty space along with the sound of the vital rush of life through her body.

As they reach the brief flight of stairs to Aledaar's private chamber, she silences her breathing and earns a growl from the big gryphon to her left. He's one to keep an eye on. Tempest didn't have much to do with him during the few months she served Aledaar since he was one of the overly prejudiced who even avoided Fury.

The dimness of Aledaar's chamber confines them in the absence of the silvery wall lights. Two small fires on either side of Aledaar's gold chair cast angular shadows. Lit from below, dark and light cleave his face to match his portrayals of both boredom and menace.

Torrent looms nearby, several feet away from Torch who kneels with her bottom resting back on her heels. It's the only position of rest a dragonkin is permitted near Aledaar. For a moment she meets Tempest's eyes, the gold light in them flares, and Tempest can make out the young gold's fear. Tempest can't place what she fears until a sudden movement by Torrent causes Torch to flinch.

God, not her. Has Tempest's absence from Bolshevik turned Torrent's aggression on Torch? Due to her age and lack of training as a ranger, she serves Aledaar as a page or errand runner. She knelt in the same spot when Tempest was first brought in and tortured with Aledaar's necklace. Tempest remembers her as a shadow against the wall through the first minutes of her trial before she followed Aledaar from the chamber, leaving Tempest to suffer with nobody but Flay to get her through.

"Ah," Aledaar sighs. "Lady Tempest, I'm intrigued to see you before me."

"My Generous Sire Aledaar," Tempest drops to one knee, wrists up. "I have come to meet your demand."

"Search her," Torrent orders but he doesn't wait for the gryphons surrounding Tempest to move. He pushes several aside before jerking Tempest up by her elbows. It only takes a small flare of her gold wings to keep her balance even though Torrent drops her with an unnecessary shove backward. His hands start over her shoulders and his fingers dig in as he covers every inch of her upper body, then each leg and finally her arms.

Tempest remains passive throughout the disgusting touching since fighting would only please Torrent.

"As Lawrence claimed," Torrent says and rests a hand on the small roundness of her stomach. "Her life is forfeit but two will take her place."

She hisses so only Torrent can hear and he answers with a cold growl. While the gash Talon left in Torrent's upper lip appears as little more than a cut when his mouth is closed, it splits half an inch from the corner of his mouth revealing some of his teeth when he smiles.

Torrent grabs the collar of her tunic and pulls, digging the back into her neck while tearing open the front to expose her scaled adornment. Then he grabs the string holding the key and yanks. The string cuts in to Tempest's skin before it snaps with an anti-climatic *pop*.

The smile of satisfaction on Aledaar's face drives dark shadowed lines up his cheeks and obscures the gleam in his eyes.

"Put her aside," he orders and Torrent tosses Tempest toward Torch. "Bring Master Lawrence."

Torch shuffles sideways enough to avoid being shoved into the wall by Tempest but the girl keeps a wing and arm out to give a measure of gentleness to Tempest's landing.

"You," he points at Torch. "Fetch Master Fury from Skyfall."

"My Generous Sire," Torch bows and hurries from the room to stay well ahead of Torrent who leaves in her wake and takes the dark passage to the dungeon instead of following her through the main chamber.

"Dragonkin," Aledaar whispers. His mouth opens as if to say something then snaps shut without uttering another word. The old gryphon appears immeasurably pleased with himself. The six gryphons who escorted Tempest into the chamber remain, three on either side of the door. The only movement comes from the fires then Aledaar hooks one foot under his chair and pushes the box forward until it rests several feet in front of him.

"I have never seen the green relic though I can imagine its beauty and power rival this one," Aledaar stands and unfolds the front of his white robes to expose the gold relic. If he knows how Tempest avoided losing her will to the thing, he must know she can free the golds. Maybe he doesn't or maybe he feels safe enough considering the guard present and Tempest's lack of weapons. Either way, she'll only get one chance and Aledaar's arrogance gives her a measure of hope.

Lawrence isn't restrained when he arrives with Torrent although the big bald gryphon looks worse than beaten. His hands hang in limp curls at his sides, barely swinging in time with the shuffle of his feet.

...my spirit is loyal but my will is gone. Lawrence said when he abandoned Tempest on the rock shelf near Welch Peak. *I hope Aledaar kills me when he's finished with me, Cherry. I really do.*

Even Lawrence's spirit has faded, withered by the pain of resistance. It's only been two days since she last saw him and the once strong and fearless gryphon's forced betrayals have left him with nothing but shattered pride evident in every move.

"Lawrence," Aledaar claps his hands together, friendly and coaxing as if Lawrence were a reluctant child. "We have a visitor."

Lawrence raises only his eyes, first to Aledaar then they roam around the room before they find Tempest. He mashes his swollen lids shut then seems to use the last of his strength to push them open. The bruises are the same dark shade as his prisoner's garb.

"Welcome," Lawrence nods before his eyes lose focus.

"Lawrence, it's me," Tempest says but the gryphon is lost again, staring into the middle of the room. If he even saw her he doesn't seem to know who she is. Darkness centers about him even though the biggest shadows are cast on the walls.

"Lawrence," Aledaar coos. "Take the key and open the box."

Torrent dangles the key before Lawrence's nose, swinging it side-to-side so it catches the light.

No, Tempest fumes at the sickening display of humiliation. Forcing Lawrence to surrender the bracelet he'd protected with his life for so many years is exceptional in its cruelty but she doesn't expect anything less of Aledaar.

"Oh, no. I..." Lawrence crumbles to his knees and tries to scream against the pain that resisting Aledaar causes. The weak cry is nothing more than a hoarse whisper as he crushes his head between his giant hands. Lawrence doesn't even get them out to arrest his fall when Torrent shoves him toward the box and there is a soft thud as his head hits the floor. A small pool of blood forms as Lawrence pushes himself up. Crimson drips from his forehead and nose as he reaches for the key.

"I can't," he moans but in spite of his protests he crawls toward the box. "Please..."

"That's it," Aledaar croons and Lawrence falls on his belly as he reaches for the box. The weight of his own wings is too much for one weakened arm to hold up. After several painful tries, the key finds the small hole at the same moment Torrent kicks Lawrence in the ribs. Tempest jumps, the sound of bone snapping isn't masked by Lawrence's agonized grunt.

"Try again," Aledaar suggests but Lawrence's next attempt is hindered by a boot placed in a soft spot just below his ribs. Torrent's long feathers snap the air as Lawrence's body stops the forward motion of his kick. The prone gryphon curls in a ball even as his legs try and kick him toward the box.

"Stop," Tempest shouts as she impulsively pushes her will at Torrent. "Stop."

Torrent freezes, one foot drawn back in preparation to strike Lawrence again, then he puts it down and stares at Tempest in anger and confusion.

"No more," she whispers and hurries to Lawrence. She ignores Aledaar's raised palm which she first thinks is an order for her to stay put. When the six red-armoured gryphon guards hold their position she knows the instruction is for them.

"Please, free him," she begs Aledaar. With Lawrence's shuddering body in her arms it's nearly impossible to stop him from kicking his way closer to the box. Tempest wraps a hand around Lawrence's to steady it as he spears the key at the box, pushing it sideways. One of the dragonkin, probably Fury, used his will on Lawrence and forced him to follow Aledaar's orders. He's as helpless as any of the golds under Aledaar's control. "It isn't the key, My Generous Sire. It's the hand which holds it. Release him from your will and I will open the box."

"Ah," Aledaar sighs. "The exile Cooper was clever but in the end his corpse will rot with yours and any others who defy me."

Soft sweat beneath Tempest's tunic makes it cling to her skin as she fights Lawrence. Even the dungeon-induced chill from his cold skin isn't enough to cool her. Soft sobs break up his difficult breaths and make her heart ache. They couldn't do more to break Lawrence's spirt than they've done already.

"Lawrence, you are of no more use to me. I release you," Aledaar hisses and Lawrence's immediately stills in

Tempest's arms. His breathing eases though pain still sends the air whistling through his tight throat.

"Don't," Lawrence gasps but he doesn't have the strength to fight as she eases the key from his shaking fingers.

Tempest's own tired hand drops the key to the stone floor before she can co-ordinate her fingers and thumb enough to point the small piece of metal at the lock. She slides the key home and after the tiniest of turns the lock yields with a soft snap.

"Kick," she orders Lawrence as she does the same. At first he doesn't move but when she repeats the command with a strong dose of her will he obliges. It can't be wrong to influence him to protect him, can it? The idea doesn't make Tempest feel any better about manipulating him with the same magic from which he had just been freed.

Soar, where the heck are you?

The crack of several discharging portals reaches her ears as she and Lawrence drag themselves up against the wall but Tempest's relief doesn't last long. There aren't enough closing portals to be Soar and the number of dragonkin they need to have a chance against the Will. No more than four have arrived and with her weariness and attention on Lawrence she didn't hear the gryphons and dragonkin arriving in the Council's main chamber. The shuffle of boots and occasional brush of metal on leather tell her the Will is gathering.

"Lord Fury," Aledaar calls. The old gryphon rises and takes the box from the floor before turning and placing it on the gold chair. His eyes don't leave the time-smoothed wood and Tempest prays he doesn't notice the absence of green light flowing from between the bottom and lid and what it really means. She needs every second she can give to Soar.

Fury strides in, pushing the gryphon guard aside. Con is close behind him and Torch slides past, kneeling briefly in Aledaar's direction before taking position next to Tempest. Aledaar doesn't notice the deep anger Fury casts at his daughter nor the disappointment on Con's face. Fury comes to a sudden stop. His axe sways, creaking against his leather trousers and for a still moment it's the only movement in the room.

"If you would be so kind, Master Fury," Aledaar's voice is barely a whisper. "Bring me that foul green bitch Flay. I believe she is in Lev's eyrie and she will come. It is time we used Conflagration's life to motivate her, yes?"

"My Generous Sire," Fury grunts before he turns his back on Tempest. He doesn't spare her a glance. Bringing Flay will spare the life of Fury's son, Tempest's brother and there is no doubt Aledaar will carry out the threat against Con if Flay doesn't come. It's a task he could have sent Torch for but instead he displays dominance by sending Fury to bring another member of his kin for enslavement.

Tempest shudders. She knows her dear friend won't hesitate to come.

"You did this," Con growls. He dives for Tempest and Lawrence only to be restrained by the gryphons at the door. His gold eyes grow in brilliance in spite of the knife at his throat.

"Shut up," the gryphon who hit Tempest in the leg barks at Con. Con quiets but doesn't stop his struggles.

Aledaar kneels before the box. He raises the gold relic to his lips and whispers before kissing it then he leans forward, hiding the box from Tempest's sight. The soft vibration of the hinge opening is quickly followed by the snap of it dropping shut and Aledaar jolts in disbelief before opening it a second time.

"Fury!" he roars and Tempest pulls Lawrence closer. "Where is the relic, Tempest?"

If Tempest could sink into the stone floor she would but she's pinned between Lawrence and the wall. Aledaar spins to his feet, the heavy gold relic swings across his chest and his wings knock the empty box to the floor before he stops and exposes his teeth to Tempest.

"No answer?" Aledaar asks and Con curses in surprise at the sight of the empty box.

"My Generous Sire?" Fury calls from the entrance. He doesn't fail to see there is no relic.

"This traitor," he spits at Tempest then he calms as he considers his next words. "Has confessed that she came to assassinate me on the order of Sire Lev."

He knows why I'm here.

Aledaar's thin smile spreads as he pleases himself with the scenario. Everyone in the room knows it's a lie, at least on Aledaar's part since it's really the truth, yet none contradict him. Even Fury remains stone-faced at the accusations brought about his daughter.

"I will have the Sire and Dame of Vancouver Island dead and the exile Daniel Cooper in chains at my feet."

"No," Tempest whispers. Even with Shadow so well protected, they can't hold out against a full assault by Fury and the Council's Will for long.

"As you will," Fury nods then departs. He's no more than a few paces out the door when Tempest's skin tingles with the ominous potential of a portal opening overhead. High above through dozens of feet of cold stone, a small rend in the sky appears. The growing power of the destination end of a portal charges everything beneath it, including her.

"Oh," Torch moans. She feels it.

Danger.

Both dragonkin instinctively tense their portalling muscles to resist the discharge they sense coming from right above. It isn't much protection but through the stone it might be enough. If they were in the open they'd have to flee or be cooked when the portal closes. When Torch cries out, Tempest knows Render's instincts about the young gold are true. She is untrained and untested and will only serve to slow an attacker for her last few breaths. Tempest's own stand against Torrent a decade earlier is proof of that.

As Tempest's skin crawls through the final second before the portal opens she reaches in her left sleeve and pulls out two pieces of the silver chain. If one will make Torch a stumbling drunk then two should knock her flat.

The mountain shakes with the simultaneous discharge of several portals. The cacophony deafens them to all but their own cries as the electrical charge ignites the silver wall lights. For a moment the room is lit in blinding white, just long enough for Tempest to see the gryphons lose their footing. The big one who hit her in the tunnel drops to his knees before collapsing over on his side.

Torch reaches for Tempest. Tempest uses her index finger to pull back the terrified young dragonkin's collar before dropping the two pieces of chain down the back of her red leather armour. She goes limp, falling against the wall before sliding sideways.

The lights brighten in timid, uneven bursts until most explode, leaving a single flickering silver glow on the wall above her head.

"Play dead," Tempest wills Lawrence as the mountain yields under its strongest and final shudder.

Chapter Thirty-Two

"Climb, Soar!" Fire shouts.

No shit.

Soar rights himself. Portals discharge all around, driving down brilliant green bolts of electricity. The heavy stink of ozone assaults with every breath as he does what Fire says. Each portal burns another messy yellow streak across his vision. None run straight up or down since he rolls and tumbles to stay clear of new portals opening above. More than once he dodges the stationary green fire of the aurora in his half-blind attempts to avoid the lightning.

The first problem isn't dodging the bolts. Rock and ice explode below as portals ground, punishing Aledaar's mountain. Jagged stone shrapnel bounces off his armour and passes through his flight feathers. They portalled in very near the mountain and Soar fell much closer as he got his bearings. More dragonkin arrive above and Soar beats his wings to follow Fire's voice. The clash of weapons and cries of attack already compete with the dragonkin thunder.

Then, instead of flying higher, Soar moves in the direction of the battle. It's a hunch but it makes sense that the most intense fighting takes place at the main entrance. Shit, judging by the crush of bodies tangling together in the air it looks like the Will was on the move.

"Dungeon is through the rear of the main chamber," Fire swoops close and barks in a hurry-up kind of voice. With his daggers drawn above his clawed hind feet, he engages a red armoured gryphon. Fire didn't tie his hair back before they departed the crevasse and in the lights of the aurora and discharging portals it's as green as the waves of scales rippling over his skin.

"I know," Soar mutters in order to keep annoyance out of his voice then realizes it's Fire's way of expressing good luck. Soar tightens his grip around the handles of his own blades. He'd be a fool to dive in unarmed and flies through the hole Fire made in the melee to reach Tundra. The gryphon is cut near his elbow but the blood is already tacky and losing its gloss. "Where are the others?"

Tundra shrugs and takes his place behind Soar, as close as he can get without causing them to foul each other's flight. A green dragonkin takes station at Soar's other shoulder, bringing his team of six up to half-strength. Soar feels the presence as scent and a slight adjustment of the airstream since the green's silent flight smooths out Soar's turbulence, speeding all three up as they get closer. The entire exchange and forming up take a split second, enough time to leave Fire behind as he drops his first kill and moves on.

Each death will be grieved. Every dead fighter will be honoured and the sooner Soar gets Tempest to Aledaar the fewer will die.

The front stoop, where Soar spent hours waiting for Tempest only to be so matter-of-factly dumped, is bottlenecked. A quick glance over his left shoulder tells him the green is Shatter, another relation of Cooper's through the gryphon branch of his family tree. Since the skies have quieted with the arrival of the last of their forces, individual battles have spread allowing Lev's forces to co-ordinate their assault.

Damned fast but not fast enough.

The disorganized Will reacts more to the appearance of so many gryphons and green dragonkin than puts up a formal defense.

Soar curses but doesn't pull up short of landing. Instead, he roars and draws a pause from nearly everyone blocking the door. Everyone but Lev, that is. He knows Soar's call as well as Soar knows his. Most of their forces battle the Will outside in the air and on the rocks and the bookend guards engage Lev and one of his gryphons. Choking dust and the flurry of blades and wings block Soar's view of the tunnel. Grit gathers in the corner of his eyes and crunches beneath his boots. Larger chunks of stone still fall from the ceiling and litter the floor. They're lucky the portals didn't bring the mountain down.

"Ass inside, Soar," Lev barks. The flash of his long, slim skyblades outlines a twelve foot wide danger zone around the Sire. He flips one of the big blades around and lands the pommel in his adversary's gut. The gryphon instinctively drops his wing to protect his flank and exposes the tunnel entrance. "My grand-daughter."

The ranger with which Lev fights is good, nearly as fast, but slows a little too much to assess two heavy dragonkin who drop down to land behind Soar. Lev doesn't turn to look and takes advantage. As Soar rushes into the tunnel, blood bubbles in the Will gryphon's throat and he's hit with the cool spray of blood. He's close enough that the Arctic air didn't have enough time to turn it to icy crimson powder.

With Tundra and Shatter on his heels, Soar makes for the main chamber. Back-up be damned. He'll get to Tempest if he has to kick her cell door down and it's all for nothing if Aledaar isn't in the mountain. The golds will fight to the death until Aledaar's spell is broken and some Will gryphons, perhaps, long after.

A half-shifted gold holds position at the end of the tunnel. Parts of him remain somewhat human, such as his distorted, scale covered face. Bands of glimmering gold strobe across his features, a mesmerizing warning thick with the promise of danger. One or two winged shapes move behind him, silhouettes of silver light and shadow cutting through the airborne dust. Tundra turns as he brings up his crossbow and

Soar prepares to charge. His wrists loosely cross and he fists his daggers in a blades down position ready to use his weight to put them through the gold's skull. A quick kill will prevent the gold from using Tundra as a weapon.

Before Soar can get ahead of Tundra and Shatter to open his wings enough to launch upward, a head-sized ball of flaming pitch roars over Soar's shoulder, singing his skin and feathers. It impacts the gold squarely in the chest and drives him back. At the same time, a second flame appears above the fire and grows with incredible speed. Believing the gold is about to immolate before his eyes, Soar eases his pace only to be knocked sideways by Shatter, hard enough to take Tundra down with him.

The fireball grew because it closed in, not because the gold made it bigger, and Soar curses himself for falling for the illusion. He'd nearly taken it in the face.

"Shit," he mutters as he and Tundra ball up on top of each other.

Sparks and sticky flaming dragonkin pitch explode as the green takes the fireball full-on. Their armour bears most of the damage but Soar's skin stings at his elbows and everywhere else he isn't covered.

"That's," Tundra sputters as Shatter charges past, unleashing a stream of flame at the gold. Pieces of his deep brown armour fall to the tunnel floor as his dragon form expands so quickly that the leather tears free from his green scaled body.

Then a second shifting, naked green bolts after him. Soar can't tell who it is.

Name tags, he decides before he can clamp down the wild thought. *Next time, fucking name tags.*

"On fire," Soar finishes and focuses on their current status while the greens get the gold out of the way. He scrapes pitch from Tundra's armour with his dagger and shoves his other in Tundra's hand to do the same for him.

"Fuck," he exclaims as another errant ball of flame brushes past, striking the wall on the opposite side of the tunnel.

"This what happened in your den?" Tundra's voice doesn't betray any nervousness but the joking does.

"Better than this," Soar answers. He's just as unhappy about jumping into a fire fight and allows Tundra the remark. Under any other circumstances he'd knock him on the chin for a jab like that. Shit, maybe not. The big gryph is only curious and Soar feels more than a little proud that his female can breathe fire. "Let's go."

Tundra stifles a chesty cough and spits. Nothing as spectacular as what Shatter let loose but the acrid stink settling in Soar's own lungs suggests they'll be hacking the stuff up for days.

They pause at the entrance to see the two greens engaged with two golds. All four are fully shifted and shake off the heavy flame with which they bombard each other as their sharp talons strike and slash. Through the dust and smoke he can make out a pair of guards at the other side, blocking the tunnel that leads to the dungeons and several others cluster at the door to Aledaar's chamber. Their attention turns to the inside of Aledaar's chamber and they ignore the dragon fight behind them. Some of the heavy red and gold drapes burn and the crash of a green impacting the wall brings down more dust and a ball of flaming fabric.

"Just like in my den," Soar exaggerates and earns a wild grin from Tundra. "I can handle this."

"How the hell do we get around without stepping into the center?"

The circular array of white tiles about fifteen feet across is more sacred to the gryphons than anywhere else. Gryphons believe it marks the spot directly overhead where the first Sire and Dame fell to earth when they were cast out by the Gods.

"That way."

Soar chooses the route that brings him closest to Aledaar's chamber since the fire and fighting dragons hold to the other side of the room, at least for the time being. If they stay wide of the stairs and keep it quick and quiet they should avoid catching the attention of the gryphons in Aledaar's chamber. Conflict continues inside but the guards at the door are content to watch. Aledaar's laugh floats through the smoke as Tundra and Soar get going. With an eye on the flaming drapes above they hustle, dodging a fiery curtain just as they reach the stairs.

The tunnel from the main entrance erupts in fire and Soar and Tundra draw back to the wall at the edge of the wide, curved stone steps.

"Go," Soar pushes Tundra toward the guarded rear door, urging him forward. Either it's Lev and the green dragonkin coming to cover his back or it's the Will in which case they need to haul ass.

The chamber shudders and the pair hug the wall as their shadows race ahead, growing in the strengthening fire light.

"Here there be gryphons," a deep voice rumbles from the direction of the entrance and Soar knows time is short.

No more safe passage bullshit, dodging fireballs and fighting dragonkin. Lord Fury is close behind, each heavy footfall causes the stone walls to exhale another gasp of dust. The distinctive sound of Lev's shout from inside the tunnel spurs Soar on but he only makes it a few steps before the massive dragonkin lord has him pinned on top of Tundra.

Shit.

Fury hauls Soar to his feet. His hands shift into huge claws and in the fire, his entire scaled, dragonkin body shimmers in the constantly changing light. Tundra disappears in the direction of the dungeons and Shatter, back in his naked dragonkin form, joins him. Over Fury's shoulder, Lev's blades cut through the smoke, mixing with a crush of bodies.

A female's pained scream filters through the smoke and Soar's stomach drops in reaction to his female's agony. It comes from Aledaar's chamber and Tundra and Shatter have disappeared to the dungeon, leaving Soar alone to get through Fury and to Tempest.

"Tempest," Soar calls but his voice cuts out as the big gold tosses him aside. He rolls but it isn't enough to stop the hard expulsion of air when he hits the stone floor. At the same time a pair of dragons tumble past, a mix of green and gold that lands on Soar's wing and pins him down long enough for Fury to catch up. For a moment the rich musk of dragonkin blood overpowers the smoke.

"Master Soar," Fury breathes as he lands on Soar, straddling his hips, and grasps his throat with his massive, serrated talons. Spots grow over Soar's eyes as Fury begins to choke him out. Fury's thighs are in the way and he can't reach his daggers so he digs his weakening fingers in to Fury's hand to relieve the pressure. The sharp cries and clashes of metal that fill the chamber ease to a rushing blur as even the most brilliant fire fades to a dull grey.

"You disrespect me, my daughter, and my kin, gryphon," he hisses. "So easy to bring down."

At the moment Soar can't agree more in spite of the fact he isn't built for tolerating such extremes of heat and smoke while a two hundred and eighty pound dragonkin keeps the air from getting where he needs it.

"Aledaar doesn't know Tempest can free us by killing him. He thinks she's only here to protect her kin, not to kill him," Fury's voice becomes an intimate whisper as the pressure on Soar's throat lessens. "He's never asked so I've never had to tell. But I know and I can't fight the order to protect the old bastard with my life.

"All you have to do is stop me from killing my daughter," Fury finishes as his hand withdraws. "And I might find some respect for you."

Soar tries to offer a solid *fuck you* but his first gasp of air is accompanied by grit, smoke and an unforgiving burn. Then he's on his feet, cursing, and stumbles backward toward the stairs and Tempest.

"You got it," Soar spits. His numb hands find his daggers but he doesn't trust himself to not drop the blades to the floor so he doesn't draw them, not yet. The battle at the main tunnel has spread, gryphons matched with gryphons and dragonkin fight each other. Several charred and bloody bodies litter the floor, as still in death as the fighting around them gives a bold demonstration of movement and life.

Until Soar recovers enough to fight, he has no choice but to keep his distance from Fury.

"I'd like to see how a *competent* dragonkin lord fights," Soar goads as he steps aside. The remark retaliation for Fury's insinuation back in Skyfall that Soar is nothing more than a competent ranger.

Fury growls, releasing smoke between his teeth and shifts his weight to hide his agitation.

Each passing second sharpens Soar's vision. Several agonizing cramps tear through his large muscles as they embrace the smoke tainted oxygen that fills his lungs but they pass quickly, each weaker than the last, until he feels about as good as he's going to get.

Fury removes the axe from his belt and swings it, rotating his wrist. The impossibly heavy head circles at the gold's side. It weighs so much that Fury has to compensate by widening his stride.

Even with Fury so close, Soar's task is to protect Tempest and not only from her sire but from all the Will. He backs away, feeling the steps one at a time as the dragonkin lord closes in.

Chapter Thirty-Three

The white wall behind Tempest scorches from the portals' discharge since the dragonkin side of the room takes most of the damage. Their physiology keeps them conscious and though the ache in Tempest's portalling muscles is far from pleasant, it restores a small measure of her energy. Lawrence breathes though his unfocused, half-open eyes suggest he's out cold. The rock diffused much of the electricity then the rest chose the easy path through her and spared Lawrence.

"Chain her in the dungeon," Aledaar growls to the two gryphons still standing then turns to Con. "With me."

Aledaar kicks at the empty wooden box, flaring his dirty, white robes. The next swing of his foot connects and sends it flying into the curtains behind his chair.

"No," Tempest growls. If Con portals Aledaar away from Bolshevik she might never find him. She can't blame Con. He has no choice but to be her enemy. She can't get past three gryphons and a dragonkin or count on a miracle from Soar and Lev. Only Aledaar's death will stop Fury from going after Shadow.

Tempest pushes back the powerful flush of nausea. Right now it's her and it just has to be done. Years of Soar's words in the training chamber, so much like Sky's, force Tempest into a state of calm.

Without taking her eyes from the two big gryphons, she feels for Torch's thigh and releases the young gold's dagger. The blade seems solid enough but the weight and small handle makes it feel useless. Again, Tempest's stomach lurches with disgust at Aledaar. Even if Torch had an idea what to do with it, she wouldn't stand a chance with the weapon. For Tempest, it's better than her bare hands.

Tempest dodges their lunge. Her smaller female frame and thinner wings give her a defensive advantage. Not much, but it helps. If all she had to do was fight, she could let her dragon free but her task requires focus and control. Beneath the surface, her agitated dragon isn't likely to allow her either.

"Torch," Aledaar barks. "Portal Torrent."

The young female draws a single, tight breath of obedience before the pieces of chain steal her awareness.

"Never mind," Torrent barks as he moves to follow Aledaar and Con. "There will be another gold."

Darn, Aledaar can't leave. Everything depends on the opportunity these minutes grant Tempest. She assesses her chance of succeeding with an armed rush but with Con and the three gryphons in the way there is no hope. Not yet.

"Don't move," Tempest wills the nearest gryphon. As long as she keeps one of them between herself and the other she'll only have a single adversary with which to concern herself. If she gets between them then she's in trouble.

He stops, allowing her to step around his still body and use him as a shield against the other then Torrent moves in her direction blocking her path to Aledaar.

"Stop," she pushes her will at Torrent, more in reaction to his menacing approach than as a result of a logical strategy. The moment she does, she frees the first gryphon from her will. If she had time, she could force a lasting thrall on him as was done to Lawrence but with only a moment to prepare he slips from her control. He seizes her wrist in his gloved hand and forces it up toward her raised wing. She has no choice but to center her focus back on him if she wants to keep hold of the knife.

"Torrent," Aledaar doesn't look back as he dives beneath the curtain with Con close behind.

The first real pain of battle appears in Tempest's wrist as the gryphon twists it then spins her, overextending her shoulder back over her gold, leather wing. As she opens her mouth to speak, he takes hold of her jaw and clamps it closed by digging his long fingers into her cheeks. The dust stirred up by their wings burns inside Tempest's nostrils as they flare to allow precious air. Then a second breath welcomes the scents of dragonkin pitch and fire.

They're inside!

Tempest shakes her head free and cries out, both to alert whomever has fought their way into the Council's main chamber and in pain as the gryphon's fingers score bruising welts in her skin.

"Tempest," Soar's voice passes through the growing smoke. Beneath the rough throaty growl, the single word is rich in strength and sheer protectiveness.

Before she can reply, a small, painful explosion lights up beneath her collarbone. Torrent's laugh draws her attention. The scarred monster pulls something that looks like one of Lev's cigarillos from his lips. The short, brown stick points at her, revealing it to be a hollow tube. Then his tongue plays at the tear in his top lip.

"The dart will keep you quiet, my pet," he leers then he's gone behind the curtain. "The next time we meet you will feel real pain."

No, Tempest screams. Her mouth opens but no sound passes her lips. Deep in her chest, the burn grows as the two gryphons drive her toward the corner between Lawrence and the stairs.

Outside, in the main chamber, the noise builds as the two gryphons charged with taking Tempest to the dungeon draw closer. Their heavy breathing fades under the clash of weapons and the thuds of heavy bodies. Even the hiss of fire from dragon throats makes it into Aledaar's chamber along with the accompanying thick smoke. Dragonkin flame doesn't bother Tempest but the smoke carries the sharp stink of burning fabric and leather and the sweetness of flesh.

Tempest's eyes dart back and forth between the two in an effort to appear overwhelmed. She is but she wants to be sure they know it. The closest gryphon bares his teeth. He draws a silver chain with one hand as the other strokes along the length.

With a snap, Tempest flares her wings and steps forward to challenge the pair. They don't react other than to pause and Tempest draws acid up into the back of her throat before she ignites it with the small remaining charge in her portalling muscles. The dart in her chest doesn't stop her from releasing a low growl that forces smoke to curl out past her lips. The glow from the fire in her throat lights up the silver chain and the gryphons move. The closest one takes a step back so the two are nearly side by side.

Tempest releases the ball of flame, spitting hard enough to pass it through their overlapping wings. A smoldering fist sized hole appears in the nearest wing as flame and smoke rise from the one behind it. Both gryphons draw away and Tempest takes advantage of the new space between them to run for the tunnel and Aledaar, slashing the small dagger at the one on her right as she goes. The blade flexes more than it should and leaves a welt instead of a cut as it jumps and skitters along the seam between his chest piece and trousers.

Three sluggish steps later, she's knocked sideways and cartwheels up against Aledaar's chair. Her attackers have no trouble damaging her before they lock her up. Their angry, shift blackened eyes reflect the flames in the main chamber and one grinds his fused tooth plates together. The mark on his stomach bleeds at one end, darkening his leathers.

Not going with you, Tempest mouths and rolls to the side just before one impacts with the chair. Fighting with these two isn't like sparring someone her own size. They will fight to get close enough to overpower her with sheer strength and Tempest has to stay clear until they make a mistake.

As she gets to her feet, the feather weight of the silver chain slides over one wing and she staggers, landing on Lawrence before the chain hits the floor. Another roll finds her pinned beneath one of the gryphons.

"Get the damn chain," he growls and the other moves to comply. In the seconds it takes for him to realize it's disappeared somewhere between Lawrence and Torch, another set of heavy boots charges in. The rustle of feathers and tang of smoke and dragonkin pitch come with him.

"Get the fuck off my female," Soar breathes and the hazy ceiling scrolls past Tempest's eyes as the gryphon holding her rolls. Patches of Soar's skin are nearly as black as his armour. Steel grates on leather as Soar draws his daggers and charges the standing gryphon. Tempest grins beneath the weight of the one holding her down. Soar could free her and deal with the other all on his own but instead he leaves Tempest to her own fight. His confidence bolsters hers and she makes a silent promise to make him proud.

Soar's collision with the gryphon cuts his warning cry short as they tumble in a mass of feathers and steel. Red and black leather ripples and twists behind flying brown feathers. Razor sharp talons slash at Soar and his daggers and Tempest claws out against her attacker. As she's pulled to her feet, she allows her fingers to shift, though with every second her hands are covered in gold scale and black talon, her real fight is with her dragon who is ready to kill everything.

Obey, Tempest thinks as she heeds Flay's lessons to culture a respectful relationship with her dragon. Only the strong mental image of a dragonkin with shifted hands holds her dragon back though her desire to taste blood lingers.

"Which one hurt you," Soar growls. The dart left a thick patch of blood on her tunic and even through the smoke Soar would have no trouble seeing it against the rough, black cloth. He doesn't slow his attack though his words are rough and indistinct. His partially shifted mouth threatens and the clack of fused tooth plates warns that Soar and his adversary will tear each other to pieces.

Tempest's attacker lunges as she slashes out with one clawed hand. She spins into a crouch to stay clear of his grip and lands the hard handle of the dagger in his belly wound as her bare feet skid to a stop on the slippery dirt floor.

Then Soar's fight ends as one pair of dark brown gryphons wings trembles and the room echoes with the wet tearing of flesh. Tempest slashes at her opponent but her attention turns to Soar. The red armoured figure in front of him seems to melt into the white stone floor as blood spills down his legs. As he drops, Soar remains standing. With an angry shake, some white returns to Soar's eyes as he pushes his inner hunter aside and regains control. Bright red blood soaks his mouth and throat in contrast to the clean shine of his skyblades.

The sight of Soar's bloodlust and victory releases Tempest's dragon and before she can hold back, her left hand moves. The lightening fast blow drives her clawed fingers deep into her opponents throat as all her dragon's power focuses on the single move. Bone snaps and the gryphon's head falls back, disappearing behind his shoulders.

Before the rest of his trembling body can fall, Tempest takes a cautious step away from Soar. Then, as the feathered form slumps over onto Lawrence she charges. Tempest's satisfied dragon retreats as she's swallowed in her gryphon's embrace.

"Little gryphon," Soar murmurs. Tempest fists the shoulders of his bloody, black armour and shuts out the stink of viscera and fire and the cries from the other room. His warm mouth sticks in her hair as his parted lips plant a heavy kiss. Only Soar and Tempest remain in their fleeting, small corner of peace. "Stand back."

She holds on, confused by his order, then as the tenderness fades from his eyes his gaze turns to the curtains covering Aledaar's back exit. The old gryphon's indignant growl follows the clash of metal.

"Talon," Soar points at the curtain and Tempest understands. Talon's forces have blocked Aledaar's escape.

"Awe, fuck me," Soar moans as Tempest reaches his side. His rough palm catches on her black tunic as he pushes her aside. A mass of dirty red hair looms over Soar and his dark brown wings rise and spread as he's lifted from the floor.

Fury's deep laugh accompanies an exhalation of smoke that pours from his nose and pools beneath Soar's feet.

"I got this," Soar breathes in spite of being suspended by a partially shifted dragonkin. "You get Aledaar."

Tempest startles at the rough tear of shredding curtains and steps back to watch as she keeps an eye on Soar and Fury. Hairy lion feet slash through the red drapes revealing glimpses of Aledaar's white robes. Behind, deeper in the tunnel. Talon's roar answers Torrent's. Panic swells and she staggers away, rocked by the sight.

Failure.

Aledaar's screech echoes through the tart smoke, chasing her from all sides and blocking escape in all directions. The last day of her simple life when she fled Sky's sparring chamber surrounds her.

Fury tosses Soar aside as Aledaar's completely shifted gryphon form emerges, held from behind in the arms of a gold dragon. Feathers surround Fury as Soar returns, clinging to the big dragonkin who shifts further and draws back a fully clawed hand.

I've fought worse, Tempest centers her spirit around the thought and finds courage. She didn't have something to fight for when she faced Sky. Today she has it.

"You waste my time, gryphon," Fury growls and Tempest doesn't think. By the time she realizes the ground up silver in her pocket will affect Aledaar's captor as well as Fury, the air around them is alight in the tiny, sparkling particles. As Fury's large, scaled talon drives claws-first toward Soar's stomach, the digits become nothing more than human fingers. Still, the crushing blow empties his lungs. Soar doesn't let go, instead he pulls Fury over with him as he falls.

"Shit, Lady Tempest," a female behind Tempest growls as Aledaar's victorious squawk echoes around them. He squirms free, crouches on his golden haunches and spreads his wings in threat. The once respectable robes of the Generous Sire hang, dingy and torn, and not a small amount of blood covers the shreds. Even the gold relic still around his neck appears to have lost its luster.

The scent of fully shifted gryphon swamps Tempest but rather than shy away, she inhales and saturates her senses with it. At first, the musk of ancient, oiled feathers gags her even worse than the smoke then her lungs relax and she lowers her chin to focus entirely on her opponent. Aledaar's scent draws her and she faces it head on. The Generous Sire stands between her and the future.

"Lady Spite," Talon shouts and without looking, the healer who treated Tempest reaches out and catches a sword as it flies from the tunnel. Her dragon form is gone and her palm doesn't have a chance to warm the grip before she tosses it to Tempest.

"Hurry it up," Soar gasps. Even with Fury sparkling in silver like everyone else, he still outweighs Soar.

Spite moves aside, allowing Torrent and Talon to rush past. Torrent drives hard, pushes his attack and swings his large, two-handed sword in aggressive circles forcing Talon to retreat with his single, lighter skyblade. Beneath Talon's fierce scowl rests a small smile of pleasure and Tempest tosses Torch's small dagger to her adopted sire.

"Seriously?" Talon mutters but he doesn't discard the weapon. Instead, he swings his skyblade down to use the pommel as a fist weapon in concert with the dagger in the other and steps closer to Torrent. He manages to land a blow on Torrent's mouth, reopening the gash he made years earlier and earning a satisfying, pained howl. Torrent's big blade isn't as effective up close and Talon's proximity forces him to yield ground.

Tempest acknowledges Spite as they turn on Aledaar. Spite stands naked, her armour presumably in pieces somewhere down the tunnel, but she isn't unarmed. A weighty axe swings in one hand, its blade smeared with blood and Tempest's breath catches. Con is nowhere to be seen.

"Lady Tempest," Spite nods and as if sensing her fears, the older gold eases them. "Your sibling rests unharmed and quite unconscious."

Then the blood belongs to Aledaar.

Good.

The Generous Sire paces, as if unsure whether to fight or escape. Blue sparks course through his flight feathers and draws hisses and balls of sticky flaming acid from Spite. Smoldering bits cling to Aledaar's ravaged robes. Only the cluster of white feathers around the base of his beak betrays his age. His ranger days are long over but fully shifted, he is as dangerous as any well trained, younger gryphon.

"Avoid the relic," Spite warns as she swings her axe to the side. The glowing path of silver light on steel blocks the tunnel entrance, marking the rumpled curtain and the dark beyond as hers. "It must belong entirely to him when he dies."

Tempest draws confidence from the older gold as a pained hiss from Soar pushes her forward, past the wall of doubt that still intrudes on conscious thought. Without waiting for Spite, she circles Aledaar and closes the route out through the main chamber. Each step steals more of her reserves as the weight of the battle, her experience with the silver chain, and her recent portals sap all but what she needs to take two steps and take Aledaar's life.

"Son of a—" Soar gasps. He must be back on his feet. Tempest discerns two sets of boots moving in the place his voice came from, one much larger than the other. His steps are quick then there is the rustle of his feathered wings against Fury's leather ones as Soar fights with the same tactic Tempest used earlier; stay out of reach until Fury makes a mistake.

Spite moves on Aledaar, spitting fire, as the old gryphon chooses the same moment to attack. Both wings flare as he rises on his hind legs, battering Spite and Tempest, then he's airborne enough to slash with his hind legs. Fear drives Tempest back a step while experience drives Spite forward.

In order to avoid Spite's axe, Aledaar moves on Tempest. Her sword comes up, slicing through the draft created by Aledaar's pounding wings. The defensive blow knocks aside his hind foot and severs tendons.

Then Aledaar's weight passes over Tempest as his feet find purchase in Fury's red armour. One talon sinks into Fury's shoulder and the pair takes Soar down as Tempest and Spite plunge after them. The chamber echoes with Aledaar's screech as he scrambles clear.

Instead of withdrawing, Tempest releases a soundless bark and clears her last mental barrier.

As Fury roars and clutches the deep and bloody wounds to his shoulder he turns his back to Aledaar. Soar takes advantage and grabs Fury from behind, wrapping himself around the dragonkin lord. Tempest spares a moment to lock her eyes with Soar. His nod as he positions his arms around Fury's throat frees her of her last worry for him.

Aledaar completes a staggering pivot on his hobbled leg and Tempest drives forward as her sword moves of its own accord. Gold leather wings shimmer and snap, tracing Spite's circle around Aledaar's flank, and Tempest's attack draws Aledaar's attention. As the shifted gryphon slashes out with his deadly talons, Spite moves. Tempest's sword arcs through the air behind her and she moves dangerously close as Aledaar wraps a claw around her free arm. The other talon grabs, coming within inches of her throat then disappears.

Spite's axe claims the limb in a flash of steel.

Aledaar screeches, a high, chilling keen only produceable by a fully shifted gryphon. The noise tapers off as Tempest buries her sword up beneath his breast feathers. Spite's arms close around Tempest and pull her away just before the relic can swing free and come into contact with her hands. As Aledaar drops back, the handle moves in time with his pierced heart.

"Bastard," Spite hisses as Fury screams in pain. Other screams echo from the main cavern as Lev shouts orders to his remaining fighters. Tempest barely listens. She can't take her eyes from the spectacle of the dying Generous Sire. Aledaar's remaining arm grasps at the blade as his body fails. His fingers tighten around the exposed blade but little blood comes from the wounds. Flight feathers fade as his exposed hind feet shorten and the fur retracts leaving the veiny calves of an elderly human.

She's seen enough and doesn't look at his face as she places a foot on his chest. With Spite's help, Tempest draws the blade free as Fury collapses and quiet overwhelms the outer chamber. Somewhere beneath Fury's prone form, Soar struggles to get out from under the big gold.

Only the frantic clash of blades from Talon and Torrent remains as Torrent backs Talon into a corner. Talon still holds the small dagger and in spite of their bloodied blades, neither shows any signs of weakening.

It's only a matter of time before one makes a fatal mistake.

"Talon," Spite whispers as she takes control of Tempest's hold on the sword. With a powerful twist of her body, the blade flies free in an elegant, arcing spin.

Torrent pauses, eyes giving away his surprise with only a slight widening. Talon doesn't look.

Torch's dagger clatters to the ground as Talon brings both arms up and takes a step back, snapping his hands together. His empty hand captures the flying blade and with nothing more than a whisper, they scissor together, cleanly removing Torrent's head.

Blood flies, both from Torrent's neck and Talon's blades as he follows through, allowing them to cross once behind his head before he gets control and drops to his knees at the same time as Torrent.

Soar, Tempest mouths as he finally pushes Fury off and gets to his feet.

"You can't talk?" Spite asks and Tempest pulls her collar back to show the wound. The older gold gives a reassuring smile. "I have others to attend to, Tempest. Then I will take care of that."

Spite moves first to Soar. His jaw tightens at her approach but he stops and lets her touch him. First, she holds a hand over his bloody nose then takes a few more seconds to pass it over his chest and belly. The she speaks quietly in his ear. Soar drops his eyes to Tempest's shoulder then acknowledges Spite with a curt nod before she moves on to Fury.

"Little gryphon," he whispers.

Soar pulls back her collar to examine the hole in her chest and his mouth tightens as he glances to her eyes. There's warmth as he grasps her shoulders then runs his hands down her arms, probing for more injuries. Then he traces the big bones of her wings, gently unfolding them and scanning the leather for tears. He checks her back and drops to his knees, probing her belly for tenderness. Each time he moves his hands, he offers her skin and their young another verse in the old tongue.

"I love you," he whispers and his breath hitches as he pulls Tempest to the floor, folds her in his wings and hides her, keeping his small family all to himself.

Epilogue

"Just once," Tempest whispers. "While this seat is still mine…"

Soar growls as she nibbles the circular bite mark below his ear.

Tempest doesn't sit on Aledaar's gold chair, Soar does. She curls up in his lap as much as she can considering her growing belly. The two months following Aledaar's death have passed in a blur of ceremonies and meetings.

Soar loses his hand in the folds of her official red robes and rubs her aching scars. The heavy salve, a gift from Lady Spite, eases the stretching as he works it into the tight, smooth marks.

"Do you think Lev will accept?" Soar asks.

"Mm," she mumbles.

The Council honoured an old law and placed Tempest at the head of the Grand Council, a position she accepted only until a permanent replacement could be chosen. The replacement, Sire Lev, has yet to learn of the appointment. If he doesn't accept then she's back to wearing a flat spot on her butt as she sits in the awful gold chair.

Lev's acceptance will make things much easier for Tempest and Soar. If he declines then she'll spend much of her time on Bolshevik Island and Soar will have duties on

Vancouver Island as master of Lev's guard. If Lev chooses to lead the Council then Tempest will be free to do as she pleases, to raise her young at home with Talon and Shadow's little gryphons. It's a 'for now' plan they both can live with.

"Tempest!"

Torch, the young gold dragonkin who delivered messages to the Vancouver Island Eyrie and has become very attached to Tempest and Soar, stumbles in interrupting their quiet moment. She chose to wear the reds of the Will when she decided to remain in Tempest's service instead of returning home to Skyfall.

"Torch," Tempest softly chides. "Apparently you are in too much of a hurry to show this chamber and its Lady the proper respect."

"Oh, right," she grins before she approaches and kneels, wrists up in submission. "My Generous Lady Tempest, Sire Lev and his delegation have arrived."

"Ah, see? That's getting easier for both of us," Tempest touches Torch's wrists.

At first Tempest refused to accept the title and greeting but Soar reminded her that acceptance of respect as the Council's head wasn't negotiable. Bearing the kneeling and deference is in itself respectful of the seat she occupies and the Council.

Soar removes his hand from Tempest's robes since it had wandered above her scars, sliding beneath her adornment and cradling her breast in his rough palm before the young dragonkin burst in. Though Soar's skin has healed from his fight with Fury and his scales, he still bears deliciously uneven calluses on his palms. She can't resist the way they vibrate against her sensitive skin.

"Um," Tempest mumbles as her cheeks turn red.

"It's okay," Torch nods. "It helps."

Torch looks at Soar. He chuckles and kisses the rough edge of Tempest's ear.

"This room," Torch continues. "So many bad memories. I can come in without fear now that there's love here."

"Up you get," Soar lifts Tempest to her feet and she pauses only long enough to kiss Torch on the forehead. Then Soar takes Torch's hand and leads her to the side of the chamber. "We'll let Lady Tempest work."

Torch catches Tempest's eye as they move out of the way. The excited young gold will finally meet the gryphons she's heard so much about. They settle to Tempest's left as the delegation enters, Sire Lev in the lead. Talon stands at Lev's right shoulder, in Soar's normal position and opposite Firn at Lev's left. Talon should be with Shadow since she's so near the end of her pregnancy but Flay stands behind him, his quick portal home. Six others including Hunter and Daniel Cooper, Fire, Agony, and Con round out the group. Agony stations herself next to Hunter and he can't conceal his displeasure.

Lev approaches Tempest while the remainder stop and kneel only half-way across the room. Protocol, as explained to Tempest, dictates Lev will offer respect on behalf of the entire group. They are all still armed, something Aledaar never would have allowed, but Tempest would never dream of disarming her brave visitors. Seeing Lev on his knees before her will be strange enough.

"My Generous Lady Tempest," Lev's pride washes away any thought this would be awkward. Then his wrists come up and he bows, pressing his head between his elbows.

Tempest leans forward and touches her forehead to Lev's wrists, the closest thing to a hug she's permitted to give her grand-sire, considering the circumstances. She hasn't seen any of them in two months. If any moment could cause tears of happiness it's this one but she takes a deep breath and with an oof, straightens up.

"Sire Lev, I've missed you all so much."

Lev stands, with much more grace than Tempest.

The heck with protocol.

Tempest staggers into Lev's arms before hugging Talon and Flay.

"I would meet with you alone, Sire Lev," she says then turns to the delegation. "Torch will make sure you receive my hospitality in the main chamber."

Lev assesses her until they are left alone.

"You have made me proud, Tempest," he smiles. His mouth broadens, wrapping his brilliant blue eyes in crinkles. "But I must ask why you have summoned me all this way. Perhaps just to fill me in on politics?"

"Well," she starts and pushes her hair behind her ears. Lev mirrors the movements so smoothly he might not even know he's done it. "The relics are safe and out of my hands for which I'm relieved. Sire Sher of Jasper has agreed to step down. Although he didn't help Aledaar and Torrent with their crimes he was complicit. I am certain Dame Arden didn't know of Aledaar's terrible manipulation of the gold dragonkin. She and Tawny raised me to keep my dragonkin blood secret even from myself. They knew of Sher's prejudice and guessed what I was. She protected me, Tawny too.

"Daniel Cooper's sibling has been released from exile, as has Daniel. She sought sanctuary in Ochre's Honour and lived there with her dragonkin mate," she sighs and rubs at her scarred side, exhausted with more than just the pregnancy. Two months of settling disputes and seeking replacements for the Council members who had been loyal to Aledaar has pushed her to the limit.

"She is mated to Lord Somebody or Other," she yawns, sure she knows the name but for the moment it escapes her. "Her young assisted us in the assault on Aledaar. She has accepted the natural course of things and will become Dame in Jasper with her mate at her side. Ironic though, after so many generations of hate for the dragonkin one will serve as Sire.

"Lord Fury, has returned to Skyfall. It will take a long time to rebuild. He has been invited to the Council and has accepted. Conflagration has been chosen as Skyfall's Emissary to the Council and Lady Flay is Ochre's Honour's Emissary.

She and Lady Spite will serve as my midwives when the time comes."

"And what of you, Tempest?" Lev asks. "Soar serves in Jasper and you here. I suppose neither of you will have much trouble dividing your duties to allow time together."

"To that question, Sire Lev, there may be a much simpler solution."

Lev raises an eyebrow and Tempest leans closer.

"What's going on in there, buddy?" Talon asks, his voice modulated so it only reaches Soar's ears.

"Council business," Soar shrugs. He knows damn well and what the implications will be for Talon should Lev agree to take over the Grand Council. And for Soar as well. If Lev leaves his post as Sire to lead the Council then his guard can choose to remain and serve Talon or accompany Lev to Bolshevik Island. Talon would become Sire at Dame Shadow's side.

A weak, cold breeze makes its way through the chamber, stirring the heavy gold fabric draping down from the ceiling. The silver wall lights don't do much to brighten the space so Tempest ordered small fires be lit around the room for the occasion. The flames warm the space not only with their heat but they also give a healthy glow to the drapes.

"Help me out," Hunter hisses. He's on his third lap around the room in his effort to avoid Agony's attention. The mark of Shadow's guard is still somewhat fresh on his upper left arm and the green dragonkin female finds it fascinating. Soar laughs. He doesn't really understand her interest with the soot blackened brand. Agony's never ending questions about gryphons and the outside world in general remind him very much of the naive, young female Talon and Shadow brought home more than a decade earlier. The same female who now carries Soar's young and sits, hopefully for not much longer, at the head of the Grand Council.

"But she's adorable," Soar protests.

"Bastard," Hunter mutters and moves on to a position behind the heavy drape next to Flay. The green dragonkin looks as amused as Soar feels and widens her wings to provide him some extra cover.

"Maybe I should tell him?" Soar says.

"About what?" Talon pulls out his phone again and sighs at the blank screen.

"A female dragonkin will only ever sleep with one male, her choice, and they are mated for life. A gryphon exchange is just a bonus if he's not dragonkin. She'll use her persuasion if that's what it takes to land him."

"Then there's nothing he can do even if you tell him?"

"Nope."

Talon's booming laugh tapers off as Tempest and Lev emerge from her chamber to stand at the top of the small rise at the opening. Heavy red and gold drapes frame them in the same fabric of the Council member's robes and the other gold drapes adorning the rest of the room. Lev holds one of her hands, her other clutches her robes to keep them from underfoot in spite of the fact her stomach lifts them off the ground.

It's endearing how she manages to turn leading the Council into something very… Cloud.

"My friends," she says clearly as the talking and shuffling cease. Lev's gaze turns to Talon and Soar. "Loyal members of the Council, my kin and my beloved family. Our friend, Sire Lev, wishes to speak."

Lev tilts his head to Tempest before addressing the assembled dragonkin and gryphons. From the corner of his eye, Soar spots Hunter peeking out from behind a curtain then has to stifle a laugh as Agony appears and glues herself to Hunter's side.

"My Generous Lady Tempest," Lev starts. His eyes seek Firn and he takes a moment to make sure he has her attention before he begins.

I'll be damned. He took Tempest's seat as head of the Grand Council.

Lev is younger than anyone ever chosen, with the exception of Tempest's temporary appointment, and at an age when many gryphons first find themselves as Sire or Dame, much less representing the body ruling the world's gryphons.

"My friends, months ago I learned my daughter, Dame Shadow and her mate, Master Talon, had conceived. I have served my eyrie for many years and planned to cede my service as Sire to Master Talon upon the birth of his young."

Talon makes a small choking sound and Soar gently takes his friends elbow to steady him. Then he grabs Talon's phone before it can slide from his fingers and fall to the stone floor.

"Before you all, I am pleased to share that I am stepping down as Sire of the Vancouver Island Eyrie. A young gryphon I have come to love as my own son, will take my place and continue to serve my home at my daughter's side."

"Easy, buddy," Soar whispers, his voice concealed by the applause that follows. Talon nods, a rough bob of his head, then locks his knees. To make sure Talon doesn't go over, Soar gets a second hand around his elbow.

Tempest takes a step forward to hold Lev's hand. He finally takes his eyes from Firn who smiles her approval, then he turns to Talon. By raising his fingers like he's tipping Talon's chin up, he tells the future Sire to hold his head high with pride.

"My friends," Tempest speaks again. "As you are aware I came to lead the Council through an old law. I claimed leadership from Aledaar through justified punishment for his crimes against the dragonkin. My actions have not only put our respected Council in turmoil but have brought much change to the great eyries of the gryphons and cities of the dragonkin.

"It has been my deep honour to serve all three.

"I believe it is time for another to fill the beautiful gold seat in the room behind me since my continued service as Your Generous Lady Tempest will only serve as reminder of the blood, both gryphon and dragonkin, let upon the very stone at our feet. There are those out there who believe my kin will never have a place among the gryphons and I expect they will not go quietly.

"Sire Lev," Tempest takes his hand. With her other she draws a small knife. The solid gold handle cradles a clear blade. Soar saw it last when Tempest claimed her rule of the Council.

In near silence, the gryphon and dragonkin guests move to the fringes of the chamber. The attending members of the Council form a circle around Tempest and Lev as they make their way down the stairs to the center of the Council chamber. Shoulder to shoulder, they form a solid wall of red robes, feathers and leather to seclude the pair. None could stand closer to Lev so they show both equality with each other and mutual support for his appointment.

For nearly a minute only the breath of Tempest's whisper as she instructs Lev can be heard. Soar jumps with the sharp drag of the blade across Lev's palm, spilling a small amount of his blood on the stone floor.

Before the raw splats of the heavy red drops even start to slow, Lev raises his hand enough that the gathered witnesses can see and his clear voice fills the room.

"My gryphons, my dragonkin" he calls, including the dragonkin as Tempest had. "My blood, my love, my service."

Soar tugs at Talon's elbow, urging him down to one knee. The other guests follow suit and almost in unison they raise their hands, wrist up. Then, with a step back, the Council members do the same. The hushed whisper of their robes drowns out the last falling drops of Lev's blood.

Finally, Tempest takes Lev's bloody hand and gently folds his fingers over the wound. She kisses his knuckles and holds tight to his elbow as she too, makes her way to the floor.

"My Generous Sire Lev," she yells as her wrists come up. Then again louder as the rest of the room joins her repeating the words.

"My Generous Sire Lev!"

Thank you for reading Skyfall. Writing it has been an amazing experience and sharing it with others has made that experience even better. Other readers would love to hear your thoughts on this book (or any others you have enjoyed!) Please take a moment to visit your favourite online retailer or website such as www.goodreads.com or www.shelfari.com and share your thoughts. Your support helps small publishers and independent writers continue to provide great and original stories!

Thank you.

GLOSSARY

Agony - Heir to the rule of Ochre's Honour.

Arden - Dame Arden is the mate of Sire Sher and together they serve the Jasper Eyrie. She is the figurative dame to all who reside in the eyrie.

Aledaar - The Generous Sire Aledaar is the leader of the gryphon Grand Council.

Bolshevik Island - Located in Northern Russia, Bolshevik Island is the location of the gryphon Grand Council.

Cherry Cooper - The human name Cloud adopts.

Cloud - Is an orphan and the only gryphon to survive the massacre at the Welch Peak Eyrie fifteen years earlier.

Common gryphon - A common gryphon is not descended from the first royal gryphons.

Condor - Sibling of Shadow and son of Sire Lev and Dame Treasure.

Conflagration - Con is the son of Lord Fury and sibling of Lady Tempest.

Cooper's - Cooper's bar is located on the street level floor of the same Calgary office tower that houses Daniel Cooper's eyrie.

Council's Will - The Council's Will are the enforcers of the Grand Council. They wear red leather armour and answer to Aledaar and the Grand Council.

Dame - Gryphon word for mother

Daniel Cooper - Leads the Calgary Eyrie, based in an office tower in downtown Calgary.

Den - A family living chamber within an eyrie. Generally a single chamber, it can vary in size and the number of rooms depending on the number of gryphons in the family.

Dove - A royal gryphon, daughter of Firn and sibling of Tundra. Her magic is in healing.

dragon - Dragons are extremely rare and have not been seen for many years.

dragonkin - The mixed breed descendants of gryphons and dragons. They take their feathered form around the age of seven, the same as gryphons. In their teens, their sire will force them to release their dragons usually through threat against the young dragonkin. The sire must then survive their offspring's dragon until he or she gets it under control.

Eviscerate - Lady Eviscerate is the green dragonkin mate of Daniel Cooper and dame to Flay and Fire.

Eyrie - The system of stone chambers and tunnels that is home to a social group of gryphons usually located within a mountain. The eyrie is ruled by a Sire and Dame.

Feather - Talon's twin sister.

Fire - The son of Daniel Cooper and Lady Eviscerate. He cares for young dragonkin who are kept hidden from Aledaar.

Firn - Dame of Dove and Tundra. She has also become Lev's life companion since both lost their mates in the rogue raids decades earlier.

Flay - Lady Flay is the green dragonkin daughter of Daniel Cooper and Lady Eviscerate. She is mated to Conflagration.

Fury - Lord Fury is the Master of the Council's Will. He is the sire of Conflagration and Lady Tempest.

George Noble - Soar's human name.

Grand Council - The governing body guiding all of gryphon society.

Grand-Dame - Grandmother gryphon.

Gryphon - Gryphons are part eagle and part lion and rightfully proud since they are kings of both the land and the sky. The females are communal and prefer the companionship and shelter of an eyrie. Males are generally loners. They are attuned with the earth and spend many months of the year listening for her to show them where to find gold which they store in a secret place known only to them.

Jasper Eyrie - The Jasper Eyrie is located in eastern British Columbia and is ruled by Sire Sher and Dame Arden.

Jenn Klein - Jenn is Shadow's human persona. She was raised as human and does not learn she is a gryphon until she is nearly thirty years old.

Lawrence - Lawrence is the longtime friend of Daniel Cooper and the Master of Cooper's Guard.

Lev - Sire Lev rules the Vancouver Island Eyrie alone since the death of his mate, Dame Treasure. He is the sire of Condor and Shadow.

Mark Williams - Mark is Talon's human name. As Mark, Talon is a trucker.

Moonwater - Moonwater is used by gryphons for a number of magic purposes. It can aid in healing and cleansing items. Females also use it in the Ritual of Blessing.

Ochre's Honour - The green dragonkin city.

portal - Dragonkin travel by portalling. A portal is an electric hole in the sky. Dragonkin create a portal using the magic of the earth and can travel to any location.

Rabid - A gossip and troublemaker known for drugging gryphons for sex or secrets.

Rapid - Rapid is a young gryphon in Dame Shadow's guard.

Render - Lord Render is the green dragonkin sibling of the leader of Ochre's Honour.

Ritual of Exchange - The Ritual of Exchange is the gryphon mating ritual. The male bites the female and if she accepts him, she returns the bite. Then she offers her tears. If he accepts her then he licks them from her cheeks.

Ritual of Blessing - The Ritual of Blessing is a secret ceremony performed only by females. Since gryphons are masters of the land and the sky, the females cleanse and bless the deceased's spirit, freeing it to return to the sky then the body is returned to the earth.

Royal gryphon - A royal gryphon is a direct descendent from the first pair of gryphons. Gryphons believe they were once pets of the Gods who were cast out because one was turned into human form by a God and that gryphon did the same to the others. Royal gryphons are descended from that God and his female.

Seth - Seth is the gryphon bartender at Cooper's.

Sher - Sire Sher serves the Jasper Eyrie as its male ruler.

Shadow - Shadow is a gryphon who was raised as Jenn Klein by the human foster parent system.

Sire - The gryphon word for father.

Sky - Master Sky is a legendary blacksmith and combat trainer. Sky is grand-dame to Soar and her son is mated to Sire Lev's sibling.

Skyblade - Any weapon made by Master Sky. The ceremony includes the blade's new owner so
the weapon will only be light, balanced and usable by him or her.

Skyfall - The gold dragonkin city.

Soar - Master Soar is Talon's best friend and Sire Lev's guard master.

Swift - Swift is Talon's ex-girlfriend and friend to Feather.

Shadow - Shadow is Jenn Klein's gryphon persona.

Talon - Talon is Mark Williams' gryphon persona. His home eyrie is in Jasper until he meets Shadow.

Tawny - Tawny is Dame Arden's dame, a royal, who ruled the Jasper Eyrie until the passing of her mate. For the past fifteen years she raised Cloud.

Tempest - The gold dragonkin name Cloud was born with.

Torch - A teenage gold dragonkin. She serves Aledaar as a page or errand runner.

Torrent - Torrent is the son of Sire Sher and Dame Arden of the Jasper Eyrie. He is in line for the eyrie's leadership since his sibling is deceased.

Treasure - Treasure is Dame Shadow's dame. She died as a result of her injuries from the rogue raid on the Vancouver Island Eyrie, shortly after giving birth to Shadow and Condor.

Tundra - Tundra is the sibling of Dove and son of Firn.

Terry Klein - Terry is the human name of Jenn/Shadow's brother, Condor.

Vancouver Island Eyrie - The Vancouver Island Eyrie is located north of Tofino, British Columbia on Vancouver Island. It is the ancestral home of Sire Lev. The eyrie was decimated twice by the same rogues that attacked Welch Peak.

Welch Peak Eyrie - The Welch Peak Eyrie is located on Welch Peak near Chilliwack, British Columbia. All but a single infant gryphon were massacred by rogue gryphons.